TOXIC
BACHELORS

Also by Danielle Steel

H.R.H	WINGS
COMING OUT	THE GIFT
THE HOUSE	ACCIDENT
MIRACLE	VANISHED
IMPOSSIBLE	MIXED BLESSINGS
ECHOES	JEWELS
SECOND CHANCE	NO GREATER LOVE
RANSOM	HEARTBEAT
SAFE HARBOUR	MESSAGE FROM NAM
JOHNNY ANGEL	DADDY
DATING GAME	STAR
ANSWERED PRAYERS	ZOYA
SUNSET IN ST. TROPEZ	KALEIDOSCOPE
THE COTTAGE	FINE THINGS
THE KISS	WANDERLUST
LEAP OF FAITH	SECRETS
LONE EAGLE	FAMILY ALBUM
JOURNEY	FULL CIRCLE
THE HOUSE ON	CHANGES
HOPE STREET	THURSTON HOUSE
THE WEDDING	CROSSINGS
IRRESISTIBLE FORCES	ONCE IN A LIFETIME
GRANNY DAN	A PERFECT STRANGER
BITTERSWEET	REMEMBRANCE
MIRROR IMAGE	PALOMINO
HIS BRIGHT LIGHT: *The Story*	LOVE: POEMS
of My Son, Nick Traina	THE RING
THE KLONE AND I	LOVING
THE LONG ROAD HOME	TO LOVE AGAIN
THE GHOST	SUMMER'S END
SPECIAL DELIVERY	SEASON OF PASSION
THE RANCH	THE PROMISE
SILENT HONOUR	NOW AND FOREVER
MALICE	GOLDEN MOMENTS*
FIVE DAYS IN PARIS	GOING HOME
LIGHTNING	

* Published outside the UK under the title PASSION'S PROMISE

DANIELLE STEEL

TOXIC BACHELORS

CORGI BOOKS

TOXIC BACHELORS
A CORGI BOOK : 9780552170857

Originally published in Great Britain by Bantam Press,
a division of Transworld Publishers

PRINTING HISTORY
Bantam Press edition published 2005
Corgi edition published 2006

12

Set in 12/14pt Garamond by
Falcon Oast Graphic Art Ltd.

Corgi Books are published by Transworld Publishers,
61–63 Uxbridge Road, London W5 5SA,
a division of The Random House Group Ltd,
in Australia by Random House Australia (Pty) Ltd,
20 Alfred Street, Milsons Point, Sydney, NSW 2061, Australia,
in New Zealand by Random House New Zealand Ltd,
18 Poland Road, Glenfield, Auckland 10, New Zealand
and in South Africa by Random House (Pty) Ltd,
Isle of Houghton, Corner Boundary Road & Carse O'Gowrie
Houghton 2198, South Africa

The Random House Group Limited supports The Forest Stewardship
Council® (FSC®), the leading international forest-certification organisation.
Our books carrying the FSC label are printed on FSC®-certified paper.
FSC is the only forest-certification scheme supported by the leading
environmental organisations, including Greenpeace. Our
paper procurement policy can be found at
www.randomhouse.co.uk/environment

MIX
Paper from
responsible sources
FSC® C016897

Printed and bound in Great Britain by Clays Ltd, St Ives plc

To my thoroughly wonderful children, Beatrix, Trevor, Todd, Nick, Samantha, Victoria, Vanessa, Maxx, and Zara, whose love, laughter, kindness, and joy light up my life.

To Sebastian, the best Christmas gift of all.

You are all God's greatest gifts to me, and I thank Him each day with awe, for the wonder of your love.

With all of my love to you.

d.s.

He Said/She Said

He said he'd always cherish me.
She said she'd love me forever.

He said he'd be my partner.
She said she'd be my best friend.

He said he'd listen to my stories.
She said she'd laugh at my jokes.

He said he'd always listen to me.
She said she'd always talk to me.

He said he'd always hug me.
She said she'd always hold my hand.

He said he'd always sleep with me.
She said she'd always kiss me goodnight.

He said he'd always love me.
She said she'd never leave me.

—Donna Rosenthal, Artist

TOXIC
BACHELORS

1

The sun was brilliant and hot, shining down on the deck of the motor yacht *Blue Moon*. She was 240 feet, eighty meters, of sleek, exquisite powerboat, remarkably designed. Pool, helipad, six elegant, luxurious guest cabins, a master suite right out of a movie and an impeccably trained crew of sixteen. The *Blue Moon* – and her owner – had appeared in every yachting magazine around the world. Charles Sumner Harrington had bought her from a Saudi prince six years before. He had bought his first yacht, a seventy-five-foot sailboat, when he was twenty-two. She had been called the *Dream*. Twenty-four years later, he enjoyed life on his boat as much as he had then.

At forty-six, Charles Harrington knew that he was a lucky man. In many ways, seemingly, life had been easy for him. At twenty-one, he had inherited an enormous fortune and had handled it responsibly in the twenty-five years since. He had made a career of managing his own investments and running his family's foundation. Charlie was well aware that few people on earth were as blessed as he, and he had done much to improve the lot of those less fortunate, both through the foundation and privately. He was well aware that he had an awesome responsibility, and even as a young man, he had thought of others first. He was particularly passionate about disadvantaged young people and children. The foundation did impressive work in education, provided medical assistance to the indigent, particularly in developing countries, and was dedicated to the prevention of child abuse for inner-city kids. Charles Harrington was a leader of the community, doing his philanthropic work quietly, through the foundation, or anonymously, whenever possible. Charles Harrington was a humanitarian, and an extremely caring, conscientious person. But he also laughed mischievously when he admitted that he was extremely spoiled, and made no apologies for the way he lived. He could afford it, and spent millions every year on the well-being of others, and a handsome amount on his own. He had never married, had no children, enjoyed living well, and when appropriate, took pleasure in sharing his lifestyle with his friends.

Every year, without fail, Charlie and his two closest friends, Adam Weiss and Gray Hawk, spent the month of August on Charlie's yacht, floating around the Mediterranean, stopping wherever they chose. It was a trip they had taken together for the past ten years. It was one they all looked forward to, and would have done just about anything not to miss. Every year, come hell or high water, on August first, Adam and Gray flew to Nice and boarded the *Blue Moon* for a month – just as they had done on her predecessors every year before that. Charlie was usually on the boat for July as well, and sometimes didn't return to New York until mid- or even late September. All his foundation and financial matters were easily handled from the boat. But August was devoted to pure fun. And this year was no different. He sat quietly eating breakfast on the aft deck, as the boat shifted gently, at anchor, outside the port of St. Tropez. They had had a late night the night before, and had come home at four A.M.

In spite of the late night, Charlie was up early, although his recollections of the evening before were a little vague. They usually were when Gray and Adam were involved. They were a fearsome trio, but their fun was harmless. They answered to no one, none of the three men were married, and at the moment none had girlfriends. They had long since agreed that, whatever their situations, they would come aboard alone, and spend the month as bachelors, living among men, indulging themselves.

They owed no one apologies or explanations, and each of them worked hard in his own way during the rest of the year, Charlie as a philanthropist, Adam as an attorney, and Gray as an artist. Charlie liked to say that they earned their month off, and deserved their annual trip.

Two of the three were bachelors by choice. Charlie insisted he wasn't. His single status, he claimed, was by happenstance and, so far, sheer bad luck. He said he wanted to get married, but hadn't found the right woman yet, despite a lifetime of searching. But he was still looking, with meticulous determination. He had been engaged four times in his younger days, although not recently, and each time something had happened to cause the wedding to be called off, much to his chagrin, and deep regret.

His first fiancée had slept with his best friend three weeks before the wedding, which had caused a veritable explosion in his life. And of course he had no choice but to call off the wedding. He had been thirty at the time. His second bride-to-be had taken a job in London as soon as they got engaged. He had commuted diligently to see her, while she continued to work for British *Vogue*, and could hardly make time to see him while he waited patiently in the flat he'd rented just so he could spend time with her. Two months before the wedding, she admitted that she wanted a career, and couldn't see herself giving up work when they got married, which was important to him. He thought she should stay home and have kids. He didn't want to be married to a career woman, so they agreed to part company – amicably of course, but it had been an enormous disappointment to him. He had been thirty-two at the time, and ever more determined to find the woman of his dreams. A year later he was sure he'd found her – she was a fantastic girl, and was willing to give up medical school for him. They went to South America together, on trips for the foundation, to visit children in developing countries. They had everything in common, and six months after they met, they got engaged. All went well, until Charlie realized his fiancée was in-separable from her twin sister, and expected to take her everywhere with them. He and the twin sister had taken an instant dislike to each other, which turned into heated debates and endless arguments each time they met. He felt certain that they would continue to dislike each other in alarming ways. He had bowed out that time too, and his would-be bride agreed. Her sister was too important to her to marry a man who genuinely despised her twin. She had married someone else within a year, and her twin moved in with them, which told Charlie he'd done the right thing. Charlie's last engagement had come to a disastrous end five years before. She loved Charlie, but even after couples counseling with him, said she didn't want children. No matter how much she said she loved him, she wouldn't budge an inch. He thought at first he could convince her otherwise, but he never did, so they parted friends. He always did. Without exception. Charlie had managed to stay friends with every woman he had ever gone out with. At Christmastime, he was deluged with cards from women he had once cared about, decided not to marry, and who had since married other men. At a glance, if one looked at the photographs of them and their families, they all looked the same. Beautiful, blond, well-bred women from aristocratic families, who had gone to the right schools, and married the right people. They smiled at him from their Christmas cards, with their prosperous-looking husbands at their side, and their towheaded children gathered around them. He was still in touch with many of them, they all loved Charlie, and remembered him fondly.

His friends Adam and Gray kept telling him to give up on debutantes and socialites and go out with a 'real' woman, the definition of which varied according to their respective descriptions. But Charlie knew exactly what he wanted. A well-born, well-heeled, well-educated, intelligent woman who would share the same values, same ideals, and had a similarly aristocratic background to his. That was important to him. His own family could be traced back to the fifteenth century, in England, his fortune was many generations old, and like his father and grandfather, he had gone to Princeton. His mother had gone to Miss Porter's, and finishing school in Europe, as had his sister, and he wanted to marry a woman just like them. It was an archaic point of view, and seemed snobbish in some ways, but Charlie knew what he wanted and needed, and what suited him. He himself was old-fashioned in some ways, and had traditional values. He was politically conservative, eminently respectable, and if he had a fling here and there, it was always done politely, with the utmost discretion. Charlie was a gentleman and a man of elegance and distinction to his very soul. He was attentive, kind, generous, and charming. His manners were impeccable, and women loved him. He had long since become a challenge to the women in New York, and the many places where he traveled and had friends. Everybody loved Charlie, it was hard not to.

Marrying Charles Harrington would have been a major coup for anyone. But like the handsome prince in the fairy tale, he had searched the world, looking for the right woman, the perfect one for him. And instead he met lovely women everywhere, who seemed delightful and appealing at first, and always had a fatal flaw that stopped him in his tracks just before he got to the altar. As much as it was for them, it was disheartening for him. His plans to marry and have children had been thwarted every time. At forty-six, he was still a bachelor, through no fault of his own, he said. Wherever the right woman was hiding these days, he was still determined to find her, and Charlie felt sure he would, one day. He just didn't know when. And for all the impostors masquerading as the right women, he was able to detect their fatal flaws every time. The one thing he consoled himself with was that he hadn't married the wrong one. He was determined not to let that happen. And he was grateful that so far he hadn't. He was ever vigilant and relentless about those fatal flaws. He knew the right woman was out there somewhere, he just hadn't found her yet. But one day he knew he would.

Charlie sat with his eyes closed and his face to the sun, as two stewardesses served him breakfast, and poured him a second cup of coffee. He had drunk a number of martinis, preceded by champagne the night before, but after a swim before he sat down to breakfast he felt better. He was a powerful swimmer, and a skilled windsurfer. He had been the captain of the swimming team at Princeton. Despite his age, he was fiercely athletic. He was an avid skier, played squash at every opportunity in the winter, and tennis in the summer. It not only improved his health, but he had the body of a man half his age. Charlie was a strikingly handsome man – tall, slim, with sandy blond hair that concealed whatever gray he'd acquired over time. He had blue eyes and, after the last month on the boat, a deep tan. He was a stunning-looking man, and his preference in women ran to tall, thin aristocratic blondes. He never thought about it particularly, but his mother and sister had both been tall blondes.

His mother had been spectacularly beautiful, and his sister had been a tennis star in college when she dropped out to take care of him. His parents had both been killed in a head-on collision while on vacation in Italy when he was sixteen. His sister had been twenty-one, and had left Vassar in her junior year, to come home and take on the responsibilities of running the family, in the absence of their parents. It still brought tears to Charlie's eyes when he thought about his sister. Ellen had said she would go back to finish college when he went to college two years later. It was a sacrifice she was more than willing to make for him. She had been an extraordinary woman, and Charlie adored her. But by the time he left for college, although he didn't know it, and she said nothing to him, Ellen was ill. She had managed to keep the seriousness of her illness from him for nearly three years. She said she was too busy working at the foundation to go back to college, and he had believed her. In fact, she had a brain tumor, and fought a valiant battle. They had determined early on that the tumor was inoperable because of its location. Ellen died at twenty-six, just months before Charlie graduated from Princeton. Charlie had no one to see him graduate. With his sister and parents gone, he was virtually alone in the world, with a vast fortune, and a great sense of responsibility for all they left him. He bought his first sailboat shortly after he graduated and for two years he sailed around the world. There was barely a day that went by that he didn't think about his sister and all she had done for him. She had even given up college for him, and had been there for him in every way until she died, just as his parents had been before. Their family life had always been harmonious and loving. The only thing that had gone wrong in his early life was that everyone who had loved him, and whom he loved, had died, and left him alone. His worst fear was of loving someone else, and having them die too.

When he'd come back from traveling the world on his yacht, he was twenty-four years old. He had gone to Columbia Business School and gotten an MBA, and learned about his investments, and how to run the foundation. He had grown up overnight and become responsible for everything in his world. Charlie had never let anyone down in his life. He knew that neither his parents nor Ellen had abandoned him intentionally, but he was alone in the world, without family, at a very young age. He had remarkable material benefits, and a few well-chosen friends. But he knew that until he found the right woman, he would be alone in important ways. He wasn't going to settle for anything less than what he felt he deserved, a woman like his mother and Ellen, a woman who would stand by him till the end. The fact that they had ultimately left him alone and terrified wasn't something he admitted to himself, not often anyway. It hadn't been their fault. It was simply a rotten turn of fate. Which made it all the more important for him to find the right woman, one he knew he could count on, who would be a good mother to his children, a woman who was nearly perfect in every way. That was vital to him. To Charlie, that woman was worth the wait.

'Oh God,' he heard a groan behind him on the deck of the boat. He laughed as soon as he heard the voice. He opened his eyes and turned to see Adam in white shorts and a pale blue T-shirt slip into a seat across the table from him. The stewardess poured him a cup of strong coffee, and Adam took several sips before he said another word. 'What the hell did I drink last night? I think someone poisoned me.' His hair was dark, his eyes nearly ebony, and he hadn't bothered to shave. He was of medium build with powerful shoulders and rugged looks. He wasn't a handsome man in the way Charlie was, but he was intelligent, funny, attractive, had charm, and women loved him. What he lacked in movie-star looks, he made up for with brains, power, and money. He had made a lot of it in recent years.

'I think you drank mostly rum and tequila but that was after the bottle of wine at dinner.' They'd had Château Haut-Brion on board, before going into St. Tropez to check out the bars and discos. Charlie wasn't likely to find his perfect woman there, but there were plenty of others to keep them all busy in the meantime. 'And I think the last time I saw you at the discothèque before I left, you were drinking brandy.'

'I figured. I think it's the rum that does me in. I turn into an alcoholic on the boat every year. If I drank like that at home, I'd be out of business.' Adam Weiss winced in the sunlight, put on his dark glasses, and grinned. 'You're a shit influence on me, Charlie, but a great host. What time did I come in?'

'Around five, I think.' Charlie sounded neither

admiring nor reproachful. He made no judgments on his friends. He just wanted them to have fun, and they always did, all three of them. Adam and Gray were the best friends he'd ever had, and they shared a bond that exceeded mere friendship. The three men felt like brothers, they'd seen each other through a lot in the last ten years.

Adam had met Charlie just after Rachel divorced him. He and Rachel had met at Harvard as sophomores, and gone to Harvard Law School together. She had graduated from law school summa cum laude, and passed the bar on the first try, although she never practiced law. Adam had had to take it a second time, but was nonetheless a terrific lawyer, and had done well. He had joined a firm that specialized in representing rock stars and major athletes – and he loved his work. He and Rachel had gotten married the day after they graduated from law school, and the marriage had been welcomed and celebrated by both families, who knew each other on Long Island. Somehow he and Rachel never met till college, although their parents had been friends. He had never wanted to meet the daughters of his parents' friends, so he had found her on his own, although he knew who she was as soon as they met. She had seemed like the perfect girl for him.

When they married, they had everything in

common, and a lifetime of happiness ahead of them. Rachel got pregnant on their honeymoon, and had two babies in two years, Amanda and Jacob, who were now fourteen and thirteen. The marriage had lasted five years. Adam was always busy working, building his career, and coming home at three in the morning, after going to concerts or sporting events with his clients and their friends. But in spite of the temptations all around him – and there had been many – he had been faithful to her. Rachel, however, got tired of being alone at night and fell in love with their pediatrician, whom she had known since high school, and had an affair with him while Adam was making money hand over fist for them. He became a partner in the firm three months before she left him, and she told him he'd be fine without her. She took the kids, the furniture, half of their savings, and married the doctor as soon as the ink was dry on their divorce. Ten years later he still hated her, and could barely bring himself to be civil to her. The last thing he wanted was to marry again and have the same thing happen. It had nearly killed him when she left with the kids.

In the decade since it had happened, he had avoided any risk of attachment by dating women nearly half his age, with one tenth the brain. And in the milieu where he worked, they were easy to find.

At forty-one, he dated women between twenty-one and twenty-five, models, starlets, groupies, the kind of women who hung around athletes and rock stars. Half the time he could barely remember their names. He was up-front with all of them, and generous with them. He told them when they met him that he would never remarry, and whatever they were doing was just for fun. They never lasted more than a month – if they lasted that long. He was only interested in a few dinners, going to bed with them, and moving on. Rachel had taken his heart with her, and tossed it in a dumpster some-where. He talked to her now only when he had to, which was less and less often as the kids grew older. Most of the time, he sent her terse e-mails about their arrangements, or had his secretary call her. He wanted nothing to do with her. Nor did he want a serious involvement with anyone else. Adam loved his freedom, and nothing on earth would have made him jeopardize that again.

His mother had finally stopped complaining about his being single, or almost, and she had finally stopped trying to introduce him to a 'nice girl.' Adam had exactly what he wanted, a rotating smorgasbord of playmates to entertain him. If he wanted someone to talk to, he called his friends. As far as he was concerned, women were for sex, fun, and to keep at a distance. He had no intention of getting close enough to get hurt again. Unlike Charlie, he wasn't looking for the perfect woman. All he wanted was the perfect bedmate for as long as it lasted, hopefully no longer than two weeks, and he kept it that way. Adam wanted no serious involvements. The only things he was serious about were his children, his work, and his friends. And as far as he was concerned, the women in his life were not his friends. Rachel was his sworn enemy, his mother was his cross to bear, his sister was a nuisance, and the women he went out with were barely more than strangers. Most of the time he was a lot happier, felt safer, and was more comfortable with men. Particularly Charlie and Gray.

'I think I had fun last night,' Adam said with a sheepish grin. 'The last thing I remember was dancing with a bunch of Brazilian women who didn't speak English, but man, could they move. I sambaed myself into a frenzy, and must have had about six hundred drinks. They were amazing.'

'So were you.' Charlie laughed out loud, as both men turned their faces to the sunshine. It felt good, even with Adam's headache. Adam played as hard as he worked. He was the top lawyer in his field these days, eternally stressed and anxious, he carried three cell phones and a pager, and spent his life either in meetings or flying somewhere to see clients in his plane. He represented a roster of major celebrities, all of whom seemed to get themselves into trouble with alarming regularity, but Adam loved what he did, and had more patience with his clients than he did with anyone else, except his kids, who meant everything to him. Amanda and Jacob were the sweet spot in his life.

'I think I made a date with two of them for tonight,' Adam said, smiling at the memory of the Brazilian beauties. 'They couldn't understand a word I said. We'll have to go back tonight and see if they're there.' Adam was beginning to revive after a second cup of coffee, just as Gray appeared, wearing dark glasses, with his mane of uncombed white hair sticking up straight. He often wore it that way, but it seemed particularly appropriate as he groaned and sat down at the table, wearing a bathing suit and a T-shirt that was clean but splattered with paint.

'I'm too old for this,' he said, gratefully accepting a cup of coffee, and opening a small bottle of Unterberg. The bitter taste settled his stomach after the excesses of the night before. Unlike Adam and Charlie, he was not in fabulously athletic shape. He was long and lean and looked somewhat under-nourished. As a boy, he had looked like a poster child for starving children somewhere. Now he just looked very thin. He was an artist and lived in the West Village, where he worked for months on intricate, beautifully done paintings. He managed to survive, though barely, if he sold two a year. And like Charlie, he had never married, nor had kids. He was respected in the art world, but had never been a commercial success. He didn't care. Money meant nothing to him. As he told them frequently, all he cared about was the integrity of his work. He offered some of the Unterberg to Adam and Charlie, and both made a face and shook their heads.

'I don't know how you drink that stuff,' Adam said, grimacing at the smell of it. 'It works, but I'd rather have the hangover than drink that.'

'It's great. It works. Maybe you should just hook me up to an IV of it, if we're going to keep drinking like this. I always forget how bad it gets. Do we qualify for AA yet?' Gray said as he downed the Unterberg, then the coffee, and then dove into a plate of eggs.

'That's usually the second week, not the first,' Charlie said happily. He loved being with his two friends. Despite their initial indulgences, they usually settled down to a dull roar after the first few days. It wasn't as bad as they both made it sound, although they had all drunk a lot the night before, and had a lot of fun, dancing with strangers, watching people, and generally enjoying each other's company. Charlie was looking forward to spending

28

the month with them. It was the high point of his year, and theirs. They lived on the anticipation of it for months every year, and reveled in the warmth of it for months after. They had a decade of memories of trips like this, and laughed at the tales of their antics whenever they met.

'I think we're early this year with a night like last night. My liver's already shot. I can feel it,' Gray commented, looking worried, as he finished the eggs, and ate a piece of toast to settle his stomach. His head was still pounding, but the Unterberg had helped. Adam couldn't have faced the breakfast Gray had just eaten. The bitters he took religiously every day while on board obviously worked and fortunately, none of them got seasick. 'I'm older than you two. If we don't slow down, it's going to kill me. Or maybe just the dancing will. Shit, I'm out of shape.' Gray had just turned fifty but looked noticeably older than either of his friends. Charlie had a youthful boyish look, even in his mid-forties, that knocked five or ten years off his appearance, and Adam was only forty-one, and was in amazing shape. Wherever he was in the world, and no matter how busy, he went to the gym every day. He said it was the only way he could cope with the stress. Gray had never taken care of himself, slept little, ate less, and lived for his work, as Adam did. He spent long hours standing in front of his easel, and did nothing but think, dream, and breathe art. He wasn't much older than the other two, but he looked his age, mainly because of his shock of unruly white hair. The women he met thought him beautiful and gentle, for a while at least, until they moved on.

Unlike Charlie and Adam, Gray never thought about pursuing women, and he made little effort, if any, in that direction. He moved obliviously in the art world, and like homing pigeons the women he wound up with found him, and always had. He was a magnet to what Adam referred to as psycho women, and Gray never disagreed. The women he went out with had always recently stopped taking their medication, or did so immediately after becoming involved with him. They had always been abused by their previous boyfriend or husband, who was still calling them, after throwing the woman in question out into the street. Gray never failed to rescue them, and even if they were unattractive or problematic for him, long before he slept with them, he offered them a place to live, 'just for a few weeks till they got on their feet.' And eventually, the feet they got on were his. He wound up cooking for them, housing them, taking care of them, finding doctors and therapists for them, putting them in rehab, or drying them out himself. He gave them money, leaving himself even more destitute than he had been before they met. He offered them a safe haven, kindness, and comfort. He did just about anything he had to, and that they needed, as long as they didn't have kids. Kids were the one thing that Gray couldn't deal with. They terrified him, and always had. They reminded him of his own peculiar childhood, which had never been a pleasant memory for him. Being around children and families always reinforced the painful realization of how dysfunctional his own family had been.

The women Gray got involved with didn't appear to be mean at first, and they claimed they didn't want to hurt him. They were disorganized, dysfunctional, more often than not hysterical, and their lives were a total mess. The affairs he had with them lasted anywhere from a month to a year. He got jobs for them, cleaned them up, introduced them to people who were helpful to them, and without fail, if they didn't wind up hospitalized or institutionalized somewhere, they left him for someone else. He had never had a desire to marry any of them, but he got used to them, and it disappointed him for a while when they moved on. He expected it. He was the ultimate caretaker, and like all devoted parents, he expected his chicks to fly the nest. Much to his amazement each time, their departures were almost always awkward and traumatic. They rarely left Gray's life with grace. They stole things from him, got into screaming fights that caused the neighbors to call the police, would have slashed his tires if he'd had a car, tossed his belongings out the window, or caused some kind of ruckus that turned out to be embarrassing or painful to him. They rarely if ever thanked him for the time, effort, money, and affection he had lavished on them. And in the end, it made it a blissful relief when they left. Unlike Adam and Charlie, Gray was never attracted to young girls. The women who appealed to him were usually somewhere in their forties, and always seriously deranged. He said he liked their vulnerability, and felt sorry for them. Adam had suggested he work for the Red Cross, or a crisis center, which would let him caretake to his heart's content, instead of turning his love life into a suicide hotline for the mentally ill and middle-aged.

'I can't help it,' Gray said sheepishly. 'I always figure that if I don't help them, no one else will.'

'Yeah, right. You're lucky one of those wackos hasn't tried to kill you in your sleep.' Over the years, one or two had tried, but fortunately, had failed. Gray had an overwhelming and irresistible need to save the world, and to rescue women in dire need. Eventually those needs always included someone other than Gray. Almost every one of the women he had dated had left him for another man. And after they left, another woman in a state of total disaster would turn up, and turn his life upside down again. It was a roller-coaster ride he had gotten used to over the years. He had never lived any other way.

Unlike Charlie and Adam, whose families were traditional, respectable, and conservative – Adam's on Long Island, and Charlie's on Fifth Avenue in New York – Gray had grown up all over the world. The parents who had adopted him at birth had been part of one of the most successful rock groups in history. He had grown up, if you could call it that, among some of the biggest rock stars of the time, who handed him joints and shared beers with him by the time he was eight. His parents had adopted a little girl as well. They had named him Gray, and her Sparrow, and when Gray was ten, they had been 'born again,' and retired. They moved first to India, and then Nepal, settled in the Caribbean, and spent four years in the Amazon, living on a boat. All Gray remembered now was the poverty they had seen, the natives they'd met, more than he remembered the early years of drugs, but he recalled some of that as well. His sister had become a Buddhist nun, and had gone back to India, to work with the starving masses in Calcutta. Gray had gotten off the boat, literally and otherwise, and went to New York at eighteen to paint. His family still had money then, but he had chosen to try and make it on his own, and had spent his early twenties studying in Paris, before he went back to New York.

His parents had moved to Santa Fe by then, and when Gray was twenty-five, they had adopted a Navajo baby and called him Boy. It had been a complicated process, but the tribe agreed to let him go. He seemed like a nice child to Gray, but the age difference between them was so great that he scarcely saw him while Boy was growing up. His adoptive parents had died when Boy was eighteen, and he had gone back to live with his tribe. It had happened seven years earlier, and although Gray knew where he was, they had never contacted each other. He had a letter from Sparrow from India once every few years. They had never liked each other much, their early life had been spent surviving the vagaries and eccentricities of their adoptive parents. He knew Sparrow had spent years trying to find her birth parents, maybe to bring some kind of normalcy into her life. She had found them in Kentucky somewhere, had nothing in common with them, and had never seen them again. Gray had never had any desire to find his, some curiosity perhaps, but he had enough on his plate with the parents he'd had, he felt no need to add more dysfunctional people to the mix. The lunatics he was already related to were more than enough for him.

The women he went out with were just more of the same. The disruptions he shared with them, and tried to solve for them, were more of what he'd seen growing up, and were familiar and comfortable for him. And the one thing he knew without wavering was that he never wanted to have children and do the same to them. Having children was something he left to other people, like Adam, who could bring them up properly. Gray knew that he couldn't, he had no parental role models to follow, no real home life to emulate, nothing to give to them, or so he felt. All he wanted to do was paint, and he did it well.

Whatever genetic mix he had come from originally, whoever his birth parents were, Gray had an enormous talent, and although never financially viable, his career as a painter had always been a respected one. Even the critics conceded that he was very, very good. He just couldn't keep his life together long enough to make money at what he did. What his parents had made in their early years, they had spent on drugs and traveling around the world. Gray was used to being penniless and didn't mind it. What he had, he gave to others whom he considered more in need. And whether on Charlie's yacht, in the lap of luxury, or freezing in his studio in the Meatpacking District in New York, it was all the same to him. Whether or not there was a woman in his life didn't matter to him much. What mattered to him were his work, and his friends.

He had long since proven to himself that although women were appealing sometimes, and he liked having a warm body in his bed to comfort him on cold nights, they were all insane – or the ones he found in his bed always were. There was no question in anyone's mind, if a woman was with Gray, more likely than not, she was nuts. It was a curse he accepted, an irresistible pull for him, after the childhood he'd had. He felt that the only way to break the spell, or the curse that had been put on him by his dysfunctional adopted family, was to refuse to pass that angst-making lifestyle on to a child of his own. His gift to the world, he often said, was promising himself never to have kids. It was a promise he had never broken, and knew he never would. He said he was allergic to children, and they were equally so to him. Unlike Charlie, Gray wasn't looking for the perfect woman, he would have just liked to find one, one day, who was sane. In the meantime, the ones he did find provided excitement and comic relief, for him and his friends.

'So, what are we doing today?' Charlie asked, as the three men stretched out on deck chairs after breakfast.

The sun was high, it was nearly noon, and the weather had never been better. It was an absolutely gorgeous day. Adam said he wanted to go shopping for his kids in St. Tropez. Amanda always loved the things he brought home for her, and Jacob was easy. They were both crazy about their dad, although they loved their mother and stepfather too. Rachel and the pediatrician had had two more children, whom Adam pretended didn't exist, although he knew that Amanda and Jacob were fond of them, and loved them like a full brother and sister. Adam didn't want to know about them. He had never forgiven Rachel for her betrayal, and never would. He had concluded years before that, given the opportunity, all women were bitches. His mother had nagged his father constantly, and was disrespectful to him. His father had dealt with the constant barrage of verbal abuse with silence. His sister was subtler than their mother, and got everything she wanted by whining. On the rare occasions when she didn't, she got out her claws and fangs and got vicious. The only way to handle a woman, as far as Adam was concerned, was to find a dumb one, keep her at arm's length, and move on quickly. Everything was fine, as long as he kept moving. The only time he stopped to smell the roses, or let his guard down, was on the boat with Charlie and Gray, or with his children.

'The shops close for lunch at one,' Charlie reminded him. 'We can go in this afternoon when they open.' Adam remembered that they didn't reopen until three-thirty or four. And it was too early to have lunch.

They had just had breakfast, even though all Adam had had, after the excesses of the night before, was a roll and coffee. He had a nervous stomach, had had an ulcer years before, and rarely ate much. It was the price he paid willingly for being in a stressful business. After all these years, negotiating contracts for athletes and major stars, he thrived on the excitement and loved it. He bailed them out of jail, got them on the teams they wanted, signed them on for concert tours, negotiated their divorces, paid palimony to their mistresses, and drew up support agreements for their children born out of wedlock. They kept him busy, stressed, and happy. And now he was finally on vacation. He took three a year, one on Charlie's boat for the month of August, which was a sacred commitment to him, and a week on the boat with him again in winter, in the Caribbean. Gray never joined them then, he had bad memories of the Caribbean from when he had lived there with his parents, and said nothing could induce him to go back there. And at the end of August each year, Adam spent a week traveling in Europe with his children. As always, he was meeting them at the end of this trip. His plane was picking them up in New

York, stopping in Nice for him, and then the three of them would go to London for a week.

'What do you say we pull out and sit at anchor for a while? We can anchor off the beach, and go in to lunch at Club 55 with the tender,' Charlie suggested, and they nodded in unison. It was what they usually did in St. Tropez.

Charlie had all the appropriate toys on board for guests – water skis, Jet Skis, a small sailboat, wind-surfing boards, and scuba equipment. But most of the time, the three men enjoyed being lazy. The time they shared was mostly spent on lunches, dinner, women, drinking, and a little swimming. And a lot of sleeping. Especially Adam, who always arrived exhausted, and said the only place he ever slept decently was on Charlie's boat in August. It was the one time of the year when he had no worries. He still got faxes from his office every day, and e-mails, which he checked regularly. But his secretaries, assistants, and partners knew not to bother him more than they absolutely had to in August. And if they did, God help them. It was the only time when Adam took his hands off the controls, and actually tried not to think about his clients. Anyone who knew him well, and how hard he worked, was well aware that he needed the breather. It made him a lot nicer to deal with in September. He coasted for weeks, and even months sometimes, on the good times he had with Gray and Charlie.

The three men had met originally as a result of their philanthropic bent. Charlie's foundation had been organizing a benefit to fund a house on the Upper West Side for abused women and children. The chairman of the event had been trying to find a major rock star to donate a performance, and had contacted Adam, who represented the artist in question. Adam and Charlie had eventually had lunch in order to discuss it, and found that they genuinely admired each other. By the time the event had taken place, the two men had become fast friends.

Adam had actually gotten the rock star he represented to donate a million-dollar performance, which was unheard-of – but he had done it. One of Gray's paintings was auctioned off at the same event, which he had donated himself, a major sacrifice for him, since it represented six months of his income. After the event, he had volunteered to paint a mural at the safe house Charlie's foundation had funded. He had met Charlie then, and Adam when Charlie invited both him and Gray to his apartment to dinner to thank them. The three men couldn't have been more different but, in spite of that, had discovered a common bond, in the causes they cared about, and the fact that none of them were married, or seriously involved with anyone at the time. Adam had just gone through his divorce. Charlie was between engagements and invited both of them on the boat he had then, to keep him company during the month of August, when he had planned to be on it for his honeymoon. He thought a trip with the two men might be a pleasant distraction, and it had turned out better than he'd hoped. They'd had a fantastic time. The girl Gray had been going out with had attempted suicide in June, and left with one of his art students in July. By August, he had been greatly relieved to leave town, and grateful for the opportunity Charlie offered to do so. Gray had been even more broke than usual at the time. And Adam had had a tough spring, with two major athletes sustaining injuries, and a world-class band canceling a concert tour, which had spawned a dozen lawsuits. The trip to Europe on Charlie's yacht had been perfect. And it had been their annual junket since then. This year promised to be no different. St. Tropez, Monte Carlo for a little gambling, Portofino, Sardinia, Capri, and wherever they felt like stopping in between. They had been on the boat for only two days, and all three men were thrilled to be there. Charlie thoroughly enjoyed their company, just as they did his. And the *Blue Moon* was the ideal venue for their shared mischief and fun.

'So what'll it be, boys? Club 55 for lunch, and a little swimming first?' Charlie pressed, so he could let the captain know their plans.

'Yeah, what the hell, I guess so,' Adam said, rolling his eyes, as his French cell phone rang and he ignored it. He could listen to the message later. He carried only one while in Europe, a vast improvement over the battery of phones and papers he carried in New York. 'It's tough work, but someone has to do it.' He grinned.

'Bloody Mary, anyone?' Charlie inquired with feigned innocence, as he signaled to the steward that they'd be leaving. The purser, who'd been standing by, a handsome young man from New Zealand, nodded, then disappeared to tell the captain, and make the lunch reservation. He didn't need to ask anything more. He knew Charlie would want to go ashore for lunch at two-thirty. Most of the time he preferred eating on board, but the scene in St. Tropez was too tempting. And everyone who was anyone went to Club 55 for lunch, just as they went to Spoon these days for dinner.

'Make mine a virgin Bloody Mary,' Gray said as he smiled at the steward. 'I thought I'd postpone my trip to rehab for a few days.'

'Make mine hot and spicy, and come to think of it, make mine with tequila,' Adam said with a broad grin as Charlie laughed.

'I'll have a Bellini,' Charlie said – they were peach juice and champagne, and an easy way to start a day of decadence. Charlie had a fondness for Cuban cigars and good champagne. They had a lot of both on board.

All three men sat drinking and relaxing on deck as they motored carefully away from the port, avoiding the many smaller boats and the daily tour boats filled with gawkers who snapped their picture as they drove by. The usual flock of paparazzi were huddled together at the end of the *quai,* waiting for big yachts to come into port, so they could see who was on board. They followed celebrities on motor-bikes, hounding them every step of the way, and they took a last picture of *Blue Moon* as she sailed away, assuming correctly that the superyacht would be back that night. Most of the time they took photographs of Charlie as he strolled through town, but he rarely if ever gave them fodder for the tabloids. Aside from the immense opulence and size of his yacht, Charlie led a relatively quiet life, and avoided scandal at all costs. He was just a very rich man, traveling with two friends, whom no one reading the tabloids had ever heard about. Even with the stars Adam knew and represented, he always stayed in the back-ground. And Gray Hawk was just a starving artist. They were three bachelors, and devoted friends, out to have some fun for the month of August.

They swam for half an hour before lunch. Afterward, Adam took out one of the Jet Skis to take a tour around the other boats, and work off some of his energy, while Gray slept on the deck, and Charlie smoked one of his Cuban cigars. It was the perfect life. At two-thirty they took the tender to lunch at Club 55. Alain Delon was there, as he often was, Gerard Départdieu, and Catherine Deneuve, which caused the three friends to discuss her at length. They all agreed that she was still beautiful, despite her age. She was very much Charlie's type, although considerably older than the women he went out with, who more often than not were somewhere in their thirties, or even slightly younger. He rarely went out with women his own age. He left the women in their forties to men in their sixties, or older. And Adam liked them much, much younger.

Gray said he would have been happy with Catherine Deneuve, at any age. He liked women closer to his own age, or even slightly older, although Ms. Deneuve was disqualified in his case, because she looked completely normal and relaxed as she laughed and talked to friends. The woman Gray was looking for, or would have noticed any-where, would have been crying softly in a corner, or talking between sobs on her cell phone while appearing distraught. The girl Adam had in mind would have been ten years older than his teenage daughter. And he would have had to buy her breast implants and a nose job. The girl of Charlie's dreams would have been wearing a halo and glass slippers. But this time, in his fairy tale, when midnight came, she wouldn't run away, or disappear, she would stay at the ball, promise never to leave him, and dance in his arms forever. He just hoped that one day he'd find her.

2

The captain docked the *Blue Moon* at the end of the *quai* in St. Tropez that afternoon. It was a major feat since dock space wasn't easy to come by in high season. Because of her size, they had to have the first spot, but as soon as they tied her up, Charlie was sorry they had gone in, instead of coming into port in the tender, as he usually preferred to do. The paparazzi were out in full force, and instantly drawn by the sheer size of the boat. They snapped a lot of photographs of all three men as they slipped into a car waiting for them. Charlie ignored them, as did Adam, and Gray waved.

'Poor bastards, what a shit way to make a living,' he said sympathetically, as Adam growled. He hated the press.

'Parasites. They're all bottom-feeders,' he said. The press constantly created problems in his clients' lives. He had gotten a call from his office just that afternoon. One of his clients had been caught coming out of a hotel with a woman other than his wife, and the shit had hit the fan. The irate wife had called the office ten times and was threatening divorce. It wasn't the first time he'd done it, and she either wanted a huge settlement in a divorce, or five million dollars to stay married to him. Nice. Nothing surprised Adam anymore. All he wanted right now was to find those Brazilian girls again, and dance the samba until the wee hours. He could deal with the rest of the crap when he got back to New York. Right now he had no interest in dealing with the tabloids, or the infidelities of his clients. They'd done it before, and would do the same things many times again. This was his time now, not theirs. Time out. He had turned his meter off.

They went into town to shop that afternoon, took naps, and had dinner at Spoon at the Hotel Byblos, where a spectacular-looking Russian super-model had come in wearing white silk pants, and a little white leather bolero, wide open, with nothing underneath. The entire restaurant got a full view of her breasts, and seemed to enjoy it. Charlie looked amused, while Adam laughed.

'She has amazing breasts,' Gray commented as they ordered dinner, and an excellent bottle of wine.

'Yeah, but they're not real,' Adam said clinically, unimpressed but also amused. It took a lot of guts to sit down to dinner in a nice restaurant with your tits hanging out, although they had seen it done before. A German girl had walked into a restaurant the year before with a see-through net blouse you couldn't even see, and no one skipped a beat. She had sat there eating dinner all night, naked from the waist up, talking, laughing, smoking, and obviously enjoying the sensation she had caused.

'How do you know they're not real?' Gray asked with interest. Her breasts were large and firm, and the nipples pointed up. He would have loved to draw them, and was already slightly drunk. They'd been drinking margaritas on the boat before they went out. Another night of decadence and debauchery had begun.

'Take my word for it,' Adam said with confidence. 'I've paid for about a hundred pair by now. Actually, a hundred and a half. A couple of years ago some girl I went out with only wanted one done. She said the other one was fine, she just wanted to match up the smaller one.'

'That sounds interesting,' Charlie said, looking amused, as he tasted the wine and nodded to the sommelier. It was fine. Better than fine. It was superb. It was a very old vintage of Lynch-Bages. 'Instead of taking them out to dinner and a movie, do you send them out for new breasts first?'

'No, every time I go out with some budding actress, she hits me up for a new pair on the way out. It's easier than arguing about it. They go quietly after that, as long as they like what they got.'

'Men used to buy women pearls or diamond bracelets as consolation prizes. I guess now they buy them implants instead,' Charlie commented drily. The women he went out with would never have asked him for new breasts, or any of the other things Adam paid for. If Charlie's dates had cosmetic work done, they paid for it themselves, from their trusts, and it was never discussed. He couldn't think of a single woman he'd gone out with who'd had plastic surgery, at least not that he knew about. Adam's girls, as he and Gray called them, had been entirely remodeled for the most part. And Gray's women needed lobotomies, or heavy sedation, more than anything else. He had paid for a number of therapists, rehab programs, shrinks, and attorneys' fees for court orders to restrain the previous men in their lives who were either stalking them or threatening to kill them, or him. Whatever worked. Maybe paying for the implants was simpler in the end. After the surgery, Adam's women thanked him and disappeared. Gray's always lingered for a while, or called when the new men in their lives began abusing them. They rarely stayed with Gray for longer than a year. He treated them too well. Charlie's women always became friends, and invited him to their weddings, to someone else, after he had left them, once their fatal flaw had been

49

unearthed. 'Maybe I should try that some time,' Charlie said, laughing over his wine.

'Try what?' Gray asked, looking confused. He was dazzled by the Russian woman and her breasts.

'Paying for implants. It might make a nice Christmas present, or a wedding gift.'

'That's sick,' Adam said, shaking his head. 'It's bad enough that I do it. The girls you go out with have too much class to want you to buy them tits.' The women Adam went out with needed them to get ahead, as actresses or models. Adam wasn't interested in class. It would have been a handicap for him. Women like the ones Charlie went out with would have been a headache for Adam. He didn't want to stick around. Charlie claimed he did. Gray just let things drift. He had no firm plans, about anything. He just lived life as it came. Adam had a schedule for everything, and a plan.

'At least it would be an unusual gift. I get so tired of buying them china.' Charlie smiled through his cigar smoke.

'Just be happy you're not paying them alimony and child support. Believe me, china is a lot cheaper,' Adam said tartly. He had stopped paying Rachel alimony when she remarried, but she had taken half of everything he had, and he was still paying hefty child support, which he didn't begrudge his kids. But he hated what he had given

50

her in the settlement. She had really put it to him ten years before when they divorced, and he had already been a partner in his firm. She got a lot more than he felt she deserved. Her parents had hired her a terrific lawyer. And he still resented it bitterly ten years later. He had never gotten over the damage she'd done, and probably never would. In his mind, buying breast implants was fine, alimony wasn't. Ever again.

'I think it's too bad you have to buy them anything, along those lines,' Gray commented. 'I'd rather just buy a woman something because I want to. Not pay for her lawyer, therapist, or a nose job,' he said innocently. Considering how little he had, whenever he got involved with someone, he wound up getting stuck for a fortune, in proportion to what he earned. But he always wanted to help them. Gray was the Red Cross of dating. Adam was the wheeler and dealer, setting clear limits and making trade-offs. Charlie was the ever polite and romantic Prince Charming. Although Gray said he was romantic too. It was just the women he got involved with who weren't, they were too desperate and needy to pay much attention to romance. But he would have liked to have some in his life, if he ever managed to get mixed up with someone sane, which seemed ever more unlikely. Adam claimed to no longer have a romantic bone in his body, and was proud of it. He said he'd rather have great sex than bad romance.

'What's wrong with having all of it?' Gray asked, starting on his third glass of the great wine. 'Why not sex *and* romance, and even someone who loves you? And that you love in return.'

'Sounds good to me,' Charlie agreed. And of course in his case, he wanted blue blood in the mix as well. He admitted readily that when it came to women, he was a snob. Adam always teased him and said he didn't want his bloodlines sullied by some peasant girl. Charlie objected to the way he put it, but they both knew it was true.

'I think you're both living in fantasyland,' Adam said cynically. 'Romance is what screws up everything, everyone gets disappointed and pissed off, and that's when the shit hits the proverbial fan. If everyone knows it's just about sex and some fun, no one gets hurt.'

'Then how come all your girlfriends get so pissed off on the way out?' Gray asked simply. He had a point.

'Because women never believe what you tell them. The minute you tell them you'll never get married, you become a challenge, and they start shopping for a wedding dress. But at least I'm honest. If they don't believe me, that's their problem. I say the words. If they don't want to hear them, that's up to them. But God knows I say them.' That was also one of the advantages of dating very young women. Twenty-two-year-olds generally weren't looking for marriage, just a good time. It was only when they started creeping up on thirty that they looked around and got panicked about where things were going. The younger ones wanted to go to clubs and bars, buy a few dresses and charge them to him, and go to concerts and expensive restaurants. If he took them to Las Vegas for a weekend, when he had to see one of his clients, they thought they'd died and gone to Heaven.

His family, however, had a different attitude. His mother always accused him of dating hookers, especially when she saw him in the tabloids. He always corrected her and said they were actresses and models, which she assured him was the same thing. His sister just looked embarrassed when the subject came up at family dinners. His brother thought it was funny, but for the past few years had told him it was time for him to settle down. Adam could not have cared less what they thought. He thought their lives were painfully boring. His wasn't. And he assured himself regularly that they were just jealous, because he was having fun and they weren't. His parents weren't jealous, they just disapproved of him on principle. And predictably, given her disapproval of Adam, or maybe just to annoy him, he thought sometimes, his mother had stayed close to Rachel. She liked her and her new husband, and always reminded Adam that she saw Rachel and stayed close to her because she was her grandchildren's mother. Whatever the issue or argument, Adam's mother always chose to be on the opposite side from him. She couldn't help herself. She had a contrary nature and a need for conflict. He suspected that beneath it all, his mother loved him. But she seemed to feel compelled to criticize him and make his life difficult. She appeared to disapprove of everything he did.

His mother still blamed him for the divorce, and said he must have done something terrible to her, to make her leave with someone else. She never sympathized with Adam for a moment that his wife had cheated on him, and left him. It had to be his fault. Somewhere, beneath the overt criticism and disapproval, he suspected she was proud of his accomplishments. But his mother never admitted that to him.

It was after eleven when they left the dinner table and wandered around St. Tropez for a while. The streets were crowded, and people were sitting at sidewalk cafés and at open-air restaurants and bars. Music was blaring from several nightclubs. They stopped for a drink at Chez Nano, and got to Les Caves du Roy at one o'clock in the morning, as it was coming to life. There were women everywhere in halter tops, tight jeans, simple little see-through dresses and shirts, artfully tousled hair, and sexy high-heeled sandals. Adam felt like a kid in a candy store, and even Charlie and Gray enjoyed it. Gray was a lot shyer about picking up women. They usually found him. And Charlie was infinitely more selective, but he loved watching the scene.

By one-thirty, all three of them were dancing, and they were still relatively sober. The Brazilian girls never reappeared, but Adam didn't care. He danced with at least a dozen others, and then settled on a little German girl who said her parents had a house in Ramatuelle, the neighboring town to St. Tropez. She looked about fourteen, until she started dancing with Adam. Then it became rapidly obvious that she knew what she was doing, and what she wanted, and was considerably older. She wanted Adam. She was practically making love to him on the dance floor. It was after three o'clock by then and Charlie began to yawn. He and Gray went back to the boat a few minutes later. Adam said he'd find his way back on his own, since they were docked at the quay that night, and Charlie had given him a radio in case he needed to call them. Adam nodded and continued dancing with the German girl, who had bright red hair and said her name was Ushi. He winked at Charlie as they walked out, and Charlie smiled. Adam was having fun. A lot of fun.

'What are we doing tomorrow?' Gray asked as they walked back to the boat. You could hear the music for a long way. But it was peaceful on the boat, once they got inside and closed the doors. Charlie offered Gray a brandy before they went to bed, but Gray said he just couldn't. They stood on deck smoking cigars instead, watching people stroll along the quay, or sit talking on other yachts docked nearby. St. Tropez was the ultimate party town – where people seemed to stay up all night.

'I was thinking we should head for Portofino, or maybe stop in Monte Carlo,' Charlie answered. After a while, even a few days, the revelry in St. Tropez got old, unless you had friends there, which they didn't. It was fun to eat in the restaurants and go to the nightclubs, but there were a number of other places they wanted to visit in the next month, some of them as festive as St. Tropez, and others a little quieter. Monte Carlo was more elegant and sedate, and all three of them enjoyed going to the casino.

'Adam might want to stick around for another night or two to see this German girl again,' Gray commented, thinking about their friend. He didn't want to spoil his fun, or blow his romance. Charlie knew him better and was more cynical. If he knew

Adam, and if past trips were any indication, one night with her was all he wanted.

It was nearly four in the morning when Charlie and Gray went to their respective cabins. It had been a long but enjoyable night. Charlie fell asleep instantly, and neither of them heard Adam come in at five that morning.

Charlie and Gray were having breakfast on the aft deck, when Adam and Ushi emerged, smiling. She looked only faintly embarrassed when she saw the two other men.

'*Gut* morning,' she said politely, as Charlie thought she looked about sixteen in the bright day-light. She wasn't wearing makeup, but she had a spectacular figure, in the jeans and skin-tight T-shirt she'd been wearing the night before, and carrying a pair of high-heeled gold sandals. Her red hair was full and long, and Adam had an arm around her.

The stewardess standing by ordered them both breakfast, and Ushi insisted all she wanted was some muesli and coffee. Adam ordered bacon, eggs, and pancakes. He seemed to be in remarkably good spirits, as his two cohorts attempted not to smile at each other.

The foursome chatted amiably, and as soon as Ushi had finished breakfast, the purser called a cab for her. Adam gave her a tour of the boat before she left, and she had stars in her eyes as he walked her off the boat to the waiting taxi.

'I'll call you,' he promised vaguely, and kissed her. It had been an unforgettable night, although his two friends knew that he would soon forget her, and a year from now they would have to remind him of her, if they chose to.

'When? Will you be at the discothèque tonight?' Ushi asked as Adam stood next to the cab.

'I think we'll probably be leaving,' he said, answering the second question, and not the first one. She had given him her phone number in Ramatuelle and said she would be there for all of August. After that she would go back to Munich with her parents. She had given him her address in Germany, as he said he went there on business occasionally. She had told him she was twenty-two years old, and studying medicine in Frankfurt. 'If we stay, I'll come back to the disco. But I doubt it.' He tried to maintain at least a minimum of honesty with the women he slept with, and not get their hopes up unduly. But he knew she couldn't have too many illusions either. She had picked a man up in a discothèque, a total stranger, and spent the night with him, knowing full well it was unlikely she would ever see him again. She had been looking for the same thing he was and, for one night at least, had gotten everything she wanted. And so had

Adam. He had enjoyed the night he had spent with her, but in the light of day, there was no hiding from the fact that they were strangers, and unlikely to ever meet again. The rules of the road were clear to both of them.

Adam kissed her as he put her in the cab, and she clung to him for a moment. 'Good-bye . . . thank you . . .' she said dreamily, and then he kissed her again.

'Thank *you*, Ushi,' he whispered, and then he patted her behind. She got into the cab, waved, and she was gone. Another evening's entertainment. It was one way to pass the time, and definitely enhanced his vacation. Her body had been even better with her clothes off, as Adam had suspected.

'Well, that was a nice little surprise,' Charlie commented with a wry smile, as Adam joined them again at the breakfast table. 'I love entertaining guests for breakfast, and such pretty ones. Do you suppose we should leave town before her parents come after you with a shotgun?'

'I hope not.' Adam grinned, looking pleased with himself. He enjoyed turning Charlie's yacht into a party boat from time to time. 'She's twenty-two years old, and a medical student. And she wasn't a virgin.' Although even Adam had to admit, she looked younger than she was.

'How disappointing,' Charlie quipped, lighting

up a cigar. In summer, on the boat, sometimes he even smoked them after breakfast. The one thing they all liked about their lives was that, however lonely they were at times, they could do anything they wanted. It was one of the great advantages of being single. They could eat at any hour, dress however they chose, drink as much as they liked, even if they got drunk, and spend time with whoever they wanted. There was no one to nag, bitch, complain, compromise with, apologize to, or accommodate. All they had was each other, and for the moment it was all they wanted. For all three of them at this precise moment in time, it was the perfect life. 'Maybe at our next stop we can find you a virgin. Around here I think they're hard to find though.'

'Very funny.' Adam grinned, pleased with himself for his conquest of the night before. 'You're just jealous. Where is our next stop, by the way?' Adam loved the way they could move from one place to another, like taking their house or hotel with them. They could live in utter luxury, design their own itinerary, and change it at a moment's notice, while being waited on hand and foot by impeccably trained crew members. As far as all three of them were concerned, this was Heaven. It was exactly what Charlie loved about having a yacht, and why he spent his summers, and several weeks in the winter, on it.

'Where do you both want to go?' Charlie inquired. 'I was thinking about Monaco or Portofino.' After considerable debate, they decided on Monaco, and Portofino the day after. Monte Carlo was just a short hop away, two hours from St. Tropez. Portofino was an eight-hour journey. As Charlie had suspected, Gray said he didn't care and Adam wanted to go to the casino in Monte Carlo.

They left the dock right after lunch, an excellent seafood buffet. It was nearly three when they departed, after stopping for a swim on the way, and then all three men dozed on the deck as they motored on toward Monaco. They were sound asleep in deck chairs when they arrived, and the captain and crew docked the *Blue Moon* expertly at the quay, using fenders to keep them from being bumped by other boats. As always, the port at Monte Carlo was filled with yachts as large as they were, or even larger.

Charlie woke up at six o'clock, saw where they were, and that his two friends were still sleeping. He went to his cabin to shower and change, and Gray and Adam woke up at seven. Adam was understandably exhausted after his revels of the previous night, and Gray wasn't used to the late hours they were keeping. It always took him a few days to adjust to their nightlife when they traveled together. But all three of them felt rested when they went to dinner.

The purser had arranged a car for them, and had made reservations at Louis XV, where they had a sumptuous dinner, in surroundings far more formal than the restaurant the night before in St. Tropez. All three of them had worn coats and ties. Charlie was wearing a cream-colored linen suit with a matching shirt, and Adam was wearing white jeans and a blazer, with alligator loafers and no socks. Gray was wearing a blue shirt, khaki slacks, and an ancient blazer. With his white hair, he looked like the senior member of the group, but there was something wild and dashing about him. He had worn a red tie, and no matter what he wore, he always looked like an artist. He gesticulated animatedly as he told them stories about his youth during dinner. He was describing a tribe of natives they had lived with briefly on the Amazon. It made for good storytelling now, but was still a nightmarish childhood to have lived through, while other kids his age were going to junior high school, riding bikes, having paper routes, and going to school dances. Instead, he had been wandering among the poor in India, living in a Buddhist monastery in Nepal, camping with natives in Brazil, and reading the teachings of the Dalai Lama. He had never really had an opportunity to enjoy being a child.

'What can I tell you? My parents were nuts. But I suppose at least they weren't boring.' Adam thought his youth had been painfully ordinary and nothing he had seen on Long Island could compare with Gray's stories. Charlie seldom spoke of his childhood. It had been predictable, respectable, and traditional, until his parents died, and then it had been heart wrenching until it became even more so when his sister died five years later. He was willing to talk about it with his therapist, but rarely socially. He knew that funny things must have happened before tragedy struck, but he could no longer remember them, only the sad parts. It was easier to keep his mind on the present, except when his therapist insisted that he remember. And even then it was a struggle to conjure up the memories and not feel devastated by them. All the worldly possessions and comforts he had did not make up for the people he had lost, or the family life that had vanished with them. And try as he might, he could not seem to recreate it. The stability and security of family, and someone to form that bond with him, always seemed to elude him. The two men he was traveling with were the closest thing he had to family in his life now, or had had in the past twenty-five years since his sister died. There had never been a lonelier time in his life than that, with the agony of knowing that he was alone in the world, with no one to care about him or love him. Now, at least, he had Adam and Gray. And he knew that, whatever happened, one or both of them would be there for him, as he would be for them. It gave all three of them great comfort. They shared a bond of unseverable trust, love, and friendship, which was priceless.

They lingered for a long time over coffee, smoking cigars, and talking about their lives, and in Adam and Gray's cases, their childhoods. It was interesting to Charlie to note how differently they processed things. Gray had long since accepted the fact that his adoptive parents had been eccentric and selfish, and as a result inadequate parents. He had never had a sense of safety in his youth, or of a real home. They had drifted from one continent to another, always seeking, searching, and never finding. He compared them to the Israelites lost in the desert for forty years, with no pillar of fire to lead them. And by the time they settled in New Mexico, and adopted Boy, Gray had been long gone. He had seen him on his infrequent visits home, but had resisted getting attached to him. Gray wanted nothing in his life that would tie him to his parents. The last time he had seen Boy was at his parents' funeral, and intentionally lost track of him after that. He felt guilty about it sometimes, but didn't allow himself to dwell on it. He had finally shed the last vestiges of a family that had been nothing but painful for him. To him, the word 'family' evoked nothing more than pain. He wondered now and then what had become of Boy since their parents' death. Whatever had happened to him, it could only be better than the life he shared with their irresponsible adoptive parents. Gray had thus far resisted any urge to feel responsible or attached to him. He thought he might try to contact him one day, but that time had not yet come. He doubted it ever would. Boy was better left as a piece of memory from the distant past, a part of his life he had no desire to revisit or touch again, although he remembered Boy as a sweet-natured child.

Adam, on the other hand, was bitter and angry about his parents. The short version, in his mind, was that his mother was a nagging bitch, and his father was a wuss. He was angry at both for their contributions to his life, or lack of them, and their depressing home life, as he viewed it. He said all he remembered of his childhood was his mother bitching at everyone, and always picking on him, since he was the youngest, and being treated as an intruder, since he had arrived so late in their lives. His vivid recollection was of his father never coming home from work. Who could blame him? As soon as Adam left for Harvard at eighteen, he had never gone home to live again. Spending holidays with them was bad enough. He said that the unpleasant atmosphere in their home had created an irreparable rift between all three children. All they had learned from their parents was how to criticize, look down at each other, nitpick, and be condescending about each other's lives. 'There was no respect in our family. My mother didn't respect my father. I think my father probably hates her, although he'd never admit it, and there's no respect between any of us kids. I think my sister is boring and pathetic, my brother is a pompous asshole with a wife just like my mother, and they think I run around with a bunch of sleazebags and whores. They have no respect for what I do, and don't even want to know what it is. All they focus on are the women I go out with, and not who I am. At this point I see them for weddings, funerals, and high holidays, and wish I didn't have to do that. If I could find an excuse not to, I would. Rachel takes the kids to see them, so I don't have to. And they like her better than they like me, and always did. They even think it's okay that she married a Christian, as long as she brings my kids up Jewish. She can do no wrong, as far as they're concerned, and I can do no right. And by now, I just figure screw them, who cares.' He sounded bitter as he said it.

'But you still see them,' Gray commented with interest. 'Maybe you care. Maybe you still need their approval, or want it. And if so, that's okay. It's just that sometimes we have to admit to ourselves that our parents aren't capable, that the love we wanted so desperately when we were kids just wasn't there. They didn't have it to give. Mine didn't, they were too busy doing drugs when they were young, and looking for the holy grail after that. They were pretty crazy. I think they liked my sister and me, as much as they could, but they had no idea how to be parents. I felt sorry for my brother Boy when they adopted him. They should have bought a dog, but they were lonely after we left, I think, so they got him.

'My poor sister is out in India somewhere, living on the streets with the poor, as a nun. She wanted to pretend she was an Asian all her life, and now she thinks she is. She has no idea who she is, and neither did they. I never knew who I was either, until I got away from them, and I still wonder sometimes about who the hell I am. I think that's the key for all of us eventually – who are we, what do we believe, what are we living, and is this the life we want to lead? I try to ask myself these questions every day, and I don't always know the answers. But at least I try to find them, and I'm not hurting anyone else while I do.

'I think the real travesty of people like my parents having kids, or adopting them, is that they really have no business having kids. I know that much about myself, which is why I don't want kids, and never did. But I try to tell myself my parents did their best, however lousy that was for me. I just don't want to recreate the same misery, and hurt someone out of my own selfish need to reproduce. I think in my case it's best for the bloodline and the insanity to stop here.' He had always felt extremely responsible about not having children, and still had no regrets about his decision not to have any. He felt utterly incapable of taking care of children, or giving them what they'd need. The thought of getting attached to them, or having them depend on him, seemed terrifying to him. He didn't want to let them down, or have them expect more of him than he could give. He didn't want to hurt or disappoint anyone as he had been in his youth. It never occurred to him that the women he constantly rescued and took care of were in effect children for him, birds with broken wings. He had an overwhelming need to nurture someone, and they met that need for him. Adam thought he would have made a good father, because he was a kind, intelligent man, with strong moral values, but Gray did not agree.

'What about you, Charlie?' Adam asked. He was bolder than Gray about moving through sacred gates and across boundaries, going where angels feared to tread. Adam always asked painful questions that made one think. 'How normal was your family when you were a kid? Gray and I are competing here for having had the shit parents of the year, and I'm not sure who would win first prize, his or mine. Mine were more obviously traditional, but they didn't have much more to give than his.' They had all had a fair amount to drink by then, and Adam wasn't shy about asking Charlie to open up about his youth. They had no secrets from each other, and Adam had always told both of them everything. As had Gray. Charlie was more private by nature, and far less expansive and forthcoming about his past.

'They were perfect, actually,' he said with a sigh. 'Loving, giving, kind, understanding, never abusive. My mother was the most loving, sensitive woman on earth. Affectionate, funny, beautiful. And my father was a truly good man. He was my hero and role model in all things. They were wonderful, and so was my childhood, and then they died. End of story. Sixteen happy years, and then my sister and I were alone in a big house, with a lot of money, and servants to take care of us, and a foundation for her to learn how to run. She dropped out of Vassar to take care of me, which she did beautifully for two years, until I went to college. She had no other life, just me. I don't think she even had a date during that time. Then I went off to Princeton, and she was sick by then, although I didn't know that for a while, and then she died. The three best people on earth, gone. Listening to you two makes me realize how lucky I was, not because of the money, but because of the kind of people they were. They were wonderful parents, and Ellen was great. But people die, people leave. Things happen, and suddenly a whole world is gone and your life is changed. I would rather have lost the money than any of them. But no one gives you that choice. You have to play with the hand you're dealt. Speaking of which, anyone for a game of roulette?' he asked in a jovial tone, changing the subject, and the other two were silent as they nodded.

It was a painful story, and both men knew it was probably why Charlie had never attached to anyone permanently. He was probably too afraid they'd die or leave or abandon him. He knew it himself. He had discussed it a thousand times with his therapist. It didn't change anything. No matter how many years he spent in therapy, his parents had still died when he was sixteen, and his last living relative, his sister, had died a horrible death when he was twenty-one. It was hard to trust anything and anyone after that. What if you loved someone and that person died or abandoned you? It was easier to find their fatal flaws and abandon them, before they could do it to you. Even with a perfect family as a child, by dying when he was so young, his parents and sister had condemned him to a life of terror forever after. If he dared to love anyone again, for sure they would die or leave him. And even if they didn't, or seemed reliable, there was always that risk. A risk he still found terrifying, and he was not willing to put his heart on the line again, until he knew he was a thousand per cent safe. He wanted every guarantee he could get. And so far, no woman had come with a guarantee, just red flags, which scared the hell out of him. So, however politely, he abandoned them. He hadn't found one yet worth risking his all for, but he felt certain that one day he would. Adam and Gray were no longer so sure. It looked to both of them as though Charlie was on his own for good. The three of them were a perfect fit, because all of them were equally sure of the same thing for themselves. The risk of coupling, for any of them, more than temporarily, was just too great. It was a curse put on them by their families, and one that none of them could erase, exorcise, or lift. The distrust and fear they lived with now was their families' final gift.

Charlie played baccarat, while Gray watched Adam play vingt-et-un, and then all three of them played roulette. Charlie put up some money for Gray, and he made three hundred dollars with a bet on the black. He gave the original hundred back to Charlie, who insisted he keep it all.

It was two in the morning when they went back to the boat, an early night for them. They went to their cabins as soon as they got home. It had been a good day, an easy companionship between friends. They were leaving for Portofino the next day. Charlie had instructed the captain to leave the dock before they got up, some time around seven. That way they would be in Portofino by late afternoon, and would have time to walk around. It was always one of their favorite stops on their summer route. Gray loved the art and architecture, and was particularly fond of the church up on the hill. Charlie loved the easy Italian atmosphere, the restaurants, and the people. It was an exceptionally pretty place. Adam loved the shops, and the Splendido Hotel high up on the hill, looking down on the harbor.

He loved the tiny port, and the gorgeous Italian girls he met there every year, as well as those from other countries who came there as tourists. It had a feeling of magic for each of them, and as they went to bed in their cabins that night, they smiled as they drifted off to sleep, thinking of arriving in Portofino the next day. As it was every year, their month together on the *Blue Moon* was a piece of Heaven for each of them.

3

They arrived in Portofino at four in the afternoon, just as the shops were opening again after lunch. They had to stay at anchor just outside the port, as the keel of the *Blue Moon* was too deep, and the depth of the water in the port too shallow. People were swimming off other boats, as Adam, Gray, and Charlie did when they woke up from their naps. By six o'clock, a number of other big yachts had come in, and there was a festive atmosphere all around them. It was a gorgeous golden afternoon. By the time dinnertime rolled around, none of them wanted to leave the boat, but they decided that they should. They were happy and relaxed, and enjoying the scenery, and the food was always delicious on Charlie's boat. But the restaurants in town were good too. There were several excellent places to eat, many of them in the port, tucked in between the shops. The shops in Portofino were even fancier than those in St. Tropez: Cartier, Hermès, Vuitton, Dolce & Gabbana, Celine, a number of Italian jewelers. It was a hotbed of luxury, although the town itself was tiny. All the action centered around the port, and the countryside and cliffs looking down at the boats were absolutely gorgeous. The Church of San Giorgio and the Splendido Hotel sat perched on separate hills, on either side of the port.

'God, I love it here,' Adam said as he grinned broadly, looking at the action all around them. A group of women had just jumped into the water topless from a nearby boat. Gray had already taken out a sketch pad and was drawing, and Charlie was sitting on deck, looking blissful and smoking a cigar. It was his favorite port in Italy, and he was happy to stay there as long as they wanted. He was in no hurry to move on. He actually preferred it to all of the ports in France. It was an easier place to be than dodging the paparazzi in St. Tropez, or wending their way through the crowds in the streets, as people ebbed and flowed out of discothèques and bars. There was something much more countrified about Portofino, and it had all the charm and ease and quaint beauty typical of Italy. Charlie loved it, as did his two friends.

All three of them wore jeans and T-shirts when they went into town for dinner. They had reservations at a delightful restaurant near the piazza, where they had gone several times before in previous years. The waiters recognized them when they walked in, and knew about the *Blue Moon*. They gave them an excellent table outdoors, where they could watch people drifting by. They ordered pasta, seafood, and a simple but good Italian wine. Gray was talking about the local architecture, when a female voice interrupted them quietly from the next table.

'Twelfth century,' was all she said, correcting what Gray had just told them. He had said that the Castello di San Giorgio had been built in the fourteenth century, and he turned his head to look at who had spoken when he heard her. A tall, exotic-looking woman was sitting at a table next to them. She was wearing a red T-shirt, sandals, and a full white cotton skirt. Her hair was dark, and she wore it in a long braid down her back. Her eyes were green, and she had creamy skin. And when he turned to look at her, she was laughing. 'I'm sorry,' she apologized, 'that was rude of me. I just happen to know it's the twelfth century, not the fourteenth. I thought I ought to say something. And I agree with you, it's one of my favorite structures in Italy, if only for the view, which I think is the best in Europe. The *castello* was actually rebuilt in the sixteenth century and built in the twelfth, not fourteenth,' she repeated, and grinned. 'The Church of San Giorgio was also built in the twelfth century.' She glanced at the paint splattered on his

T-shirt, and identified him immediately as an artist. She had managed to impart the information about the *castello* without sounding pompous, but knowledgeable and funny, and apologetic about her intrusion into her neighbors' conversation.

'Are you an art historian?' Gray asked with interest. She was a very attractive woman, although not young or eligible by Gray or Charlie's standards. She looked about forty-five years old, maybe a little younger, and she was with a large table of Europeans who were speaking Italian and French. She had been speaking both fluently with them.

'No, I'm not,' she answered his question. 'Just a busybody who comes here every year. I own a gallery in New York.' Gray squinted at her then, and realized who she was. Her name was Sylvia Reynolds, and she was well known in the art scene in New York. She had launched a number of contemporary artists, who were now considered important. Most of what she sold was very avant-garde, and very different from Gray's work. He had never met Sylvia before, but had read a lot about her, and was impressed by who she was. She glanced at him, and the two men at his table, with a look of interest, and a warm smile. She seemed to be full of life, energy, and excitement. She was wearing an armful of silver and turquoise bracelets, and everything about her said she had style. 'Are you an artist?

Or did you get paint on the T-shirt painting your house?' She was anything but shy.

'Probably both.' Gray smiled back at her, and held out a hand. 'I'm Gray Hawk.' He introduced the others to her, and she smiled easily in their direction and then back at Gray. She responded instantly to his name.

'I like your work,' she said with a warm tone of praise. 'I'm sorry I interrupted you. Are you staying at the Splendido?' she asked with interest, momentarily ignoring her European friends. There were several attractive women in the group, and a number of very good-looking men. There was also a very pretty young woman speaking to the man next to her in French. Adam had noticed her when they sat down, and couldn't decide if the man next to her was her husband or her father. She seemed to be on very close terms with him, and that sector of the group was obviously French. Sylvia appeared to be the only American in the group, which didn't seem to bother her at all. She seemed equally at ease in French, Italian, and English.

'No, we're on a boat,' Gray explained in answer to her question about where they were staying.

'Lucky you. One of those nice big ones, I assume,' she said, teasing them. She didn't really mean it, and at first Gray didn't answer, he just nodded. He knew that she'd been joking, and he didn't want to show off. She looked like a nice woman, and her reputation was that, in spite of her success, she was.

'Actually, we came here in a rowboat from France, and we're pitching a tent on the beach tonight,' Charlie quipped amiably, and she laughed. 'My friend was embarrassed to tell you. We managed to scrape up enough for dinner, but couldn't manage the hotel. The story about staying on a boat was just to impress you. He lies constantly, whenever he finds women attractive.' She laughed at him, and the others smiled.

'In that case, I'm flattered. I can think of worse places to pitch a tent than Portofino. Are the three of you traveling together?' she asked Charlie, intrigued by the three attractive men. They were an interesting-looking lot. Gray looked in fact exactly as an artist should, she thought Adam looked like an actor, and Charlie looked as though he owned or ran a bank. She loved guessing about what people did. In some ways she wasn't far off the mark. There was something theatrical and intense about Adam, it would have been easy to imagine him onstage. Charlie looked extremely proper, even in T-shirt and jeans and Hermès loafers without socks. They didn't look like three playboys to her. They had an aura about them that suggested they were men of substance. She found Gray easiest to talk to, because he had opened the conversation first. She had been listening to their conversation, and liked what he said about the local architecture and art. Other than his one mistake about the date of the *castello*, everything he had said had been intelligent and accurate. He obviously knew a lot about art.

Her dinner partners had paid the check and were ready to leave by then, and the whole group stood up. Sylvia followed suit, and as she walked around the table, all three of her new American friends noticed that she had great legs. Her friends glanced at the group at the table behind them then, and Sylvia made polite introductions as though she knew Gray and his friends better than she did.

'Are you going back to the hotel?' Adam asked Sylvia. The French girl had been looking at him, and he decided the man she was with had to be her father, since she was flirting openly with Adam, and showed no obvious interest in anyone else.

'Eventually. We're going to walk around for a while. The shops are open till eleven, unfortunately. I do too much damage when I come here every year. I can never resist,' Sylvia answered.

'Would you like to have a drink later?' Gray asked, getting up his courage. He wasn't pursuing her, but he liked his new friend. She was easy and open and warm, and he wanted to talk to her more about the local art.

'Why don't you all come up to the Splendido?' she suggested. 'We seem to spend half the night in the bar. I'm sure we'll still be there at whatever hour.'

'We'll be there,' Charlie confirmed, as she hurried off to join her friends.

'Score!' Adam said, as soon as she was out of earshot, and Gray shook his head.

'I don't think so. She just wanted to talk about art,' Gray corrected, and Adam shook his head.

'Not you – me, dummy. Did you see that French girl at the other end of the table? She's with some old fart I thought was her husband, but I don't think he is. She was giving me hot eyes.'

'Oh, for chrissake,' Gray said, rolling his eyes. 'You just got some last night. You're obsessed!'

'Yes, I am. She's very pretty.'

'Sylvia Reynolds?' Gray looked surprised, she didn't look like Adam's type. She was about twice the age of what he usually liked. She was more in Gray's range, although he had no romantic interest in her, just artistic, and she was a good connection for him to have. She was an extremely important woman in the New York art world. Charlie said he hadn't recognized her at first, but was now fully aware of who she was.

'No, the young one,' Adam corrected again. 'She's a pretty little thing. She looks like a ballerina, but you can never tell in Europe. Every time I see a cute young thing, it turns out she's in medical school, or law school, or studying to be an engineer or a rocket scientist.'

'Well, you'd better behave yourself. She could be Sylvia's daughter, for all you know.' Although that wouldn't have stopped Adam. When it came to women, he was fearless, and without conscience or remorse – to a point, of course. But he thought everyone was fair game unless they were married. There he drew the line, but nowhere else.

Like everyone else in the tiny port, they walked around the square and the shops after dinner, and close to midnight they walked up to the hotel from the port. And just as Sylvia had predicted, her entire group was sitting in the bar. They were laughing and talking and smoking, and when she saw the three men walk in, she waved with a broad smile. She introduced them to her friends again, and conveniently, the chair next to the young woman Adam had found pretty was vacant, and he asked her if he could sit down. She smiled and pointed to the seat. When she spoke to him, her English was excellent, although he could tell from her accent she was French. Sylvia explained to Gray that the young woman Adam was talking to was her niece. Charlie found himself sitting between two men. One was Italian, and the other French, and within minutes they were deeply engaged in a conversation about American politics and the situation in the Middle East. It was one of those typically European conversations that go straight to the core of things, without messing around, with everyone expressing strong opinions. Charlie loved exchanges like that, and within minutes, Sylvia and Gray were talking about art. It turned out that she had studied architecture, and lived in Paris for twenty years. She had been married to a Frenchman, and was now divorced, and had been for ten years.

'When we got divorced, I had no idea what to do, or where to live. He was an artist, and I was dead broke. I wanted to go home, but I realized I no longer had one. I grew up in Cleveland, and my parents were gone by then, and I hadn't lived there since high school, so I took both my kids and moved to New York. I got a job in a gallery in SoHo, and as soon as I could, I started a gallery on a shoestring, and much to my amazement, it worked. So here I am, ten years after I went back, still running the gallery. My daughter is studying in Florence, and my son is getting a master's at Oxford. And now I'm wondering what the hell I'm doing in New York.' She took a breath and smiled at him. 'Tell me about your work.'

He explained the direction he had been taking for the past ten years and the motivations behind it.

She understood exactly what he meant when he told her about the influences behind his painting. It all made sense to her, although it wasn't the kind of art she showed, but she had great respect for what he said, and what she'd seen of his work several years before. He said his style had changed considerably in the meantime, but she had been impressed by his earlier work. They discovered that they had lived within blocks of each other in Paris at roughly the same time. And she said without embarrassment that she was forty-nine years old, although she looked about forty-two. There was something very warm and sensual about her. She didn't look American, or French, but with her hair pulled back and her big green eyes, she looked very exotic, perhaps South American. She seemed completely at ease in her own skin, and with who she was. She was only a year younger than Gray, and their lives had run parallel many times. She also loved to paint, but said she wasn't very good. She did it more for fun. She had a deep love and respect for art.

They all sat there until nearly three o'clock, and then finally the threesome from the *Blue Moon* stood up.

'We'd better get back,' Charlie said. It had been an enjoyable evening for all of them. He had pursued his conversation among the other men for many hours. Gray and Sylvia hadn't stopped talking all night, and although Sylvia's niece was an undeniably pretty girl, Adam had gotten drawn into a conversation with a lawyer from Rome, and had enjoyed a heated debate, even more than he had enjoyed flirting with Sylvia's niece. It had been a terrific evening for all concerned, and their hosts stood up with regret.

'Would you like to spend the day on the boat tomorrow?' Charlie offered to the group at large, and everyone smiled and nodded their heads.

'All of us in a rowboat?' Sylvia teased. 'I suppose we could take turns.'

'I'll try to come up with something more suitable by tomorrow,' Charlie promised. 'We'll pick you up in the port at eleven.' He wrote down the phone number of the boat for her then, in case something changed. They left each other fast friends a few minutes later, and all three men looked pleased as they walked back down the hill to the tender waiting for them in the port. It was exactly what they loved about their trips together. They went to fun places and met interesting people. They all agreed that the evening they'd spent with the group that night had been one of their best.

'Sylvia is an amazing woman,' Gray commented admiringly, and Adam laughed.

'Well, at least I know you're not attracted to her,' Adam said as they reached the port. The tender was waiting for them with two crew members standing by. They were on duty at all hours, whenever Charlie and his friends were on the boat.

'How do you know I'm not attracted to her?' Gray asked with a look of amusement. 'Actually, I'm not. But I like her head. I loved talking to her. She's incredibly honest and perceptive about the art scene in New York. She's a no-nonsense kind of person.'

'I know. I could see that while she was talking to you. And I know you're not attracted to her, because she's not nuts. She looks about as normal as it gets. No one's threatening her life, she doesn't look as though she'd put up with being abused by anyone, and she doesn't look as though her prescription for antipsychotic medication just ran out. I don't think there's a chance in hell you'll fall for that one, Gray,' Adam teased. She was nothing like the women Gray normally wound up with. She looked entirely put together, totally competent, and completely sane. Saner than most in fact.

'You never know,' Charlie said philosophically. 'Magical things happen in Portofino, it's a very romantic place.'

'Not that romantic,' Adam countered, 'unless she has a nervous breakdown by tomorrow at eleven.'

'I think he's right,' Gray said honestly. 'I have a fatal weakness for women who need help. When her husband left her for someone else, she picked up her kids and moved to New York without a penny. Two years later she was running a gallery, and now it's one of the most successful in New York. Women like that don't need to be rescued.' He knew himself well, and so did his friends, but Charlie was still hopeful. He always was, even about himself.

'That could be a refreshing change,' Charlie suggested, smiling at him.

'I'd rather be her friend,' Gray said sensibly. 'It lasts longer.' Charlie and Adam both agreed as they got back on the boat, said goodnight, and went to their cabins. It had been a terrific night.

The entire group came on board the next morning, as the three friends were finishing breakfast. Charlie gave them a tour of the boat, and they motored out to sea shortly after. They were all immensely impressed. It was quite a boat.

'Charlie tells me you travel together for a month every year. What a fabulous thing to do,' Sylvia said, smiling at Gray, as they both drank virgin Bloody Marys. Gray had decided that it would be a lot more fun to talk to Sylvia and stay sober. None of them had a drinking problem, but they readily agreed, they drank far too much on the boat, like bad teenagers who had run away from their parents. Around Sylvia, it was more of a challenge to be an adult. She was so bright, and so on top of things, he didn't want his senses dulled when he talked to her.

They were deep in conversation about Renaissance frescoes in Italy, when the boat stopped and they threw anchor.

Within minutes everyone was in bathing suits, diving off the boat into the water. They cavorted like kids, two of Sylvia's friends water-skied, and Gray noticed Adam on the Jet Ski with the niece astride behind him.

They swam and played until nearly two o'clock, and by then the crew had set out a fabulous buffet of seafood and pasta. They sat down to an enormous lunch, with Italian wine, and at four o'clock they were still at the table in animated conversation. Even Adam was forced to be intelligent with Sylvia's niece – it turned out that she was studying political science in Paris, and was planning to enter a doctoral program. Like her aunt, she wasn't anyone to take lightly. Her father was the minister of culture, and her mother was a thoracic surgeon. Both of her brothers were doctors, she spoke five languages, and she was thinking of getting a law degree after her doctoral degree in political science. She was considering a career in politics. This was not a girl who wanted implants from him. She expected intelligent conversation, which came as a shock to Adam. He wasn't used to women her age being as direct as she was, or as serious about their studies. Charlie laughed at him as he walked by – she was discussing foreign money markets, and Adam looked nervous. She had him on his toes, or on the ropes, as he ruefully admitted later. He was no match for her, despite her age.

Sylvia and Gray spent the afternoon discussing art, interminably, much to their delight. They went from one period of history to another, drawing parallels between politics and art. Charlie watched them all with fatherly pleasure, making sure that his crew was making them feel at home on the boat, and that his guests had everything they wanted.

The day was so beautiful that they decided to stay and have dinner on the boat, at Charlie's invitation. It was nearly midnight before they motored slowly closer to the port, after stopping for a moonlight swim on the way back. For once, Gray and Sylvia stopped talking about art, and just enjoyed the water. She was a powerful swimmer, and seemed capable in all things she did, whether athletics or art. Gray had never met a woman like her. They swam back to the boat, as he found himself wishing he was in better shape than he was. It wasn't something he thought about often. But she was extremely fit, and scarcely out of breath as they got back on board. For a woman her age, or even a younger one, she looked great in a bikini, but she seemed unaware of herself around him, unlike her niece, who had been flirting relentlessly with Adam.

Her aunt made no comment, she was well aware of the fact that her niece was a grown woman, and was free to do whatever she wanted. Sylvia wasn't in the habit of running anyone else's life. Her niece could run her own.

Before they left, Sylvia asked Gray if he'd like to go to San Giorgio with her the following morning. She had been there often before, but loved seeing it again and again. She said she saw something new each time she went there. He accepted readily, and agreed to meet her in the port at ten. There was nothing coy about her invitation to him, it was simply a bond between two art lovers. She said they were leaving the day after, and Gray was happy for a chance to see her again.

'What nice people,' Charlie commented after they left, and Adam and Gray agreed with him. It had been a terrific day and evening. The conversations had been fascinating, the swimming fun, the food plentiful, and their new friends an unusually intelligent, attractive lot. 'I notice Sylvia's niece isn't spending the night. Did you strike out on that one?' Charlie teased him, and Adam looked chagrined.

'I'm not sure I'm smart enough to pull that off. That girl makes my education at Harvard look like high school. Once we got off the subject of law, torts in the American judicial system, and constitutional law, as opposed to the French legal system, I felt like a total dummy. I damn near forgot to put the make on her, and when I thought of it, by then I was exhausted. She can run rings around any guy I've ever met. She should be dating one of my Harvard law professors, not me.' In a funny way, she had reminded him a little of Rachel when they were young, she was so damn smart, graduating from Harvard Law School summa cum laude, and the similarity had turned him off. He had decided not to pursue her, it was too much work, and he had long since forgotten half the things she asked him. She had fenced with him intellectually all day and night, and he liked it and found it challenging, but in the end, it made him feel tired and old. His mind just didn't work that way anymore. It was easier to buy girls implants and new noses than to try and wrestle with their brains. It made him feel slightly inferior to her, which left his ego somewhat deflated, and wasn't exactly an aphrodisiac for him. Unlike Gray, who had loved his conversations with her aunt, and felt invigorated by the information they'd shared, and the things he'd learned from her. Sylvia was extremely knowledgeable on many subjects, though mainly art, which was her passion, just as it was his. But Gray didn't want to have sex with her, although he found her beautiful and appealing. All he wanted was to get to know her better, and talk to her, for as many hours as he could. He was thrilled they'd met.

The three men shared a last glass of wine on the deck before they smoked cigars and went to their cabins, happy and relaxed after a fun day on the boat. They had no plans for the next day, and Adam and Charlie said they were going to sleep late. Gray was already excited about meeting Sylvia to visit the church. He mentioned it to Charlie on their way downstairs, and his host looked pleased. He knew Gray led a lonely life, and thought she'd be a good friend for him, and a useful person for him to know. He had struggled for so long with his art, and was so talented, Charlie hoped he'd get a break one of these days, and was hopeful Sylvia could introduce him to the right people in the art scene in New York. She might not be a potential romance for him, or the kind of woman he was attracted to, but he thought she'd make a great friend. He had enjoyed talking to her himself. She was cultured and knowledgeable, without being pompous or pretentious about it. He thought she was a very nice woman, and he was surprised she wasn't linked to any of the men in the group. She was the kind of woman a lot of men would have been attracted to, especially Europeans, although she was a good fifteen years older than the women Charlie went out with, even though she was barely three years older than he. Life wasn't fair that way, he knew, particularly in the States. Women in their twenties and thirties were at a premium, it was all about youth. A woman Sylvia's age was a specialty, and would only appeal to a rare few, and only then to a man who was not threatened by how smart and capable she was. The kind of girls Adam went out with were generally considered a lot more desirable, in most cases, than a woman of substance and intellect like Sylvia. Charlie knew that there were a lot of women like her in New York who were just too damn smart and successful for their own good, and wound up alone. Although for all he knew there was a man waiting for her in New York or Paris or somewhere else. But he doubted it. She put out a vibe that suggested she was independent and unattached, and liked it that way. It didn't seem to bother her at all, and she was obviously not on the make, for them, or anyone. Charlie had shared his assessment of her with Gray over cigars the night before.

The next morning, as they walked up the hill to San Giorgio, Gray discovered that Charlie's thoughts about Sylvia were correct.

'You're not married?' Gray asked her cautiously, curious about her, as well as what she knew about the church. She was an interesting woman, and he wanted to be her friend.

'No, I did that once,' she said carefully. 'I loved it

92

when I was married, but I'm not sure I could ever do that again. Sometimes I think I love the commitment and lifestyle more than the man. My husband was an artist, and a total narcissist. Everything was about him. I adored him, almost as much as he adored himself. Nothing else ever existed for him,' she said in a matter-of-fact tone. She wasn't bitter, she was just finished with it, and Gray could hear that in her voice. 'Not the children, or me, or anyone. It was always about him. After a while, that gets old. I'd still be married to him, though, if he hadn't left me for someone else. He was fifty-five when he left me, I was thirty-nine, and over-the-hill as far as he was concerned. She was nineteen. It was a bit of a blow. They got married and had three more kids in three years, then he left her too. At least I lasted longer. I had him for twenty. She had him for four.'

'I assume for a twelve-year-old that time?' Gray snapped, feeling angry on her behalf. It sounded like a rotten deal to him, knowing what he knew of her now, that she had gone to New York after that, penniless with two kids, and no help from him.

'No, the last one was twenty-two. Old for him. I was also nineteen when we got married, and an art student in Paris. The last two were models.'

'Does he see your kids?'

She hesitated in answer to the question, and then

shook her head. The answer seemed painful for her. 'No, he saw them twice in nine years, which was hard for them. And he died last year. It leaves a lot of things unresolved for my kids, about what they meant to him, if anything. And it was sad for me. I loved him, but with narcissists, that's just the way it is. In the end, the only ones they love are them-selves. They just don't have it in them to love anyone else.' It was a simple statement of fact. Her tone was regretful but not bitter.

'I think I've known women like that.' He didn't even try to explain to her the level of insanity he had tolerated in his love life. It would have been impossible to try and she probably would have laughed at him, just as everyone else did. Insanity in his home life was all too familiar to him. 'And you never wanted to try again, with someone else?' He knew he was being nosy, but had the feeling she didn't mind. She was remarkably honest and open about herself, and he admired that. One had the feeling there were no dark secrets, no hidden agendas, no confusion in her head about what she felt or wanted or believed. Although inevitably, there were probably scars. Everyone had them at their age, no one was exempt.

'No. I've never wanted to marry again. At my age, I don't see the point. I don't want more children, not my own at least. I wouldn't mind someone else's kids. Marriage is a venerable institution, and I believe in it, for those purposes anyway. I just don't know if I believe in it anymore for myself. Probably not. I don't think I'd have the guts to do it again. I lived with a man for six years, after my divorce. He was an extraordinary person, and an amazing artist, a sculptor. He suffered from severe depression and refused to take medication. He was basically an alcoholic, and his life was a mess. I loved him anyway, but it was impossible. More impossible than I can tell you.' She fell silent after she said it, and he watched her face. There was something agonizing lurking there, and he wanted to know what it was. He sensed that in order to know her, he needed to know the rest.

'You left him?' He was cautious with the words, as they approached the church.

'No, I didn't. I probably should have. Maybe he would have stopped drinking then, or taken his medication, or maybe not. It's hard to say.' She sounded peaceful and sad, as though she had accepted a terrible tragedy and inevitable loss.

'He left you?' Gray couldn't imagine anyone doing that to her, and surely not twice. But there were strange people in the world, who lost opportunities, sabotaged themselves, and destroyed lives. There was nothing you could do about it. He had learned that himself over the years.

'No, he committed suicide,' Sylvia said quietly, 'three years ago. It took me a long time to get over it, and accept what happened, and it was hard when Jean-Marie, the children's father, died last year. The loss brought some of it back, grief does that, I think. But it happened, I couldn't change it, no matter how much I loved him. He just couldn't do it anymore, and I couldn't do it for him. That's a hard thing to make your peace with.' But he could hear in her voice that she had. She had been through a lot, and come out the other end. He knew just looking at her that she was a woman determined to survive. He wanted to put his arms around her and give her a hug, but he didn't know her well enough. And he didn't want to intrude on her grief. He had no right to do that.

'I'm sorry,' he said softly, with all the emotion he felt. With all the insane women he'd been involved with who turned every moment into a drama, here was a sane one who had lived through real tragedy and had refused to let it destroy her. If anything, she had learned from it and grown.

'Thank you.' She smiled at him, as they walked into the church. They sat quietly for a long time, and then walked around the church, inside and out. It was a beautiful structure from the twelfth century, and she pointed things out to him that he had never seen before, although he'd been there many times. It was another two hours before they walked slowly down to the port.

'What are your children like?' he asked with curiosity. It was interesting to think of her as a mother, she seemed so independent and so whole. He suspected she was a good mother, although he didn't like thinking of her that way. He preferred to think of her as he knew her, just as his friend.

'Interesting. Smart,' she said honestly, and sounded proud, which made him smile. 'My daughter is a painter, studying in Florence. My son is a scholar of the history of ancient Greece. In some ways he's like his father, but he has a kinder heart, thank God. My daughter inherited his talent, but nothing else from that side of the gene pool. She's a lot like me. She could run the world, and maybe will. I hope she'll take the gallery over one day, but I'm not sure she ever will. She has her own life to lead. But genetics are an amazing thing. I see both of us in them, mixed in with who they are themselves. But the history and the ancestry are always there, even in the flavors of ice cream they like, or the colors they prefer. I have a great respect for genetics, after bringing up two kids. I'm not sure that anything we do as parents actually makes a difference, or even influences them.'

They stopped at a small café then, and he invited her to have coffee with him. They sat down, and she turned the tables on him again. 'What about you? Why no wife and kids?'

'You just said it. Genetics. I'm adopted, I have no idea who my parents were, or what I'd be passing on. I find that terrifying. What if there's an ax murderer somewhere in my ancestry? Do I really want to burden someone else with that? Besides, my life was insane when I was a child. I grew up thinking childhood was a singular kind of curse. I couldn't do that to someone else.' He told her a little about his childhood then. India, Nepal, the Caribbean, Brazil, the Amazon. It read like an atlas of the world, while being parented by two people who had no idea what they were doing, were burnt out on drugs, and finally found God. It was a lot to explain over two cups of espresso, but he did his best, and she was intrigued.

'Well, somewhere in your history, there must have been a very talented artist. That wouldn't be such a bad thing to pass on.'

'God knows what else there is though. I've known too many crazy people all my life, my parents and most of the women I've been involved with. I wouldn't have wanted a child with any of them.' He was being totally honest with her, just as she had been with him.

'That bad, huh?' She smiled at him. He hadn't told her anything that had frightened her. All she felt was deep compassion for him. He had had a tough life as a kid, and had complicated things for himself, by choice, ever since. But the beginning hadn't been his choice. It had been destiny's gift to him.

'Worse.' He grinned at her. 'I've been doing heavy rescue work all my life. God knows why. I thought it was my mission in life, to atone for all my sins.'

'I used to think so too. My sculptor friend was a bit of that. I wanted to make everything right for him, and fix everything, and in the end, I couldn't. You never can, for someone else.' Like him, she had learned that the hard way. 'It's interesting how, when people treat us badly, we then feel responsible, and take on their guilt. I've never really understood it, but it seems to work that way,' she said wisely. It was obvious that she had given the subject considerable thought.

'I've been beginning to get that myself,' he said ruefully. It was embarrassing to admit how dysfunctional the women in his life had been, and that after all he'd done for them, almost without exception they had left him for other people. In a slightly less extreme way, Sylvia's experience wasn't so different from his. But she sounded healthier than he felt.

'Are you in therapy?' she asked openly, as she

would have asked him if he'd been to Italy before. He shook his head.

'No. I read a lot of self-help books, and I'm very spiritual. I've paid for about a million hours of therapy for the women I've been involved with. It never occurred to me to go myself. I thought I was fine, and they were nuts. Maybe it was the other way around. You have to ask yourself at some point why you get involved with people like that. You can't get anything decent out of it. They're just too fucked up.' He smiled and she laughed. She had come to the same conclusion herself, which was why she hadn't had a serious relationship since the sculptor committed suicide.

She had taken about two years to sort it out, working on it intensely in therapy. She had even gone on a few dates in the past six months, once with a younger artist who was a giant spoiled brat, and twice with men who were twenty years older than she was. But after the dates she realized she was past that now, and a twenty-year age difference was just too much. Men her age wanted women younger than she was. Then she had had a number of very unfortunate blind dates. For the moment, she had decided that she was better off by herself. She didn't like it, and she missed sleeping with someone, and having someone to curl up to at night. With her children gone, the weekends were agonizingly lonely, and she felt too young to just give up. But she and her therapist were exploring the possibility that maybe no one else would come along, and she wanted to be all right with it. She didn't want someone turning her life upside down again. Relationships seemed too complicated, and solitude too hard. She was at a crossroads in her life, neither young nor old, too old to settle for the wrong man, or one who was too difficult, and too young to accept being alone for the rest of her life, but she realized now that that could happen. It frightened her somewhat, but so did another tragedy or disaster. She was trying to live one day at a time, which was why there was no man in her life, and she was traveling with friends. She said it all as simply as possible to Gray, and managed not to sound pathetic, desperate, needy, or confused. She was just a woman trying to figure out her life, and perfectly capable of taking care of herself while she did. He sat staring at her for a long time as he listened, and shook his head.

'Does that sound too awful, or slightly insane?' she asked him. 'Sometimes I wonder about myself.' She was so agonizingly honest with him, both strong and vulnerable at the same time, which knocked him off his feet. He had never known anyone like her, neither man nor woman, and all he wanted was to know more.

'No, it doesn't sound awful. It sounds hard, but real. Life is hard and real. You sound incredibly sane to me. Saner than I am, surely. And don't even ask about the women I've gone out with, they're all in institutions somewhere by now, where they belonged when I met them. I don't know what made me think I could play God, and change every-thing that had happened to them, most of which they did to themselves. I don't know why I thought I deserved that torture, but it stopped being fun a long time ago. I just can't do it anymore, I'd rather be alone.' He meant it, particularly after what he had just heard from her. Solitude was a lot better than being with the lunatics he'd been with. It was lonely, but at least it was sane. He admired her for what she was doing, and learning, and wanted to follow her example. She was a role model of health and normalcy to him. As he listened, he didn't know if he wanted her as his woman, or just his friend. Either one sounded good to him. She was beautiful, as he sat and looked at her, but above all, he valued her friendship. 'Maybe we could go to a movie some time when we get back to New York,' he suggested cautiously.

'I'd like that,' she said comfortably. 'I warn you, though, I have lousy taste in movies. My kids won't even go with me. I hate foreign films and art films, sex, violence, sad endings, or gratuitous bullshit. I like movies I understand, with happy endings, that make me laugh and cry and stay awake. If you have to ask what it meant when you walk out, take someone else, not me.'

'Perfect. We'll watch old *I Love Lucy* reruns, and rent Disney movies. You bring the popcorn, I'll rent the films.'

'You've got a deal.' She grinned at him. He walked her back to the hotel then, and when he left her, he hugged her and thanked her for a wonderful morning in her company.

'Are you really leaving tomorrow?' he asked, looking worried. He wanted to see her again, before they both left Portofino. Otherwise, in New York. He could hardly wait to call her when he got back. He had never met a woman like her, not one he had been willing to talk to. He'd been too busy rescuing women to ever bother looking for one who could be his friend. And Sylvia Reynolds was that person. At fifty, in Portofino, it seemed crazy even to him, but he felt as though he had found the woman of his dreams. He had no idea what she'd say if he shared that piece of information with her. Probably run like hell, and call the police. He wondered if he had caught a good case of insanity from the women he'd gone out with, or had always been as crazy as they. Sylvia wasn't crazy. She was beautiful and smart, vulnerable, honest, and real.

'We are leaving tomorrow,' she said quietly, sad to leave him too, which made her somewhat nervous. Although she'd told her therapist she was ready to meet someone, now that she had, all she wanted to do was run away before she got hurt again. But she also wanted to see him one more time before she did. There was a strange push-me-pull-you going on in her head as she smiled at him. 'We're going to Sardinia for the weekend, and then I have to go to Paris to see some artists. After that, I'm spending a week in Sicily with my kids. I'll be back in New York in two weeks.'

'I'll be back in about three,' he said, beaming as he looked at her. 'I think we'll be in Sardinia this weekend too. That's where we're going after this.' As soon as she left Portofino, he wanted to leave too, if Charles and Gray were willing.

'Well, that's a stroke of good fortune,' she said, smiling at him, feeling young again. 'Why don't the three of you join us for dinner in the port tonight? Good pasta and bad wine, not the kind of stuff you and the others are used to.'

'Don't be too impressed. If you come to dinner at my place, I'll serve you the rotgut I usually drink myself.'

'I'll bring the wine.' She grinned at him. 'You cook. I'm a rotten cook.'

'Good. It's nice to know there's something you

can't do. I'm told I'm a halfway decent cook. Pasta, tacos, burritos, goulash, meat loaf, salad, peanut butter and jelly, pancakes, scrambled eggs, macaroni and cheese. That's it.'

'Pancakes. I love pancakes. I always burn them. No one will ever eat them.' She laughed, and he smiled at the prospect of cooking for her.

'Perfect. *I Love Lucy*, and pancakes. What kind of ice cream for dessert? Chocolate or vanilla?'

'Mint chocolate chip, mountain blackberry, or banana walnut,' she said confidently. She was beginning to like the way it felt being with him. It was scary, but nice, all at the same time. The roller coaster of life. She hadn't been on it in a long time, and realized now how much she had missed it. She hadn't seen a man who had appealed to her in years. This one did.

'Oh, Jesus. Designer ice cream. What's wrong with Rocky Road?'

'I'll bring the ice cream and the wine, if you're going to be that way about it.'

'And don't forget the popcorn!' he reminded her. It wasn't going to be fancy, but he knew it was going to be good. Anything he did with her would be, like going to San Giorgio that day. It had been very good. 'What time's dinner tonight?' he asked as he hugged her again. It was just a friendly hug, nothing that would scare her or commit them to

105

more than an easy dinner at his place. The rest was to be discovered and decided at some later date, if it felt right to both of them. He hoped it would.

'Nine-thirty, at Da Puny. See you then.' She smiled easily and waved, and then disappeared into the hotel. He walked down to the port with a spring in his step, where the tender and a crew member were waiting for him. He smiled all the way back to the boat, and was still smiling when Charlie saw him as he came on board. It was one o'clock by then, and they were waiting for lunch with him.

'That was a long time to spend in church with a woman you barely know,' Charlie commented mischievously, as he looked at his old friend. 'Did you propose?'

'I probably should have, but I blew it. Besides, she has two kids, and you know how I hate kids.' Charlie laughed at his response, and didn't take him seriously.

'They're not kids, they're grown-ups. Besides, she lives in New York, and they live in Italy and England. I think you're safe.'

'Yeah, maybe. But kids are kids, whatever age.' Family scenes were not his thing, as Charlie knew. Gray told him then about the dinner invitation for that night, and it appealed to all of them, as Adam eyed him more carefully than Charlie had.

'Is something going on with you two?' Adam

looked suspicious, and Gray pretended to be amused. He wasn't ready to share it with them. Nothing had happened. He just liked her, and he hoped that she liked him. There was nothing to say.

'I wish. She's got great legs, but one fatal flaw, from what I can see.'

'What's that?' Charlie asked with interest. Flaws in women always fascinated him. He was obsessed with them himself.

'She's sane. Not my type, I fear.'

'Yeah. I knew that,' Adam agreed.

Gray told them then that the group was leaving for Sardinia the following day, which also appealed to all of them. Portofino was delightful, but they all agreed it would be less amusing once the others left. Charlie suggested they move on that night after dinner, and travel through the night. If they left by midnight, they could be in Sardinia the following night in time for dinner. It would be fun to see the same group again in Porto Cervo, and would make for a great weekend. And in case he changed his mind, it gave Adam another shot at Sylvia's niece. But even without that, they enjoyed all the others in the group. It was a great mix.

Charlie told the captain their plan, and he agreed to organize the crew. Night crossings were easier for the passengers, but harder on the crew. But they did it frequently. The captain said he'd sleep while

Charlie and his guests were out for dinner, and leave as soon as they came on board again. And they'd be in Sardinia well in time for dinner the next day.

Gray told Sylvia at dinner that night, and she smiled at him, wondering what he'd said to the others, and faintly embarrassed by her attraction to him. She hadn't felt anything like it in years, and wasn't ready to share that information with Gray either. But she sensed that the feelings were reciprocal, and he also liked her. She felt like a kid again.

They had a nice time at dinner. Sylvia sat across the table from Gray, but nothing she said or did gave her feelings for him away. She kissed him and the others on both cheeks when they left them, and promised to meet for dinner at the Yacht Club in Porto Cervo the next day. Gray turned to look at her one last time as they walked away, but she never turned to look at him. She was talking to her niece intently, as they stopped to buy a gelato in the piazza, and Gray noticed again that Sylvia had a lovely figure. And a remarkable brain. He wasn't sure which he liked best.

'She likes you,' Adam commented as they got into the tender. It reminded him of high school, and Charlie laughed at them both.

'I like her too,' Gray said casually, as he sat down and looked across the water at the *Blue Moon,* waiting for them.

'I mean she *really* likes you. I think she wants to go to bed with you.'

'She's not that kind of woman,' Gray said, looking stone-faced, and wanting to protect her from the kind of comments Adam made. It suddenly seemed disrespectful to him.

'Don't give me that. She's a beautiful woman, she has to go to bed with someone. It might as well be you. Or do you think she's too old for you?' Adam pondered the question as Gray shook his head.

'She's not too old. I told you, she's too sane.'

'Yeah, I guess she is. But even sane women like to get laid.'

'I'll keep it in mind, in case I ever run into another one,' Gray said, smiling at Charlie, who was watching him with interest. He was beginning to wonder if there was something between them too.

'Don't worry, you won't.' Adam laughed, as the three men boarded the *Blue Moon,* and Charlie poured them each a brandy before they went to bed. As they sat on the aft deck in the moonlight, the crew weighed anchor and they took off. Gray sat watching the moonlight dance on the water, thought of her in her hotel room, and wished that he could be there. He couldn't imagine being lucky enough to have something like that happen to him. But maybe one day. First, they had a date for pancakes and ice cream in New York. And after that, who knew. Before that, there would be the weekend in Sardinia. For the first time in a long time, he felt like a boy again. A fifty-year-old boy, with an absolutely incredible forty-nine-year-old girl.

4

Sardinia was as much fun as they all hoped it would be, with Sylvia and her friends. Two more Italian couples joined them in Porto Cervo, and Charlie took everyone out on the boat for lunches and dinners, water-skiing and swimming. It gave Gray and Sylvia an opportunity to get to know each other better, even with all the others around. And after watching them for the entire weekend, Adam decided they were just friends. Charlie wasn't as convinced, but kept his impressions to himself. He knew if Gray wanted to say something to him, he would. Charlie talked to her quite a bit himself. They talked about his foundation, and the work they did, her gallery, and the artists she represented. It was obvious that she loved her work. It was equally obvious that she liked his friend. And Gray liked her. They chatted quietly with each other on several occasions, they swam together, danced in the nightclubs, and laughed a great deal. By the end of the weekend, all of them felt as though they had become great friends. And when Sylvia and her group left, Charlie and the others went to Corsica for two days. They'd had enough of Sardinia by then, and it wouldn't have been as much fun without them. Gray had spoken to Sylvia quietly before she left the boat for the last time, and told her he'd call her in New York as soon as he got home. She smiled at him, hugged him, and wished them all a great trip.

From Corsica they went to Ischia, and from there to Capri. They came up the west coast of Italy after that, came back to the French Riviera for the last week, and anchored in Antibes. As always, when they were together, it was incredible. They went to nightclubs, restaurants, walked, swam, shopped, met people, danced with women, and turned strangers into friends. And on one of their last nights, they had dinner at the Eden Roc. It had been the perfect trip, they all agreed.

'You should come to St. Bart's this winter,' Adam urged Gray. He always flew there to meet Charlie on the boat for a week or two over New Year's. Gray always said that a month on the boat in the summer was enough for him, and they all knew why he hated the Caribbean. It had too many bad memories for him.

'Maybe some time I will,' Gray said vaguely. Charlie said he hoped he would.

The last night was always nostalgic, they hated to leave each other and go back to real life. Adam was meeting Amanda and Jacob for a week in London, and taking them to Paris for a weekend, and staying at the Ritz. It would be a gentle transition for him after the luxuries of the *Blue Moon*. Gray was flying straight from Nice to New York, which was going to be a shock for him. Back to his walk-up studio in the Meatpacking District, which had grown trendy, but his studio was still as uncomfortable as it had ever been. But at least it was cheap. He was looking forward to calling Sylvia as soon as he got home. He had thought of calling her from the boat, but didn't want to make expensive calls on Charlie's bill, which seemed rude to him. He knew she'd gotten back the previous week, after her trip to Sicily with her kids. Charlie was staying in France, on the boat, for another three weeks, in splendid solitude. But it was always lonely for him when the other two were gone. He hated to see them go.

The morning they left, Gray and Adam drove to the airport together in a limo the purser had rented for them. Charlie stood on the aft deck and waved, and was sad when they were gone. They were his closest friends, and both good men. For all their vagaries and hang-ups, Adam's comments about women, and weakness for very young ones, Charlie knew they were decent people and cared a great deal about him, as he did about them. He would have done anything for them, and he knew they would for him too. They were the Three Musketeers, through thick and thin.

Adam called Charlie from London, to thank him for a fantastic trip, and the next day Gray sent him an e-mail saying the same thing. The best ever, they all agreed. It was hard to imagine, but their trips got better every year. They met terrific people, went to wonderful places, and enjoyed each other more with each passing year. It made Charlie feel sometimes that life wouldn't be so bad if he never met the right woman. If that happened, at least he had two remarkable men as friends. Life could be worse.

He spent his last two weeks on the boat doing business by computer, setting up meetings for his return, and making a list of things he wanted the captain to attend to to maintain the boat. In November, they'd be making the crossing to the Caribbean, and Charlie would have loved to be on it. He found it relaxing and peaceful to do so, but he had too much going on this year. The foundation had given nearly a million dollars to a new children's shelter, and he wanted to be around to see how it was being spent. When he finally left the boat in the third week of September, he was ready. He wanted to see friends, and get to his office. He had been gone for nearly three months. It was time to go home, whatever that meant. To him, it meant an empty apartment, an office where he upheld his family's traditions, sitting on the boards and committees he served on, and spending time with friends, going to dinner parties or cultural events. It never meant a person he could come home to, someone waiting for him, or to share his life with. It was beginning to seem less and less likely that he would ever find that person, but even if he didn't, he still had to go home. There was nowhere else to go. He couldn't hide from reality forever, sitting on his boat. And there were always Gray and Adam in New York. He was going to call them as soon as he got home, and see if they wanted to go out for dinner somewhere. They were in fact someone to go home to, and the brothers he had come to love. He was grateful he had them.

The flight to New York was uneventful, and unlike Adam, Charlie flew commercial. It had never seemed worthwhile to him to buy a plane. But Adam traveled more than he did, and it made sense to him. Charlie knew, from an itinerary Adam's secretary had sent him, that he was flying back to New York that night too. He had been in Las Vegas for an entire week, after his travels in Europe with his kids. He'd had an e-mail from Adam himself too, asking Charlie if he wanted to go to a concert with him the following week. It was one of those megaevents that Charlie loved and Gray said he hated, and it sounded like fun to him, so he had e-mailed back that he would join him. Adam wrote back that he was pleased.

News from Gray had been scarce in the past few weeks. Charlie assumed he was working, and was lost in his own world at the studio, after not painting for a month while he was on the trip. Sometimes Gray disappeared for weeks, and emerged victorious when a particularly tough spell with a painting had been beaten into submission. Charlie suspected he was in one of those. He was planning to call him some time that week. And Gray would be surprised to hear from him, as always. He totally lost track of time whenever he was at work. Sometimes he had no idea what time of year it was, and he didn't leave the studio for days or weeks. It was just the way he worked.

The weather in New York was hot and muggy, and it was late afternoon when Charlie arrived. He went through customs quickly, with nothing to declare. His office had a car waiting for him, and as they approached the city, the bleakness of Queens depressed him. Everything looked dirty, people looked hot and tired, and when he opened the window in the car, the air was like a blast of bad breath in his face, tainted with exhaust fumes. Welcome back.

When he got to his apartment, things were even worse. His cleaning staff had aired out the apartment, but it still smelled musty and looked sad. There were no flowers, no sign of life anywhere. Three months was a long time. All his mail was waiting for him at the office, whatever hadn't been sent to him in France. There was food in the refrigerator, but no one to prepare it, and he wasn't hungry. There were no messages on the machine. No one knew he was coming back, and worse yet, no one cared. For the first time, it made Charlie stand there in his empty apartment and wonder what was wrong with him and his friends. Was this what they wanted? Was this what Adam aspired to, with his constant efforts to stay unattached and go out with coeds and bimbos? What the hell were they thinking? The question was hard to answer. He had never felt as lonely in his life as he did that night.

For the last twenty-five years, he had been sifting through women like so much flour, looking for some microscopic point of imperfection, like a mother monkey searching her baby for fleas. And inevitably, he found them, and had an excuse to discard them. Which left him here, on a Monday night, in an empty apartment, looking out at Central Park, and couples wandering there, holding hands or lying on the grass, looking up at the trees together. Surely, none of them were perfect. Why was that good enough for them, and not for him? Why did everything have to be so perfect in his life, and why was no woman good enough for him? It had been twenty-five years since his sister died. Thirty since his parents' death in Italy. And all these years later, he was still standing guard over his empty life, watching with ever greater vigilance for barbarians at the gate. He was beginning to wonder, in spite of himself, if it was time to let one of the barbarians in. However frightening that had seemed till now, it might finally be a relief.

5

In spite of a desire to seem 'cooler' than that, Gray had called Sylvia the night he got back to New York on the first of September. It was the Labor Day weekend, and he wondered if she'd be away. It turned out she wasn't, much to his relief. She had sounded surprised to hear from him, and for a moment, he wondered if he had heard her wrong, or misread her, and was doing the wrong thing.

'Are you busy?' he asked nervously. She sounded distracted, and not entirely pleased.

'No, I'm sorry. I have a leak in my kitchen, and I have no idea what to do with this goddamn thing.' Everyone in her building was off over the long weekend.

'Did you call your super?'

'Yes, his wife is having a baby tonight. And the plumber I called said he can't get here till tomorrow afternoon, for twice the rate since it's a holiday. My neighbor called that it's dripping through his ceiling.' She sounded exasperated, which was at least familiar to him. Damsels in distress were his specialty.

'What happened? Did it just start out of nowhere, or did you do something?' Plumbing was not his area of expertise either, but he had a sense of how things worked mechanically, which she didn't. Plumbing was one of the few things she couldn't do.

'Actually' – she started to laugh sheepishly – 'I dropped a ring down the sink, so I tried to take the damn thing apart, before it wound up in the Manhattan sewer system. I got the ring, but something went wrong, and I couldn't get it back together fast enough. I seem to have sprung a major leak. Now I have no idea what to do.'

'Give up the apartment. Find a new one immediately,' Gray suggested, and Sylvia laughed at him.

'You're a big help. I thought you were an expert at rescue work. Some help you are.'

'I specialize in neurotic women, not plumbing issues. You're too healthy. Call another plumber.' And then he had a better idea. 'Do you want me to come over?' He had just arrived from the airport ten minutes before. He hadn't even bothered to glance at his mail. He had gone straight to the phone and called her.

'Something tells me you don't know what to do either. Besides, I look disgusting. I haven't combed my hair all day.' She had stayed home doing paper-work, and the Sunday *Times* crossword puzzle. It was one of those lazy days when she had nothing important to do. Sometimes it was pleasant being in town while everyone else was away, although by the end of the day, the solitude usually got to her, with no one to talk to, which made it nice to hear from him.

'I look disgusting too. I just got off a plane. Besides, you probably look better than you think.' How disgusting could she look? He couldn't imagine her looking anything but terrific, even with uncombed hair. 'Tell you what, you do your hair, I'll do the sink. Or I can do your hair, and you do the sink. We can take turns.'

'You're crazy,' she said, sounding good-natured and amused. It had been a boring, lonely Sunday on a holiday weekend and she was happy to hear from him. 'I'll tell you what. If you fix the sink, I'll buy you a pizza. Or Chinese takeout, you pick.'

'Whatever you want. I ate on the plane. I'll change into my plumbing clothes, and be over in ten minutes. Hang on to your hat till then.'

'Are you sure?' She sounded embarrassed, but pleased.

'I'm sure.' It was an easy way for them to see each other again. No anticipation, no fancy clothes, no awkward first date. Just a leak in her kitchen sink, and uncombed hair. He washed his face, brushed his teeth, shaved, put on a clean shirt, and was out the door ten minutes later. He was at her door another ten minutes after that. She lived in a loft south of him, in SoHo. The building had been renovated, and looked very sleek. She lived on the top floor, and the art he saw everywhere as soon as he got off the elevator looked serious and impressive. It wasn't the kind of work he did, but he knew it was what she sold. She had some major artists in her own collection, which caught his eye immediately. It was easy to see from the look of the apartment that she had great taste.

She had made the same effort he had, washed her face, combed her hair, brushed her teeth, and put on a clean T-shirt. Beyond that, she was barefooted, wearing jeans, and she looked happy to see him. She gave him a quick hug and looked him over.

'You don't look like a plumber to me.'

'I couldn't find my overalls, sorry. This will have to do.' He was wearing good shoes and a clean pair of jeans. 'Did you turn off the water?' he asked, as she led him to the kitchen. It was all black granite and chrome. It was a beautiful place, and she told him she had done most of the design work herself.

'No,' she said, looking blank, in answer to his question about the water. 'I don't know how.'

'Okay,' he said, muttering to himself, as he

slipped under the sink. There was a steady cascade of water, flowing from the sink through the cabinet beneath, and she had towels all over the floor. Gray was on his knees looking for the shut-off valve, and asked her for a wrench. She handed it to him, and a minute later, the water stopped. Problem solved, or at least put on hold for the moment. He emerged from under the sink with a broad smile, and wet jeans from the knees down, from where he had knelt.

'You're a genius. Thank you.' She smiled back at him and then glanced down at his jeans. 'Sorry, you're all wet. I'd offer to dry your pants, but it might be a little forward to ask you to take them off on a first date. I'm a little out of practice, but I think that's probably not the thing to do.' On the other hand, she knew that if she didn't, he would be miserable sitting through dinner in wet jeans. And besides, she assumed correctly, he was tired from the trip, he didn't need to be wet and uncomfortable too. 'Maybe we ought to skip dating etiquette for this time. Take off your pants. I'll put them in the dryer. I'll get you a towel. We can order a pizza delivered.' She came back with a white bath towel five minutes later. It was a big fluffy luxurious one. She pointed at her guest bathroom, where he could change. He came out a minute later, carrying his jeans, and with the towel wrapped around his waist.

He looked funny wearing it with a shirt, socks, and shoes.

'I feel a little silly,' he admitted with a sheepish grin, 'but I'd probably feel sillier eating dinner in my boxers.' She laughed at him then, and he followed her into the loft's main room. She had an enormous living room filled with sculpture and paintings. It was an incredible backdrop for her art. He noticed a number of important artists represented as he looked around the room. 'Wow! You've got some great stuff.'

'I've been collecting for years. One day I'll give them to my kids.' What she said reminded him again that this was not as simple as it looked, for him at least. Hearing her mention her children was like a roll of thunder in the background. He had never wanted to deal with a woman who had kids. But Sylvia was different. Everything about her was different from any woman he'd ever known. Maybe her kids were different too. And at least they weren't his. He had a psychotic terror of small children, or a phobia about them. He wasn't sure what it meant, but he knew it wasn't good.

'Where are they?' he asked, looking around nervously, as though expecting them to spring out of a closet and leap at him, like pet snakes, or a pair of pit bulls. She saw the look on his face and was once again amused.

'In Europe. Remember? Where they live. In Oxford and Florence. They won't be home till Christmas. You're safe. Although I wish they were here.'

'Did you have a nice trip with them?' he asked politely, as she went back to the kitchen and adjusted the setting on the dryer, and then came back to the living room.

'Very nice. How about you? How was the rest of the trip?' She sat down on the couch, and he sat in an enormous black leather chair, facing her. She looked beautiful in her bare feet and jeans, and he was happy to see her. Happier than he'd ever been in recent years. He had missed her, which seemed crazy even to him. He hardly knew her, but he had thought about her constantly during the last weeks of the trip.

'It was great,' he said, sitting in the leather chair in the towel, while she tried not to laugh, looking at him. He looked funny and vulnerable and sweet. 'Actually,' he corrected himself, 'it wasn't. It was good. But not as good as Portofino and Sardinia with you. I thought about you a lot after you left.'

'I thought about you too,' she admitted, and then smiled at him. 'I'm glad you're back. I didn't expect you to call me so soon.'

'Neither did I. Or actually, yes I did. I wanted to call you as soon as I got back.'

'I'm glad you did. What kind of pizza do you want, by the way?'

'What do you like?'

'Anything. Pepperoni, pesto, meatball, plain.'

'All of the above,' he said, watching her. She looked at ease in her domain.

'I'll order the one with everything on it, just no anchovies. I hate anchovies,' she said, as she left the room.

'Me too.'

She went back to check on the dryer again then, came back with his jeans, and held them out to him.

'Put your pants on. I'll order the pizza. Thanks again for fixing my sink.'

'I didn't,' he reminded her, 'I just turned off the water to stop the leak. You've got to get a plumber here on Tuesday.'

'I know.' She smiled at him, as he disappeared into the bathroom again, carrying his jeans. He came back and handed her the folded towel, and she looked surprised as she took it from him.

'What's wrong?'

'You didn't leave it crumpled up on the floor. What's wrong with you? I thought that's what all men do.' She was smiling at him, and he grinned. For a minute, she'd had him worried, she had looked so startled when he handed her the towel.

The apartment was so impeccably neat, he couldn't figure out what else to do with the towel other than hand it back to her.

'Do you want me to go back and leave it on the floor?' he offered, and she shook her head, and then called in the order for the pizza. As soon as she did, she offered him a glass of wine. She had several bottles of excellent California wine in the refrigerator, and opened one for him. It was a Chardonnay, and when he tasted it, it was delicious.

They went back to the living room again then and sat down. This time she sat next to him on the couch, instead of across the glass coffee table from him. He had an overwhelming urge to reach out and pull her close to him, but he wasn't ready to do that yet, and neither was she. He could sense the palpable awkwardness between them. They scarcely knew each other, and hadn't seen each other now in several weeks. 'You're not exactly typical for me either,' he commented, in response to her astonishment that he hadn't thrown her clean white towel on the floor. 'If you were, you'd be having some kind of hysterical fit over the leak in your kitchen, or maybe even telling me it was my fault, or something your last boyfriend or ex-husband was doing to terrorize you, because he wants both of us dead. And any minute, he'll be coming up the fire escape with a gun.'

'I don't have a fire escape,' she said apologetically, laughing at what he said. She couldn't even begin to imagine the women he had been involved with before. And now neither could he.

'That simplifies things,' he said quietly, admiring her. 'I love your apartment, Sylvia. It's beautiful and elegant and simple, just like you.' It wasn't pretentious, or showy, but everything in it had style and was of great quality.

'I like it too. I have a lot of treasures here that mean a lot to me.'

'I can see that,' he said, thinking that she was rapidly becoming a treasure that meant a lot to him. Now that he saw her again, he realized that he liked her even better than he had before. There was something very real and meaningful about seeing her where she lived. It was different than seeing her in restaurants, or on Charlie's boat. She had looked beautiful and appealing to him then, but now she seemed more real.

They talked about her gallery then, and the artists she represented, while they waited for the pizza to arrive.

'I'd love to see your work,' she said thoughtfully, and he nodded.

'I'd like you to see it too. It's not the kind of work you show.'

'Who's your gallery?' She was curious, he had

never mentioned it to her, and he shrugged when he answered.

'I don't have one at the moment. I was really unhappy with my last dealer. I have to do something about finding someone else. I don't have enough for a show yet anyway, so I'm in no rush.'

The pizza arrived then, and Sylvia paid for it, although Gray offered to. She told him it was his fee for stopping her leak. They sat at her kitchen table, and ate the pizza as they chatted comfortably. She shared the wine with him, turned down the lights, lit candles, and served the pizza on good-looking Italian plates. Everything she did or touched or owned had a sense of elegance and style. Just as she did, in her simple ponytail, bare feet, and jeans. She was wearing the same stack of turquoise bracelets he had noticed her wearing in Italy.

They sat there for a long time, talking about nothing in particular. They just enjoyed being together, and she was glad he had come over to help her with the leak. It was ten o'clock when he finally admitted that the jet lag was getting to him. That with the wine was putting him to sleep. He got up from the table regretfully, helped her put the dishes in the dishwasher, although she insisted she could do it herself after he left. He liked helping her, and he could see it wasn't familiar to her. She was used to doing things herself, just as he had been all his life. But it was nicer doing things together, and he was sorry to leave. He liked being with her, and when he turned to her before he left, she was looking up at him.

'Thanks for coming by, and helping me, Gray. I appreciate it. I'd be swimming around my kitchen by now if you hadn't turned the water off for me.'

'You'd have figured it out. It was a great excuse to see you,' he said honestly. 'Thanks for the pizza, and the good company.' He reached out and hugged her then, and kissed her on both cheeks, and then he stopped and looked at her, and held her there, wondering if it was too soon. There was a question in his eyes, and she answered it for him. She reached up to him and pulled him closer to her, and as she did, their lips met, and it was hard to tell if he had kissed her, or she had kissed him. It no longer mattered, they were holding tightly to each other, with all the longing they had felt for each other in the past few weeks, and the emptiness they had lived with for months and years before that. It was an endless, breath-consuming, life-giving kiss. And when he held her afterward, she leaned her face against his.

'Wow!' she whispered. 'I wasn't expecting to do that. . . . I thought you just came over to fix my sink.'

'I did,' he whispered back. 'I wanted to do this in

Italy, but I thought it was too soon.' She nodded, knowing it probably would have been. She wanted to go to bed with him, but she knew it was much, much too soon, according to all the rules. They had barely known each other for a month, and hadn't seen each other in weeks. One day at a time, she told herself. She was still savoring their first kiss. And just as she thought about it, he kissed her again. This one was more passionate, and she couldn't help wondering how many times he had done this with other women, how many affairs he'd had, how many crazy women had come into his life, wanting him to rescue them, how many times it had ended, and how many times he had started over again with someone else. He had had a lifetime of meaningless relationships, like a merry-go-round of women, and in her whole life, she had loved only two men. And now him. She didn't love him yet. But she thought she could one day. There was something about him that made her want him to stay and stay and stay, and never leave. Like the man who came to dinner, and never left, and just moved in.

'I'd better go,' he said in a gentle sexy voice that aroused her just listening to him. She nodded, thinking she should agree, but she didn't. She opened the door for him, and he hesitated.

'If I turn the water on tomorrow,' she whispered, 'will you come back to turn it off again?' She looked at him innocently, her hair slightly tousled, her eyes full of dreams, and he chuckled at her.

'I could turn it on right now, and give us an excuse for me to stay,' he whispered hopefully.

'I don't need an excuse, but I don't think we should,' she said demurely.

'Why's that?' He was playing with her neck, and running his lips across her face tantalizingly. She ran her hands through his hair, and pulled him close to her.

'I think there's a rule book somewhere about situations like this. I think it says you're not supposed to sleep with each other on the first date, after eating pizza and fixing a sink.'

'Damn, if I'd known that, I wouldn't have fixed the sink or eaten the pizza.' He smiled at her and kept kissing her. He wanted her more than he ever had any woman he could remember. And he could see she wanted him just as badly, but still felt she shouldn't. She was savoring the moment and thoroughly enjoying him.

'See you tomorrow?' she said softly. It was nearly a tease, but not quite, and he was surprised to find he liked it, waiting for her, and the right moment, whenever that was. For him, it would have been right then, or whenever she wanted. He was willing to wait, if Sylvia preferred it. She was worth waiting for. He had waited fifty years for her.

'Your place or mine?' he whispered. 'I'd love you to come to mine, but it's a mess. I've been gone for a month and no one's cleaned it. Maybe this weekend. Why don't I come back here tomorrow and see how your sink is doing?' The gallery was closed for the Labor Day holiday, and she was planning to work at home. She had nothing else to do the next day.

'I'll be here all day. Come whenever you want. I'll cook you dinner.'

'I'll cook. I'll call you in the morning.' He kissed her again, then left, and she stood silently, looking at the door after she'd closed it. He was a remarkable man, and it was a magical moment. She walked into her bedroom, as though seeing it for the first time, and wondered how it would look with him in it.

And as he walked out into the street and hailed a cab, he felt as though everything in his life had changed in a single evening.

6

Gray called Sylvia at ten o'clock the next morning. His whole apartment looked a mess, and he hadn't even bothered to unpack his suitcase. He had fallen into bed the night before, thinking of her, and the moment he woke up, he called her. She had been working on some papers, and smiled when she heard him.

They asked each other how they'd slept. She had been awake half the night, thinking about him, and he had slept like a baby.

'How's your sink holding up?'

'It's fine.' She smiled.

'Maybe I'd better come over and check on it.' She laughed at him, and they chatted for a few minutes. He said he had some things to do at home after his trip, but offered to bring her lunch around twelve-thirty.

'I thought we were doing dinner,' she said, sounding surprised, although she had told him she'd be home all day, which was a tacit invitation, and she'd meant it.

'I don't think I can wait that long,' he said honestly. 'I waited fifty years for you to come along. Another nine hours might kill me. Are you free for lunch?' he asked nervously, and she smiled. She was free for anything he wanted. She had decided the night before when he kissed her that she was ready to let him into her world, and share her life with him. She didn't know why it felt right to her, but everything about him did. She wanted to be with him.

'I'm free anytime you want to come over.'

'Can I bring anything? Quiche? Cheese? Wine?'

'I've got some stuff here. You don't need to bring anything.' There were so many things she wanted to do with him, walk through Central Park, wander around the Village, go to a movie, lie in bed and watch TV, go out to dinner, stay home and cook for him, see his work, show him her gallery, or just lie in bed and hold him. She hardly knew him, and yet at the same time, she felt as though she had always known him.

In his studio, Gray opened his mail, checked his bills, and haphazardly took his clothes out of his suitcase. He left most of them lying on the floor, and took out what he wanted. He showered, shaved, dressed, quickly wrote some checks, ran out the door, mailed them, and went to the only florist he found open. He bought her two dozen roses, hailed a cab, and gave the driver her address in SoHo. At noon, he rang the bell, and was standing in her doorway. The plumber had just left, and her eyes widened instantly when she saw the roses.

'Oh my God, they're beautiful . . . Gray, you shouldn't.' And she meant it, she knew he was a starving artist, and she was bowled over by the tenderness and generosity of the gesture. He was a true romantic. After a lifetime of narcissists, she had finally found a man whom she not only cared about, but to whom she mattered.

'If I could afford to, I'd send you roses every day. This may be the last of it for a while,' he said regretfully. He still had to pay his rent and his phone bill, and the ticket to France had been fearfully expensive. He wouldn't let Charlie pay for it. He thought the least he could do was pay his own way to get there. He had hoped to hop a ride on Adam's plane, but Adam had flown straight to Europe from Las Vegas on the way over, and to London with his kids after. 'I wanted to get you roses today, because today is special.'

'And why is that?' she asked, still holding the roses in her arms and looking up at him with eyes that seemed enormous. She was excited, and at the same time a little frightened.

'Because today is the beginning . . . This is where we begin . . . where it all starts. After today, neither of us will ever be quite the same again.' He looked at her then, took the roses from her, and set the enormous bundle down on a nearby table. And then he took her in his arms, kissed her, and held her. He could feel her trembling, and then he looked down at her. 'I want you to be happy,' he said gently. 'I want this to be a good thing for both of us.' In time, he wanted to make it up to her for the pain and disappointments she'd suffered. He wanted to make up for the absurdity and affronts in his own life. This was their chance to do it right, and make a difference to each other.

She went to put the roses in a vase, and set them down in the living room on a table.

'Are you hungry?' she called out to him, as she walked back into the kitchen. He followed her and stood in the doorway, smiling at her. She was beautiful. She was wearing a white shirt and jeans, and without saying a word, he walked over to her and began unbuttoning her shirt. She just stood there, motionless, and watched him. He slipped the shirt gently off her shoulders, and dropped it on a chair, and then admired her like a work of art, or something he had just painted. She was perfect. Her skin showed no signs of age, and her body was young and tight and athletic. No one had seen it in a long time. There had been no man to mirror who she was or what she felt, and care about what she needed or wanted. She felt as though she'd been alone for a thousand years, and now finally he had come to join her. It was like sharing a journey with him. Their destination was unknown, but they were fellow travelers setting out together.

He took her by the hand then, and led her quietly to her bedroom. They lay down on the bed together, and gently took each other's clothes off. She lay naked next to him, and he kissed her, as her hands began discovering him, and then her lips, and he slowly began exploring her. What he did was tantalizing, and the long, slow unraveling of his hunger for her would have been excruciating, if it hadn't been so exactly what she wanted. It was as though he had always known her. He knew exactly where to be and what to do and how to get there, and she did the same for him. It was like a dance they had always known how to do together, their rhythms perfectly matched, their bodies fitting together like two halves of one whole. Time seemed to stand still, until everything began to move quickly, and then finally, they both exploded into the stratosphere together, and she lay in his arms, silently, kissing him and smiling.

'Thank you,' she whispered as she lay in his arms and he pulled her closer. Their bodies were still woven together, and he smiled at her.

'I've been waiting for you forever,' he whispered

back. 'I didn't know where you were . . . but I always knew you were out there somewhere.' She hadn't been as wise as he, she had lost hope years before, of ever finding him. She had been certain that she had been condemned to be alone for the rest of time. He was a gift she had long since stopped expecting, and no longer even knew she wanted. And now he was here, in her life, in her head, in her heart, in her bed, and in every nook and cranny of her body. Gray had become a part of her forever.

They lay in her bed until they both fell asleep, and woke up hours later, sated, tranquil, happy. They walked into the kitchen finally, and made lunch together, naked. She had no shame with him, and neither did he, and even though their bodies were no longer as perfect as they once had been, they were totally comfortable with each other. They took their lunch back to bed, and ate it, talking and laughing with each other. Everything between them was simple and fun and easy.

They took a shower together afterward, and then dressed and went for a long walk around SoHo. They stopped in shops, looked into art galleries, bought gelato on the street and shared it. It was six o'clock when they went back to her place finally, after renting two old movies. They climbed back into her bed, and watched them together, made love again, and at ten o'clock that night, she got up and fixed him dinner.

'I want you to come to my place tomorrow,' he said when she came back to bed with their dinner, and handed him his. She had made scrambled eggs with cheese in them, and English muffins. It was the perfect end to their special day, one which they both knew they would never forget. And there was still so much left for both of them to discover.

'I want to see your recent work,' she said, thinking of it again, as they ate the eggs.

'That's why I want you to come over.'

'If you want, I'll go home with you in the morning. I have to be at the gallery at noon, but we can go to your place before that.'

'I'd like that,' he said, smiling. They finished the eggs, turned off the TV, curled up together in the bed, with their arms around each other.

'Thank you, Gray,' she whispered to him again. He was half-asleep by then, and only smiled and nodded. She kissed him gently on the cheek, moved even closer to him, and moments later, they were both sound asleep, looking like peaceful, happy children.

7

Sylvia was up early the next morning. She woke and saw Gray sleeping next to her, and for a fraction of an instant, she was startled, and then she lay nestled next to him, smiling at what had happened. If anything serious happened between them, this was going to be an enormous change for her. And even more so for him. He had never had a normal woman in his life, and she hadn't had a partner and companion in her life in years.

She slipped out of bed quietly, and went to take a shower. She let him sleep for as long as possible, and then made breakfast for both of them. She woke him up by serving him breakfast in bed on a tray. It was a far cry from the women he had fed, served, taken care of, nursed back to health, or doled out their medication to because they were too irresponsible or whacked-out to be responsible for it themselves. He looked up at Sylvia in amazement, as she set the tray down on the bed, and kissed his shoulder. He looked handsome and sexy lying in her bed, even with his uncombed hair. She loved his looks, he was strong and powerful and interesting and very male.

'Did I die and go to Heaven, or is this just a dream?' He put his arms behind his head and lay smiling at her. 'I don't think I've ever had breakfast in bed, unless cold two-day-old pizza on a paper towel counts.' She had even put a small vase with a rose in it on the tray. It was fun spoiling him. She had missed having someone to fuss over and take care of. For most of her adult life she had had a husband and children to nurture. Now everyone was gone. And she was excited to be pampering him.

'I'm sorry to wake you,' she apologized. It was ten o'clock, and she wanted to go to his studio with him, as they had discussed, before she went to work. Gray glanced at the clock in consternation.

'Good Lord. What time did you get up?'

'Around seven. I very rarely sleep late.'

'Neither do I. But I slept like a baby last night.' He smiled at her, and then got up to comb his hair and brush his teeth. He came back a minute later, and settled back into her comfortable bed with the tray. 'You're going to spoil me, Sylvia. I'll get fat and lazy.' There was no risk of that, she suspected. She was just enjoying being with him, and doing for him. She handed him the newspaper, which she'd read herself, while she had coffee and toast in the kitchen. He glanced at it, and put it away. He would much rather talk to her.

They chatted while he ate, and then he got up and got ready. They left for his studio at eleven, and walked out of her apartment hand in hand. She felt like a teenager with a new romance, but it had been so long since she felt that way that she was enjoying every minute of it. She was smiling as they walked out into the September sunshine, and he hailed a cab. It was a short ride to his apartment, and as they walked up four flights of stairs in the dilapidated old brownstone, he apologized for the mess in advance.

'I've been gone for a month, and to be honest, it was a mess before that. In fact' – he grinned broadly at her, slightly out of breath as they reached his landing – 'it's been a mess for years.' So had his life, but he didn't point that out to her. He had appeared to be a pillar of stability to the women he went out with, but compared to Sylvia, he seemed haphazard and disorganized. She ran an extremely successful gallery, had had two long relationships in her life, raised two normal, healthy children to adulthood, and everything about her life and apartment was impeccable, orderly, and neat as a pin. When he opened the door to his apartment, they could hardly get through the door. One of his suitcases was blocking it, there were packages the super had just shoved in, and a stack of mail had fallen and was spread all over the floor. The bills he'd paid the day before lay open and in disarray on a table. There were clothes on the couch, his plants had died, and everything in the apartment looked tired and worn. It had a comfortable, masculine feeling to it. The furniture was decent looking, although the upholstery was worn. He had bought everything in the place secondhand. There was a round dining table in the corner of the room, where he entertained friends for dinner sometimes, and beyond it was what had once been the dining room, and had always been his studio. It was why she had come.

She walked straight toward it, as he tried in vain to make order in the place, but it was beyond hopeless, he realized. Instead, he followed her into the next room, and stood watching her reaction to his work. He had three paintings on easels in various states of development. One was nearly finished, another he'd just begun before his trip, and the third he was pondering and planned to change because he didn't think it worked. And there were at least another dozen or so paintings leaning against the walls. She was stunned by the power and beauty of his work. They were representational and meticulous, dark in most cases, with extraordinary lights in them. There was one of a woman's face, in a peasant dress from the Middle Ages, that was reminiscent of an Old Master. His paintings were truly beautiful, and she turned to him with a look of admiration and respect. It was completely different from what she showed in her gallery, which was hip and new and young. She had a real passion for emerging artists, and what she showed was easy to look at and fun to live with. She sold some very successful young artists as well, but none had the obvious training he did, the masterly skill, and the expertise that showed in his work. She had known Gray was a painter of the first order, but what she saw in his work now was maturity, wisdom, and infinite ability. She stood next to him then, looking at the work, wanting to absorb it and drink it all in.

'Wow! It's absolutely amazing.' She understood now why he only did two or three paintings a year. Even working on several at once, as most artists did, it had to take him months, or even years, to complete each one. 'I'm blown away.' He looked thrilled with her reaction. There was one of a water scene that was absolutely mesmerizing with sunlight on the water at the end of day. It made you want to stand and stare at it forever. Sylvia knew, looking at his work, that he needed an important gallery to see his work and represent him, not hers.

145

He knew the kind of work she sold, he had just wanted her to see it so she could see what he did. He had a great respect for her understanding of art history, and even modern painting. He knew that if she reacted favorably to it, it would be a major compliment to him. And whether she liked it or not, it was what he did. 'You have to find a gallery to represent you, Gray,' she said sternly. He had told her he had been without representation for nearly three years. He sold his work to people who had bought them previously, and to friends, like Charlie, who had bought a number of his paintings and also thought they were very good. 'It's a crime to leave all these paintings just sitting here, without a home.' There were stacks and stacks of them leaning against the walls.

'I hate all the dealers I meet. They don't give a damn about the work, just the money. Why give my work to them? It's not about money, at least not for me.' She could see that easily from the way he lived.

'But you have to eat,' she chided him gently. 'And not all dealers are that greedy and irresponsible. Some really care about what they do. I do. I may not sell work of this caliber, or as masterful as these, but I believe in the work I show, and my artists. In their own way, they have tremendous talent too. They just express it differently than you.'

'I know you care about it. It's written all over

you, that's why I wanted you to see my work. If you were like the rest of them, I wouldn't have invited you in. But then again, if you were like them, I wouldn't be falling in love with you either.' It was a big statement after their first night together, and for a moment she didn't answer. She loved being with him, and wanted to get to know him better, this was serious for her too, but she didn't know if she loved him yet. However excited she was about him, it was still too soon. It was for him too. But he was getting there faster than either of them had planned, and so was she. Seeing his work, and knowing he had dared to be vulnerable with her, made her care about him even more. She gave him a look that had no need of words, and he took her in his arms and kissed her.

'I love your work, Gray,' she whispered.

'You're not my dealer,' he teased her. 'All you have to love is me.'

'I'm getting there,' she said honestly. In fact, faster than expected.

'Me too,' he said clearly.

She stood staring at his work for a long moment, as though she were on another planet. Her mind was going a million miles a minute. 'I want to find a gallery for you. I have some ideas. We can go look at their work this week and see what you think.'

'Never mind what I think. It depends on what

they think too. You don't have to worry about that. You have enough to do, and I don't have enough for a show right now anyway,' he said modestly. He didn't want to take advantage of her connections. What he felt for her was entirely personal and private, it had nothing to do with his work, or wanting an introduction from her, and she knew that.

'The hell you don't have enough for a show,' she said forcefully, as she would have to one of her young artists, half art dealer, half pushy stage mother. But a lot of them needed to be pushed. Few if any of them ever realized how talented they were. Not the good ones anyway. The young show-offs were rarely as good. 'Look at all this,' she said, gently moving things so she could see what was in his stacks. It was gorgeous stuff, as good as what was in progress on the easels, or better.

Once finished, his paintings seemed to be lit from within, some by candlelight, some by fire. There was a luminous quality to them that she had never seen in recent work. It was straight out of the Renaissance and the work of the Old Masters. And yet it had a modern-day feeling to it. It was the technique that was so remarkable, and which was a lost art. She knew he had studied in Paris and Italy, just as her daughter was doing. In Gray's case, it had given him a great foundation. She thought his work was nothing less than brilliant and inspired. 'Gray, we have to find you a gallery, whether you like it or not.' It was the kind of thing he would have done for one of his previous women, helping them to find a gallery, an agent, or a job, more often than not with disastrous results. No one had ever offered to help him, except maybe Charlie. But Gray didn't like to impose on anyone, particularly his friends, or those he loved.

'I don't need a gallery, Sylvia. Honestly, I just don't.'

'What if I find you one you like? Will you at least look at it, and talk to them?' She was pushing hard, but he loved her for it. She had nothing to gain from it, all she wanted was to help him. Just as he had done for so many for so long. He smiled and nodded in answer. She had already decided who to call, there were at least three possibilities that were perfect for him. And she knew that if she thought about it, there would be others, uptown galleries, important ones, that showed work like his. Definitely not galleries in SoHo like her own. He needed an entirely different venue. Also London and New York. The right galleries would have connections in other cities. That's where he belonged, in her opinion.

'Don't worry about this,' Gray said gently, and meant it. 'You have enough on your plate as it is.

149

You don't need another project. I don't want to make more work for you. I just want to be with you.'

'Me too,' she said, smiling at him. But she also wanted to help him. Why not? He deserved it. She knew that artists were typically terrible businessmen and incapable of selling their own work. That was why they had dealers. Gray needed one too. She was determined to help him. And hopefully, to have a relationship with him. That still remained to be seen. But whether she did or not over time, there was no reason not to give him a hand with the right connections for his art. She knew damn near everyone in New York in the art world. She had proven herself to be so honorable and decent that doors opened for her with ease, and always had. And once she opened the right door for him, the rest would be up to him. All she wanted to be was the conduit, which was a perfectly respectable goal between them, even if all they turned out to be were friends who'd had a brief romance.

Sylvia glanced at her watch then. It was nearly noon and she had to get to her office. He promised to call her later, as she kissed him good-bye, and a moment later she was scampering down the stairs as he called out to her.

'Thank you!' he shouted down the stairwell, and she looked up with a broad smile. She waved then, and was gone.

There was the usual chaos once she got to her office. Two artists had called in frantic about their next show. A client was upset because a painting hadn't arrived yet. Someone else called to check on a commission they'd ordered. The installer had had a motorcycle accident, broken both arms, and couldn't put up their next show. She had an appointment with their graphic designer that afternoon, about the brochure for the next show. She had to meet a deadline for their next ad in *Artforum,* and the photographer hadn't delivered the four-by-fives yet of the piece of sculpture in the ad. She didn't have time to breathe until four o'clock that afternoon. But as soon as she did, she made some calls for Gray. It was easier than she had expected. The dealers she called trusted her reputation, her taste, and her judgment. Most people who knew her thought she had a good eye, and an instinct for great art. Two of the dealers she called asked her to send slides. The third was coming home that night from Paris, so she left a message for him to call her. She called Gray as soon as she hung up. She was a woman on a mission. And he laughed the minute he heard her. She sounded like a whirlwind, and he assured her he had slides. If he hadn't, she was going to send a photographer over to do some.

'I have sheets of them, if that's all you want.'

'That'll do for now,' she said cheerfully, and told him she'd have a messenger at his studio in half an hour to pick them up.

'Wow, you don't mess around, do you?'

'Not with work as great as yours . . . besides,' she said, slowing down a little. This wasn't business for her after all, it was romance. She had to remind herself of that for a minute. 'I want good things to happen for you.'

'They already did, in Portofino. The rest is gravy.'

'Well, let me take care of the gravy,' she said, sounding confident, and he smiled.

'Be my guest.' He was loving the attention, it was completely unfamiliar to him. He didn't want to take advantage of her, but he was fascinated watching her work, and seeing how she lived her life. She was not a woman to be daunted by obstacles, nor to accept defeat or failure. She just rolled up her sleeves and got to work, whatever the task at hand.

The messenger appeared at Gray's door at exactly four-thirty, brought the slides to Sylvia, and shortly after five she had them and a cover letter in the hands of the dealers she'd called about Gray's work. She left her gallery at six, and as soon as she got home, Gray called her, and suggested dinner together. He wanted to take her to a small Italian restaurant in his neighborhood. She was thrilled. It was funny and cozy and the food was delicious, and she was relieved to see on the menu that it was cheap. She didn't want him spending money on her, but she didn't want to humiliate him by offering to pay either. She suspected they would be doing a lot of cooking for each other in the future. And after dinner that night, he took her home, and stayed at her place. They were falling into a delicious routine.

They made breakfast together the next morning, and the next day he served her breakfast in bed. He said it was her turn. She had never had a turn before, but this time they were partners, spoiling and pampering each other, listening to each other, consulting each other on what they thought. For the moment, everything about it was perfect. It frightened her to look into the future, or have too much hope that this meant more than it did. But whatever it was, and however long it lasted, it suited them both for now, and was all they had ever wanted. And the sex was beyond terrific. They were old and wise enough, and had just enough experience, to care about each other, and make sure that each was pleased. Nothing in their relationship was self-serving. Each of them enjoyed making the other happy, whether in or out of bed. After a lifetime of mistakes, they were both wise and well seasoned. Like a fine wine that had ripened perfectly with age. Not too old yet, but just old enough to be vibrant and delicious. Although her children might have thought them old, in fact they were the perfect age to enjoy and appreciate each other. Sylvia had never been happier in her life. Nor had Gray.

Both art dealers she had sent his slides to called her on the same day. Both were interested, and wanted to see samples of his work. The third dealer called two days after he got home from Paris, and said pretty much the same thing. Sylvia told Gray about it over dinner the day they called.

'I think you're going to have some options here,' she said, looking ecstatic. Gray was floored. In a matter of days, she had swept him out of his lethargy, gotten slides of his work to the right places, and opened several doors.

'You are an amazing woman,' he said with eyes that said it all.

'You are an amazing man, and an extraordinary artist.' She made a date with him to take his work to all three galleries on Saturday afternoon. She said they could use her van. And as promised, she showed up in the morning in a sweatshirt and jeans to help him load up. It took them two hours to take everything he wanted downstairs, and he was embarrassed to have her work. She had already played fairy godmother to him, he hated to use her as delivery person too, but she was game.

She had brought a sweater and better shoes to

change into when they went to the galleries that were expecting them. And by five o'clock it was over. He had offers from all three galleries, who were wildly impressed with his work. Gray couldn't believe what she had done, and even she had to admit she was pleased.

'I'm so proud of you,' she said, beaming at him. They were both exhausted but delighted. It took another two hours to get all his work back upstairs. He hadn't made a decision yet about which gallery to choose. But that night he did, and she thought he had made the right choice. It was an important gallery on Fifty-seventh Street, with a large branch in London, and a corresponding gallery in Paris, with whom they exchanged work. It was perfect for him, she said confidently, thrilled with his choice.

'You are incredible,' he said, smiling at her. He didn't know whether to laugh or cry, he was so moved by what she'd done. They were sitting on the couch in his living room as he said it. The room was an even bigger mess than it had been earlier in the week. He had been painting all week, inspired by her energy, and hadn't bothered to tidy up. She didn't care and didn't seem to see it. He loved that about her too, in fact there was absolutely nothing he didn't. As far as Gray was concerned, she was the perfect woman, and he wanted to be the perfect man for her, and give her all that she had never had and needed. There was little he could do for her except be there for her, and love her, which was precisely what he wanted to do. 'I love you, Sylvia,' he said quietly, as he looked at her.

'I love you too,' she said softly. She wasn't even sure if she wanted to, but the days and nights they had spent together meant something. She liked the way he thought, and what he believed. She loved his integrity and what he stood for. She even admired his work. There was nothing they needed to do about it, nowhere to go with it, no decisions they had to make. All they had to do was enjoy it. It was all so simple, for the first time in both their previously complicated lives. 'Do you want me to cook dinner?' she asked, smiling at him. The only decisions they had to make were where to eat, and whose place to sleep at. He liked sleeping at her apartment, and she preferred it. His was too big a mess, although she liked visiting him there and seeing the progress on his work.

'No,' Gray said firmly, 'I do not want you to cook dinner. I want to take you out and celebrate. You got me a terrific gallery this week. I would never have done that myself. I would just have sat here, on all of it, too lazy to move.' He wasn't lazy, far from it. But he was modest about his work. She knew many artists like him. They needed someone to make the moves and bridge the gap for them. She had been happy to do it for him, with remarkably good results.

They had dinner at a small French restaurant on the Upper East Side that night, with good French food and fine French wine. It was a genuine celebration, of them, of his new gallery, of everything that lay ahead. And as they went back to her place in a cab, they talked about Charlie and Adam. Gray hadn't seen Adam since he got back, or even called him, and he knew Charlie wasn't back yet, and Gray hadn't called him either. He often didn't call either of them, especially when he was engrossed in his painting. They were used to his dropping off the face of the earth, and called him when they didn't hear from him. He described his friendship with them to Sylvia that night, the depth of it, and their kindness to him. They talked about why Charlie had never married, and why Adam never would again. Sylvia said she felt sorry for them. Charlie seemed like a lonely man to her, and it saddened her to hear about his sister and parents, enormous irreversible losses for him. In the end, losing them had cost him the opportunity to be loved by someone else, which multiplied the tragedy exponentially for him.

'He says he wants to get married, but I don't think he ever will,' Gray said philosophically. They both agreed that Adam was another story. Bitter

157

about Rachel, angry at his mother, all he wanted was bimbos and girls who were young enough to be his daughters. It sounded like an empty life to her. 'He's a great guy, once you get to know him,' Gray said loyally about his friend. Sylvia was not as convinced. It was easy to see the merit and quality in Charlie. Adam was the kind of man who never failed to annoy her. Smart, confident, cocky, successful, with no real use for women, except as sex objects and decorations. He would never have dreamed of going out with a woman his own age. She didn't say it to Gray, but she had a profound disrespect for men like him. As far as she was concerned, he needed therapy, a good swift kick in the ass, and a powerful lesson. She hoped that one of these days, some smart young thing would deliver it to him. From what she could see, he had it coming. Gray didn't see it that way. He thought he was a great guy, who'd had his heart broken when Rachel left him.

'That doesn't justify using people, or disrespecting women.' Sylvia had had her heart broken too, more than once, but it hadn't made her use men as disposable objects. Far from it. It had made her retreat and lick her wounds, and think about how and why it had happened, before venturing out into the world again. But then again, she was a woman. Women functioned differently than men,

158

and came to different conclusions. Most women who had been badly burned retreated to nurse their wounds, whereas most men who had been wounded ran headlong into the world, wreaking vengeance on others. She was sure, as Gray said, that Adam was nice to the women he went out with. The problem was that he had no respect for them, and would never have understood what she and Gray were sharing. He would never have let it happen, or dared to trust it. Which made her realize once again what a miracle it was that she and Gray had found each other.

She cuddled up next to him in bed that night, feeling safe and warm and lucky. And if, in the end, he went away again, at least they would have had this magical moment. She knew now that she could survive whatever happened. Gray loved that about her. She was a survivor, and he had proven over a lifetime that he was as well. If anything, their dis-appointments had made them kinder, wiser, and more patient. They had no desire to hurt each other or anyone else. And whatever else happened, or didn't, between them, along with the dreams, the hope, the romance, and the sex, best of all, they had become friends and were learning to love each other.

8

'I'm back. Are you all right?' Charlie called Gray at his studio on a Monday, and sounded concerned. 'I haven't heard from you in weeks. I called you a few times after I got back, but your phone is always on the machine, at whatever hour,' Charlie complained, as Gray realized he'd probably been at Sylvia's when Charlie called, but Gray said nothing to him. It had been a blissful weekend for Sylvia and Gray, and Charlie had no idea what had happened since Gray's return to New York. Charlie had realized while at friends' in the Hamptons over the weekend that he hadn't heard a word from Gray since shortly after he got home. Charlie had a couple of e-mails from him in early September while he was still on the boat, but nothing since. Usually, if all was well in his world, Gray eventually checked in, and this time he hadn't.

'I'm fine,' Gray said happily. 'I've just been working.' He said nothing about Sylvia yet, but they had both agreed over the weekend that it was time to say something to his two friends. She wanted to wait to tell her children. He and Sylvia had been seeing each other for nearly a month, and from what both of them could discern, it was real. She was faintly worried that Charlie and Adam would be jealous, or even resentful. With a serious relationship in his life, Gray would be less available to them, and she had a feeling it wouldn't sit well with them. Gray had insisted that wasn't the case, but Sylvia was not convinced.

He told Charlie about his new gallery then, and Charlie whistled. 'How did that happen? I can't believe you finally got off your duff and found a gallery to sell your work. It's about goddamn time.' Charlie was delighted for him.

'Yeah, I thought so too.' He didn't give Sylvia credit for it yet, but he intended to the next time he and Charlie met. He didn't want to talk about it over the phone.

'How about lunch one of these days? I haven't seen you since the boat,' Charlie said. He was going to a concert with Adam later that week. It was harder to get together with Gray. He tended to get involved in his work, and isolate himself for weeks on end. But he sounded in good spirits these days, and if he had signed up with a major gallery, things were obviously going well for him.

'I'd love to have lunch with you,' Gray said

quickly. 'When?' It was rare for him to be that anxious or enthusiastic about getting together. Most of the time, he had to be pried from his lair and dragged from his easel. Charlie didn't comment. He assumed that Gray was ebullient about the deal he'd made.

Charlie quickly consulted his book. He was swamped with meetings for the foundation, many of which included lunch. But he had an opening at lunchtime the following day. 'How's tomorrow?'

'Sounds good to me.'

'The Yacht Club?' It was Charlie's favorite venue for lunch, either that or one of his other clubs. Gray found the Yacht Club painfully stuffy at times, as did Adam, but they humored him anyway.

'That sounds fine,' Gray said, sounding pensive.

'See you at one,' Charlie confirmed, and both men went back to work.

Gray told Sylvia the following morning that he and Charlie were having lunch, and she looked at him over the stack of pancakes he had just made.

'Is that good or bad?' she asked, looking nervous.

'Good, of course.' He sat down across the table from her with a plate of pancakes of his own. He loved cooking for her. He was becoming the breakfast chef, and she cooked for him at night, or they went out. Everything was falling into place, and they had settled into an easy routine. He left in the

162

morning to go to his studio, where he no longer slept. She went to the gallery, and they met back at her place around six, when they both got home. He usually brought a bottle of wine, or a bag of groceries. He had bought lobsters for them over the weekend, which reminded them both of the golden days on the boat. He hadn't officially moved in with her, but he was sleeping there every night.

'Are you going to tell him about us?' she inquired cautiously.

'I thought I would. Is that still okay with you?' Knowing how independent she was, he tried not to step on her toes.

'It's okay with me,' she said easily. 'I'm just not so sure it will be okay with him. It might be a bit of a shock, you know. He might have liked me fine as a passing face in Portofino, but he may be a little less enthused at the thought of this becoming a full-time deal,' which clearly it had become in the four weeks since Gray got home. And it was more than fine with them. Very, very fine.

'Don't be silly. He'll be happy for me. He's always been interested in the women I've been with.'

Sylvia laughed as she poured him a cup of coffee. 'Yeah, because they were no threat to him. He probably figured they'd wind up in jail or an institution before they could cause a lot of trouble between the two of you.'

'Are you planning to cause trouble?' Gray asked with interest, looking slightly amused.

'No, of course not. But Charlie could perceive it that way. The three of you have been inseparable for ten years.'

'Yeah. And I'm still planning to see them. There's no reason why they can't see me with you.'

'Well, see what Charlie says. Maybe we should have him over for dinner. I've actually thought of that a couple of times recently. And Adam too, if you want,' although she liked him a great deal less. 'I'm just not too crazy about having dinner with women the same age as my kids. Or younger, in Adam's case. But I'll do whatever you think is a good idea.' To Sylvia, it seemed like the diplomatic thing to do.

'Why don't we have Charlie over on his own first,' Gray suggested amiably. He knew she didn't approve of Adam, and he didn't want to push it. At least not quite so soon. But he liked the idea of including her with his two friends. They were an important part of his life, and so was she.

Both of them knew that including friends in their private world was going to be important to the health of the relationship in the long run. They couldn't sit there alone forever, holding hands, watching movies on TV, and spending their weekends in bed, although they both loved it, and it was certainly fun. But they needed more people in their life than that. Adding friends to the mix was yet another step toward achieving some kind of stability between them. Sylvia always felt as though there was some kind of rule book somewhere about relationships, and others knew its contents better than she. First you slept together, then he spent the night, eventually with increasing frequency. At some point, he needed to have a closet and some drawer space, they hadn't gotten there yet, and his clothes were hung all over her laundry room. She knew she was going to have to do something about that one of these days. After that he'd get a key, once you were sure that you didn't want to date anyone else, in order to avoid awkward moments, if he arrived at the wrong time. She had already given him one, there was no one else in her life, and sometimes he came home from the studio before she got back from the gallery. There was no point having him sit on the front stoop, waiting for her. She wasn't sure what came after that. Buying groceries, he had done that. Dividing up the bills. Answering the phone. She was definitely not there yet, in case she got calls from her kids, who knew nothing about Gray. Asking him to live with her, changing his address, putting his name on the mailbox and bell. Friends were a part of all that. It was going to be important that they like at least some of the same people. And in time, her kids. She wanted Gray to meet them too. She knew he was uneasy about that. He had said as much to her. She knew that was the easy part. Her kids were great, and she was sure he would love them too. All Emily and Gilbert wanted was for her to be happy. If they saw that he was kind to her, and they loved each other, then Gray would be welcomed into the family. She knew her kids.

They still had a long way to go, but they were on their way. Some of the hurdles ahead still frightened her, and she wasn't ready for them yet, and neither was he. But she knew that telling Adam and Charlie was a big one for him. She had no idea how they'd react to the news that she and Gray were as serious as they were. She hoped that Charlie wouldn't discourage him, or frighten him about her kids. She knew that that was Gray's one big Achilles' heel. He was phobic about kids, not only about having his own but about relating to someone else's. It didn't seem to matter to him that hers were adults and no longer children. He was panicked about getting attached to anyone to that degree. For a man who had spent a lifetime nurturing some of the most dysfunctional women on the planet, the one thing that terrified him was meeting, dealing with, or relating to their kids. To Sylvia, it appeared to be a completely irrational fear. But to Gray, it was real.

Gray helped her clean up the breakfast dishes, and he left for the studio first. She had some calls to make before she left for work. She wanted to call Emily and Gilbert. With the time difference, it was usually too late to call them when she got home from work. She hadn't said anything to them about Gray yet. Neither of them was coming home till Christmas. Sylvia thought there was plenty of time between now and then, three months in fact, to see how things were going with Gray, before she said anything to them. Both were out when she called that day, and she left loving messages on their answering machines. She stayed in close touch with her kids.

By the time Sylvia left for the gallery that day, Gray was already at the Yacht Club with Charlie. They were seated at his favorite table. It was an enormous elegant dining room, with vaulted ceilings, portraits of previous commodores, and ship models under glass around the room. Gray thought Charlie looked terrific, tan, fit, and rested.

'So how was the end of the trip?' Gray asked conversationally, after they both ordered chef's salads.

'It was fine. We didn't really go anywhere after you left. I had work to do, and the crew started doing some repairs. It was just nice to be on the boat, instead of here in the apartment.' He had been finding it lonely and depressing of late, and he was feeling restless. 'So tell me about the gallery you signed with. Wechsler-Hinkley, isn't it?' It was an impressive name in the art world. 'How did that happen? Did they just find you?' Charlie was happy for him. No one deserved it more than Gray. He had an enormous talent. 'Or did you find them?' Charlie was smiling broadly in anticipation of the story.

'Actually, a friend gave me an introduction,' he said cautiously. Sylvia had made him nervous about Charlie's reaction, which he knew was silly. But now he felt anxious, and he looked it.

'What kind of friend?' Charlie asked with interest. He didn't know what or why, but there was something smoky about the story.

'A friend friend . . . you know . . . actually . . . a woman,' Gray said, feeling like a schoolboy reporting to his father.

'Now there's a twist,' Charlie said, looking amused. 'What kind of woman? Do I know her? Is there a new wounded bird in your nest these days? One who works at a gallery, with good connections? If so, how clever of you,' Charlie praised him. But it wasn't what he thought. Gray wasn't dating some secretary who had asked her boss to see him. There was no wounded bird in Gray's nest, but rather a dynamo who had taken him under her wing, and flown like an eagle.

'Actually, I don't think it was clever. More like lucky.'

'There's no luck involved in this, and you know it,' Charlie said, echoing Sylvia's words to him. 'You've got a major talent. If anyone got lucky, my friend, they did. But you're not answering my question.' Charlie's eyes met Gray's and held them. 'Who's the woman? Or is she a secret?' Maybe she was married. That had happened to him before too, runaway wives who claimed they were separated, and weren't, or had an 'arrangement.' And then their husbands showed up and tried to kill him. He had played out every disastrous scenario possible in the years of his eternal bachelorhood. Occasionally, Charlie worried about him. One of these days, an abusive ex-boyfriend of one of his nutcases was going to shoot him. 'You're not in a mess again, I hope, are you?' Charlie looked worried, and Gray laughed ruefully as he shook his head.

'No, I'm not. But I've got a hell of a reputation, don't I? I guess I deserve it. I've dated some lulus.' He sighed and shook his head again, and decided to brave it. 'But not this time. And yes, I'm seeing someone. But this one is different.' He said it proudly.

'Who is she? Do I know her?' Charlie was curious who the woman of the hour was. But who-ever she was, Gray looked happy, Charlie had noticed. He looked relaxed, and pleased with life, very content, almost complacent. He looked as though he were on tranquilizers, or happy pills, but Charlie knew he wasn't. But there was an almost euphoric air about him.

'You've met her,' Gray said cryptically, still stalling, thinking of Sylvia's warnings.

'And? Do we need a drumroll?' Charlie teased him.

'You met her in Portofino.' He finally spat it out, but still looked nervous.

'I did? When?' Charlie's mind suddenly went blank. He couldn't remember anyone that Gray had dated on the trip. The only one who had scored on the trip was Adam in St. Tropez, Corsica, and Capri. Neither he nor Gray had dated anyone, as he recalled.

'Sylvia Reynolds,' Gray said calmly. 'She was part of that whole group we met up with in Portofino and Sardinia.'

'Sylvia Reynolds? The art dealer?' Charlie looked stunned. He remembered Gray liking her and Adam teasing him about it, saying she wasn't his type, that she wasn't crazy enough, or in fact at all. Charlie remembered her perfectly. He had liked her. And apparently so did Gray. It was hard to believe that they had gotten into mischief somewhere along the way. 'When did that happen?' he asked, still looking somewhat astounded. He had suspected on the trip that they liked each other, but not necessarily enough to see each other after.

'It happened when I got back. We've been seeing each other for nearly a month. She's a lovely woman. She introduced me to Wechsler-Hinkley, and two other galleries, as soon as she saw my work. The next thing I knew, I'd been signed. She doesn't let much grass grow under her feet,' he said admiringly, smiling at his friend.

'Well, you certainly look happy,' Charlie said, adjusting to the concept. Gray had never spoken of any woman as he had now. 'I hate to admit it, but I agreed with Adam. I didn't think she was your type.'

'She's not,' Gray laughed ruefully again. 'I guess that's a good thing. I'm not used to being around a woman who can take care of herself, and really doesn't need me for anything except a good time and a roll in the hay.'

'Is that what it is?' Charlie asked with a look of interest. He was going to have a lot to report to Adam when he saw him the following night.

'No, it's not. Actually, it's a lot more than that. I've been staying with her every night.'

Charlie looked shocked. 'You've been seeing her for a month, and you *moved in*? Isn't that a little hasty?' It sounded to Charlie as though Gray had traded places with the little birds with broken wings.

'I didn't move in,' Gray said quietly. 'I said I'm sleeping there.'

'*Every night?*' Gray felt like a naughty schoolboy again. Charlie did not look pleased. 'Don't you think things are moving a little too quickly here? You're not giving up your studio, are you?' Charlie sounded panicked.

'Of course not. I'm just having a good time with a wonderful woman, and enjoying her company. She's a hell of a woman. Smart, capable, normal, decent, funny, giving, loving. I don't know where she's been all these years, but in three and a half weeks, my whole life has changed.'

'Is that what you want?' Charlie asked him pointedly. 'From the sound of it, you're in it up to your neck. That can be a dangerous thing. She could get ideas.'

'About what? Like she'd want to move into my shithole of an apartment? Or steal my thirty-year-old luggage maybe? She has better art books than I do. I guess she could always steal my paints. My couch is pretty well shot, and hers looks pretty good to me. My plants died while I was in Europe. And I don't have a decent towel to my name. I own two frying pans, six forks, and four plates. I'm not sure what you think she could get out of me, but whatever it is, I'd actually be happy to give it to her. Relationships can be difficult, but believe me,

172

Charlie, this is the first woman I've ever gone out with who *doesn't* look dangerous to me. The others definitely were.'

'I don't mean she's after your money. But you know how women get. They have a lot of illusions, and construe things differently. You ask them out to dinner, and the next thing you know, they're trying on a wedding dress, and registering at Tiffany. I just don't want to see you get dragged into anything.'

'I promise you, Charlie, I'm not being dragged anywhere. Wherever this thing is going, I'm a willing passenger on the train.'

'Good Lord, are you going to marry her?' Charlie stared at Gray, his eyes huge in his face.

'I don't know,' he said honestly. 'I haven't thought about marriage in years. I don't think she wants to. She's been married, and it doesn't sound like it was a great experience for her. Her husband walked out on her with a nineteen-year-old girl, after twenty years of marriage. She has kids, she says she's too old to want more. Her gallery is a huge success. She has a hell of a lot more money than I ever will. She doesn't need me for that. And I have no desire to take advantage of her. We can each support ourselves, although she better than I. She has a terrific loft in SoHo, a career she loves. She's only had one man in her life since her divorce, and he committed suicide three years ago. I'm the first man she's been involved with since. I don't think either of us wants more than we have right now. Would I ever marry her, one day down the road? Probably. If she was willing, which I doubt, I'd be nuts if I didn't give it a shot. But right now, our biggest decision is where to have dinner every night, or who's going to cook breakfast. I haven't even met her kids,' he said calmly. Charlie was staring at him wide-eyed. It was quite a speech. He hadn't seen Gray in slightly over three weeks, and he was not only living with a woman, but talking about possibly marrying her one day. Charlie looked as if he'd been shot. And for a fraction of a second, seeing the look on his face, Gray realized that there was a distinct possibility that Sylvia had been right. Charlie was very obviously not pleased with the recent turn of events in Gray's life.

'You don't even like kids,' Charlie reminded him, 'of any age. What makes you think that hers are any different?'

'Maybe they're not. Maybe that will be the dealbreaker for me. Maybe she'll get tired of me first. They live three thousand miles away, they're both grown up. And maybe at that distance, I can even stand her kids. All I can do is give it a shot. That's the best I can do. Maybe it'll work. Maybe not. All I know is that it's working now, and we're having a great time together. Beyond that, who the hell knows? I could be dead by next week. In the meantime, I'm having a hell of a good time. The best in my life.'

'Hopefully not,' Charlie said somberly, referring to his comment about being dead in a week. 'But you may wish you were, if she turns out to be different than you think she is, and by then you'll be trapped.' He sounded ominous, and Gray smiled at him. Charlie was looking panicked, and Gray wasn't sure if it was for himself or on Gray's behalf. Either way, it was unnecessary. He was feeling anything but trapped. At the moment, he was a more than willing love slave in Sylvia's elegant loft.

'I'm not trapped,' Gray said quietly. 'I'm not even living there. I'm just staying there. We're trying it out. And if it doesn't work for either of us, I'll go back to my studio, and that's that.'

'It never works that way,' Charlie said knowingly. 'Some women cling, they hang on, they accuse, berate, they get hysterical, they call lawyers. They claim you made promises you never made. Somehow they get their claws into you, and the next thing you know they think they own you.' Charlie looked utterly terrified for him as he said it. He'd seen it happen to other men over the years, and didn't want something like that to happen to Gray. He knew how innocent he was at times.

'Trust me, neither Sylvia nor I want to be owned.

We're too old for that. And she's a lot healthier than you give her credit for. If she walked away from her husband of twenty years without a backward glance, she's not going to be hanging around my neck like an albatross, trying to get her claws into me. If anyone walks, she's a lot more likely to do it first.'

'Is she commitment phobic? If she is, you could get seriously hurt.'

'And I haven't been hurt before? Charlie, be serious, life is about getting hurt. We get hurt every day when people we scarcely know won't take our calls. I've probably had more women walk out on me than any guy in New York. I survived it. I will again, if that happens. And yes, she probably is commitment phobic, so am I. Christ, I don't even want to meet her kids. I'm scared to death to get hurt or too attached, but this is the first time I've actually felt that the upside of the ride just might be worth a little pain, or even a lot of risk. No one's made any promises. No one's talking about marriage. All we're saying to each other right now is, where do you want to have dinner tonight? For the moment, we're both still safe.'

'You're never safe once you get involved,' Charlie said with a worried frown. 'I just don't want you to get hurt.' But he had tipped his hand about how he felt about relationships. It wasn't just about the fatal flaws he found in his debutantes, it was about the pain he had been trying to avoid ever since his entire family died. Charlie was terrified to take a risk. Gray no longer was. It was a major milestone for him. And the fact that he was doing so was a huge threat to Charlie. It was as though an alarm bell had gone off somewhere. One of the members of the Bachelors' Army had defected. Gray saw everything in Charlie's eyes that Sylvia had feared, not only distrust and disapproval, but total panic. She was smarter than Gray knew, about people anyway, and she had Charlie pegged. Maybe Adam too. What Gray didn't like about it was that Charlie's reaction to his situation with Sylvia made him feel not only disloyal to him, but as though he was a total fool for feeling as he did. It was an unpleasant feeling, and put a pall on things, as Charlie signed the check. From Gray's perspective, it hadn't been an easy lunch, to say the least.

'Sylvia and I were hoping that you would come down to the loft for dinner one night.' Charlie put the pen down and stared at him.

'Do you realize what you sound like?' Charlie said with a grim look, as Gray shook his head. He wasn't sure he wanted to hear. 'A married man, for God's sake. And don't forget you're not.'

'Is that the worst thing that could happen to me?' Gray finally snapped back. He was disappointed by

Charlie's reaction. Severely so, in fact. He hadn't wanted Sylvia to be right. And she was. Dead on. 'Somehow, I think colon cancer would be worse.'

'Sometimes it's hard to tell the difference,' Charlie said cynically. 'Committing yourself to that extent can be a very insidious thing. You have to give up who you are to do it, and become someone no sane man would ever want to be.' He said it with total conviction, as Gray sighed and looked at him. Who had they become in all these years? How high a price had they paid for the freedom they were hanging on to so desperately? Maybe too high a price. In the end, after defending their independence for a lifetime, they were all going to wind up alone. And suddenly since he'd met Sylvia, it had occurred to Gray that that might not be such a worthy goal. He had said it to her only days before. He had finally realized that one day, when it came to that, he didn't want to die alone. One day the crazy, needy women, and the debutantes and Adam's bimbos, would stop hanging on, or even coming around. They would be at home with someone else. The paradise of freedom wasn't looking quite so good to Gray as it had till then.

'Do you really want to spend your old age with me?' Gray asked Charlie, looking him dead in the eye. 'Is that what you want? Or would you like a better-looking pair of legs than mine across the

178

table from you when you're floating around on the *Blue Moon*? Because if you don't think about that one of these days, I'm what you're going to wind up with. I love you a lot, you're my best friend, but when I get old and sick and tired and lonely one day, much as I'd like to see your face across the lunch table, it could just be that I'll want to crawl into bed with someone else who'll hold my hand. And unless you want to end up with Adam or me, maybe you'd better start thinking about it too.'

'What's happening to you? What's she feeding you? Ecstasy? Why the hell are you worrying about your old age now? You're fifty years old. You don't have to worry about that for another thirty years, and God knows what'll happen to us between now and then.'

'Maybe that *is* the point. I'm fifty years old. You're forty-six. Maybe it's time for us to grow up one of these days. Adam can still get away with it, he's a lot younger than we are. I just don't know if I want to live my life this way anymore. How many more women can I rescue? How many more restraining orders can I help them get? How many more boob jobs does Adam want to pay for? And how many more debutantes do you want to find something wrong with? If they're not good enough for you, Charlie, then to hell with them. But maybe it's time for you to find someone who is.'

179

'Spoken like a true traitor,' Charlie said, toasting him with the last of his wine. He emptied the glass and set it down. 'I don't know about you, but I find this a very depressing conversation. You may be feeling Father Time nipping at your heels, which seems ridiculous to me, if you want to know what I think. But I'm not. And I'm not about to settle for some half-assed relationship with just any woman, because I'm afraid to die alone. I'd rather kill myself tonight. I'm not settling down, or even thinking about it, until I find the right one.'

'You never will,' Gray said sadly. The conversation had depressed him too. He had hoped that Charlie would share his joy, but instead he acted as though Gray had betrayed the cause. And in Charlie's eyes, he had.

'Why would you say a thing like that?' Charlie asked him, sounding annoyed.

'Because you don't want to. And as long as you don't, no one will ever measure up. You won't let them. You don't want to find the right one. Neither did I. And then suddenly Sylvia walked into my life and everything got turned around.'

'Sounds to me like your head got turned around. Maybe you should be on antidepressants and take another look at the relationship then.'

'Sylvia is the best antidepressant I've ever had. The woman is a total dynamo, and a joy to be around.'

'I'm happy for you if that's the case, and I hope it lasts. But until you figure that out, at least don't try to convert the rest of us, till you know if the theory works. I'm not convinced it does.'

'I'll let you know,' Gray said quietly as they both stood up. Gray followed Charlie out of the Yacht Club, and they stood looking at each other on the sidewalk for a long moment. It had been a tough lunch for both of them, and a disappointing one for Gray. He had wanted more from his friend – celebration, support, excitement. Anything but the cynicism and harsh comments they had traded over lunch.

'Take care of yourself,' Charlie said, patting him on the shoulder, as he hailed a cab with his other hand. He couldn't wait to get away. 'I'll call you . . . and congratulations on the gallery!' he shouted as he got into the cab.

Gray stood on the sidewalk, watching him, waved, put his head down, and walked away. He had decided to walk back to his apartment. He needed some air, and time to think. He had never heard Charlie be as blunt and cynical as that, and he knew he was right in his own assessment of his friend's situation. Charlie didn't want to find 'the right one.' Gray had never seen it quite that way before. But it was clear to him now. And contrary to what Charlie believed, Sylvia hadn't brainwashed him, she had opened his mind and filled his life with sunlight. Standing next to her, he could see what he had always wanted, and never dared to find. She made him brave enough to be the man he wanted to be, but had been too frightened to be before. Charlie was still afraid, and had been for a long time. Ever since Ellen and his parents died. No matter how much therapy he had had, and Gray knew he'd had a lot of it, Charlie was still terrified. And he was still running. Maybe he always would. It saddened Gray to think that that could happen. It seemed like a terrible waste to him. He had only known Sylvia for six weeks, but now that he knew her, and was opening his heart to her, his whole life had changed. It had cut him to the quick when, instead of celebrating with him, Charlie had called him a traitor. Gray had felt it like a physical blow, and the words were echoing in his head when his cell phone rang.

'Hi. How did it go?' It was Sylvia, sounding cheerful and bright, calling him from the office. She had finally convinced herself that Gray knew Charlie better than she did, and her assessment of his reaction to their romance was probably all wrong. She told herself Gray was right, and she was just being paranoid. 'Did you tell him? What did he say?'

'It was terrible,' he said honestly. 'It sucked.

Among other things, he called me a traitor. The poor guy is scared shitless of any kind of commitment or relationship. I never saw it quite that clearly before. I hate to say it, but you were right. It was a very depressing lunch.'

'Shit. I'm sorry. You finally convinced me I was wrong.'

'You weren't.' He was learning that she seldom was. She had a good sense about people and their reactions, and she was remarkably tolerant of their quirks.

'I'm sorry. That must have been really upsetting for you. You're not a traitor, Gray. I know you still love them. There's no reason why you can't have a relationship, and them in your life too.' She wasn't trying to pull him away from them. But he had a strong sense that Charlie would, if Gray allowed him to.

'If they'll still let me play. I was pretty candid about what I said.'

'About us?'

'About him, too. I told him he's wasting his life, and he's going to die alone.'

'You could be right,' she said gently, 'but he has to figure that out for himself. And maybe that's what he wants. He has that right. From what you've said, he's had some pretty major abandonment issues since his family died. That's hard to get over.

Everyone he ever loved as a kid died. It's hard to convince someone like that that the next person he loves won't abandon him and die too. So he dumps them first.'

'That's pretty much what I said.' They both knew it was true. And beyond all his defenses, Charlie did too. He just wasn't prepared to admit it, even to his best friend. It was a lot easier to say that there was something wrong with the women in his life, to justify his rejecting them.

'I don't suppose he enjoyed hearing it much.'

'It didn't look that way,' he said, sounding sad. 'But I didn't like what he said about us.'

'Hopefully, he'll get over it. If he'll come, we'll have him to dinner some time. Let him simmer down for a while. You gave him a lot to swallow at one gulp. Us. And a lot of honesty about him.'

'Yeah, I did. I think he was pretty shocked about us. The last time he saw me, on the boat, I was a member in good standing of the Boys Club, and as soon as he was out of sight, I jumped ship. At least that's how he sees it.'

'How do you see it?' she asked, sounding worried.

'Like I'm the luckiest guy in the world. I told him that too. I don't think he believed me. He thinks you've got me on drugs.' At that, Gray laughed. 'If you do, don't detox me now. I'm loving it.' He sounded happier again.

'Me too.' She smiled, thinking about him, and he could hear it in her voice. She had a client waiting for her then, and told him she'd see him at the apartment after work. 'Try not to worry about it too much,' she told him again. 'He loves you. He'll calm down.' Gray wasn't as sure. He thought about it long and hard as he walked to his apartment. Their lunch had come as a shock not only to Charlie, but to Gray as well . . . *'Spoken like a true traitor.'* . . . he could still hear Charlie's words ringing in his head, block after block, after block . . .

Charlie was thinking of everything Gray had said all the way uptown. He had plenty of time to think about it. His appointment was at the children's center they had just funded, in the heart of Harlem. He still couldn't believe all that Gray had said. And more of it than he wanted to admit had hit its mark. He had had the same concerns as Gray recently, about dying alone. But he wasn't prepared to discuss terrors like that with anyone but his therapist. He knew Adam was too young to get it, but Gray did. At forty-one, Adam was still building his career, and playing hard. Charlie and Gray had already reached the top of their game, and were making their way down the other side of the mountain. And Charlie was no longer as sure as he once had been that he was willing to go it alone. In the end, he might have no other choice. He envied Gray more than he wanted to admit that he had found someone he wanted to make the final leg of the journey with. But who knew if it would last? Probably not. Nothing ever did.

He was thinking about it with a sorrowful look, and remembering bits and pieces of the conversation to share with his therapist, when the cab stopped at the address he'd given.

'Are you going to be okay here?' the driver asked with a look of concern. Charlie looked as though he should have been stopping somewhere on Fifth Avenue rather than in the heart of Harlem. He was wearing a Hermès tie, a gold watch, and an expensive suit. But he didn't like going to the Yacht Club looking like a slob.

'I'll be fine.' He thanked the driver with a smile, and handed him a handsome tip.

'Do you want me to wait? Or come back?' He hated to leave him there.

'Don't worry about it, but thanks a lot.' He smiled again, and tried to force his conversation with Gray from his head, as he looked up at the building. It was in serious need of repair. Their million dollars could do a lot, and he hoped it would.

In spite of himself, he was still thinking about

Gray as he walked to the front door. The worst of it was that he felt as though he was losing him to Sylvia. He hated to admit to himself that he was jealous of her, but in his heart of hearts, he knew he was. He didn't want to lose his best friend, to some pushy dynamo of a woman, as Gray described her – the dynamo, not the pushy part – just because she had the connections to find a gallery for him. She was obviously sucking up to him, and wanted something from him. And if she was manipulative enough, which he hoped she wasn't, she could blow their friendship right out of the water, and banish Charlie forever. The worst fear he had was of losing his friend. Death by marriage, or cohabitation, or spending the night, or whatever the hell Gray said it was. Charlie didn't trust her. Gray already seemed as though he'd been possessed. She was brainwashing him, and the worst of it was that some of what he had said made sense. Too much, in fact. Especially about Charlie. It had to come from her. Gray would never have spoken to him that way on his own. Never. She had turned him inside out and upside down. And Charlie didn't like it one bit.

He stood at the door of the Children's Center for a long time after ringing the bell. Finally a young man with a beard, in jeans and a T-shirt, came to open it for him. He was African American, and had a wide white smile and velvet chocolate-colored eyes. When he spoke, it was with the lilt of the Caribbean in his voice.

'Hello. Can I help you?' He looked at Charlie as though he had been dropped from another planet. They never saw people come to the center dressed as he was. The young man managed to conceal his amusement and led him in.

'I have an appointment with Carole Parker,' Charlie explained. She was the director of the center. All Charlie knew about her was that she was a social worker, and her credentials were excellent. She had gone to Princeton as an undergraduate, got her MSW at Columbia, and was working toward her doctorate. Her specialty and area of expertise was abused kids.

This was a safe house for abused children and their mothers, but unlike other similar establishments, the main focus was on the children, more than their mothers. An abused woman without a child, or one whose children hadn't been abused, could not stay there. Charlie knew that they were doing a research study, in conjunction with NYU, on preventing child abuse, rather than just putting balm on the end result. There were ten full-time staff working there, six part-time employees, who mostly worked nights and were, for the most part, graduate students, two psychiatrists who worked closely with them, and a flock of volunteers, many of whom were inner-city teenagers who had themselves been abused. It was a new concept to use survivors of child abuse to help younger kids who were enduring the same thing. Charlie liked everything he'd read about it. Parker had started it herself three years before, when she got her master's degree. She was planning to become a psychologist, specializing in urban problems, and inner-city kids. She was running the place on a shoestring. She herself had raised over a million dollars to buy the house and start it, and his foundation had matched the funds she'd been able to raise on her own. From what he'd read of her, she was an impressive young woman, and the only other thing he knew about her was that she was thirty-four years old. He had no idea what she looked like, and had only spoken to her on the phone. She had been professional and businesslike, but had sounded kind and warm. She had invited him to come and see the place, and had promised to give him a tour herself. Everything on paper had checked out so far, including the director herself. She was young, but allegedly capable. The references she'd supplied to the foundation board had been extremely impressive. Some of them were from the most important people in New York. No matter how well trained and capable she was, she also had some powerful connections. The mayor himself had written a reference for her. She had met a lot of important people, and impressed them favorably, while putting the center together.

The young man led Charlie to a small, battered waiting room, and offered him a cup of coffee as soon as he sat down, which Charlie declined. He'd had enough to drink with Gray over lunch, and most of what had happened there was still sticking in his throat, but as he waited for her, he forced it from his mind.

He glanced at the people walking by the open door of the waiting room. There were women, young children, teenagers wearing T-shirts that identified them as volunteers. There was an informal basketball game going on in a courtyard outside, and he noticed a sign inviting neighborhood women to come to a group twice a week, to talk about preventing child abuse. He wasn't sure what their impact on the community had been so far, but at least they were doing what they said. As he watched the kids throw basketballs through the hoop, a door opened, and a tall blond woman stood looking down at him. She was wearing jeans, running shoes, and one of their T-shirts herself. He realized as he stood up to shake hands with her that she was nearly as tall as he was. She was statuesque, six feet tall, with a patrician face. She looked as though she should have been a model not a social worker. She smiled when she greeted him, but her manner was official and somewhat cool. They needed the funds the foundation had given them, but it went against the grain with her to grovel or kiss his feet, although she knew it would help. She still had trouble doing that on command, and she wasn't sure what he expected of her. She seemed slightly suspicious and on the defensive as she invited him into her office.

There were posters on the walls everywhere, and schedules, memos, announcements, federal warnings to staff. Suicide hotlines, poison control, a diagram showing how to do the Heimlich. There was a bookcase full of reference books, at least half of which had spilled onto the floor. Her desk was buried, her in-box was full, and she had framed photographs of children on her desk, all of whom had come through the center at some point. It was definitely a working office. Charlie knew that she ran all the community and children's groups herself. The only one she didn't run was the one for abused mothers. There was a woman from the community who had been trained and came to do that. Carole Parker did just about everything else herself, except scrub the floors and cook. Her bio had said that in a pinch she was willing to do that too, and had. She was one of those women who were interesting to read about, but were sometimes daunting to meet. Charlie hadn't decided yet if she was. She was certainly striking, but when she sat down at her desk, she smiled at him and her eyes got warm. She had piercing, big blue eyes, like a doll.

'So, Mr Harrington, you've come to check us out.'

But even she had to admit that for a million dollars, he had the right to do so. The foundation had actually given them exactly $975,000, which was precisely what she'd asked for. She hadn't had the guts to ask for a full million. Instead, she'd asked him to match what she had raised herself over the past three years. She had been stunned when she was notified by the foundation that their grant request had been approved. She had applied to at least a dozen other foundations at the same time, and all of the others had turned her down. They said they wanted to follow the center's progress for the next year, before they committed funds to her project. So she was grateful to him, but she always felt like a dancing monkey when money people came to look around. She was in the business of saving lives and repairing damaged kids. That was all that interested her. Raising money to do it was a necessary evil, but not one she enjoyed. She hated having to charm people in order to get money out of them. The acute need of the people she served had always been convincing enough for her. She hated having to convince others, who led golden lives. What did they know about a five-year-old who had had bleach poured in her eyes and would be blind for the rest of her life, or a boy who had had his mother's hot iron put on the side of his face, or the twelve-year-old who had been raped by her father all her life and had cigarettes stubbed out on her chest? Just how much did it take to convince people that these kids needed help? Charlie didn't know what she was going to say to him, but he could see her passion in her eyes, and a certain degree of disapproval, as she glanced at his well-tailored suit, expensive tie, and gold watch. Whatever he had spent on them, she knew she could have put to better use. He instantly read her thoughts, and felt foolish for coming there looking like that.

'I'm sorry not be dressed more appropriately. I had a business lunch downtown.' It wasn't true, but he couldn't have gone to the Yacht Club dressed as she was, in T-shirt, Nikes, and jeans. As he said it to her, he took his suit jacket off, unbuttoned his cuffs, rolled up his sleeves, took off his tie, and stuffed it in his pocket. It wasn't much of an improvement, but he'd made an effort at least, and she smiled.

'Sorry,' she said apologetically. 'PR isn't my strong suit. I love what we do here. I'm not so great at rolling out the red carpet for VIPs. For one thing, we don't have one, and even if we did, I wouldn't have time to roll it out.' Her hair was long, and she was wearing it in a thick braid down her back. She looked almost like a Viking as she sat there, with her long legs stretched out under the desk. She looked like anything but a social worker, but her credentials said she was. And then he remembered that she had gone to Princeton, and he said it was his alma mater too, hoping to break the ice.

'I liked Columbia better,' she said easily, visibly unimpressed that they had gone to the same school. 'It was more honest. Princeton was a little too full of itself for my taste. Everyone is so wrapped up in the history of the place. It seemed to me that it was a lot more about the past than the future.'

'I never thought of it that way,' Charlie said cautiously, but nonetheless was impressed by her remarks. In some ways, she was as daunting and earnest as he had feared, in others not at all. 'Were you in an eating club?' he asked, still hoping to score points with her, or find a common bond.

'Yes,' she said, looking embarrassed, 'I was. I was in Cottage.' She paused for a beat and then smiled knowingly at him. She knew his type. Aristocratic men like him attended Princeton in abundance. 'And you were in Ivy.' It didn't accept women even while she was there. She had hated the boys who belonged to it. Now it just seemed sophomoric and foolish. She smiled when he nodded.

'I won't say something stupid like "How did you guess?"' It was obvious that she knew the type, but she knew no more than that about him. 'Is there a possibility you'd forgive me?'

'Yes,' she laughed at him, and suddenly looked younger than she was. She wore no makeup, and never bothered to when she was at the center. She was too busy to care about vanity or details. 'Nine hundred and seventy-five thousand dollars from your foundation says I can forgive you just about anything, as long as you don't abuse your children.'

'I don't have any. So at least I'm not guilty on that one.' He sensed that she didn't like him, which quickly became a challenge to him to turn it around. She was a very pretty woman after all, no matter how many degrees she had. And few women were able to resist Charlie's charm, when he chose to turn it on. He wasn't sure yet if Carole Parker was worth the effort. In some ways, she seemed like a hardened case. She was politically correct to her core, and sensed that he wasn't. She was surprised to hear that he didn't have kids, and then vaguely remembered hearing that he wasn't married. She wondered if he was gay. If Charlie had known that, he would have been crushed. She didn't care what his sexual preferences were. All she wanted was his money, for her kids at the center.

'Would you like to take a look around?' she

offered politely, standing up again, and looking him right in the eye. In high heels, she would have been exactly as tall as he was. Charlie was six foot four, and their eyes were the same color. Their hair was equally blond. For a shocking instant, he realized that she looked like his sister, and then he did everything he could to forget it. It was too unsettling.

She didn't see the look on his face as he followed her out her office door, and for the next hour she took him into every room, every office, dragged him down every hallway. She showed him the garden that the children had planted on the roof, introduced him to many of the children. She introduced him to Gabby with her Seeing Eye dog, and told him his foundation had paid for it. They were both currently in training. Gabby had named the big black Lab they'd given her Zorro. Charlie stopped and patted it, with his head bent, so Carole wouldn't see the tears in his eyes. The stories she told him, when the children weren't around, were heartbreaking. For a few minutes, they watched a group in progress, and he was vastly impressed as he listened. Carole normally led the group, but she had taken the afternoon off from her duties to meet him, which she usually thought was a waste of time. She felt that her time was better spent with their clients.

She introduced him to their volunteers, working

hard at occupational therapy with the younger kids, and a reading program for those who had reached high school without being able to read or write. He remembered reading about the program in her brochure, and also that she had won a national award for the results they had achieved so far. Every one of their clients was literate by the time they left the outpatient services of the center after a year. And the kids' parents were welcome to join the adult reading program too. They also offered counseling and therapy for kids and adults alike.

She took him from top to bottom, introduced him to everyone, and finally to her assistant, Tygue, the young man who had opened the door for him. Carole told Charlie that he was on loan from a doctoral program from Yale. She had pulled in some incredible people to work with her, many of whom she had known before, and some of whom she had found along the way. She explained that she and Tygue had gotten their master of social work degrees together. She had started the center after that, and he had gone to Yale to continue his studies. He was originally from Jamaica, and Charlie loved listening to him speak. After they had chatted with him for a few minutes, she walked Charlie back into her office. He looked drained.

'I don't know what to say to you,' he said, sounding humble as he looked at her. 'This is quite a place. You've done an amazing job. How did you put this together?' He was in awe of what she'd done, and however ornery she'd been with him at first, and contemptuous about his eating club, it was obvious to him that she was quite an extra-ordinary human being. A lot more so than he, he felt. At thirty-four, she had created a place that literally turned people's lives around, and made a difference for a number of human beings, old and young.

He had been so busy listening to every word she said, once they started the tour, that he had com-pletely forgotten to charm her. Instead, she had knocked him right off his feet, not with her charm, or her striking good looks, but with her tireless work and achievement. The center she had created, however dilapidated it still looked, was an amazing place.

'This was my dream since I was a kid,' she said simply. 'I saved every penny I ever got from the time I was fifteen. When I was in my teens, I waited on tables, mowed lawns, sold magazines, coached swimming. I did everything I could to make this place happen, and I finally did. I saved about three hundred thousand dollars of my own, including some money I made in the stock market later on. The rest I shook out of people, until I finally had enough to put a down payment on the building and get started. It was pretty touch and go at first. But it won't be anymore,' she said honestly, and gratefully at last, 'thanks to your foundation. I'm sorry I wasn't more welcoming at first. I hate having to justify what we're doing. I know we're doing great work, but sometimes people who come here don't see it, or don't understand the value of what we're doing. When I saw the suit and the watch,' she said sheepishly, 'I figured you wouldn't get it. It was stupid of me. I think I have a prejudice against people who went to Princeton, including myself. We're all so privileged, and don't know it. What I see here is the real deal. The rest just isn't, or at least not to me.' He nodded. Charlie didn't know what to say to her, she was an awe-inspiring woman, and he was in fact in awe of her. Not daunted or cowed, but in awe. He was suddenly embarrassed about the suit and gold watch too.

He pointed to the watch apologetically. 'I promise I'll throw it out the window on the way home.'

'You won't have to.' She laughed openly. 'One of our neighbors will probably take it off your arm. I'll have Tygue walk you out. You'll never make it to the curb.'

'I'm tougher than I look,' he said, smiling at her, and she had warmed up to him considerably. After all, whatever his eating club had been, he had given them nearly a million dollars, and she was grateful to him for that. She wondered if she had been a little tough on him at first, and knew she had. She just hated guys like him, who had never seen the other side of life. On the other hand, he ran a foundation that supported some impressive causes, so he couldn't be all bad, no matter how spoiled he was. She would have gagged on the spot if she had known he had a 240-foot yacht, but he didn't tell her that.

'I'm tougher than I look too,' she said honestly, 'but you still have to be careful in this neighborhood. If you come back, wear your sweats and running shoes.' She had noticed his expensive John Lobb shoes, custom made for him at Hermès.

'I will,' he promised, and meant it. If only to avoid irritating her. He liked it a lot better when she looked as though she approved of him, as she did now. The look in her eyes when he walked in had been more than a little chilly. Now things were going a lot better, and he liked the idea of coming back to visit the center again. He said as much to her as she and Tygue walked him to the front door.

'Come back anytime,' she said with a warm smile. And just as she did, Gabby came confidently down the stairs with Zorro. She was holding fast to his harness, and recognized Tygue and Carole's voices.

'What are you doing down here?' Carole said with a look of surprise. The children usually didn't come downstairs, except to eat or play in the garden. The offices were all on the ground floor, which made more sense. Particularly if abusive parents showed up to look for their kids, or assault them again, when they had been mandated to Carole's care by the courts, as was Gabby's case. They were safer out of sight upstairs.

'I came down to see the man with the nice voice. Zorro wanted to say good-bye.' This time even Carole saw the tears in Charlie's eyes. Fortunately, Gabby didn't, as Carole gently touched his arm. The child was impossible to resist, and she ripped out his heart, as she approached them with a broad smile.

'Good-bye, Zorro,' Charlie said, first patting the dog, and then gently touching the child's hair. He looked down at her, but his smile was wasted on her. And nothing he could do for her now would ever change what had happened to her, neither the memory, nor the result. All he had been able to do was indirectly pay for her dog. It seemed so much less than enough, which was what Carole always felt about what she did. 'Take good care of him, Gabby. He's a handsome dog.'

'I know,' she said, with a sightless grin, bending down to kiss Zorro's snout. 'Will you come back and see us again? You're nice.'

'Thank you, Gabby. You're nice too, and very beautiful. And I will come back to see you again. I promise.' He looked right at Carole as he said it, and she nodded. In spite of her initial prejudices about him, she liked him. He was probably a decent human being, just very fortunate and very spoiled. She had been fleeing from men like him all her life. But at least this one cared about making a difference. A million dollars' worth of difference. It said something about him. And he had cared enough to come up and see the place. Even more than that, she liked the way he talked to the little girl. It seemed too bad that he didn't have kids himself.

Tygue had found a cab for him by then, and came back inside to tell him it was waiting outside.

'Put your helmet on,' Carole teased, 'and hide the watch.'

'I think I can make it from here to the cab.' He smiled at her again, and thanked her for the tour. It had made not only his day, but possibly his year. He said good-bye to Gabby again, and turned one last time on his way out the door to look at her and the dog. He shook hands with Tygue, and carrying his jacket over his shoulder, with his sleeves still rolled up, he slipped into the cab and gave the driver his address. He sat in silence, thinking of all he had seen that afternoon, feeling a lump in his throat every time he thought of Gabby and her dog.

Charlie walked through his front door and picked up the phone when he got home. He called Gray on his cell phone. A lot of things had come clear to him that afternoon, about what mattered and what didn't.

Gray answered his cell phone on the second ring. He and Sylvia were cooking dinner, and he was surprised to hear it was Charlie. He had been telling her about the lunch again, and how upset he still was by Charlie's reaction to his announcement that he and Sylvia were dating.

'I'm sorry I was such an asshole at lunch today,' Charlie said without preamble. 'I can't believe I'm saying this, but I actually think I was jealous.' Gray's mouth was hanging open as he listened and Sylvia watched him. She had no idea who it was or what they were saying, but Gray looked dumbstruck.

'I don't want to lose you, pal. I think it scared me, thinking that things were different. But what the hell, if you love her, I guess I can get used to her too.' There were tears in his eyes again as he said it. It had been an emotional afternoon, and the last thing he wanted was to lose a friend like Gray. They loved each other like brothers.

'You're not going to lose me,' Gray said in a choked voice. He couldn't believe what he was hearing. This was the friend he had always known Charlie was. In the end, Sylvia was wrong.

'I know,' Charlie said, sounding like himself again. 'I figured it out this afternoon. And then I fell in love.'

'No shit,' Gray said with a grin. 'With who?'

'A six-year-old blind girl with a black Lab Seeing Eye dog named Zorro. She's the cutest kid I've ever seen. Her mother poured bleach in her eyes, and she's never going to see again. Apparently we bought her the dog.' The two men were silent for a moment, as tears ran down Charlie's cheeks. He couldn't get the memory of her out of his head, and knew he never would. Whenever he thought about the Children's Center, he knew he would always think of Gabby and Zorro, long after she was gone.

'You're a good man, Charlie Harrington,' Gray said, overcome with emotion. All afternoon he had thought he was losing his friend. Charlie had sounded so angry, and so bitter, especially when he'd called Gray a traitor. But he seemed to have forgiven him. It had only taken a few hours.

'You're a good man too,' Charlie said, looking around his empty apartment, which suddenly seemed emptier than ever. And as he did, he couldn't help thinking about Sylvia and Gray. 'Invite me to dinner sometime. I hope she cooks better than you do. The last dinner you cooked for me damn near killed me. Whatever you do, don't make her your secret goulash.'

'As a matter of fact, it's bubbling away on the stove at this very moment. I was teaching her how to do it.'

'Take my advice, flush it now, or the romance will be over. I nearly had to get my stomach pumped. Call in for Chinese takeout.'

'O ye of little faith . . . she's already had it. She loves it.'

'She's lying. Believe me, no one in the world could love your goulash. Either she's crazy or she loves you.'

'Maybe both. I'm kind of hoping that's the case.'

'It's not in my best interest,' Charlie admitted cautiously, 'but for your sake, so am I. You deserve a good one for a change. I guess maybe so do I. If I ever find one.' He hesitated, and then went on. 'Some of what you said today is true. I'm not sure what I want, or if, or who. My life is a lot simpler like this.' Simpler, but lonely. He had been more aware of it recently than ever in his life, ever since he had come back to New York.

'You'll find one, if you want to. You'll know when it's right, Charlie. I did. One day it just walks into your life and hits you on the head.'

'I hope so.' They talked for a few more minutes and hung up. Gray said the goulash was burning, which Charlie commented was a blessing.

After he hung up, he sat in the silence of his

apartment, thinking of the tour he'd taken of the Children's Center. All he could think of at first was Gabby and Zorro . . . then Tygue, the doctoral student from Jamaica, by way of Yale . . . and then Carole Parker. They were an amazing group of people. He found himself staring into space then, thinking of the way she had looked at him when they first met. She had absolutely hated him, and had nothing but contempt for him as she took in his suit and watch. And in spite of that, he liked her. He liked what she had done, what she believed in, how hard she had worked to set it up. She was an impressive woman, with an extraordinarily bright mind and a lot of guts. He had no idea how or why or when, but he knew he wanted to see her again. He had a lot to learn from her, not only about what she was doing with his money at the center, but about life. And he hoped that one day, with luck, in spite of the suit and gold watch, they could be friends.

9

Adam picked Charlie up in a ridiculously long limousine on his way to the concert. One of his most important clients was singing. The whole concert tour had been an agony for him, and the contracts relating to it a nightmare to negotiate, but now that the big night had come, he was in great spirits. The star herself was one of the most important artists in the country, if not the world. Vana. A single word. A singular woman. They had booked her into Madison Square Garden, and every screaming teenager would be there, along with every groupie, weirdo, and adult rock-and-roll fan in New York. It wasn't the kind of event Charlie went to often, but Adam had convinced him it would be fun and said he had to go.

Scalpers were selling seats at four and five thousand dollars a ticket. People had stood on line for two or three days to buy them when the box office opened. It was the hottest show of the year, and Adam had warned Charlie to wear jeans. He didn't want him showing up in a suit, and getting the shit kicked out of him. He had enough to worry about that night, without worrying about him. And of course, Adam not only had backstage passes but front-row seats. It was a night no one would forget. He just hoped everything would go smoothly. All three of his cell phones kept going off all at once as they rode to Madison Square Garden. He couldn't even talk to Charlie until they were halfway there. He had gesticulated hello to him, and poured himself a drink in the limo, as they stopped at a red light.

'Jesus, and my doctor wonders why my blood pressure is so high,' he finally said, grinning at Charlie, who was vastly amused by his antics. Listening to Adam scream at everyone who called him was half the fun. 'This business is going to kill me. What's happening with Gray? Is he okay? He never calls me.' But then again, with the insanity of Vana coming to town and performing at the Garden, he hadn't had time to call him either. Adam said he was up to his ears in concert shit.

'He's fine,' Charlie said cryptically, and then decided to tell him. 'Actually, he's in love.'

'Yeah, sure. I'll bet he is. Where'd he find her? Coming out of rehab or an institution?' Adam laughed as he finished his drink, and Charlie grinned.

'Portofino,' Charlie said, looking smug, and ever more amused. Adam was never going to believe it, and at first neither had he. He was still getting used to the idea himself.

'What, Portofino?' He was looking stressed beyond belief and totally distracted. One of his assistants had just called him to say that Vana's hairdresser hadn't shown up with her wigs, and she was having a fit. They were rushing someone to her hotel to pick them up, but they might have to start late. It was all he needed. The unions would go nuts if they ran late, although they always did. He wasn't producing the show, but if she violated her contract, there would be endless lawsuits. He was there to protect her from herself. Vana was famous for walking right off the stage.

'Gray met her in Portofino,' Charlie said quietly, as Adam stared at him.

'Met who in Portofino?' He looked blank, and Charlie laughed at him. This was no time to be discussing Gray's love life, but it was something to talk about, as they sat in traffic and Adam fumed. He wanted to get to Vana before she did something illegal, insane, or quit.

'The woman Gray's in love with,' Charlie continued. 'He says he's staying with her, not living with her, *staying* with her. I gather that's not the same thing.'

'Of course it isn't,' Adam said, sounding irritable. 'Staying with her means he's too tired to get out of bed after he makes love to her, which is probably just due to laziness and age. Living with her is a commitment he'd be a fool to make. He can get just as much out of her, and have a better sex life, if he just stays with her. Once he lives with her, it's all over. He'll be taking the garbage out, picking her dry cleaning up, and cooking for her.'

'I don't know about the dry cleaning and the garbage, but he's cooking for her.'

'He's insane. If he's only staying with her, he doesn't have a closet or a key. And he can't answer the phone. Does he have a key?'

'I forgot to ask.' Charlie was laughing by then. Adam looked like he was going to have a nervous breakdown while they waited for the light to change. Talking about Gray at least distracted him. And Charlie was fascinated to hear the rules, according to Adam. There seemed to be a whole list of things that translated to what one's status was. Charlie had never qualified for most of them, though once he'd had a key.

'Who the hell is she?'

'Sylvia Reynolds, the art dealer we met in Portofino. Apparently, Gray got closer to her than we realized, while you were chasing her niece.'

'Oh Jesus, the girl with the face of an angel and

the brain like Albert Einstein. You can never get girls like that into bed, they talk you to death and you die of old age trying to get into their knickers. She had great legs, as I recall,' Adam said regretfully. He always missed the ones that got away. The ones that didn't faded for him in a day.

'The niece had great legs?' Charlie asked, trying to remember. All he could recall now was her face.

'No, Sylvia. The art dealer. What the hell is she doing with Gray?'

'She could do a lot worse,' Charlie said loyally, and Adam agreed. 'He's crazy about her, I hope she's as crazy about him as he thinks she is. But if she's eating his goulash, maybe she is.' He didn't tell Adam how upset he'd been when Gray first told him about it over lunch at the Yacht Club. It had been a momentary lapse that still embarrassed him, remembering his own lack of grace. Gray seemed to have gotten over it, and hearing that Gray was 'staying' with Sylvia didn't seem to bother Adam a bit. He had other, more important things on his mind that night, like Vana walking off the stage if they didn't find her wigs. The lawsuits that would generate, given the size and importance of the concert, would keep him busy for the next ten years.

'It won't last long,' Adam commented about Gray's new romance. 'She's too normal. He'll be tired of her in a week.'

'He doesn't seem to think so. He says that's why he likes her, and he doesn't want to die alone.'

'Is he sick?' At that, Adam looked genuinely worried, and Charlie shook his head.

'Just thinking about his life, I guess. He leads a pretty solitary life, when he's painting. She got him into a terrific gallery, so I guess this isn't entirely a bad thing.'

'Maybe it's more serious than we think, if she's doing things like that for him. I'd better call him. We don't want him going off the deep end over a great pair of legs.' Adam started to look worried again, as Charlie shook his head.

'From the sound of it, he already did. We'll have to watch how this one plays out,' Charlie said cautiously, as they pulled up to Madison Square Garden in the long black limousine. Charlie couldn't believe the crowds. It took them nearly twenty minutes to push their way in, with the help of the police. There were two plainclothes cops waiting to take them to their seats.

Adam disappeared to check on things backstage, as soon as they found their seats. Charlie said he'd be fine, and sat watching the crowds swirling around him. And as he did, he noticed a pretty blond girl in the shortest skirt he'd ever seen. Her hair was long and teased. She was wearing high-heeled black leather boots, and a bright red leather jacket. She was wearing a lot of makeup and looked about seventeen. She asked him politely if there was anyone sitting in the empty seat, and he said there was. With that, she disappeared. He saw her again a few minutes later, speaking to someone else. He had the feeling she was cruising the theater, looking for a place to sit, and eventually she came back to him.

'Are you sure there's someone sitting there?' she asked somewhat doggedly. He could see that she was older than he had first estimated, but not much, she was a striking-looking girl, and she had an incredible figure, most of which seemed to be straining at the seams of a black see-through blouse that gave him a generous view of her voluptuous curves. She would have looked like a hooker if there hadn't been something so innocent about her face.

'Yes, I'm sure,' Charlie assured her again that the seat was occupied. 'My friend just went backstage.'

'Oh my God!' she said with an incredulous look. 'Does your friend know Vana?' She said it as though asking if he knew God, and Charlie smiled at her and nodded.

'He works for her. More or less.'

'Do you mind if I sit down until he gets back?' she asked, and he wondered if she was cruising him, but he didn't think so. She was far more interested in meeting Adam, once she knew he was backstage. 'My ticket is in the back row, and I can't see anything. I just thought I'd see if there were any empty seats up here, but I guess not. I waited on line for mine for two days. I brought a sleeping bag and camped out. My friend and I took turns.' He nodded, looking slightly dumbfounded as she sat down next to him. She looked no worse than the rest of the crowd, although she would have stood out like a sore thumb almost anywhere else. She looked like Julia Roberts in *Pretty Woman* before Richard Gere transformed her on Rodeo Drive, and she had the same kind of breathtaking good looks. The outfit she was wearing was pretty breathtaking too, especially the boots, which had six-inch heels, and went well over her knees. Her skirt was barely decent, and the blouse would have blown from here to kingdom come if she sneezed. It was quite a look. But it seemed to work for her.

Charlie couldn't help wondering what she looked like without the makeup, with her hair pulled back, in a clean pair of jeans. Probably even more striking than she did. He wondered if she was some kind of model, or an aspiring actress, but he was cautious about talking to her. He didn't want to encourage her to stay. She was perched on the edge of Adam's seat, and he looked stunned when he returned. He thought Charlie had picked her up, and he was impressed. He didn't think he had it in him to pursue a girl like her, in five minutes or less.

'They found her wigs. Her hairdresser was drunk off her ass in the hotel. But they got her someone else. Whoever got her saved the day,' Adam explained, and looked with interest and confusion at the girl sitting in his seat. 'Is there some reason why you're sitting here?' he asked her bluntly. 'Have we met?' He couldn't help looking straight into her blouse, and then up at the perfect face. She was a knockout-looking girl, and just his type, on a lucky day.

'Not yet.' She smiled at him. 'My seat sucks. I was just talking to your friend. He says you work for Vana. I bet that's cool.' She was all goo-goo eyes and hero worship as she smiled at him.

'Sometimes it's cool. Tonight it wasn't so cool.' Vana had been threatening to walk out when he got backstage. And then she calmed down when they found her wigs and someone else's hairdresser, but he didn't bother to try and explain it to this girl. He wasn't sure she would have understood. He assumed her IQ was questionable, but he thought her tits were great. IQ was never a huge issue for him. He preferred tits to brains, ever since Rachel. 'Look, I hate to bother you, and I'd love to sit here and talk to you, but she's going to start in about five minutes, after they do her hair. You'd better go back to your seat.' The girl in the denim miniskirt and black patent-leather boots looked like she was going

215

to burst into tears. Adam looked exasperated, but there was nothing he could do for her. There were no empty seats, and then he had an idea. He had no clue as to why he was helping her, and he figured he'd probably regret it, but he grabbed her arm, pulled her out of the seat, and beckoned her to come with him. 'If you promise to behave yourself, I can get you a seat on the stage.' They always saved a few in case someone unexpected turned up.

'Are you serious?' She was awestruck, as he led her quickly toward the stage, and showed his pass to one of the guards keeping the riffraff out. They instantly let him through. The girl knew he was completely serious by then. She hadn't had a stroke of luck like that in years. Her friend had told her she was crazy to head for the front row, but it had paid off big-time for her that night, as Adam helped her up the steps in her short skirt and high-heeled boots. He got a fabulous view of her bottom while she did, and had no qualms about checking it out. He figured that if she wore a skirt like that, she probably expected him to.

'What's your name, by the way?' he asked for no particular reason, as he led her to a row of folding chairs tucked in at the back of the stage. They had to step over wires, and sound equipment, but she was going to get a fabulous view of the show, and she looked up at him as though she'd had a religious vision, and he was it.

'Maggie O'Malley.'

'Where are you from?' He looked down at her with a smile, as she took her seat and crossed her legs. From where he stood, he had a totally unobstructed view down her shirt. He wondered if she was as racy as she looked, or had just dressed the part for the concert. Being more experienced than Charlie with women who looked like that, he pegged her at about twenty-two.

'I was born in Queens, but I live in the city now. On the West Side. I work at Pier 92.' It was a bar that catered to a rough crowd sometimes. It was essentially a restaurant and pickup bar, and the waitresses all looked like her. The prettier ones danced on the bar at hourly intervals and set the tone for sex and booze. Adam guessed correctly that she made a lot in tips. Sometimes the girls who worked there were young actresses out of work, and desperate for money.

'Are you an actress?' he asked with interest.

'No, I'm a waitress. But I dance a little. I used to tap-dance and take ballet as a kid, more or less.' She didn't tell him that what she'd learned, she'd picked up from TV. There'd been no formal dance lessons in her neighborhood. She had been born in the poorest, toughest part of Queens, and got out as soon as she could. Where she lived now on the Upper West Side, in a building that was barely more than a tenement, was a palace compared to where she'd grown up. And then she looked at Adam breathlessly with tears in her eyes. 'Thank you for my seat. If I can ever do anything for you, look me up at Pier 92. I'll buy you a drink.' It was all she had to offer him, although there were other things he would have preferred to get from her. But she looked so innocent, despite the outrageous outfit, that he felt guilty for his thoughts. She seemed like a sweet girl, despite her sexy clothes.

'Don't worry about it. Happy to do it. Maggie, was it?'

'Mary Margaret actually,' she said, looking wide-eyed, and he could easily imagine her in a parochial school uniform. Mary Margaret O'Malley. He couldn't help wondering how she had come to dress the way she did. She had the face of an angel, and the body of a stripper, and her outfit needed to be burned. She would have looked incredible with the right hairdo and decent clothes, but life dealt the hands it did. And she had done all right for tonight, for a poor girl from Queens who worked at Pier 92. She was sitting on the stage at Vana's show, in a special seat.

'I'll come find you after the show,' he promised her, and meant it for a minute, and then suddenly she bounced up from the seat and gave him a hug like a little kid. There were tears in her eyes.

'Thank you for what you did for me. It's the nicest thing anyone's ever done.' The look in her eyes made him feel guilty for his earlier lascivious thoughts. Putting her on the stage had been easy for him.

'Don't worry about it,' he said as he turned to leave, and then she grabbed his arm.

'What's your name?' She wanted to know who her benefactor was, and he looked startled. They weren't likely to meet again.

'Adam Weiss,' he said, and then ran back to his own seat. The lights were being dimmed. Two minutes later, as he sat next to Charlie, the show began. Charlie leaned toward him briefly just before Vana came out.

'Did you find her a seat?' He had been mesmerized by her. Charlie had never seen anyone quite like her up close. Girls who looked like that were definitely not his thing.

'I did,' Adam whispered. 'She said she wants to go out with you,' he said with a mock-serious look, and Charlie laughed.

'Not likely. Did you get her phone number, blood type, and address?'

'No, just her bra size. It's a lot bigger than her IQ,' Adam said with a wicked grin.

'Don't be mean,' Charlie scolded him. 'She was sweet.'

'Yeah, I know. Maybe we'll take her to the party with us, after the show.' Charlie gave him a grim look. He thought the concert would be enough for him. This was not his scene, although he had always liked Vana's music. And he did that night too.

The show was fabulous, and Vana played seven encores. She had never looked or sounded better. Maggie came back to visit them during intermission, to thank Adam again. He put an arm around her shoulders and invited her to the party then. She threw her arms around his neck and hugged him again, while Adam felt the impact of her breasts on his chest. Hers were real, and so was her nose. Everything she had had been God's gift, not store-bought. He hadn't seen a girl like her in years.

'You shouldn't do that,' Charlie said quietly after she went back to her seat, before the second act began.

'Do what?' Adam asked innocently. He could still feel her breasts on his chest. He had liked it a lot. He always did. He knew a million women like her, but none of them were real.

'Take advantage of young girls. She may dress like a hooker, but you can see she's a sweet kid. Don't be a shitheel, Adam. It'll come back to haunt you one day. You wouldn't want someone doing that to your kid.'

'If my kid dressed like that, I'd kill her, and so would her mother.' He had wanted to bring both his kids to the show, but Rachel wouldn't let him. She said it was a school night, and she didn't want their kids in an atmosphere like that. She said they were too young. He had nice, wholesome kids.

'Maybe Maggie doesn't have anyone to tell her not to dress like that.' She looked like she'd gone to a lot of trouble to put her outfit together that night, but somewhere along the way, in her enthusiasm, it had gone wrong. But there wasn't much you could do too wrong to a face and body like hers. She'd been blessed. And maybe one day, when she grew up, she'd learn to tone it down, rather than up.

'I guess not,' Adam commented drily, 'if she works at Pier 92.' He had been there once and couldn't believe how bad it was. Every sleazeball on Broadway came in to paw the girls while they ate and drank. The waitresses weren't topless or naked, but they might as well have been, given how little they wore. They wore dresses that looked like mini–tennis skirts, and underneath them thongs, and on top cheesy satin bras that they were forced to wear several sizes too small. The place was a dump. 'Stop feeling sorry for her, Charlie. There are worse things, like being born in Calcutta, or the little blind kid you told me about the other day at the place you visited in Harlem. That girl is gorgeous, and she'll figure it out one day. For all you know, she'll be discovered by some shithead agent and wind up a big star.'

'I doubt it,' Charlie said sadly, thinking about her. Girls like that were a dime a dozen, and most of them never got out of the hell where they lived, particularly with guys like Adam chasing after them and taking advantage of them. It made him sad for her. And then the second act began.

When it was over, the crowd went wild. Groupies, fans, photographers, and practically half the audience tried to crawl up on the stage. It took a dozen cops to get Vana off in one piece, and Adam couldn't even get backstage. He used his cell phone to call the stage manager, who told him that Vana was okay, and thrilled at how it had gone. He said to tell her he would see her at the party, and when he turned around to talk to Charlie, Maggie was there. She had nearly lost her blouse and jacket trying to get off the stage, but she had managed to get back to them, and thanked Adam profusely again. She had no idea what had happened to her friend. It would have been next to impossible to find anyone in that mob.

'Do you want to come to the party?' Adam asked her. She looked fine for that crowd. He wasn't embarrassed to take her with him, although Charlie would have been. But Charlie wanted to go home anyway. The concert had been more than enough for him, although he had thoroughly enjoyed it. He just didn't need any more stimulation that night. Adam always did. He loved the seamy side of that life, and Maggie would fit right in. She was thrilled to go.

It took the three of them half an hour to get back out to the sidewalk, and another twenty minutes to find the limousine, but they finally did, and the three of them crawled in. They were heading to the East Side to a private club that had been rented for the party. Charlie knew there would be lots of women, booze, and drugs. Not his scene. Adam didn't do drugs either, but he had nothing against women and drink. And lots of both. Maggie sat on the banquette opposite them with a look of ecstasy on her face, as Adam casually glanced up her skirt. Her legs were even better than he had realized at first. She had an absolutely unbelievable body. Charlie had noticed it too, but rather than look up her skirt, he had glanced out the window. And then she crossed her legs.

'Where are we going?' she asked excitedly in a childlike voice, with a slight New York accent. It wasn't excessive, but it was recognizable. Adam seemed not to notice.

'We're going to drop Charlie off first. Maybe we'll stop for a drink somewhere, and then I'll take you to the party.' And afterward, hopefully he'd take her home with him, if she was willing. He never forced anyone to do anything. He didn't have to. There were enough women in his life to keep him happy at all times. But she looked as though she'd go home with him, he didn't think there would be a problem. He had picked up plenty of girls like her, and they were so excited to be taken along, particularly on a night like this, that they almost always wound up in his bed. It was a rarity when they didn't. He was sure Maggie would. So was Charlie.

Charlie said goodnight to her politely when they dropped him off. He said he hoped he'd see her again sometime, which he knew was unlikely. But what else could he say? Have a nice night in bed with Adam? For an odd moment, he hoped she wouldn't. It was like shooting fish in a barrel, and he wanted her to be better than that, or at least have a fair chance. She was much too impressed with where Adam was taking her, and the seat he'd gotten her on the stage. Charlie wanted to tell her to have more self-respect than that. But there were some things one couldn't change. And it was Adam's life, and hers. It was up to them what happened after he left, not up to him. He almost wanted to protect her from Adam, and herself, but there was no way he could do that. He rode up in the elevator, looking thoughtful, and when he let himself into his apartment, he stood looking out at the park in the dark. It had been a fun night, and he'd had a good time. He was tired, and a few minutes later he went to bed.

Adam took Maggie to a bar, as he had promised, and she had a glass of wine. He had a margarita, followed by a mojito, and let her take a sip. She liked it, but said she didn't drink hard liquor, which surprised him. He was even more surprised when she said she was twenty-six. He had figured her for younger than that. She said she modeled at trade shows sometimes, and had done some catalog work, but mostly she just worked at Pier 92, and said she made a fortune on tips. It was easy to see why. She had a body that just wouldn't quit.

They got to the party by one o'clock, and it was just starting. Adam knew there were a lot of drugs around. Cocaine, Ecstasy, heroin, crack, crystal meth. The crowd was wilder than usual, and it didn't take him long to figure out it was not a good scene to be in. It happened that way sometimes after concerts. He danced with Maggie for a few minutes, and then got her out, and back into the limousine. He invited her back to his place then for a nightcap, and she looked at him and shook her head.

'I'd better not. It's pretty late. I have to be at work tomorrow, but thanks anyway.' He made no comment, and gave the driver her address. He was horrified when he saw where she lived. It was one of the most dangerous streets he'd ever seen. It was hard to imagine a girl who looked like her living there. Her life had to be a fight for survival every day, and he felt sorry for her, but he was also mildly annoyed that she hadn't spent the night with him.

'I hope you don't mind that I didn't go to your apartment, Adam,' she said apologetically, particularly after all he'd done for her. 'I don't do things like that on the first date.' He stood staring at her, wondering if she actually thought there would be a second one. She had written down her number for him, and he had shoved it in his pocket. He was going to throw it away when he got home. She was fun for a night, on a lark, or would have been, but there was no reason to ever see her again. He could have a hundred like her anytime he wanted to. He didn't need a waitress from Pier 92, no matter how pretty she was, or how good her legs were. It wouldn't have been any different if she'd gone home with him. It just would have been fun.

'No, I understand. Why don't I walk you upstairs?' The building looked as though she could get murdered just trying to get home, but she was used to it, and shook her head.

'That's okay,' she said easily, smiling at him. 'I have three roommates. Two of them sleep in the living room, it would be too weird if you came in. By now, they're all asleep.' He couldn't even imagine living that way, and had no desire to. He just wanted to leave her there, and forget that people led lives like hers. She wasn't his problem, and he didn't want her to be. All he wanted now was to go home.

'Thank you, Miss Mary Margaret O'Malley, it was a pleasure meeting you. See you again some-time,' he said politely.

'I hope so,' she said honestly, but even she knew it was unlikely. He led a charmed life. He knew people like Vana, had backstage passes, rode in limousines, and lived in a different world. She was innocent, but not as stupid as he wanted her to be. Instead of goodnight, he might as well have said 'Have a nice life.' But he knew that more than likely, she wouldn't. How could she? What could life possibly have in store for a girl like her, no matter how beautiful she was? What way out did she have? He knew the answer. None.

'Take care of yourself,' he said as she let herself into the building with a key, and turned to look at him for the last time.

'You too. And thanks, I had a fantastic time. Thanks again for my great seat.' He smiled at her, wishing he was in bed with her. It would have been a lot more fun than standing in the stench of her neighborhood and freezing on the street while he watched her go in. She waved then and was gone. He wondered if she felt like Cinderella as she walked into the building where she lived. The ball was over, and the limousine and driver were going to turn into a pumpkin and six mice by the time she got upstairs.

He got into the car again, and could smell her perfume. It was cheap, but it suited her and had a nice scent. He had noticed it when he danced with her, and he was startled to realize, as he drove back to his apartment in the East Seventies, that he was depressed. It was depressing to see people live like that, and know they had no way out. Maggie O'Malley would live in buildings like that forever, unless she got lucky, married some slob with a beer belly, and moved back to Queens again, where she could reminisce about the tenement she'd lived in in Manhattan, or the terrible job she'd had where drunken idiots reached up her skirt every night. And he was just as bad. He would have gone to bed with her, if she'd been willing to. And the next day he would have forgotten her. For the first time in years, he felt like a total cad as he rode home. It made him question his own morality. Charlie was right. What if some guy treated Amanda like that one day? It could happen to anyone. But in this case it was happening to a girl called Maggie, whom he didn't know and never would. He drank a shot of tequila when he got home, thinking about her. He walked out on the terrace of his penthouse, and wondered what it would have been like if she'd been there. Exciting probably. For a minute or two, an hour, or a night. That's all she was to him, and would have been. A bit of fluff and some fun. He took his clothes off then, and dropped them on the floor next to his bed. He slipped into bed in his jockey shorts, as he always did, and forgot about her. For him, Maggie was gone. She had to go back to her own life, whatever it was.

10

In spite of the fact that Charlie told himself there was no reason to, he went back to the Children's Center to look around again. He brought dough-nuts and ice cream for the children, a little teddy bear for Gabby, and treats for her dog. He had been haunted by them since he'd been there. But it wasn't Gabby who had drawn him back there, and he knew it the moment he walked in. It was Carole who had haunted him, as much as Gabby and her dog. In fact, even more. He knew it was a crazy thing to do, but he couldn't stop himself. She had been on his mind all week.

'What brings you back here?' she asked with a look of curiosity when she saw him. He had come in jeans and an old sweater this time, and a pair of running shoes. He'd been standing in the courtyard, talking to Tygue quietly when she came out of group and saw him.

'Just taking another look.' He had come without warning, and for a minute she thought he was checking up on them, and thought it was rude. And then Tygue told her about the ice cream he'd brought for the kids, and Gabby showed her the little bear and told her about the treats for Zorro.

'They get under your skin, don't they?' she said to him, as she led him back to her office, and offered him a cup of coffee.

'No, thanks, I'm fine. I know you're busy. I won't stay long.' He couldn't tell her he'd been in the neighborhood, because the only thing in it was the Children's Center and a lot of people in tenements, while dealers sold drugs in doorways. The only thing he could have done in the neighborhood was buy heroin or crack.

'It was nice of you to bring things for the children. They love it when people visit. I wish we could do more for them, but we never have enough money. I have to save what we've got for the important stuff like salaries, heat, and medication. They'd much rather have ice cream,' she said, smiling at Charlie. And as she did, he was suddenly glad he'd come.

He had wanted to see her again, but now that he had, he couldn't think of a reason to justify it. He told himself he admired the work she did, which was true, but there was more to it than that. He enjoyed talking to her and wanted to know her better. But he couldn't explain it to himself. She was a social worker, and he ran the foundation. Now that they had given her the money she needed, other than financial reports, there was no real excuse for further contact. Their lives were too different for there to be an excuse for social contact between them. He already knew that she had nothing but contempt for the life he led, and the world he came from. She was a woman who was sacrificing herself for a bunch of kids who were fighting for survival. He was a man who lived a life of luxury and self-indulgence.

'Is there anything I can do for you?' she asked him helpfully, as he shook his head. He couldn't think of a single excuse to linger, although he would have liked to.

'No, I'll come back and see the kids again, if you don't mind. I'd like to check on Gabby.'

'She's doing fine, now that she has Zorro. She's going to start at a special school next month. We think she's ready.'

'Will she leave here then?' he asked, worried about the child, as he looked at Carole.

'Not for a while. Eventually, we'll try to get her into foster care, and feed her back into the system. But a special-needs kid like her isn't easy to place, for obvious reasons. People who provide foster homes aren't ready to deal with a blind kid and a Seeing Eye dog.'

'Then what?' He had never thought about it before, but for a child like Gabby, life was going to be hard, harder than most. Probably forever.

'If we can't find foster parents for her, then we'll put her in a group home. There are a lot of them in upstate New York. She'll be fine.'

'No, she won't,' he said, looking distraught. It was as though he had discovered a whole other world full of people with problems no one could solve. In this case, all of them were kids. And none of what had happened to them had been their fault.

'She'll be as fine as any of them are,' Carole said carefully. 'Maybe better, thanks to your gift. Zorro is going to be a big plus in her life.'

'Don't you wonder what happens to all of them, after they leave here?' The plight of the children she tended to tugged at his heart.

'Of course I do. But we can only do so much, Mr Harrington,' she said coolly, guarded again.

'Charlie, please,' he interrupted her.

'We only do what we can. It's like emptying the ocean with a thimble sometimes. But there are success stories too. Kids who find great foster homes with good people and thrive. Others who get adopted by people who love them. Kids we get operations for, who wouldn't have otherwise. Gabby and her dog. Some of their problems we can solve, some we can't. You just have to accept where the limits are, otherwise it breaks your heart.' He had never seen as closely where their money went, or who it was going to. He had never looked into faces like theirs, or met a woman like her, who was devoting her life to changing the world for a handful of souls on a backstreet in Harlem. Since he'd come there the first time, only days before, it had turned his life upside down, and his heart. 'They told us in school that you have to be professional, keep a distance, and not get too involved. But sometimes you just can't. Sometimes I go home at night, and I just lie in bed and cry.' It was easy for him to imagine now. He had done the same himself.

'You must need to take a breather sometimes,' he said thoughtfully, wanting to suggest lunch or dinner to her, but he didn't have the guts.

'I do.' She smiled innocently at him. 'I go to the gym, swim, or play squash, if I'm not too tired.'

'So do I,' he said, smiling at her. 'Play squash, I mean. Maybe we should play some time.' She looked surprised. She had no idea why they would. As he looked at her, her eyes were blank. As far as Carole knew, he was the head of the foundation that had just given them a million dollars, and not much else. She couldn't imagine being friends with him. Her only contact with him was what it was now. Professional and courteous. And all she owed him was financial reports. She had no idea that he was trying to be friends. It never occurred to her that he would.

She walked him out a few minutes later, before she went into another group. When she left him, he was still chatting with Tygue, and said he'd come back soon. A few minutes later, Charlie left, and took a cab downtown. He was having dinner with Gray and Sylvia that night. Carole forgot about him as soon as he walked out.

When he got to Sylvia's apartment, Gray was in the kitchen, and she opened the door for him. She was wearing a pretty embroidered black peasant skirt, and a soft white blouse. She had set the table beautifully for him, with tall white candles and a big basket of tulips in the center. She had wanted everything to be just right for him, because she knew how much he meant to Gray, and she had liked him when they first met. She wanted Gray's friendship with him to remain solid. She didn't want to disrupt Charlie's life. She felt she had no right to. And she didn't want him disrupting theirs. There was room for both of them in Gray's life, and she wanted to prove that to Charlie, by welcoming him into their lives. As she looked at him, her eyes were warm. She knew how suspicious he had been of her, once Gray told him that he was involved with her. And she suspected correctly that it wasn't personal. He had liked her when they met in Portofino, he was just worried about what their relationship would mean to him, and how it would impact him. Like a child facing a new nanny, or a man his mother was going out with. What did it mean for him? Charlie and Gray were like brothers, and any weight added to the balance could change everything for them. She wanted to reassure both of them now that although her weight had been added to the scale, they were still safe in their private world. She felt like Wendy in *Peter Pan* sitting down to dinner with the Lost Boys, as they all sat down at the table, and Gray opened a bottle of wine.

Charlie had looked around the apartment before he sat down, and was impressed by how elegant it was, how many interesting treasures she had, and how well she'd put it all together. She had a great eye, and a light touch in conversation. She wisely stayed mostly in the background that night, and they were well into their second bottle of wine when Charlie mentioned Carole, and described his visit to the center in Harlem.

'She's an amazing woman,' he said, in a tone of deep admiration.

He told them about Gabby and her dog, the others he'd met, and the stories she'd told him. He had known of incidents of child abuse before, but none as ugly or as disheartening as the ones she'd told him. She didn't pull any punches. He realized now that other organizations had dressed it up for them. But Carole went straight to the bone of what she was dealing with and why she needed his money. She made no apology for wanting a lot from him, and had alluded to wanting more. Her dream for the center was a big one. For the moment she had no choice but to keep the center small, but one day she wanted to open an even bigger place deep in the heart of Harlem. There were few places that needed her more, and she had been quick to point out to him that child abuse was not just a disease of the inner city. It existed in homes on Park Avenue, right in the lap of luxury. In fact in middle-class homes, it was a lot harder to uncover. She assured him that people were committing hideous acts against children in every town, in every state, in every country, and at every socioeconomic level. Where she was, in some ways, it was easier to deal with. She had sworn a war against poverty, child abuse, neglect, hypocrisy, indifference. She had taken a big bite into the woes of the world, and she had no time or patience for the kind of world he lived in, where people turned a blind eye, ignored what was going on around them, and got dressed up and went to parties. She had no time herself to waste on things like that, and no desire to pursue them. What she wanted was to help her fellow man, and save their children. Charlie's eyes lit up like a bonfire as he spoke of her, and Sylvia and Gray watched him. She had set his mind and heart ablaze with what she'd showed him.

'So when are you taking her out to dinner?' Gray teased, as he sat with an arm around Sylvia's shoulder. Charlie had enjoyed his evening with them, the food had been edible for once, and the conversation lively. He was surprised to find he liked Sylvia even better than he had in Portofino. She seemed softer now, and gentler, and he had to admit that she was wonderful to his friend. She had even been kind and welcoming to him.

'How about never?' Charlie said with a rueful grin. 'She hates everything I stand for. When I met her, she looked at me like dirt under her shoes because I was wearing a suit.' Not to mention the gold watch.

'She sounds a little tough to me. You gave her a million bucks, for chrissake. What did she expect you to do? Show up in shorts and flip-flops?' Gray said, looking annoyed on his behalf.

'Maybe,' Charlie said, willing to forgive her for being tough on him. What she was doing, hand to hand, was more important, he thought, than anything he'd done in his entire lifetime. All he did was sign checks and give away money. She was in the trenches with those kids every day, fighting for their lives. 'She has no patience with the way we all live, the things we do. She's practically a saint, Gray.' Charlie sounded convinced of it, and Gray looked suspicious.

'I thought you said she went to Princeton. She's probably from some fancy family, trying to atone for their collective sins.'

'I don't think so. My guess is that she went there on a scholarship. There were a lot of people like her when I was there, and more lately. It's not as elitist as it used to be. And that's a good thing. Besides, she said she hated Princeton.' Although the eating club she'd been in had been a good one. But there were many ways to get in. Even Princeton was no longer the good old boys' club it used to be. The world had changed, and people like Carole had changed it. He was a throwback to another era, living off the glory of his aristocratic family. Carole was a whole new breed.

'Why don't you ask her out?' Gray encouraged him, and Sylvia agreed. 'Or is she a dog?' That hadn't occurred to him, given the way Charlie was raving about her. Somehow he had assumed that she was attractive. He couldn't imagine Charlie getting excited about an ugly woman, although maybe in this case he had. He described her like Mother Teresa.

'No, she's very beautiful, although I don't think

she gives a damn about that either. She doesn't have patience for much in her life, except the real thing.' And in her eyes, he knew, he wasn't it, although he knew she hadn't really given him a fair chance, and probably never would. He was nothing more than the head of the foundation to her.

'What does she look like?' Sylvia asked with interest.

'She's about six feet tall, blond, pretty face, blue eyes, good figure, no makeup. She says she swims and plays squash when she has time. She's thirty-four years old.'

'Not married?' Sylvia inquired.

'I don't think so. She wasn't wearing a ring, and I didn't get that impression, though I doubt that she's alone.' A woman who looked like her couldn't be, he told himself, which made it even more ridiculous to invite her to dinner. Although he could pretend it was for foundation business, and learn more about her then. It was a ruse that appealed to him somewhat, although he felt dishonest hiding behind the foundation to get to know her better. But maybe Sylvia and Gray were right, and it was worth a shot.

'You never know with women like that,' Sylvia said wisely. 'Sometimes they give up a lot to support their causes. If she puts that much time and energy and passion into what she does, it may be all she's got.'

'Find out,' Gray said, encouraging him again. 'Why not? You've got nothing to lose. Check it out.' Charlie felt weird talking about her, and sharing it with them. He felt vulnerable discussing her with them, and more than a little foolish.

By the time Gray brought out a bottle of Château d'Yquem Sylvia had bought for them, they almost had Charlie convinced, but as soon as he got home that night, he knew how foolish it was to think of inviting Carole to dinner. He was too old for her, too rich, too conservative, too established. And whatever her background was, it was obvious that she had no interest in guys like him. She had even laughed at him about his watch. He couldn't even imagine telling her he had a yacht, although most people in his world had heard about the *Blue Moon*. But yachting magazines were about as far from her field of interest as it got. He laughed to himself thinking about it as he got into bed that night. Gray and Sylvia's intentions were good, but they just couldn't fathom how different and what a zealot she was. It was written all over her, and her scathing comments about eating clubs at Princeton hadn't fallen on deaf ears. He had heard her loud and clear.

He called Gray the next morning to thank them for dinner, and tell him what a nice time he'd had. He had no idea where their relationship was going, or if it would last, he doubted it, but for now it seemed like a nice thing for both of them. And he was relieved to see that Sylvia wasn't trying to interfere or shut him out. He said as much to Gray, who was happy to hear Charlie so relaxed about Sylvia, and promised to have him over again soon.

'Your cooking has even improved,' Charlie teased, and Gray laughed.

'She helped,' he confessed, as Charlie chuckled.

'Thank God.'

'Don't forget to call Mother Teresa and invite her out to dinner,' Gray reminded him, and Charlie paused for a minute, and then laughed hollowly this time.

'I think we all had a lot to drink last night. It sounded good, but it doesn't sound like such a hot idea in the bright light of day.'

'Just ask her. What's the worst that could happen?' Gray said, sounding like an older brother, as Charlie shook his head at the other end.

'She could call me an asshole and hang up. Besides, it would be awkward when I see her again.' He didn't want to expose himself, although he had nothing else to do at the moment. There was no other woman in his life, and hadn't been for months. He was tired these days, and imperceptibly slowing down. The chase was not quite as much fun. It was easier going to dinner parties and social events alone. Or spending an evening with good friends, like Gray and Sylvia last night. He enjoyed that more than the effort he had to put into dating, and courting someone to wind up in bed with them. He'd done it all before too many times.

'So what?' Gray commented about Carole possibly hanging up on him. 'You've lived through worse. You never know, this could be the right one.'

'Yeah, sure. I could sell the *Blue Moon* and build her dream center in Harlem, and maybe then she'd agree to go out with me on a date.'

'Hell,' Gray laughed at him, 'no sacrifice is too great for love.'

'Don't give me that. What did you give up to be with Sylvia? The cockroaches in your apartment? Give me a break.'

'Give her a call.'

'Okay, okay,' he said, to get Gray off his back, and a few minutes later, they promised to talk again soon, and hung up.

Charlie was determined not to call her, but the thought of her haunted him all afternoon. He went to his office at the foundation, then to his club, had a massage, played squash with a friend, and called Adam to thank him for the concert, but he was in a meeting. Charlie left his thanks on voice mail, and wondered what had happened between Adam and Maggie that night. The usual, probably,

Adam had dazzled her with his fancy footwork, poured a gallon of champagne into her, and she wound up in his bed. He still felt sorry for her when he thought of her. Despite her outfit, there was something sweet and innocent about her. There were times when Adam's behavior with women, and lack of conscience about it, made his skin crawl. But as Adam always pointed out, if they were willing, they were all fair game. He hadn't knocked anyone unconscious and raped them yet. They lay down at his feet adoringly, and what happened after that was between two consenting adults. Charlie just wasn't so sure that Maggie had been quite as adult as she looked, or as practiced at his game. She wasn't looking for implants or a nose job. All she had wanted was a better seat at the concert. Charlie couldn't help wondering what she'd had to give up in exchange. He thought about it as he left his club after the squash game, took a cab home, and told himself he was getting old. Adam's morality, or lack of it, and the way he treated women, had never bothered him before. And as Adam always reminded him, anything was fair in the pursuit of sex and fun. Or was it? Somehow it no longer sounded quite as amusing anymore.

It was nearly six o'clock when he walked into his apartment, listened to his messages, and stood staring at the phone. He wondered if she'd still be in her office, or in group, or maybe she'd gone home. He remembered that he had her card in his wallet, took it out, looked at it for a long moment, and then called her, feeling nervous and foolish. She was the first woman he'd ever met who made him feel as though he was doing something wrong. He wanted to apologize to her for his indulgences and privilege, and yet that same privilege had allowed him to give her a million dollars so she could continue saving the world. He felt like an anxious schoolboy as he heard the phone ring at the other end. He was suddenly praying she wouldn't be there, and was about to hang up, when she answered, sounding out of breath.

'Hello?' She forgot to say who she was, but he knew her voice immediately. He had called on her private line.

'Carole?'

'Yes.' She didn't recognize his voice.

'It's Charlie Harrington. Did I catch you at a bad time?'

'Not at all,' she lied, rubbing her shin. She had just rammed it, dashing for the phone. 'I just got out of group. I ran down the stairs when I heard the phone.'

'Sorry. How's my little friend?' He was referring to Gabby, as Carole knew immediately. She smiled and said she was fine. He asked how things were going at the center, if there were any new developments, and Carole found herself wondering if he was going to be checking on them constantly for the next year. It was a little unusual to hear from the heads of foundations who gave them grants. She wondered why he'd called. 'I don't want to make any promises we can't live up to, or raise false hopes, but you mentioned that there were other programs you wanted to implement, and other grant proposals you might want to explore. I wondered if you'd like to do that over lunch or dinner with me some time.' He had taken the coward's way out, he knew, hiding behind the foundation, but at least he'd called. There was a long pause.

'To be honest, we're not ready to make any more grant requests. We don't have the staff to man the programs I want, or even to write the proposals right now, but yes, actually, I wouldn't mind picking your brain to see what you think of our plans.' She didn't want to head in directions the foundation wasn't open to, and waste a lot of energy and time.

'I'd be happy to listen and give you an honest assessment of where our interests lie. For a later date of course.' It would be tough asking the foundation board to give her more money, when they had just granted her a million dollars. But talk was cheap. 'We couldn't really do a lot for you until next year.

But it's a good thing for you to think of now, so you can plan your attack accordingly, at the beginning of our next fiscal year.'

'Whose side are you on?' She laughed at him, and he laughed as he answered her, more honestly than she knew.

'Yours, I think. You're doing a great thing.' He had fallen in love with her child abuse center, and if he wasn't careful, he knew he'd be falling in love with her. For a week or two anyway, or if they were lucky, maybe more. Love never lasted long with him. Fear was a more powerful emotion for Charlie than love had ever been.

'Thank you.' She was touched by the kindness of his words. He sounded sincere to her. She let her guard down slowly as she listened to him, and he was a good connection to have.

'When would you like to get together?' he asked her casually, pleased with the way the conversation was going. He had given her the option of lunch or dinner, so she didn't feel pressured by him. That was usually a good first move. And maybe the last one in this case. There was nothing in her voice to suggest that she was interested in him. She probably wasn't, but he'd get a better sense of it when they met and talked over a meal. If she had no interest whatsoever, he wasn't going to stick his neck out and make a fool of himself with her. But so far so good.

'I can't really get away at lunchtime. I always stay here and eat a banana at my desk, if I get that far. Most of the time, in the middle of the day, I'm in group. And I meet with clients one-on-one in the afternoon.' She had taken a big chunk out of her day for him when he had come to take the tour, but she didn't want to make a habit of it, even for him.

'What about dinner, then?' He held his breath. 'Tomorrow maybe?' He was going to a deadly dinner party and would gladly cancel it to be with her.

'Sure,' she said hesitantly. She sounded a little confused. 'I'm not sure I'll have all my ducks in order by then. I have a list of programs I want to start, it's in rough form, and it's around here somewhere. But I can tell you what I have in mind.' That was all he wanted from her, and not about the programs she was starting, but she had no idea. He sounded as offhand as she.

'We'll just talk about it, and see what we come up with, talking it through. That works better for me sometimes, doing it free form. A brainstorming session with food. Which reminds me, where do you like to eat?'

She laughed at the question. She rarely went out to dinner. By the time she got home at night, she was exhausted. Most nights she didn't even have the energy to go to the gym, which she liked to do too.

'Let's see. My usual haunts? Mo's hamburgers on 168th Street and Amsterdam . . . Sally's spareribs on 125th, near the subway stop on my way home . . . Izzy's deli on West 99th Street and Columbus . . . I only go to the best places. I don't think I've been to a decent restaurant in years.' Charlie wanted to change that, and other things in her life, but not all in one night. He wanted to go easy with her, until he knew the lay of the land.

'I'm not sure I can compete with Mo and Izzy's. Where do you live, by the way?'

She hesitated for a minute, and he wondered suddenly if she was living with someone. She sounded as though she was afraid Charlie wanted to drop by. 'On the Upper East Side, in the Nineties.' It was a respectable neighborhood, and he got the feeling she was embarrassed to admit it. He wondered suddenly if Gray was right, and her background was more traditional than her ideologies would suggest. She was very dogmatic about what she believed. He had expected her to say that she lived somewhere on the Upper West Side, not on the East Side, but he didn't question it, or push. He could sense her skittishness. Charlie knew women well, he'd been doing this for a long time. A lot longer than Carole, who didn't have the faintest idea how experienced he was, or what he had in mind. Given even a hint of encouragement, which she hadn't given him so far, he wanted to change her life.

'I know a nice quiet Italian place on East Eighty-ninth. How does that sound?' he offered.

'Perfect. What's it called?'

'Stella Di Notte. It's not quite as romantic as it sounds. It means Night Star in Italian, but actually it's a play on words. Stella is the owner, she does all the cooking, and she weighs about three hundred pounds. I don't think they'd ever get her more than an inch or two off the ground, but the pasta is fantastic. She makes it all herself.'

'It sounds great. I'll meet you there.' Charlie was a little startled by her suggestion. He hadn't expected her to say that, and more than ever, he now suspected that there was a man living at her place. He was determined to find out.

'Wouldn't you rather I pick you up?'

'No,' she said honestly. 'I'd rather walk. I'm cooped up here all day, and I live on Ninety-first. I need the exercise, even for a few blocks. It clears my head after work.' A likely story, he said to himself. There was probably a handsome thirty-five-year-old, lying on the couch, watching TV with the remote in his hand.

'See you there then. Seven-thirty? Does that give you enough time after work?'

'That's fine. My last group is at four-thirty

tomorrow, so I can be home by six-thirty. I assume it's not fancy or anything?' she asked, suddenly sounding nervous. She almost never went out, and never dressed. She wondered if he expected her to wear a little black dress and pearls. She didn't own either, nor did she want to. He looked the type, but this was work. She wasn't going to get dressed up for him. She'd rather have gone to Mo's in that case. She wasn't about to change her lifestyle for him, no matter how much money the foundation had to give them. There were some things she no longer did, and never would again. Dressing up was one of them.

'It's not fancy,' he reassured her. 'You can even wear jeans if you want.' Although he hoped she wouldn't. He would have loved to see her in a dress.

'If you don't mind, I will. I won't have time to dress. I never do anyway. What you see is what you get.' Apparently. Jeans and Nikes. Oh, well. So much for the dress.

'I'll do the same,' he said quietly.

'At least you can wear your watch in that neighborhood,' she chuckled at him, and he laughed.

'That's too bad. I pawned it yesterday.'

'What'd you get for it?' She liked teasing him. He seemed like a nice guy. In spite of herself, she was looking forward to dinner with him. She hadn't been out to dinner with a man in nearly four years.

And that wasn't about to change, except for one business dinner with him. Just one, she told herself.

'Twenty-five bucks,' he answered her question about the watch.

'Not bad. See you tomorrow night,' she said, and hung up a moment later. And suddenly, after she did, a bolt of lightning ran through him that terrified him. What if he really was insane? Maybe the jeans and running shoes were about something else? What if the gorgeous six-foot Viking with the heart of Mother Teresa didn't have a man living with her? What if he was even more obtuse? What if she was gay? It hadn't even occurred to him till then. But anything was possible. She was clearly no ordinary girl.

'Oh, great,' he said to himself as he put the card back in his wallet, and called the restaurant to make a reservation. Whatever she was, he would know more tomorrow. And until then, all he could do was guess and wait.

11

Charlie got to the restaurant before Carole did. He had told no one he was meeting her, not even Sylvia and Gray. There was nothing to tell them yet, except that he was having an informal foundation dinner with her, since he had used a ruse to get her there. It wasn't a date. He had walked to the restaurant himself. It was a longer walk for him, but like her, he needed the air. He'd been anxious about it all day. And by then, he really was convinced she was gay. It was probably why he'd gotten no re-action from her. Usually, women responded to him in some way. Carole hadn't. She was all business, and had been, both times they met. Professional to her fingertips, although she seemed warm with everyone else, especially the kids. And then he remembered how friendly and congenial she and Tygue had been. Maybe there was a man in her life, and it was him. All he knew by the time he got to the restaurant was that there was a knot in his stomach, which was unfamiliar to him, and she was a complete mystery, and maybe still would be after they had dinner together that night. He wasn't at all sure that she was going to open up to him. She had seemed sealed tight, like a shell, which only seemed more challenging, along with her very impressive brain.

She was totally different from the socialites he pursued normally. They dressed, they danced, they smiled, they went everywhere with him, they played tennis and sailed, and for the most part they bored him to extinction, which was why he was having dinner with Carole Parker that night, who appeared to have absolutely no interest whatsoever in him, and he didn't even know if she was gay or straight. And he had lied to get her there. The whole thing was absurd.

Carole arrived five minutes after he did, and joined Charlie at the corner table Stella had given them. She looked smiling and relaxed as she walked in, in a pair of white jeans and sandals and a crisp white shirt. Her hair was still damp from the shower, and she had woven it quickly in a braid. She wore no makeup or nail polish. Her nails were short, and everything about her looked crisp and clean. She had a pale blue sweater draped over her shoulders, and it occurred to him that with what she wore, she would have looked perfect on the *Blue Moon*. She looked like a sailor or a tennis player, she was a long, lean, athletic-looking woman, and her eyes were a clear bright blue, the same color as her sweater. She looked like a Ralph Lauren ad, although she would probably have hated him if he said it. In her heart, she was more Che Guevara than anything as prosaic and fashionable as a Ralph Lauren model. She smiled at Charlie as soon as she saw him.

'I'm sorry I'm late,' she apologized, and sat down, as he stood up to greet her. It was only five minutes, and it had allowed him to compose himself as he waited for her. He didn't want to order wine until she got there, and they figured out what they were eating.

'No problem. I didn't notice since I no longer have a watch anyway. I thought I'd spend the twenty-five bucks I got for it on dinner,' he said, smiling at her, and she laughed at him. He had a nice sense of humor. She hadn't bothered to bring a handbag with her, she had her key in her pocket, and she didn't need to carry a lipstick since she didn't wear any. And surely not for him. 'How was your day?'

'Busy. Crazy. The usual. What about you?' she asked, looking interested. That was new for him too. He couldn't remember the last time a woman had asked him how he was, and actually seemed as though she gave a damn about it. This one did.

'Interesting. I was at the foundation all day. We're trying to figure out how much we want to spend internationally. There are some very good programs in dire need in developing countries, but they have a hell of a time implementing them once they get the money. I had a conference call with Jimmy Carter today, on that subject. They do a lot of really great work in Africa, and he gave me some good advice about how to get through the red tape.'

'Sounds good to me,' she said, smiling at him. 'Projects like that make me realize how small our scope is here. Mine, anyway. I'm dealing with kids in a radius of forty blocks of me, sometimes less. It's pathetic when you think of it.' She sighed as she sat back in her chair.

'Not pathetic. You're doing great work. We don't give a million dollars to people who aren't doing impressive work.'

'How much does the foundation give away every year?' She'd been wondering about that since she met him. His foundation was greatly respected in philanthropic circles, and it was all she knew about him.

'About ten million. You kicked us up to eleven, but you're worth it.' He smiled at her, and then pointed to the specials. 'You must be starving if all you eat is a banana for lunch.' He remembered what she'd said. They both ordered the gnocchi because Charlie told her it was fabulous and Stella's specialty. She was serving it that night with fresh tomatoes and basil, and in the lingering warm weather of Indian summer, it sounded perfect to Carole too. He ordered a bottle of inexpensive white wine, and once it was served, she took a sip.

The food was as delicious as he had promised, and they talked about her ideas for the center until dessert. She had some big dreams and hard work ahead of her, but after what she'd accomplished so far, he knew she was capable of achieving all she set out to do. Especially with help from foundations like his. He assured her that others would be equally impressed, and she'd have no trouble getting money from him or anyone else the following year. He was vastly impressed by all she did, and how carefully she was already planning for the future.

'That's quite a dream you have, Ms Parker. You really are going to change the world one day.' He believed in her 1,000 per cent. She was a remarkable young woman. At thirty-four, she had accomplished more than some people in a lifetime, and most of it by herself, with no one's help. It was clear that the center was her baby, which once again made him curious about her.

'What about you? What else do you do with your spare time? I say that jokingly, believe me. It's no wonder you have no time to eat. You mustn't sleep much either.'

'I don't,' she reassured him. 'It seems like such a waste of time to me.' She laughed as she said it. 'That's all I do. Work and kids. Groups. Most of the time I hang out at the center on the weekends, although officially I'm not working. But being there and keeping an eye on things makes a difference.'

'I feel that way about the foundation,' he admitted, 'but you still have to make time for other things, and have some fun sometimes. What does fun mean for you?'

'Work is fun for me. I've never been happier than since we opened the center. I don't need other things in my life.' She said it honestly, and he could see she meant it, which worried him a little. Something was wrong with this picture, or at least the one she presented. Other than work, much was missing.

'No men, no babies, no ticking clock telling you to get married? That's unusual at your age.' He knew she was thirty-four, and had gone to Princeton and Columbia, but he knew nothing else about her, even after dinner. All they had talked about was the center and the foundation. His work and hers. Their respective missions.

'Nope. No men. No babies. No biological clock. I threw mine away several years ago. I've been happy ever since.'

'What does that mean?' he pressed her a little,

but she didn't seem to mind it. He sensed that whatever she didn't want to answer, she wouldn't.

'The kids at the center are my children.' She seemed comfortable as she said it.

'You say that now, but maybe one day you'll regret it. Women aren't lucky that way. They have decisions to make at a certain age. A man can always make a fool of himself and have a family when he's sixty or seventy or eighty.'

'Maybe I'll adopt when I'm eighty.' She smiled at him, and for the first time he smelled tragedy in there somewhere. He knew women well, and something bad had happened to this one. He didn't know why or how he knew it, but he suddenly sensed it. She was too pat in her answers, too firm in her decisions. No one was that sure of anything in life, unless heartbreak got them there. He had been there himself.

'I don't buy it, Carole,' he said cautiously. He didn't want to scare her, or make her back off completely. 'You're a woman who loves children. And there has to be a man in your life somewhere.' After listening to her all evening, she didn't seem gay to him. Nothing she had said to him suggested it, although he could be wrong, he knew, and had been once or twice. But she didn't seem gay to him. Just hidden.

'Nope. No man,' she said simply. 'No time. No

interest. Been there, done that. There hasn't been anyone in my life in four years.' A year before she'd opened the center, as he figured it. He wondered if some heartbreak in her life had turned her in another direction, to heal her own wounds as well as others'.

'That's a long time at your age,' he said gently, and she smiled at him.

'You keep talking about my age as though I'm twenty. I'm not that young. I'm thirty-four. That seems pretty old to me.'

He laughed at her. 'Well, not to me. I'm forty-six.'

'Right.' She turned the tables on him quickly, to get the focus off herself. 'And you're not married and have no kids either. So what's the big deal? What about you? Why isn't your clock ticking if you're twelve years older than I am?' Although he didn't look it. Charlie didn't look a day over thirty-six, although he felt it. Lately, he felt every moment of his forty-six years, and then some. But at least he didn't look it. Nor did she. She looked somewhere in her mid-twenties. And they looked handsome together, and were very similar in type, almost like brother and sister, as he himself had noticed when he had first observed that she looked a lot like his sister, Ellen, and his mother.

'My clock is ticking,' he confessed to her. 'I just

haven't found the right woman yet, but I hope I will one day.'

'That's bullshit,' she said simply, looking him dead in the eye. 'Guys who've been single forever always say they haven't met the right woman. You can't tell me that at forty-six, you've never met the right one. There are a lot of them out there, and if you haven't found one, I think you don't want to. Not finding the right woman is really a poor excuse. Find something else,' she said matter-of-factly, and took a sip of her wine as Charlie stared at her. She had cut right to the quick, and worse yet, she was right, and he knew it. So did she. She looked convinced of what she'd said.

'Okay. I concede. A few of them might have been right, if I'd wanted to compromise. I've been looking for perfection.'

'You won't find it. No one's perfect. You know that. So what's the deal?'

'Scared shitless,' he said honestly, for the first time in his life, and nearly fell off his chair when he heard himself say it.

'That's better. Why?' She was good at what she did, although he didn't realize it till later. Getting into people's hearts and heads was her business, and what she loved doing. But he sensed instinctively that she wasn't going to hurt him. He felt safe with her.

'My parents died when I was sixteen, my sister took care of me, and then she died of a brain tumor when I was twenty-one. That was it. End of family. I guess I've figured all my life that if you love someone they either die, or leave, or disappear, or abandon you. I'd rather be the first one out the door.'

'That makes sense,' she said quietly, listening to him, and watching him closely. She knew he had told her the truth. 'And people do die and leave and disappear. It happens that way sometimes. But if you're the first one out the door, you wind up alone for sure. You don't mind that?'

'I didn't.' Past tense. Lately he was minding it a lot, but he didn't want to say that to her. Yet.

'You pay a big price in life for being scared,' she said quietly, and then added, 'scared to love. I'm not so good at that myself.' She decided to tell him then. Just as he did with her, she felt safe with him. She hadn't told the story in a long time, and kept it short. 'I got married at twenty-four. He was a friend of my father's, the head of a major company, a brilliant man. He had been a research scientist, and started a drug company we all know. And he was totally nuts. He was twenty years older than I was, and an extraordinary man. He still is. But narcissistic, crazy, brilliant, successful, charming, and alcoholic, dangerous, sadistic, abusive.

They were the worst six years of my life. He was a total sociopath, and everyone kept telling me how lucky I was to be married to him. Because none of them knew what went on behind closed doors. I had a car accident, because I wanted to, I think. All I wanted to do was die. He kept torturing me, and I'd leave him for a day or two, and then he'd bring me back, or charm me back. Abusers never lose sight of their prey. When I was in the hospital after the car accident, I got sane. I never went back again. I hid out in California for a year, met a lot of good people, and figured out what I wanted to do. I opened the center when I got home, and never looked back.'

'What happened to him? Where is he now?'

'Still here. Torturing someone else. He's in his fifties now. He married some pathetic debutante last year, poor kid. He's about as charming as it gets, and as sick. He still calls me sometimes, and wrote me a letter telling me she meant nothing to him, and he still loves me. I never answered him, and I won't. I screen my calls, and I never return his. It's over for me. But I haven't had any inclination to try again. I guess you could reasonably say that I'm commitment phobic,' she said, smiling at Charlie, 'or relationship phobic, and I intend to stay that way. I have no desire whatsoever to have the shit kicked out of me again. I never saw it coming. No one did. They just thought he was handsome and charming and rich. He comes from a so-called "good family," and my own family thought I was nuts for a long time. They probably still do, but they're too polite to say it. They just think I'm weird. But I'm alive, and sane, which looked questionable for a while until I ran my car into the back of a truck on the Long Island Expressway, and scared the hell out of myself. Believe me, running into a truck was a lot less painful and dangerous than my life with him. He was a total sociopath, and still is. So, I threw my biological clock out the window, and my high heels and makeup with it, all my little black cocktail dresses, my engagement and wedding rings. The good news is that I never had kids with him. I probably would have stayed with him if I did. And now instead of one kid or two, I have forty of them, a whole neighborhood, and Gabby and Zorro. And I'm a whole lot happier than I was.' She sat and looked at him and the sorrow and pain in her eyes was unveiled. He could see that she had been to hell and back, which was why she cared so much about the children she worked with. She had been there herself, although in a different way. He had felt cold chills run up his spine at the story she told him. She had made it sound simple and quick, but he could see that it wasn't. She had lived a nightmare, and finally woken up. But it had

264

taken her six years to do so, and she must have suffered incredibly during those six years. He was sorry that it had happened to her. Sorrier than she knew. But she was still alive to tell the tale, and doing wonderful work. She could have been sitting in a chair somewhere, drooling, or on drugs or drunk out of her mind, or dead. Instead, she had made a good life for herself. But she had given up so much.

'I'm sorry, Carole. Some awful stuff happens to all of us at some point, I guess. Life is about what you do afterward, how many pieces you can fish out of the garbage and glue back together.' He knew there were still some big pieces missing in himself. 'You have a lot of guts.'

'So do you. For a kid to lose his whole family at the age you were is a crippling blow. You never totally get over it, but you may get brave enough not to hit the door one day. I hope you do,' she said gently.

'I hope you do too,' he said softly as he looked at her, grateful for the honesty they had shared.

'I'd rather put my money on you.' She smiled at him. 'I like the way my life is now. It's simple and easy and uncomplicated.'

'And lonely,' he supplied bluntly as she stopped talking. 'Don't tell me it's not. You'd be lying and you know it. I'm lonely too. We all are. If you choose to be alone, you may not get hurt by any-one, but you pay a big price for it. It's a big-ticket item, and you know that. So you may not have any obvious bumps and bruises this way, no fresh scars. But when you go home at night, you hear the same thing I do, silence, and the house is dark. No one asks you how you are, and no one gives a damn. Maybe your friends do, but we both know that's not the same thing.'

'No, it's not,' she said honestly. 'But the alternative is scarier than shit.'

'Maybe one day the silence will be scarier yet. It gets to me at times.' Particularly lately. And time wasn't on his side. Or even hers for much longer.

'And then what do you do?' She was curious about that.

'I run away. I go out. I travel. See friends. Go to parties. Take women out. There are lots of ways to fill that void, most of them artificial, and wherever you go in the world, you take yourself, and all your ghosts. I've been there too.' He had never been as honest with anyone in his life, other than his therapist, but he was tired of artifice, and pretending that everything was all right. Sometimes it just wasn't.

'Yeah, I know,' she said softly. 'I just work till I drop, and tell myself I owe it to my clients. But it's not always about them. Sometimes it is, but sometimes it's about me. And if there's anything left when I go home, I swim or play squash or go to the gym.'

'At least it looks good on you.' He smiled at her. 'We're a mess, aren't we? Two commitment phobics having dinner and sharing trade secrets.'

'There are worse things.' She looked at him cautiously then, wondering why he had asked her out. She was no longer sure it was entirely about her plans for the center, and she was right about that. 'Let's be friends,' she said gently, wanting to make a deal with him, to set the ground rules early on, and the boundaries that she was so good at. He looked at her for a long, hard time before he answered. This time, he wanted to be honest with her. Last time, when he had invited her to dinner, he hadn't been. But he wanted to be before too late.

'I won't make you that promise,' he said as their equally blue eyes met and held. 'I don't break promises, and I'm not sure I can keep that one.'

'I won't go out to dinner with you unless I know we're just friends.'

'Then I guess you'll have to start having lunch with me. I'll bring you a banana or we can meet at Sally's and get spareribs all over our faces. I'm not telling you we can't be friends, or that we won't be. But I like you better than that. Even commitment phobics have romances occasionally, or go out on dates.'

'Is that what this was?' She looked at him, startled. It had never occurred to her when he invited her to dinner. She genuinely thought it was foundation business, but she liked him better than that now, enough to want to be friends.

'I don't know,' he said vaguely, not ready to admit that he had lied to her, or used a ruse to get her to have dinner with him. All was fair in sex and fun, as Adam said. Or something along those lines. This had been fun, and interesting even more than fun, but there was no sex yet, and Charlie guessed there wouldn't be for a long time, if ever. 'I'm not sure what it was, other than two intelligent people with similar interests getting to know each other. But next time I'd like it to be a date.'

She sat there miserably for a minute, without answering him, wanting to run away, and then she looked at him with anguish on her face. 'I don't date.'

'That was yesterday. This is today. You can figure out tomorrow when it happens, and see what you feel like doing then. You don't have to make any big decisions yet. I'm just talking about dinner, not open-heart surgery,' he said simply. He made sense, even to her.

'And which one of us do you think would be out the door first?'

'I'll toss you for it, but I warn you, I'm not in as

good shape as I used to be. I don't sprint quite as fast as I once did. You might get there first.'

'Are you using me to prove your abandonment theory, Charlie? That all women leave you sooner or later? I don't want to be used to confirm your neurotic script,' she said, and he smiled as he listened.

'I'll try not to do that, but I can't promise that either. Remember, just dinner. Not a lifetime commitment.' Not yet at least. He warned himself silently to beware of what he wished for. Stranger things had happened. Although he couldn't imagine anything better than spending time with her, for however long it lasted, and whoever hit the door first.

'If you're looking for the "right woman," having dinner with a confirmed commitment phobic should not be high on that list.'

'I'll try to keep that in mind. You don't have to be my therapist, Carole. I have one. Just be my friend.'

'I think I am.' They didn't know about the rest yet, but they didn't need to. The future was up for grabs, if she was willing.

He paid the check then, and walked her back to her house. She lived in a small elegant brownstone, which surprised him, and she didn't invite him in. He didn't expect her to. He thought things had gone better than well for a first date.

She told him that she lived in a small studio

apartment, at the back of the building, that she rented from the owners. She also mentioned that it was incredibly cheap, and she'd been lucky to find it. He wondered if she had gotten any kind of settlement out of her marriage, since she had mentioned that her husband was rich. He hoped so, for her sake, she should have gotten something out of it instead of only grief.

'Thank you for dinner,' she said politely, and then more firmly, 'It wasn't a date.'

'I know that. Thank you for the reminder,' he said with a twinkle in his eye as he looked at her. He was wearing a blue shirt, with no tie, jeans, and a sweater the same color as hers, with brown alligator loafers and no socks. He looked very handsome, and she looked beautiful as she said goodnight to him. 'How about dinner next week?'

'I'll think about it,' she said, as she fitted her key into the front door, waved, and disappeared.

'Goodnight,' he whispered to himself with a small smile, as he walked up the block with his head down, thinking of her, and all the information they'd shared. He didn't look back, and never saw her watching him from an upstairs window. She wondered what he was thinking, just as he did about her. Charlie was pleased. Carole was scared.

12

Two days after Charlie's dinner with Carole, Adam pulled up in front of his parents' house on Long Island in his new Ferrari. He already knew he was in for trouble. They expected him to go to services with them, and he had been planning to, as he did every year. But one of his star athletes had just called him in a panic. His wife had been arrested for shoplifting, and he admitted that his sixteen-year-old son was dealing cocaine. It may have been Yom Kippur for him and his parents, but a football player from Minnesota didn't know shit about Yom Kippur and needed Adam's help. He was always there for them, and this time was no different.

They were sending the kid to Hazelden in the morning, and luckily Adam knew the assistant DA on the wife's shoplifting case. They had made a deal for a hundred hours of community service, and the DA had agreed to keep it out of the papers. The quarterback he represented said he owed him his life forever. And at six-thirty Adam was on his way.

It took him an hour to get to his parents' house on Long Island. He had missed the services at the synagogue entirely, but at least he had made it in time for dinner. He knew his mother would be furious, and he was disappointed himself. It was the one day of the year he actually liked to go to synagogue to atone for his sins of the past year and remember the dead. The rest of the time, his religion meant little to him. But he loved the tradition of high holidays, and was grateful that Rachel observed all the traditions with his kids. Jacob had been bar mitzvahed the previous summer, and the service where his son had read from the Torah in Hebrew had reduced him to tears. He had never been so proud in his life. He could remember his own father crying at his.

But tonight he knew there would be no such tender moments. His mother would be livid that he hadn't made it in time to go to synagogue with them. It was always something with her. His taking care of his clients in a crisis meant nothing to her. She had been furious with her younger son ever since his divorce. She was closer to Rachel, even now, than she had ever been to him, and Adam always felt his mother liked her better than her own son.

They were all sitting in the living room, just back from synagogue, when Adam walked in. He was wearing a tie and a beautifully cut dark blue Brioni suit, a custom-made white shirt, and perfectly polished shoes. Any other mother would have melted when she saw him. He was well built and good looking, in an exotic, ethnic way. On rare good days, when he was younger, she had said he looked like a young Israeli freedom fighter, and had occasionally been willing to let on that she was proud of him. These days all she ever said was that he had sold his soul to live in Sodom and Gomorrah, and his life was a disgrace. She disapproved of everything he did, from the women she knew he went out with, to the clients he represented, the trips he took to Las Vegas on business, either to see title fights for his boxers, or to see his rappers do concert tours. She even disapproved of Charlie and Gray, and said they were a couple of losers who had never been married and never would be, and hung out with a bunch of loose women. And every time she saw pictures of Adam in the tabloids with one of the women he was dating, standing behind Vana or one of his other clients, she called him to tell him that he was a complete disgrace. He was sure tonight wasn't going to be much better.

Missing services on Yom Kippur was about as bad as it got, as far as she was concerned. He hadn't come home for Rosh Hashanah either. He'd been in Atlantic City cleaning up a contract dispute that had erupted when one of his biggest musical artists had shown up drunk, and passed out onstage. High Jewish holidays meant nothing to his clients, but they meant a lot to his mother. Her face looked like granite when he let himself into the house and walked into the living room. He was so stressed and anxious, he was pale. Coming home always made him feel like a kid again, which was not a happy memory for him. He had been made to feel like an intruder and a disappointment to them since birth.

'Hi, Mom, I'm sorry I'm so late,' he said as he walked toward her, bent to kiss her, and she turned her face away. His father was sitting on the couch staring at his feet. Although he had heard Adam come in, he never looked up to see him. He never did. Adam kissed the top of his mother's head, and moved away. 'I'm sorry, everybody, I couldn't help it. I had a crisis with a client. His kid's selling drugs, and his wife was about to go to jail.' His excuse meant nothing to her, it was just more cannon fodder for her.

'Lovely people you work for,' she said, with an edge to her voice that could have sliced through a side of beef. 'You must be very proud.' Sarcasm dripped from her voice, as Adam saw his sister glance at her husband, and his brother frowned and turned away. He could tell it was going to be one of those great evenings that left his stomach aching for days.

'It feeds my kids,' Adam said, trying to sound

lighthearted, as he went to the sideboard and poured himself a drink. A stiff one. Straight vodka over ice.

'You can't even wait to sit down before you have a drink? You can't go to synagogue on Yom Kippur, or say a decent hello to your family, and you're already drinking? One of these days, Adam, you're going to wind up at AA.' There was little he could say. He would have made a joke of it with Charlie and Gray, but nothing that happened in his family was ever a joke. They looked like they were sitting shivah, as they waited for the maid to tell them that dinner was served. She was the same African American woman who had worked for them for thirty years, though Adam could never figure out why she did. His mother still referred to her as 'the *schwartze*' in front of her, although she spoke more Yiddish than he did by now. She was the only person Adam enjoyed seeing on his rare visits home. Her name was Mae. His mother always said with a look of disapproval, what kind of name was Mae?

'How was synagogue?' he asked politely, trying to strike up conversation while his sister Sharon spoke in hushed tones to their sister-in-law Barbara, and his brother Ben talked golf to their brother-in-law, whose name was Gideon, but no one liked him, so they pretended he had no name. In his family, if you didn't make the cut, everyone pretended you

275

had no name. Ben was a doctor, and Gideon only sold insurance. The fact that Adam had graduated magna cum laude from Harvard Law School was canceled out by the fact that he was divorced because his wife had left him, a fact for which, in his mother's opinion, he was almost certainly to blame. If he were a decent guy, why would a girl like Rachel leave him? And look what he'd been dating ever since. The mantras were endless, and he knew them all by then. It was a game you could never win. He still tried, but never knew why he did.

Mae finally came to call them in to dinner, and as they sat down at their usual places, Adam saw his mother stare down the length of the table at him. It was a look that would have wilted concrete. His father was at the opposite end, with both couples lined up on either side. Their children were still being fed in the kitchen, and Adam hadn't seen them yet. They'd been shooting basketball hoops and secretly smoking cigarettes outside. His own children never came. His mother saw them alone with Rachel, on her own time. Adam's place was between his father and sister, like someone they had made room for at the last minute. He always got the table leg between his knees. He didn't really mind it, but it always seemed like a sign from God to him that there wasn't room for him in this family, even more so in recent years. Ever since his divorce from

Rachel, and his partnership in his law firm shortly before that, he had been treated like a pariah, and a source of grief and shame to his mother in particular. His accomplishments, which were considerable in the real world, meant absolutely nothing here. He was treated like a creature from outer space, and sat there sometimes feeling like ET, growing paler by the minute, and desperate to go home. The worst part of it for him was that this was home, hard as that was for him to believe. They all felt like strangers and enemies to him, and treated him that way.

'So, where have you been lately?' his mother asked in the first silence, so that everyone could hear him list off places like Las Vegas and Atlantic City, where there were gambling and prostitutes and roving bands of loose women, all of whom had been summoned there for Adam's use.

'Oh, here and there,' Adam said vaguely. He knew the drill. It was tough to avoid the potholes and pitfalls, but he usually gave it a good try. 'I was in Italy and France in August,' he reminded her, he had spoken to her since.

There was no point telling her he'd been in Atlantic City the week before, dealing with another crisis. Mercifully, she had no idea where he'd been on Rosh Hashanah and didn't expect him to come home. He only made the effort on Yom Kippur. He glanced at his sister then, and she smiled at him. For an instant, in a momentary hallucination, he saw her hair get tall with white streaks in it, and fangs come out. He always thought of her as the Bride of Frankenstein. She had two kids, whom he rarely saw, who were just like Gideon and her. He went to everyone's bar and bat mitzvahs, but other than that, he never saw them. His nephews and nieces were all strangers to him, and he admitted to Charlie and Gray that he preferred it that way. He insisted that everyone in his family were freaks, which was precisely what they thought of him.

'How was Lake Mohonk?' he asked his mother. He had no idea why she still went there. His father had made a fortune in the stock market forty years before, and they could have afforded to go anywhere in the world. His mother liked to pretend they were still poor. And she hated planes, so they never ventured far.

'It was very nice,' she said, foraging for something else to spear him with. She usually used whatever he told her to clobber him. The trick was not to give her any information, other than what she read in the tabloids, which she purchased religiously, or what she saw on TV. Generally, she sent him clippings of the ugliest pictures of him, standing behind one of his clients being handcuffed and taken to jail. She always wrote little notes on what she sent, 'In case you missed this . . .' When they were particularly bad, she sent them in triplicate, mailed separately, with little notes on them that began, 'Did I forget to send you . . .'

'How're you feeling, Dad?' was usually Adam's next attempt at conversation, which always had the same response. He had been convinced as a boy that his father had been replaced by a robot left there by creatures from outer space. The robot they had left had a piece of defective machinery that made it difficult for it to speak. It was capable of it, but you had to kick the robot into action first, and then you realized the battery was dead. His father's standard answer to the question eventually was 'pretty good,' as he stared into his plate, never looked at you, and continued to eat. Removing himself mentally entirely, and refusing to enter into the conversation, had been the only way his father had survived fifty-seven years of marriage to his mother. Adam's brother Ben was turning fifty-five that winter, Sharon had just turned fifty, and Adam had been an accident nine years later, apparently one that was neither worth discussing, nor addressing, except when he did something wrong.

He couldn't remember his mother ever telling him she loved him, or wasting a kind word on him since he was born. He was, and had been even as a child, an embarrassment and an annoyance. The kindest thing they had ever done for him was ignore him. The worst was scold him, shun him, berate him, and spank him, all of which had been his mother's job when he was growing up, and she was still doing it now that he was in his forties. All she had eliminated over the years was the spankings.

'So who are you dating now, Adam?' his mother asked as Mae brought in the salad. He assumed that because he hadn't gone to synagogue, and had to be punished for it, she had brought the big guns out early this time. As a rule, she waited to level that one at him till after dessert, with coffee. He had learned long since that there was no correct answer. Telling her the truth, on that or any subject, would have brought the house down.

'No one. I've been busy,' he said vaguely.

'Apparently,' his mother said, as she walked swift and erect to the sideboard. She was slim and spare and in remarkably good shape although she was seventy-nine years old. His father was eighty, but going strong, physically at least.

She took a copy of the *Enquirer* out of the sideboard then, and passed it down the table, so everyone could see it. She hadn't sent him the clippings of that one yet. She'd apparently been saving it for the high holidays, so everyone could enjoy it, not just Adam. He saw that it was a photograph taken of him at Vana's concert. There was a girl standing next to him with her mouth wide open and her eyes closed, in a leather jacket, and her breasts exploding out of a black blouse. Her skirt was so short it looked like she had none on. 'Who is *that*?' his mother asked in a tone that suggested he was holding out on them. He stared at it for a minute, and had absolutely no recollection, and then he remembered. Maggie. The girl he'd gotten a seat on the stage for, and whom he had taken home to the tenement she lived in. He was tempted to tell his mother not to worry about it, since he hadn't slept with her, so obviously she didn't count.

'Just a girl I was standing next to at the concert,' he said vaguely.

'She wasn't your date?' She was torn between relief and disappointment. She'd have to choose another weapon.

'No. I went with Charlie.'

'Who?' She always pretended she didn't remember. To Adam, forgetting the names of his friends was just another form of rejection.

'Charles Harrington.' The one you always pretend you don't remember.

'Oh. *That* one. He must be gay. He's never been married.' Her point on that one. She was in control now. If you said he wasn't gay, she'd want to know how you knew, which could be incriminating. And if you threw caution to the winds and agreed with her, just to get the hot potato out of your lap, it would inevitably come back to haunt you later. He had tried it with other topics. It was best to say nothing. He smiled at Mae instead as she passed the rolls again, and she winked at him. She was his only ally, and always had been.

He felt like he'd been in hell for several hours by the time they got up from the table after dinner. The knot in his stomach was the size of his fist by then, as he watched them settle into the same chairs where they always sat, and had been sitting before dinner. He looked around the room then, and he realized he just couldn't do it. He went to stand close to his mother, in case she had an urge to hug him. It didn't happen often.

'I'm sorry, Mom. I have an incredible headache. It feels like a migraine. It's a long drive, I think I'd better go.' All he wanted to do was bolt for the door and run for his life.

She looked at him for a long moment with her lips pursed, and nodded. She had punished him adequately for not going to synagogue with them. He was free to go. He had done his duty, as whipping boy and scapegoat. It was a role she had assigned him for his entire life, since he had had the audacity to arrive in her life at a time when she thought she was finished having children. He had been an unexpected and unwelcome assault on her tea parties and bridge games, and had been soundly punished for it. Always.

And still was. He had been a major inconvenience to her, and never a source of joy. The others took their cues from her. At fourteen, Ben had been mortified to have his mother pregnant again. At nine, Sharon had been outraged by the intrusion on her life. His father had been playing golf, and unavailable for comment. And as their final revenge, he had been brought up by a nanny, and never saw them. As it turned out, the punishment that had been meted out to him had been a blessing. The woman who had taken care of him until he was ten had been loving and kind and good and the only decent person in his childhood. Until his tenth birthday, when she was summarily fired and not allowed to say good-bye. He still wondered sometimes what had happened to her, but as she hadn't been young then, he assumed that she was dead by now. For years, he had felt guilty for not trying to find her, or at least write her, to thank her for her kindness.

'If you didn't drink so much and go out with such loose women,' his mother pronounced, 'you wouldn't get migraines.' He wasn't sure what the loose women had to do with it, but he didn't ask her. He took her word for it, it was simpler.

'Thanks for a great dinner.' He had no idea what he'd eaten. Probably roast beef. He never looked at what he was eating in their house. He just got through it.

'Call me some time,' she said sternly. He nodded and resisted the urge to ask her why. It was another question no one could have answered. Why would he want to call her? He didn't, but called anyway, out of respect and habit, every week or so, and prayed that she'd be out so he could leave a message, preferably with his father, who barely managed to squeeze three words in between hello and good-bye, which were almost always 'I'll tell her.'

Adam said good-bye to each of them, then said good-bye to Mae in the kitchen, let himself out the front door, and slipped into the Ferrari with an enormous sigh.

'Holy fucking shit!' he said out loud. 'I hate those people.' After he said it out loud he felt better, and gunned the car. He was on the Long Island Expressway ten minutes later going well over the speed limit, but his stomach already felt better. He tried to call Charlie, just so he could hear the voice of a normal human being, but he was out, and he left an inane message on the machine. And as he drove home, he found himself thinking of Maggie. The picture of her in the *Enquirer* was awful. He remembered her looking better than that. In her own way, she was a cute girl. He thought about her for a few minutes and wondered if he should call her. Probably not, but he knew he needed to do something that night to restore his battered guts and ego. There were plenty of others he could call, and when he got home, he called them. Everyone was out. It was a Friday night, and all the women he knew would be out on dates with someone. All he needed was a little human touch, someone to smile at, talk to him, and hold him. He didn't even need to have sex with them, he just wanted someone to recognize the fact that he was a human being. Seeing his family took all the air out of him, it was like having his blood sucked out of him by vampires. Now he needed a transfusion.

Sitting in his apartment, Adam ran through his address book. He called seven women. All he got were their answering machines, and then he thought of Maggie. He figured she was probably working, but just for the hell of it, he decided to call her. It was after midnight by then, and maybe she was home. He fished into the leather jacket he'd worn that night, at Vana's concert, looking for the little scrap of paper where he'd written her number. He went through all the pockets, and then he found it. Maggie O'Malley. He dialed the number. He knew it was ridiculous to reach out to her, but he had to talk to someone. His mother drove him crazy. He hated his sister. He didn't even hate her. He disliked her, nearly as much as she disliked him. She had never done anything with her life except get married and have two children. He would have been happy talking to Gray or Charlie. But he knew Gray was with Sylvia, and it was too late to call. And he remembered that Charlie was gone for the weekend. So he called Maggie. He felt a rising wave of panic, as he always did when he went home, and now he really was getting a migraine. Somehow, just being with them, brought back the worst memories of his childhood. He let the phone ring a dozen times, and no one answered. A message machine finally came on with several girls' names on it, and he left his name and number for Maggie, wondering why he'd bothered. Like everyone else he knew, Maggie was out that night, and as soon as he set the receiver down, he knew it was stupid to have called her. She was a total stranger. He couldn't explain to her what seeing his family did to him, or how much pain his mother always caused him. Maggie was some silly girl he had dragged around with him that night, for lack of someone better. She was just a waitress. Seeing her in the clipping his mother had used to torture him had reminded him of her, and he was relieved now that she hadn't answered. He hadn't even slept with her, and the only reason he had kept her number was because he had forgotten to take it out of his jacket and toss it.

In spite of his mother's dire warnings about potential alcoholism, and telling him that even migraine headaches could result, he poured himself a drink before he went to bed, and lay there after he did, trying to recover from the strain of the evening on Long Island. He hated going home and seeing them. It was an exquisite form of torture. It always took him days to recover from it. What was the point of having him, if they were going to treat him like an outcast all his life? He lay in bed, thinking of them, as the headache his mother had warned him about began to pound. It took him nearly an hour after that to fall asleep.

An hour later, he was in a deep sleep when the telephone rang. He dreamed that it was monsters from outer space, trying to eat him alive, and making strange buzzing sounds while they did. And all the while, his mother stood laughing at him, waving newspapers in his face. He put the covers over his head, and dreamed that he was running screaming from them, until he realized it was the phone. He put the receiver to his ear, and was still more than half asleep when he answered.

'. . . llo . . .'

'Adam?' He didn't recognize the voice, and realized as he woke up that the headache was even worse than it had been when he went to bed.

'Who is this?' He didn't know, and no longer cared, as he rolled over in bed and started to go back to sleep.

'It's Maggie. You left a message on my machine.'

'Maggie who?' He was still too out of it to understand.

'Maggie O'Malley. You called me. Did I wake you up?'

'Yeah. You did.' His mind was a little clearer then, as he glanced at the alarm clock next to his bed. It was just after two. 'Why are you calling me at this hour?' As his head cleared, the headache did too. But he knew that if he talked to her, he would have trouble going back to sleep.

'I thought it was important. You called me at midnight. I just got home from work. I thought you'd still be up.'

'I'm not,' he said, lying in bed and thinking about her. His call to her must have sounded like a booty call to her at that hour. But calling him back at two A.M. was hardly any better. In fact, slightly worse. And now it was too late to see her anyway. He was half asleep.

'What were you calling me about?' She sounded curious, and somewhat ill at ease. She had liked meeting him, and was grateful for the seat he'd gotten her. But she was disappointed he hadn't called her afterward. When she mentioned it to them, her friends at the restaurant where she worked didn't think he would. They thought the fact that she hadn't slept with him might make him less interested. Maybe if she had, he might have felt some bond to her. Although the maître d' insisted it was just the reverse.

'I was just wondering if you were busy,' Adam said sleepily.

'At midnight?' She sounded shocked, and as he woke up and turned on the light, he was faintly embarrassed. Most of the women he knew would have hung up on him at that point, except those who were truly desperate. Maggie wasn't, and sounded insulted by his explanation. 'What was that, a booty call?' She had called it. Except in his case, it had been an antidote to the venom of his mother. Her particular brand was singularly potent, and he'd been hoping some sympathetic soul would provide the antivenom he needed. And if sexual favors were involved, that wouldn't hurt either. It was just slightly more awkward in Maggie's case, because he really didn't know her.

'No, it wasn't a booty call, I was just lonely. And I had a headache.' Even to his own ears, he sounded pathetic.

'You called me because you had a headache?'

'Yeah, sort of,' he said, sounding embarrassed. 'I had a shit evening with my parents on Long Island. It's Yom Kippur.' He guessed correctly that with a name like O'Malley, she wouldn't know beans about Yom Kippur. Most of his dates didn't.

'Well, Happy Yom Kippur,' she said a little tartly.

'Not exactly. It's the Day of Atonement,' he informed her.

'How come you didn't call me before this?' She was justifiably suspicious.

'I've been busy.' He was growing sorrier by the minute. The last thing he needed was to deal with this girl he had planned never to call, at two o'clock in the morning. It served him right, he realized, for calling her in the first place. So much for booty calls to strangers at midnight.

'Yeah, I've been busy too,' she said in her distinctly New York accent. 'Thanks for the seat anyway, and a nice evening. You weren't going to call me again, were you?' She sounded sad when she said it.

'Apparently I was, since I did call you. Two hours ago in fact,' he said, sounding irritated. He didn't owe her any explanations, and now his headache was coming back with a vengeance. Evenings on Long Island always did that. And Maggie wasn't helping, contrary to what he'd intended.

'No, you weren't going to call me. My girlfriends said you wouldn't.'

'You discussed this with them?' It was embarrassing to think about. Maybe the entire neighborhood had been polled about whether or not he'd call her.

'I just asked what they thought. Would you have called me if I slept with you?' she asked, curious, as

290

Adam groaned, closed his eyes again, and rolled over.

'For God's sake, what do I know? Maybe. Maybe not. Who knows? Depends if we liked each other.'

'To be honest, I'm not sure I like you. I thought I did the night I met you. Now I think you were just playing with me. Maybe you and Charlie thought I was funny.' She sounded insulted. With his limousine and the places he'd taken her to, it was obvious that he had money. Guys like him took advantage of girls like her all the time, and afterward they never called them. That's what her friends had said, and when he didn't call, she decided they were right. She was even happier now that she hadn't slept with him, although she'd thought about it and decided against it. She didn't know him. And she wasn't willing to trade a seat on the stage for her body.

'Charlie thought you were very nice,' Adam lied to her. He had no idea what Charlie had thought. He couldn't remember. Neither of them had ever mentioned her again. She was just someone who had quickly crossed their radar screen one night, and vanished, never to be seen again. She was right. He wasn't going to call her. Until the nightmare on Long Island, and no one else answered. He'd been desperate for human contact. And now he was getting more than he wanted.

'And what about you, Adam? Did you think I was nice too?' She was pushing. He opened his eyes again, and stared at the ceiling, wondering why he was talking to her. It was all his mother's fault. He had had just enough to drink to believe that most things in his life were his mother's fault. The rest were Rachel's.

'Look, why are we doing this? I don't know you. You don't know me. We're strangers. I have a headache, a big one, my stomach hurts. My mother thinks I'm an alcoholic. Maybe I am. I don't think so. But whatever I am, I feel like shit. I was born into the family from hell, and I just spent an evening with them. That's nothing to mess around with. I'm pissed off. I hate my parents, and they don't like me either. I don't know why I called you, but I did. You weren't home. Why don't we just let it go at that? Just pretend you never got the message. Maybe it was a booty call. I don't know why the hell I called you, except that I feel like shit. And I always feel like shit after I see my mother.' He was getting seriously worked up over it, as Maggie listened quietly at her end.

'I'm sorry, Adam. I didn't have such great parents either. My father died when I was three. And my mother was an alcoholic. I haven't seen her since I was seven.'

'So who did you grow up with?' He had no idea

why he was pursuing the conversation, but he was curious about her.

'I grew up with an aunt until I was fourteen. Then she died, and I was in foster care till I graduated from high school. Actually, I didn't really graduate. I got my GED at sixteen. I've been on my own ever since.' She said it matter-of-factly, and seemed to have no need for pity.

'Jesus. That sounds like a bunch of bad breaks.' But a lot of the women he knew had histories like that. The kind of women he went out with had rarely had easy lives, most of them had been molested by male relatives, left home at sixteen, and had gone to work as actresses and models. There were few women he knew who had had normal lives, or were debutantes like the ones who went out with Charlie. Maggie was no different. She just sounded more philosophical about it, and she didn't sound as though she expected him to do anything about it. She didn't expect him to pay for implants for her, in order to make up for the fact that her mother had been a hooker, or she'd been molested by her father. Whatever had happened to her, she sounded as though she'd made her peace with it. If anything, she sounded sympathetic to Adam.

'Do you have any family at all?' He was intrigued.

'Nope. It kind of sucks on holidays, but I see my foster parents once in a while.'

'Believe me,' Adam said cynically, 'not having a family is a blessing. You wouldn't have wanted to have one like mine.' Maggie wasn't sure she agreed with him, but she wasn't about to debate it with him at two-thirty in the morning. They had been chatting aimlessly for half an hour. And she still believed his call to her had been a booty call, which she thought was just plain rude and downright insulting. She wondered how many other women he had called, and if he would have bothered to call her at all, if one of the others had come to his aid. Apparently, they hadn't, since he was obviously alone, and had been sleeping soundly when she called him.

'Most of the time, I think I'd like to have a family, even a bad one.' And then she thought of something. She was wide awake, despite the hour, and by now so was he. 'Do you have brothers and sisters?'

'Maggie, could we talk about this some other time? I'll call you tomorrow. I'll give you my entire family history. I promise.' And with that, she heard a crashing sound, he groaned, and shouted a single word: 'Shit!' He sounded like he'd gotten hurt.

'What happened?' She sounded worried.

'I just got out of bed and stubbed my toe on the night table, and the alarm clock fell on my foot. Now I'm not only tired and upset, I'm injured.' He sounded like a five-year-old about to burst into tears, and she repressed a giggle.

'You're a mess. Maybe you should go back to sleep.'

'No kidding. I've been suggesting that for the past half hour.'

'Don't be rude,' she chided him. 'You know, sometimes you're very rude.'

'Now you sound like my mother. She always says things like that to me. Just how polite is it to send me tabloid clippings of me looking like shit, or when my clients go to jail? How rude is it to call me an alcoholic and tell how much she loves my ex-wife, although she cheated on me and dumped me, and then married someone else?' He was getting worked up again, as he got back in bed, and Maggie listened.

'That's not rude. It's mean. She says stuff like that to you?' Maggie sounded surprised, and sympathetic yet again. Although he was nearly yelling at her, he realized she was a sweet person. He had realized it the night they met. He just didn't have room in his life for someone like her. He wanted sex, glamour, and excitement. She was none of the above, although her figure was fantastic. But since she hadn't been willing to share her body with him, he had no way of knowing just how much fun it was. She had made him some silly speech about not

295

doing things like that on a first date. And if so, with Adam, there would be no second. And now she was talking to him at nearly three A.M., and listening to him complain about his mother. She didn't even seem to mind, although his call to her had clearly been a booty call. She disapproved of that, and told him so, but she still hadn't hung up. 'You shouldn't let her say things like that to you, Adam,' she said gently. Her mother had been mean to her too, and then one night, without saying good-bye, she was gone.

'Why do you think I have a headache?' Adam said, almost shouting again. 'Because I bottle it all up inside.' He realized he sounded like a nutcase, and felt like one. This was phone therapy, without sex. It was the weirdest conversation he'd ever had. He was almost sorry he'd answered the phone, and yet not. He liked talking to Maggie.

'You shouldn't bottle up your feelings. Maybe you should talk to her sometime, and just tell her how you feel.' Adam lay in bed and rolled his eyes. She was a little simplistic in her point of view, but she was not without compassion. But she also didn't know his mother. Lucky for her. 'What did you take for your headache?'

'Vodka and red wine at my mother's house. And a shot of tequila when I got home.'

'That's really bad for you. Did you take aspirin?'

'Of course not, and believe me, brandy and champagne are worse.'

'I think you should take aspirin or a Tylenol or something.'

'I don't have any,' he said, lying in bed and feeling sorry for himself. But in a weird way, it was nice talking to her. She really was a nice person. If she weren't, she wouldn't have been listening to him complain about his parents, and tell her all his woes.

'How come you don't have Tylenol in the house?' And then she thought of something. 'Are you a Christian Scientist?' She had known one once. He never took any medicine, or went to the doctor. He just prayed. It seemed strange to her, but it worked for him.

'No, of course not. Remember. Tonight is Yom Kippur. I'm Jewish. That's what started this whole mess. That's why I had dinner with my parents. Yom Kippur. And I don't have aspirin in the house because I'm not married. Married people have things like that. Wives buy all that stuff. My secretary buys me aspirin at the office. I always forget to buy any for here.'

'You should go out and buy some tomorrow, before you forget again.' She had a childlike voice, but it was soothing to listen to. In the end, she had given him just what he needed. Sympathy, and someone to talk to.

'I should get some sleep,' he reminded her. 'And so should you. I'll call you tomorrow. And this time I really will.' If nothing else, to thank her.

'No, you won't,' she said sadly. 'I'm not fancy enough for you, Adam. I saw the kind of places you went that night. You probably go out with some pretty jazzy women.' And she was only a waitress from Pier 92. It had been an accident of fate that they had met at all, and yet another that he had left a message on her machine that night. Accident number three: she had called him back, and woken him up.

'You're sounding like my mother again. That's the kind of thing she says. She doesn't approve. She thinks I should have found another nice Jewish girl years ago, and remarried. And now that you mention it, the women I go out with are no fancier than you.' Their clothes were a little more expensive maybe, but whenever that was the case, they had been paid for by someone else. In many ways, although his mother wouldn't have agreed with him, Maggie was more respectable than they were.

'Then how come you never remarried?'

'I don't want to. I got burned once, badly in fact. My ex-wife turned out to be just like my mother. And I have no desire to try the experiment again.'

'Do you have kids?' She had never asked him the

night they met, there had been too much going on. She hadn't had time.

'Yes. Amanda and Jacob, respectively fourteen and thirteen.' He smiled as he said it, and Maggie could hear it in his voice.

'Where did you go to college?'

'I can't believe this,' he said, amazed at himself that he was continuing to answer her questions. It was addictive. 'Harvard. Undergraduate and law school. I graduated from law school magna cum laude.' It was a pompous thing to say to her, but what the hell, he couldn't see her anyway, and anything they said on the phone was fair game.

'I knew it,' she said, sounding excited. 'I just knew it. I knew you'd gone to Harvard! And you're a genius!' For once, the appropriate reaction. He lay in bed and grinned. 'That's amazing!'

'No, it's not,' he said more modestly this time. 'A lot of people do it. In fact, much as I hate to admit it to you, Rachel the Horrible graduated summa cum laude and passed the bar on the first try. I didn't.' He was confessing all his weaknesses and sins.

'Who cares, if she was a bitch?'

'That's a nice thing to say.' He sounded pleased. Without even intending to, he had found an ally.

'I'm sorry. I shouldn't say that about your children's mother.'

299

'Yes, you should. I say it all the time. She is. I hate her. Well,' he corrected himself, 'I don't hate her, I dislike her strongly.' It was a religious holiday after all. But Maggie was Catholic presumably. She could say it. 'You're Catholic, aren't you, by the way?'

'I used to be. I'm not much of anything these days. I go to church and light candles sometimes, but that's about it. I guess I'm nothing. When I was a kid, I wanted to be a nun.'

'That would have been a terrible waste of a beautiful face and a great body. Thank God you didn't.' He sounded as though he meant it.

'Thank you, Adam. That was a nice thing to say. I really think you should go to bed now, or you're going to have a worse headache tomorrow.' He hadn't thought about it for the past half hour, while talking to her, but he realized suddenly, as he glanced at the clock, that his headache had gone away. It was four A.M.

'What about breakfast tomorrow? What time do you get up?'

'Usually around nine o'clock. Tomorrow I was going to sleep in. I have the day off from work.'

'Me too. On both counts. I'll pick you up at noon. I'll take you somewhere nice for brunch.'

'How nice?' She sounded worried. Most of what she wore belonged to her roommates. None of what she had had on the night they met had belonged to her, which was why the blouse was so tight. She had the biggest boobs in the house, but she said none of that to Adam. And he had guessed what she was worried about. A lot of the girls he went out with were in the same boat.

'How about blue jeans nice, or denim skirt nice? Or shorts nice?' He was trying to give her options.

'Denim skirt nice sounds good.' She sounded relieved.

'Perfect. I'll wear one too.' They both laughed, and he jotted down her address again, on the pad he kept next to his bed. Usually, when he wrote something down in the middle of the night, it was because one of his clients had been arrested. This had been a lot more fun. 'Thanks, Maggie. I had a nice time tonight.' Nicer possibly than if he'd seen her. This way he had actually talked to her, it hadn't been about trying to seduce her, and he wasn't at all sure that brunch the next day would be about seducing her either. Maybe they would just wind up friends. They were off to a good start.

'I had a nice time, too. I'm glad you called me, even if it was a booty call,' she teased him.

'It was *not* a booty call,' he insisted, but she wasn't convinced, and neither was he. It had been a booty call, but came to a much better end. And his headache was gone too.

'Yeah, right.' Maggie hooted at him. 'It was too.

Anything after ten o'clock is a booty call, and you know it.'

'Who made up those rules?'

'I did,' she said, laughing into the phone.

'Get some sleep. If you don't, you'll look like hell tomorrow. No, I guess you won't. You're too young to look like hell, but I will.'

'No, you won't,' she said practically. 'I think you're very handsome.'

'Goodnight, Maggie,' he said quietly. 'You'll recognize me by the fat head I'll still have tomorrow.' Between her comments about Harvard and his good looks, he had begun to really like her. She made him feel like a million dollars, with or without a headache. It had been a nice end to a terrible evening. She had made it up to him for all the abuse he always endured on Long Island. 'See you tomorrow.'

'Night night,' she said softly, and hung up. And as she got into bed and crawled under the blanket, she wondered if he'd actually show up. Guys did things like that. They made promises and then broke them. She decided to get dressed and wait for him anyway, just in case. But even if he didn't show up the next day, it had been nice talking to him. He really was a nice guy, and she liked him.

13

Maggie was sitting on the couch in the living room waiting for him the next day. It was nearly noon, and it was a gorgeous day. The first Saturday in October. She was wearing a denim miniskirt, a tight pink T-shirt she had borrowed from one of her roommates, and gold sandals. She had pulled her long hair straight back this time, and had tied a pink scarf around it in a long ponytail that made her look even younger than she was. This time, she had worn very little makeup. She had gotten the feeling that he thought she was wearing too much the night they met.

The next time she looked at her watch, it was five after twelve and he hadn't shown up yet. Everyone else in the apartment had gone out, and she was beginning to wonder if he really was going to come. Maybe not. She decided to give it till one, and if he didn't, she was going to go for a walk in the park. There was no point being depressed if it didn't happen. She hadn't told anyone, so no one was going to laugh at her if he stood her up. She was thinking about it when the phone rang. It was Adam, and she smiled the minute she heard his voice. Then just as quickly, she wondered if he was calling to cancel. It seemed weird that he was calling her, and not downstairs ringing the bell.

'Hi, how are you?' She tried to sound casual, so he wouldn't think she was too disappointed. 'How's your headache?'

'What headache? I forgot, what number is your apartment?'

'Where are you?' She was stunned. He was coming after all. Better late than never, and it was only twelve-ten.

'I'm downstairs.' He was calling from his cell phone. 'Come on down. I made a reservation for lunch.'

'I'll be right down.' She hung up and bounded down the stairs, before he could disappear or change his mind. It was rare in her life, and always had been, for people to actually do what they said. And he had.

She walked out her front door, and he was sitting there looking like a movie star in his brand-new red Ferrari. It was the one he had driven to Long Island the night before, which his entire family had politely ignored. His parents drove matching Mercedes, as did his sister-in-law and brother, his brother-in-law drove a BMW, and his sister didn't drive at all. She expected other people to turn their lives upside down, stop whatever they were doing, and drive her. As far as they were concerned, a Ferrari was so beyond the pale and so vulgar as to not even be worth discussing. But Adam loved it.

'Oh my God! Look at that car!' Maggie was standing there, looking at him, and jumping up and down on the sidewalk. Adam grinned while he watched her, and then opened the door and told her to get in. She had never seen anything like it, except in movies, and she was riding in it with him. She couldn't believe it. She wished that someone she knew could see them driving by. 'Is this yours?' she asked him excitedly.

'No. I stole it.' He laughed at her. 'Of course it's mine. Hell, let's face it, I went to Harvard.' They both laughed, and then she handed him a small package. 'What's that?'

'A present for you. I went to the grocery store and got it for you this morning.' She had bought him a bottle of Tylenol in case he got another headache.

'That was nice of you,' he said, smiling at her. 'I'll save it for the next time I see my mother.'

Adam drove through Central Park. It was a beautiful afternoon. He stopped on Third Avenue at a restaurant that had a sidewalk café and a garden. He ordered eggs Benedict for both of them, after she assured him that she liked them. She had never had them before, but they sounded good to her when he described them. Afterward, they sat at their table in the garden and drank wine, and when they finally left the restaurant, they went for a walk. She loved looking in the shop windows with him, and talking about the people he represented. He talked about his children, the demise of his marriage, and what an agony it had been for him, and then he talked about his two best friends, Charlie and Gray. By the end of the afternoon, she felt as though she knew everything about him, and she had cautiously told him some things about herself.

Maggie was more reserved than he was, and she seemed to prefer talking about him. She told him little anecdotes about her childhood, her foster parents, the people where she worked. But it was obvious to both of them, and always had been, that her life was a lot less exciting than his. Most of the time, all she did was eat, sleep, go to movies, and work. She didn't seem to have a lot of friends. She said she didn't have time to spend with them. She worked long hours at Pier 92, and she was vague when he asked what else she did with her time. She smiled and said, 'Just work.' He was surprised at how easy it was being with her. She was nice to talk to, and although she'd led a simple life, she seemed wise in the ways of the world. She'd seen a lot, some of it none too pleasant, for a woman of twenty-six. She looked younger than she was, but she was a lot older in her head. Older even than Adam in some ways.

They got back in his car at six o'clock, and she was thinking to herself that she hated to see the day end. It was almost as though he read her mind. He turned to her with a hopeful expression. 'How about if I barbecue some steaks for us on my terrace? How does that sound to you, Maggie?'

'Extremely good,' she said, beaming at him. He said he had some in the fridge.

She had only seen buildings like the one he lived in in movies. The doorman greeted them on the way in, and smiled at her. She was a pretty woman, and people looked at her everywhere they went. Adam pressed the elevator button marked Penthouse, and as soon as he let her into the apartment, she stood there in silence, staring at the view.

'Oh my God,' she said, just as she had about the Ferrari. 'Just look at that.' He was on the thirty-second floor, and he had a wraparound terrace complete with hot tub, deck chairs, and barbecue. 'This *is* a movie,' she said, staring at him, dumbfounded. 'How did this happen to me?'

'Just lucky, I guess.' He teased her. The thing that made him sad for her, now that he knew her better, was that it hadn't happened to her. It had happened to him. After dinner, she would have to go back to the miserable tenement where she lived. He hated the realities of her life, for her sake. She deserved so much more than fate had dished out to her. Some things really weren't fair. All he could do was give her a pleasant evening, feed her well, spend some time together, and send Maggie back to her own world. Nothing he did would change the stark realities for her, but the funny thing was, she didn't seem to mind. She didn't have a jealous bone in her body, and whatever facet of his life she saw or heard about, she was happy for him.

Maggie was a totally different kind of woman from anyone he had ever met before. She looked like all the others, but absolutely nothing about her was the same. She was kind and gentle and funny, and everything about her was real. She was smart, and enjoyed sparring with him. And much to his delight, she thought he walked on water. The other women he went out with all wanted to use him. They wanted wardrobes, jewelry, charge cards, apartments, new cars, plastic surgery, and introductions for jobs or parts in movies. All the women he knew appeared to have multiple agendas. Maggie seemed as though all she wanted was to be with him and share a good time. There was an irresistible quality of innocence about her in contrast to all the women who had crossed his path in the past several years.

She made a big salad while he got the steaks out of the fridge and lit the barbecue. The steaks were huge and made an enormous meal, and afterward, they ate ice cream in cones on the terrace and dripped it all over themselves while they laughed at each other. Maggie had strawberry ice cream all over her feet, but didn't seem to care.

'Here,' Adam said helpfully, 'stick them in the hot tub. No one will ever know.' He pulled the lid off for her, and the water was bubbling and warm. It was big enough for at least a dozen people, and she sat on the edge, stuck her feet in, and giggled.

'You must give a lot of wild parties,' Maggie said, looking at him, as she sat on the edge of the hot tub in her denim skirt and pink T-shirt. She looked more than ever like a little kid.

'What makes you say that?' he answered non-committally. He never liked talking about the other women in his life, and he thought Maggie was about to ask him about that.

'Look at this setup,' she said, glancing around and then back at him. 'Hot tub, penthouse, terrace, barbecue, great apartment, killer view. Hell, if I lived in a place like this, I'd have friends over all the time.' She hadn't gone at all in the direction he expected.

'Sometimes I do,' he said honestly. 'Sometimes I like being here by myself. I work hard, sometimes it's nice to just chill out.' She nodded. When she got home from work at night, she felt that way too. And then he added with a gentle look, 'I'm having a good time being here with you.'

'Me too,' she said simply, watching him from where she sat. 'How come you don't want to get remarried?'

'How do you know that?' He looked puzzled.

'You said it on the phone last night,' she explained, and he nodded. He had been so sleepy much of the time that he had forgotten a lot of what he'd said. All he remembered was how nice it had been to talk to Maggie. 'Don't you want more kids? You're young enough to have them.' It was the kind of exploration most women made with him, and never liked the answers they got. But he was always honest with them. He believed in truth in advertising, whether or not the women chose to believe him. Most of them didn't. He just became a bigger challenge once he told them the truth.

'I like the two I've got. I don't need to get married. I don't want more kids. And marriage wasn't such a great experience for me. I have a lot more fun being single than I ever did being married.'

'I'll bet you do,' Maggie said, laughing at him.

'So would any guy with all the toys you've got.' She was the first woman who had ever acknowledged that to him. Most of them tried to convince him that marriage would be better. Maggie didn't. She seemed to think he was right.

'That's kind of how I see it,' he agreed with her. 'Why give up all this for one woman who could disappoint you and make you unhappy?' Maggie nodded. He couldn't even imagine one who would not disappoint him and might make him happy. That seemed sad to her.

'Do you have a lot of girlfriends?' She suspected he did. He looked like the kind of man who would. If nothing else, the Ferrari said he was a pretty racy guy.

'Sometimes,' he said honestly again. 'I don't like to be tied down. My freedom means a lot to me.' She nodded. She liked the fact that he didn't try to hide who he was. It was all open and easy to see. 'Sometimes I don't go out with anyone for a while.'

'And now?' she asked with a look of mischief. 'Lots, or none at all, or just a few?'

He smiled at her from where he sat. 'Are we filling out a questionnaire again?' She had asked him a lot of questions the night before too. It seemed to be her style. 'I'm not seeing anyone particular right now.'

'Are you auditioning?' she teased, looking more

womanly than she had before. She was a beautiful girl. In broad daylight, he could see it more clearly than he had the night they met.

'Are you applying for the job?'

'Maybe,' she said honestly. 'I'm not sure.'

'What about you?' he asked her quietly. 'Are you seeing someone?'

'Nope. I haven't dated anyone in a year. The last guy I went out with turned out to be a drug dealer and wound up in jail. He seemed like a real nice guy for a while. I met him at Pier 92.'

'I'm not dealing drugs, if you're worried about that,' he reassured her. 'Everything you see, I made from the sweat of my brow.'

'I wasn't worried about that with you.' He got up then, and went to put some music on. The evening seemed to be taking a romantic turn. When he came back, she asked him another question, one that was important to her. 'What if we go out with each other one day? Would you be going out with other women at the same time?'

'I might. I won't put you at risk, if that's what you're worried about. I'm careful and I had an AIDS test recently.'

'So did I,' Maggie said matter-of-factly. She'd had it after the drug dealer went to jail.

'If you're asking if I would promise to be totally exclusive to you, Maggie, probably not. At least not at first. Where it goes after that, who knows? I like keeping my options open, and at your age, so should you.' She nodded. She didn't love what she was hearing, but it made sense to her too, and at least he was honest. He wasn't going to make promises and then cheat on her. But he was going to see other people. And so could she. 'Even if we were dating, I like having separate lives. I've been single for a long time, nearly eleven years, and as far as I know, it's going to stay that way. I don't want to get all tangled up in someone else's life.'

'I still think you're wrong on that one,' she said easily, 'about getting remarried, but that's up to you. I don't want to get married for a long time either. I'm too young. There's a lot I still want to do, at least for the next few years. But one day I'd like to get married and have kids.'

'You should.'

'I want to give my kids everything I never had. Like a mother for instance,' she said quietly.

'I never had one either,' he said, as he walked over to where she was sitting at the edge of the hot tub, dangling her feet in like a kid. 'Not all mothers really are. Mine sure wasn't. I came along as a surprise nearly ten years after my sister, and fourteen after my brother, and everyone was pissed off all my life. They never should have had me.'

'I'm glad they did,' she said softly as he stood

next to her. 'I would have been really sad if they didn't.' She smiled up at him.

'Thank you,' he said softly, and then leaned down and kissed her. And then he suggested they take a hot tub together. He had a brand-new bathing suit for her to wear, in exactly the right size. He had a stack of them in the closet, and told her to pick one she liked. It really was the perfect, fully equipped bachelor pad. If he hadn't been as honest with her, it would have bothered her, but since he had, there were no hidden agendas and no secrets between them.

She put on the bathing suit and got into the hot tub, and a minute later he came out in his bathing suit and got in with her. They sat there talking and kissing for a long time, and then they took their bathing suits off, as night fell over New York, on a warm October night. They lay together side by side for a long time, and then he wrapped her in a towel and carried her inside. He laid her on his bed, and then unwrapped her like a gift. She looked exquisite as she lay there on his bed. He had never seen a body as beautiful as that in his life. He had even been startled to realize she was a natural blonde. There was nothing fake about Maggie O'Malley. Every inch of her was real.

He made love to her, and they were both surprised at how perfectly they fit, how much they enjoyed each other, and even laughed or said something silly from time to time. She was totally comfortable with him. Afterward, they lay side by side on his bed, and then went back to the hot tub again. She said it was the best night of her life, which was easy to believe. She'd had such a hard life until then, and still did. It was more than a little surreal for her, knowing that she would be going back to her tenement and her job, that nothing in her existence would change, but in her moments with him, she shared a life she had never even imagined before. He knew it was going to be interesting and challenging for her, if they continued seeing each other, while she went back and forth between two worlds.

They made love again one more time before she left. And this time, they were totally spontaneous, and their passion caught them by surprise.

He invited her to spend the night. Although ordinarily he didn't do that, he wanted to with her. He hated to send her back to the nightmare where she lived. But they were both going to have to get used to that, she to going back, and he to letting her. He wasn't offering her permanence, just respites from the life she led, and Maggie said that was good enough for her. But she still thought it was better for her to go back to her own place that night.

He insisted on driving her back to her

apartment. He didn't want her taking a cab. It was too dangerous where she lived. She had been good to him, he wanted to be good to her. She felt like Cinderella again on the drive home, even more so this time, because the Ferrari was his, and not a rented limousine.

'I won't ask you to come up,' she said as he kissed her.

'You probably have a husband and ten kids you're hiding from me,' he whispered, teasing her, and she laughed.

'Only five.'

'I had a wonderful time with you,' he said, and meant it.

'So did I,' she said as she kissed him again.

'I'll call you tomorrow,' he promised, and she laughed.

'Yeah . . . sure . . .' She got out of the Ferrari then, ran up the steps, let herself into the building, waved, and as she disappeared into the building and remembered his last words to her, she hoped he would, but she wasn't counting on it. Maggie knew better than anyone that nothing in life was sure.

14

Adam called Maggie often the week after Yom Kippur. She spent the night with him several times. She had just been moved to the day shift at Pier 92, so her schedule worked well for him. And she loved sleeping with him at night. Everything seemed perfect with them, and they both stuck to their deal. She asked him no questions about the future, she had no reason to, and on the nights she spent at home, neither of them asked the other who'd they'd seen or what they'd been doing when they saw each other again.

In fact, Adam was so taken with her that on the nights he didn't see her, he called her anyway, usually late before he went to bed. On two occasions he was surprised and slightly upset to discover that she was out. But he didn't tell her he'd called, and left no message on the machine. She never said anything about having been out when he saw her again. But he admitted to himself privately that not finding her at home, waiting for his call, had bothered him. But he never said a word about it to her. They both continued to claim and reap the benefits of their freedom. Adam wasn't sleeping with anyone else during the early weeks of their relationship, he didn't want to, he was becoming increasingly addicted to her. And she told him openly that there was no one else for her. But as the weeks went by, there were nights when he called, that no one was home. He found as time went by, he hated that more and more. It made him think that he should start seeing other women one of these days, just so as not to get too attached to her. But as Halloween approached, he hadn't done anything about it. He was still being totally exclusive to her, after a month. It was the first time he had done that in years.

Adam was mildly bothered that he and Charlie hadn't seen much of each other since Charlie had gotten back a month before. But every time he called and invited him somewhere, Charlie was busy these days. Adam knew he had a heavy social schedule, and a lot of work to do for the foundation, but it irked him that they hadn't had time to get together. The good news was that it gave him more time to spend with Maggie. He was getting increasingly antsy about her, and worried about what she did when he wasn't around. As time went on, there were still a number of nights they didn't spend together, when she just wasn't home. And she never told him where she'd gone. She just re-appeared bright and cheerful the next day, fell back into bed with him, happy as can be, with her utterly irresistible body. He was crazier about her every day. Without even knowing it, she was beating him at his own game. All the options he had so grandly told her he wanted in the beginning meant less to him every day. Judging by the number of times she was out when he called her late at night, she seemed to be taking advantage of her freedom more than he.

And Adam had seen even less of Gray. He had talked to him several times, but Gray was enjoying his blissful domestic scene with Sylvia and didn't want to go anywhere. Adam finally sent e-mails to both of them, and got Gray and Charlie to agree to a boys' night out, two days before Halloween. It had been over a month since any of them had seen each other. It was the first time in years it had been that long, and all three complained that the others had disappeared.

They met at a steak restaurant downtown, which was one of their favorite haunts, and Adam got there first. The other two walked in just behind him, and he could see that Gray had put on weight. Not a lot, but just enough to look fuller in the face. He said that he and Sylvia were cooking together a lot, and he looked happier than ever. They had been dating for two months, and known each other for three. As far as he was concerned, he said there were no red flags yet. His two cohorts were happy for him, but thought it was still early days. Gray said they never argued, and were happy with each other. He no longer stayed at his studio, but spent every night with her. But he still insisted that he wasn't living with her officially. Just 'staying' with her. The semantics seemed like splitting hairs to Adam and Charlie, but apparently it made Gray feel better than saying they were living together.

'What about you?' Adam questioned Charlie somewhat querulously. 'Where the hell have you been all month?'

'I've been out a lot,' Charlie said cryptically, as Gray grinned. Charlie had admitted to him a few days before that he had taken his advice and was seeing Carole Parker. Nothing major had happened yet, but they were having dinner a lot, and getting to know each other. They were seeing each other several times a week, but so far he hadn't even kissed her. They were moving slowly, and Charlie readily admitted that they were both scared to death of getting hurt.

Adam had seen the conspiratorial look on Gray's face, and forced Charlie to tell him too.

'Christ, you two, what's happening to you?

Gray's practically living with Sylvia, or *is* living with her, but doesn't want to admit it to himself, and you sound like you're about to go over the hill too. Talk about traitors to the bachelors' code of ethics.' He complained good-naturedly, but he was happy for both his friends. They had both wanted to find someone, and were long overdue. He wasn't as sure about himself. His relationship with Maggie seemed to be steadily on track, but was destined to go nowhere, as they had agreed from the first. They were just dating and maintaining separate lives and doing whatever they wanted whenever they weren't together. But when they were, she was one hot mama, and he loved being with her. He could never seem to get enough of her, and was occasionally even irritated by her independent spirit. That had never happened to him before. He was always the independent one in his relationships, but Maggie was more so. She seemed to need a lot of time to herself, which he always wanted too, but not with her.

'What about you?' Charlie asked Adam pointedly over dessert. 'You've been awfully quiet about what you've been up to. Seeing anyone? Or just the lucky hundred, as usual?' Adam went out with more women than Charlie had ever counted. Preferably at the same time.

'I've been seeing someone for about a month,'

Adam said casually. 'It's no big deal. We agreed not to get serious. She knows I don't want to get married.'

'What about her? Is her clock ticking yet?' Charlie asked with interest, and Adam shook his head.

'She's too young to have a clock. That's the advantage of young ones.'

'Oh, Jesus,' Gray said, rolling his eyes, 'tell me she's not fourteen. You're going to wind up in jail one of these days if you don't watch out.' They loved teasing him about the young women he went out with. Adam always said it was mostly envy on their part.

'Relax, guys, she's twenty-six, and a really nice person, with a totally great body.' And a great mind, which he didn't bother to list, or they'd know he had totally lost it, which he was beginning to fear he had. When he was falling in love with a woman's mind, he knew he was in deep shit. In truth, they all were, but none of them were ready to admit it to each other, or themselves. And none of their relationships had stood the test of time yet. They hadn't survived first arguments, or the ordinary disappointments that happened to everyone. They were still up to their ears in the novelty and the fun. What happened after that remained to be seen.

The three men sat around until after midnight,

talking and drinking and enjoying one another's company. They had missed each other in the past month, and hadn't even known it. They were so busy doing other things, and spending time with the women they were involved with, that they hadn't realized how vital a part of each other's lives they were, and how vast a void it left when they didn't see each other. They promised to get together more often. And in the meantime they reveled in talking politics, money, investments, art, in honor of Gray's new gallery thanks to Sylvia, and their respective occupations. Adam had added two new major clients, and Charlie was pleased with the progress at the foundation. They left the restaurant reluctantly, and were the last to leave.

'Let's make each other a promise,' Gray said before they got into cabs and dispersed in different directions. 'No matter what happens with the women we're seeing, or others who might come after them, let's see each other whenever we can, or at least talk on the phone. I've missed you two. I love Sylvia, and I love *staying* with her' – he looked at them both with a grin – 'but I love you too.'

'Amen,' Charlie seconded the motion.

'Damn right,' Adam agreed.

A moment later, they got into separate cabs, and went back to their own lives and women. Adam called Maggie when he got home, even though it was late, and this time he was furious to find that she was out. It was nearly one o'clock in the morning. What the hell was she doing? And with who?

Two days later, Charlie went to the Halloween party Carole had organized for the children at the center. She had asked him to come in costume, and he had promised to bring cupcakes for the kids. He loved visiting her there. He had taken her to lunch twice, once to Mo's and once to Sally's, but most of the time he saw her for dinner after work. It was more relaxing, and seemed more discreet. Neither of them wanted to get tongues wagging. They still hadn't decided whether what they were doing was friendship or romance, it was a little of both, and until they figured it out, they didn't want the pressure of other people knowing. Adam and Gray were the only people Charlie had told, and he didn't even tell Carole he had when he spoke to her the next morning. He just told her he'd had a great time with his friends, and she said that she was glad. She hadn't met either of them yet, but from everything Charlie said, she knew they were both interesting, worthwhile men to whom he was not only loyal, but deeply attached. He said both men had been like brothers to him, and she respected that. For

Charlie, with no blood relations left in the world, his friends had become family to him.

The children looked adorable in their costumes at the Halloween party. Gabby was dressed as Wonder Woman, and Zorro was wearing a T-shirt with an S on it, and she said he was Super Dog. There were Raggedy Anns and Minnie Mouses, Ninja Turtles and Spider-Man, and a veritable coven of witches and ghosts. Carole was wearing a tall, pointed black hat and a green wig, a black turtleneck, and black jeans. She said she had to move around too much with the kids to wear a more elaborate costume. But she had painted her face green, and had worn black lipstick. She was actually wearing makeup these days when they went out at night. Charlie had noticed it immediately, and complimented her, when they went on their first official dinner date. She had actually blushed when he noticed, and said she felt silly, but she kept wearing it anyway.

Charlie had come to the Halloween party as the Cowardly Lion in *The Wizard of Oz*. His secretary had gotten the costume for him at a theatrical costume shop.

The kids all had a terrific time, the cupcakes were a big success, and he had brought a ton of Halloween candy for them, since they couldn't go trick-or-treating in the neighborhood. It was too dangerous, and most of them were too young. It was nearly eight o'clock by the time Carole and Charlie left. They had talked about going to dinner afterward, but they were both exhausted, and had eaten too much candy themselves. Charlie had eaten a handful of Snickers bars, and Carole had an irresistible weakness for the chocolate pumpkins with marshmallows inside.

'I'd invite you to my place,' she said cautiously, 'but it's a total mess. I've been out all week.' They had had dinner together almost every night, except the night when he'd had dinner with Adam and Gray.

'Do you want to come to my apartment for a drink?' he asked comfortably. She hadn't been there yet. He always took her out, they had been to a number of restaurants they both liked, and some they didn't.

'I'd like that' – she smiled at him – 'but I won't stay long. I'm beat.'

'Me too,' he agreed.

The cab sped down Fifth Avenue, and stopped at his address. He got out wearing his lion suit, and she with her green wig and green face, and the doorman smiled and greeted them as though he were wearing a business suit and she an evening dress. They rode up in the elevator in silence, smiling at each other. And when he opened the door to the apartment, he flipped on the lights and walked in. She followed him in cautiously, and looked around. It was a beautiful, elegant place. There were handsome antiques everywhere, most of which he had inherited, and some of which he had bought over the years. Carole walked slowly across the living room, and admired the view of the park.

'This is wonderful, Charlie.'

'Thank you.' It was a handsome apartment, without question, but recently, he had found it depressing. Everything seemed so tired and old to him, and the place was always so deadly silent whenever he came home. It was odd, but lately he'd been happier on his boat. Except for the time he spent with her.

Carole stopped and looked at a table full of photographs, while he went to get them a glass of wine, and turned on the rest of the lights. There were several of his parents, a beautiful one of Ellen, and a number of other friends. And there was a funny one of him, Gray, and Adam on the boat that summer. It was while they'd been in Sardinia with Sylvia and her friends, but only the Three Musketeers were in the picture, and no one else. There was another photograph of the *Blue Moon* in profile, as she sat in the port.

'That's quite a boat,' she said, as he handed her the glass of wine. He still hadn't told her about the boat, he had been waiting for the right moment to do so. It was embarrassing, but he knew that sooner or later he'd have to tell her that he owned a yacht. At first it had seemed pretentious to him, but now that they were seeing so much of each other, and exploring the possibility of dating, he wanted to be honest. It was no secret that he was a wealthy man.

'Gray and Adam and I spend the month of August on her every year. That photograph was taken in Sardinia. We had a great time,' he said, somewhat nervously, as she nodded her head and sipped the wine, and then followed him to the couch, and sat down.

'Whose boat is it?' she asked casually. She had told him earlier that her family were all sailors, and she'd spent a lot of time on sailboats in her youth. He was hoping she'd like his boat, even though it was a powerboat, and generally sailors called them 'stinkpots.' But there was no question that his was a beauty. 'Do you charter it?' She was acting normal, and he smiled at her green face. His lion suit looked just as silly, as he relaxed on the couch and crossed his furry legs, while his lion's tail stuck straight up behind him, and she giggled. They were quite a pair.

'No, we don't charter her.' He answered her second question before her first.

'Is it Adam's?' Charlie had mentioned that he was

enormously successful, and that his family had money. He shook his head. And then took a breath.

'No. It's mine.' There was dead silence in the room as she looked into his eyes.

'Yours? You never told me that,' she said, with a look of total surprise. It was an enormous yacht.

'I was afraid you'd disapprove. I'd just come back when we first met. I spend three months on her in Europe every summer, and a couple of weeks in the Caribbean in winter. It's a wonderful place to be.'

'I'm sure it is,' she said pensively. 'Wow, Charlie . . . that's a big deal.'

It was such a visible sign of Charlie's enormous wealth, and in sharp contrast to the way Carole worked and tried to live, and all that she believed. Charlie's fortune was no secret to her, but she lived far more simply and discreetly than he. The hub of her world was the center in Harlem, and the people in it, not a yacht, floating around the Caribbean. In spirit, Charlie knew she was more spartan than he. And he didn't want her to think less of him for his extravagant indulgences. He didn't want to frighten her.

'I hope it's not a deal-breaker for you,' he said quietly. 'I'd love you to come on her one day. She's called the *Blue Moon*.' He felt better having told her about it, although he wasn't sure yet how she felt. She looked a little shocked.

'How big is she?' Carole asked out of curiosity.

'Two hundred and forty feet.' Carole whistled in response, and took a long sip of her wine.

'Jesus . . . I work in Harlem . . . and you have a two-hundred-and-forty-foot yacht . . . there's a discrepancy for you. But on the other hand,' she said, excusing him for the extravagance of it, 'you just gave me a million dollars to spend on my kids. I guess if you didn't have that kind of money, you couldn't help us either. So maybe it's a wash.'

'I hope so. I don't want something stupid like a boat to come between us.'

She looked at him solemnly, with loving eyes. 'It won't,' she said slowly. 'At least I hope it won't.' There was nothing showy about him otherwise, and she could see that it was important to him, and how much he loved his boat. It was just a very, very big boat. 'That's a long time to be gone in the summer,' she said pensively.

'Maybe next year you can come with me,' he said hopefully. 'And I don't have to stay away as long. I had no pressing reason to come back this year, so I stayed away longer than I usually do. Sometimes I dread coming back here. I get lonely.' He looked around the apartment as he said it, and then back at her. And then he smiled. 'I have fun on the boat, especially with Gray and Adam. I can't wait for you to meet them.' But Carole and Charlie weren't quite ready for that yet. They both wanted more time to establish the relationship, and then he thought of something as he looked at her, and put an arm around her. He'd been wanting to do it for days. 'So now you know my darkest secret. I have a yacht.'

'Is that as bad as it gets?'

'Yes. I've never been in jail. I've never been prosecuted for a felony, or even a misdemeanor. I have no children, legitimate or otherwise. I've never declared bankruptcy. I've never been married, or stolen someone's wife. I brush my teeth every night before I go to bed, even if I'm drunk, which doesn't happen too often. I always floss. I pay for my parking tickets. Let's see, what else . . .' He paused for breath, and she laughed at him. The lion's tail was sticking straight up in the air at the back of the couch.

'You look so silly with that tail.'

'And you, my darling, look absolutely wonderful with a green face.' As soon as he said it, he kissed her, and when he stopped she was out of breath. It had been an evening full of surprises, but so far they were pleasant ones, even though she was a little shocked over the size of his yacht. To her, it looked more like an ocean liner than an ordinary boat. 'I've always wanted to kiss a woman with black lips and a green face,' he whispered, and she laughed at what he said. And he kissed her again. She clung to him this time as he did. He was awakening things in her that she had forgotten and repressed for years. She had put her heart and soul into her work, and had forgotten all else. But in Charlie's arms, she remembered now how sweet it was to be kissed, and how much sweeter still to be cherished by a man.

'Thank you,' she whispered as he held her close. She had been so frightened to do that with him, to be close to him, and to let herself take the risk of falling in love again. He had gently led her over the threshold into his private world, and she felt safe with him. Just as he did with her.

He walked her around the apartment then, showed her some of his treasures, and the things he loved most. Photographs of his parents and sister, paintings he had bought in Europe, including a remarkable Degas that hung over his bed. And after she had looked at it for a moment, he led her from the room. It still felt too soon for them to linger in his bedroom, but seeing his Degas led them to talk about the ballet. She told him she used to dance.

'I was very serious about it until I was sixteen, and then I quit,' she said with regret, but he understood her posture better now, and the graceful way she moved.

'Why did you quit?'

She smiled sheepishly as she answered. 'I got too

tall. I would have been condemned to the back row of the corps de ballet forever. Primas are always small, or they used to be. I think they're taller now, but not as tall as I am.' There were occasional disadvantages to her height, though not many as far as Charlie was concerned, he loved how tall and lithe she was. She managed to remain both elegant and feminine at the same time, and he was considerably taller than she was, so he didn't mind at all.

'Would you like to go to the ballet some time?' Her eyes lit up as he asked her, and he promised her they'd go. There were so many things he wanted to do with her. The fun had only just begun.

She stayed till nearly midnight, and he kissed her again several times. They wound up in the kitchen finally, where they had a snack before she left. They'd never eaten a proper dinner that night, just a lot of cupcakes and candy, until they made sandwiches and sat at the kitchen table, chatting.

'I know this sounds ridiculous, Charlie.' She was trying to explain to him how she felt. 'All my life I've hated extravagance, and the snobbishness and arrogance of rich people. I never wanted to be special, unless I'd earned it. Not because someone I was related to had. I wanted to help poor people, and people who never had any luck. I feel guilty when I do things other people can't, or spend more money than they, so I don't. Not that I can anyway.

But if I could, I wouldn't. It's just who I am.' He already knew that about her, so he wasn't surprised. She never spoke of her family, so he had no idea if they had money. Given the way she lived and the life she had devoted herself to, he suspected they didn't. Maybe some, but not much. There was nothing about her, other than her aristocratic good looks, that suggested she came from money. Maybe a good solid family of modest means, and sending her to Princeton had probably been a stretch.

'I understand,' he said quietly as they both finished their snack. 'Are you horrified that I have a boat?'

'No,' she said thoughtfully. 'It's just not something I would do even if I could. But you have a perfect right to spend your money any way you like. You do a lot of good for people through the foundation. I just always feel I should be living in abject poverty, and giving whatever I have to someone else.'

'Sometimes you have to keep a little and enjoy it yourself.'

'I do. But I'd rather give mine back. I feel guilty for taking a salary at the center. I just figure other people need it more than I do.'

'You have to eat,' he pointed out to her. He felt far less guilty than she. He had inherited an enormous fortune at an early age, and had lived up to the responsibility of it fully over the course of many years. He enjoyed his luxuries, his paintings, the objects he collected, and most of all his boat. He never apologized to anyone for it, except indirectly to Carole now. Their philosophies were very different, but not too different, he hoped.

'Maybe I've been a little too extreme,' she admitted. 'Austerity allows me to feel I'm atoning for my sins.'

'I don't see any sins,' he said seriously. 'I see a wonderful woman who has given of her life's blood to others, and works herself to the bone. Don't forget to have some fun.'

'I have fun with you, Charlie,' she said softly. 'I always do when we're together.'

'So do I.' He smiled and kissed her again. He loved kissing her, and longed to go further, but he didn't dare to yet. He knew how frightened Carole was, of getting too attached, of getting hurt again, and he had his own fears to contend with too. He worried about the same thing, and he was always waiting for the fatal flaw to surface. In her case it was an obvious one, and not a hidden flaw. It was right out in front, like a flag. She came from a different background than he did. She was a social worker, devoted to her work in Harlem, and she was skittish about his world. She wasn't a debutante or a socialite, and if anything she disapproved of his way of life, although she totally approved of him.

But the big question for him was whether or not she could overcome her reservations and accept the way he lived. If they were going to be together, and stay together, she was going to have to make her peace with that discrepancy, and so was he. At the moment, he thought they could. It rested more on Carole, at this point, than on him. She was the one who was going to have to be willing to forgive the frivolous extravagances of his world, without wanting to run away from him.

He took her home in a taxi, and kissed her at her front door. She didn't invite him up, but she had told him earlier that her place was a mess. He had never seen her studio, but could well imagine how challenging it was to live in one room. And she led a busy life.

He kissed the tip of her nose before he left her, and she laughed when she saw that he had green lips. Her face was still painted green from the Halloween party that night.

'I'll call you tomorrow,' he promised, as he got back in the cab. 'And I'll see about ballet tickets, maybe for next week.' She waved and thanked him again, and then disappeared into the house as he drove off.

His apartment seemed empty without her when he got back. He liked the way she filled his space, his life, his heart.

15

Charlie's secretary told him the next morning that she'd gotten tickets to the ballet for Friday night. It was a supposedly excellent production of *Giselle*, and he left a message for Carole to tell her, and then sat down to open his mail. His new Princeton alumni directory had come, and just for the fun of it, he looked up Carole's name. He knew the year she'd graduated, so it was easy to look up. He flipped through the correct pages, and then frowned when he didn't see her name.

He thought about the year she'd told him, and he went through it again. She wasn't there, which was strange. There was obviously a mistake. He mentioned it to his secretary later that morning, and decided to do Carole a favor, and save her some time, since he was sure she'd want it corrected herself. He asked his secretary to call the alumni office and report the omission to them. He gave her Carole's full name, Carole Anne Parker, and gave the correct year of her graduation.

He was hard at work on some financial reports later that afternoon, when his secretary called him on the intercom, and he picked it up, looking distracted. He was trying to make sense of some extremely complicated financial projections far into the future, and had to concentrate on what she had just said.

'I called the alumni office, as you asked me to, Mr Harrington. And I gave them Miss Parker's name and graduation. They said that no one by that name has ever graduated from Princeton. I asked them to check again, and they did. I don't think she went to Princeton. Maybe that's the mistake. The alumni office insists she didn't.'

'That's absurd. Give me the number. I'll call them myself.' He was annoyed at their stupidity, and he was sure Carole would be too. He even knew her eating club. It was all over her CV that she had gone to Princeton.

But when he called them five minutes later, they told him the same thing. They were in fact extremely disagreeable about it, and said they didn't make mistakes like that. Carole Anne Parker had never graduated from Princeton. In fact, according to their records, when they checked further, no one by that name had ever attended the school. As he hung up the phone, a cold chill ran down his spine. And five minutes later, feeling like a monster, he called Columbia's School of Social Work. They told him the same thing. She had never attended Columbia either. When he hung up the phone, he knew he had found the fatal flaw. The woman he was falling in love with was a fraud. Whoever she was, and however well intentioned her work for the center had been, she had none of the degrees she claimed she did, and had even conned a million dollars out of his foundation, based on falsified credentials and a phony reputation. It was nearly criminal, except for the fact that she hadn't wanted the money for herself, but to help others. He had no idea what to do with the information. He needed time to think about it and digest it.

When she called him that afternoon, for the first time since he'd met her six weeks before, he didn't take her call. He couldn't just disappear out of her life, and he wanted an explanation. But first he needed time to absorb it, and two days later, he was taking her to the ballet. He made a decision that afternoon to say nothing until then, and deal with it after that. He called her late that afternoon, and said the board of trustees was having a crisis and he couldn't see her until Friday. She said she understood perfectly, and those things happened to her too. But when she hung up at her end, Carole wondered why he had sounded so chilly. In fact, he'd nearly been crying. He felt completely ripped off and disillusioned. The woman he had admired so totally since the day they met was a liar.

He spent an agonizing two days waiting to see her again, and when he picked her up on Friday for the ballet, she looked lovely. She was wearing the regulation little black cocktail dress, high heels, and a simple black fur jacket. She was beautifully dressed, and had even worn a pair of very proper pearl earrings that she said had been her mother's. He believed not a single word she said now. She had tainted everything between them with her lies about Columbia and Princeton. He no longer trusted her, and she thought he looked stiff and unhappy. She asked him if everything was all right, as the curtain went up, and he nodded. He had barely spoken to her in the cab, nor when they got to Lincoln Center. Carole thought he looked awful. She could only assume that since she'd last seen him, something terrible had happened at the foundation.

At intermission, they went to the bar to have a drink, and before they went back to their seats, she excused herself to go to the ladies' room, and just as she was about to leave him, a couple swooped down on her before Carole could avoid them. She turned her head away, as though she were trying to hide from them, which Charlie noticed instantly and cringed inside. All she said to him was that they were friends of her parents and she couldn't stand them, and then she vanished. Charlie then realized who they were, as the woman in question bore down on him, and her husband quickly followed. He knew them too, and had to admit he didn't like them either. They were unbearable social climbers.

The woman prattled on endlessly about the performance, and said she had liked the previous season's production of it better. She went on ad nauseam about the strengths and weaknesses of the dancers, and then fixed her gaze on Charlie with beady eyes, and made a cryptic comment that meant nothing to him when she first said it.

'Well, you've made quite a coup, haven't you,' she said, sounding both knowing and nasty. Charlie had no idea what she was talking about as he stared at her, wishing Carole would come back. As angry as he was at her, standing awkwardly next to her was a lot more pleasant than being trapped by this dreadful woman and her mealymouthed husband, both of whom were glued to him because of who he was. 'I hear she nearly had a nervous breakdown when her husband left her. I don't know what she needed him for anyway, the Van Horns have a lot more money than he does. All he ever was was new money. The Van Horns are the oldest fortune in the country.' He had no idea why she was talking to him about the Van Horns. He knew Arthur Van

Horn himself, though not well. He was one of the most conservative men he'd ever met, surely the most uptight, and definitely the most boring, and how much money they had was of absolutely no interest to Charlie.

'The Van Horns?' Charlie asked blankly. She sounded like a madwoman as she spewed gossip and details of a situation that completely bemused him. She was talking about some woman whose husband had left her who had apparently been a Van Horn. It all sounded more than a little crazy to Charlie, as she looked at him as though he were completely stupid.

'The Van Horns. I was talking about the Van Horn girl. Wasn't that who I just saw you with when I walked over?' She looked at him as though he were demented, and then suddenly as he looked at her, he realized what she was saying. He felt as though he had been struck by lightning.

'Of course. I'm sorry. I was distracted. Miss Van Horn, of course.'

'Are you two seeing each other?' she asked him boldly. Women like her had no shame about asking questions. They thrived on gathering information to use later to impress others that they were insiders in the social group, though more often than not they weren't. They were acquainted with the 'right' people, but disliked by all.

'We're business connections,' he said, nodding. 'The foundation has been involved with her children's center. They're doing a great job with abused children. What was her married name, by the way? Do you remember?'

'Wasn't it Mosley? Or Mossey? Something like that. Dreadful man. He made an absolute fortune. I think he married a girl even younger than Carole after her. It's a shame it shook her so badly.'

'His name wasn't Parker, was it?' Charlie was now a man on a mission. He wanted to know the truth, from whatever source he got it. Even from the likes of this repulsive social climber.

'Of course not. That's her mother's maiden name. The Parker Bank, in Boston. Not quite as big as the Van Horn fortune, but very handsome. Nice for Carole she has two fortunes to inherit from, not just one. Some people are just born lucky,' she said, as Charlie nodded, and he saw Carole approaching. It was easy to spot her in the crowd in high heels, and he signaled to her that he would join her where she was, as he thanked his informant and departed. He had discovered so many lies in the past two days, that he no longer knew what to believe about Carole.

'I'm sorry I left you with that awful woman. I figured if I stuck around, she'd stay forever. Did she chew your ear off?'

'Yes,' he said succinctly.

'She always does. She's the biggest gossip in New York, all she ever talks about is who married who, who someone's grandfather was, and how much money they inherited or made. God knows where she gets her information. I just can't stand her.' He nodded, and they followed the crowd back to their seats. The curtain went up immediately, and Charlie sat, leaning away from her, looking wooden. Carole's fatal flaw, he had discovered in the past few days, was not the obvious one that she came from a different world, and a simple background, and was uncomfortable in his world, or even that she was a fraud, as he had thought on Wednesday. Her fatal flaw, as it turned out, was a much simpler one. She was a liar.

When the performance ended and the curtain went up, she smiled at him, and thanked him.

'It was really lovely. Thank you, Charlie. I loved it.'

'I'm glad,' he said politely. He had promised to take her to dinner afterward, but he no longer wanted to. What he had to say to her he didn't want to say in public. He suggested they go back to his apartment. She smiled at the suggestion, and said she could make him scrambled eggs. He nodded, and barely managed to make idle chitchat with her on the short ride back to his apartment. She had no idea what was wrong with him that night, but it was very obvious to her that he was upset about something. And she didn't have long to wait to find out what it was.

He opened the front door for her, turned the lights on, strode into the living room with her following him, and didn't even bother to sit down. He turned to face her with a look of outrage.

'Just what exactly did you think you've been doing all this time with all your goddamn pretentious bullshit about not liking eating clubs and the social scene, and people with money? Why the hell did you lie to me? You're not just some simple girl who devoted herself to slaving away to save the poor in Harlem. You come from the same world I do, you went to the same school I did. You're doing the same things I am for the same reasons I am, and you're every goddamn bit as rich as I am, Miss Van Horn, so don't give me any more lofty bullshit about how uncomfortable and ill at ease you are in my world.'

'Where did all of that come from? And it's none of your goddamn business how rich I am. That's the whole point, Charlie. I don't want to be admired and pursued and respected and kowtowed to because of who my grandfather was. I want to be

345

respected and liked because of who I am. And there's no goddamn way on earth to do that with a name like Van Horn. So I use my mother's name. So what? So sue me, for chrissake. I don't owe you or anyone else any explanations.' She was as angry as he was.

'I didn't want you to lie to me. I wanted you to tell me the truth. How am I supposed to trust you if you even lie to me about who you are? Why didn't you tell me, Carole?'

'For the same reason you didn't tell me about your yacht. Because you thought it would scare me or shock me or put me off, or maybe you were afraid I was after your money. Well, I'm not, you idiot. I have my own. And everything I said about being uncomfortable in your world is true. I hated that world all my life, I grew up in it, I had it coming out of my ears. All the pomp and ceremony and bullshit and pretentious garbage I want no part of. I love what I do. I love those kids. And that's all I want now. I don't want a fancy life. I don't need it. I hated it when I had it. I gave it up four years ago, and I'm a lot happier now. And I'm never going back to that world, for you, or anyone else.' She nearly had steam coming out of her ears.

'But you were born there. You belong there, even if you don't want to be there. Why was I crawling around apologizing to you? You could have at least let me off the hook on that one. You could have at least told me who you are instead of making a fool of me. When were you going to tell me? Ever? Or were you going to pretend to be Little Miss Simple forever, and make me crawl around on my hands and knees apologizing to you for what I have, and who I am, and the way I live? And now that I think about it, I don't believe you live in a studio apartment either, do you? You own that whole house, don't you?' His eyes blazed at her. She had lied to him about everything. She bowed her head for a moment and then looked at him.

'Yes, I do. I was going to move to Harlem when I opened the center, but my father wouldn't let me. He insisted I get that house, but I didn't know how to explain it to you.'

'At least someone in your family has some sense, even if you don't. You'd have gotten yourself killed up there, and you still could. You're not Mother Teresa, for chrissake. You're a little rich girl, just like I was a rich boy, at way too early an age. And now I'm a rich man. And you know what? If people don't like it, screw them. Because this is who I am. Maybe one of these days you'll stop apologizing too. But until that happens and you figure out that it's okay to be who we are, you can't go around lying to people and pretending you're not who you are. It

347

was a stupid, rotten thing to do, and you made me feel like a fool. I called the goddamn Princeton alumni office this week and told them they'd made a mistake and dropped you off the roster. They told me you'd never gone to school there, because I thought your name was Parker, of course. And then I thought you were a fraud. As it turns out, you're not a phony, you're just a liar. In relationships, people owe it to each other to be honest, no matter what that is. Yes, I have a boat. Yes, I have a lot of money. So do you. Yes, you're a Van Horn. So fucking what? But once you lie to me like that, I don't trust you, I don't believe you, and to tell you the truth, I don't want to be with you. Until you figure out who you are, and who you want to be when you grow up, I don't think there's a damn thing left for us to say to each other.' He was so upset he was shaking from head to foot, and so was she. She hated the fact that it had come out this way, but in some ways, she was relieved. She had hated lying to him. It was one thing not telling people who she was at the center, but it was an entirely different thing not telling him.

'Charlie, I just wanted you to like me for me, not because of my father's name.'

'What did you think? That I was after your money? That's ridiculous and you know it. You turned this whole relationship into a farce, and your lying to me about any of it was a complete disrespect to me.'

'I only lied to you about my name, and about where I come from. It's not important. I'm still me. And I apologize. You're right, I shouldn't have done it. But I did. Maybe I was just plain scared. And once you knew me as Carole Parker, it was a lot harder to explain who I really was. I didn't kill anybody, for God's sake, I didn't steal your money.'

'You stole my trust, which is worse.'

'Charlie, I'm sorry. I think I'm falling in love with you.' As she said it, tears rolled down her cheeks. In her own eyes, she had screwed up everything, and she felt terrible about it. She loved everything about him.

'I don't believe you.' He spat the words at her. 'If you were falling in love with me, you wouldn't have lied to me.'

'I made a mistake. People do that sometimes. I was scared. I just wanted you to love me for me.'

'I was beginning to. But God only knows who you really are. I was falling in love with Carole Parker, a simple girl from nowhere with no money and nothing to her name. Now you turn out to be someone else. A fucking heiress, for chrissake.'

'Is that so terrible? You can't forgive me for that?'

'Maybe not. What was terrible was lying to me, Carole. That's the terrible part.' As he said it, he turned away from her, and stared out the window at the park. He stood that way, with his back to her, for a long time. They had said enough for one night, and possibly forever.

'Do you want me to leave?' she asked in a choked voice.

He didn't answer at first, and then he nodded, and finally spoke. 'Yes, I do. It's over. I could never trust you. You lied to me for nearly two months. That's a hell of a long time.'

'I'm sorry,' she said softly. He still had his back to her. He didn't want to see her face again. It hurt too much. The fatal flaw was hanging in the breeze.

She walked quietly out of the apartment, and closed the door behind her. She was still shaking when she got into the elevator, and when she got downstairs. She told herself that the whole thing was ridiculous. He was angry at her for being rich, when in fact he was richer still. But it wasn't about that, and she knew it. He was furious with her because she had lied to him.

She took a cab back to her house, and hoped that he would call her that night. He didn't. He didn't call her that night or the next day. She checked her voice mail constantly. Weeks later, he still hadn't called her. Finally, she realized that he never would again. What he had said to her that night was true. He had told her it was over for him, that he could

350

no longer trust her. However good her intentions, she had broken the sacred trust between them, which was the essence of a relationship. He didn't want to see her anymore, or talk to her, or be with her. She knew she was in love with him now, but she knew that it wouldn't change anything. Charlie was gone for good.

16

Two weeks before Thanksgiving, Adam and Maggie were spending a quiet evening at his place, when out of the blue she brought up Thanksgiving. She hadn't thought about it before, but now that they were spending so much time together, she wanted to spend it with him, and wondered if he was going to be with his kids. She hadn't met either of them yet, and they had both agreed it was still too soon. They were together nearly every night, and he loved being with her, but as he told her, this was still the test drive, and they were taking their relationship out for a spin.

'Thanksgiving?' He looked at her blankly. 'Why?'

'Are you going to be with your kids?'

'No, Rachel is taking them to her in-laws in Ohio. We alternate holidays. This is my off year.'

She smiled at him then. She hoped that meant good news for her. She hadn't had a real Thanksgiving, with people she cared about, in years. Not since she was a very little kid, if then.

She'd cooked a turkey with her mother once, who had been too drunk to eat it and passed out before it was cooked. Maggie had wound up eating it at the kitchen table alone. But at least her mother was there, even if unconscious in the next room.

'Do you suppose we could spend it together?' she asked, cuddling up to him, and looking at him.

'No, we can't,' he said, looking grim.

'Why not?' She took it as an immediate rebuff. Things had been going really well between them, and the brusqueness of his answer took her by surprise and hurt her feelings.

'Because I have to go to my parents'. And I can't take you with me.' With a name like O'Malley, his mother would have a heart attack. Besides, who he was dating was none of her business.

'Why are you going there? I thought you had a terrible time on Yom Kippur.' What he was saying made no sense to her.

'I did. That has nothing to do with anything. In my family, you have to turn yourself in for holidays anyway. Like a warrant for your arrest. It's not about having a good time. It's about tradition and obligation. As much as they drive me nuts, I think family is important. Mine stinks, but I still feel I need to go and show respect. God knows why, but I feel I owe it to them. My parents are old, they're not going to change, so I suck it up and go. Don't

353

you have somewhere to go?' He looked miserable when he asked her. He hated the reminder that he had to spend another rotten holiday with them again. He hated the holidays, and always had, because of that. His mother managed to ruin every single one of them for him. The only mercy was that his parents celebrated Chanukah and not Christmas, so he got to spend Christmas with his kids. That was fun at least. Holidays on Long Island never were. 'Where are you going to be for Thanksgiving?'

'In my apartment, alone. The others are all going home.' And she, of course, had nowhere to go.

'Stop trying to make me feel guilty,' he nearly shouted at her. 'I have enough of that with my mother as it is. Maggie, I'm really sorry you have nowhere to go, but I can't do anything about it. I have to go home.'

'I don't understand that,' she said unhappily. 'They treat you like shit. You told me so. So why would you go home?'

'I feel like I should,' he said, looking stressed. He didn't want to defend his decisions to her. It was hard enough as it was. 'I have no choice.'

'Yes, you do,' she insisted.

'No, I don't. I don't want to discuss this with you again. That's just the way it is. I'll be home that night. We can do something over the weekend.'

'That's not the point.' She was pushing, and he didn't like it. She was treading on dangerous ground with him. 'If this is a relationship,' she pressed on at her own peril, 'then I want to spend holidays with you. We've been together for two months.'

'Maggie, don't push me,' he warned her. 'This isn't a relationship. We're dating. That's different.'

'Well, pardon me,' she said sarcastically. 'Who died and made you king?'

'You knew the rules when we started. You lead your life. I lead mine. We meet in between when it works for both of us. Well, Thanksgiving doesn't work for me. I wish it did. Believe me, I wish it did. And I'd be happy to spend it with you if I could. But I can't. Thanksgiving with my parents is a command performance for me. I'll come home with a migraine, a stomachache, and a giant pain in the ass, but come hell or high water, they expect me to be there.'

'That sucks,' she said, pouting.

'Yes, it does,' he agreed. 'For both of us.'

'And what was that bullshit about this not being a relationship? And all that meeting-in-the-middle crap?'

'That's what we've been doing. Not to mention the fact that I've been seeing you every weekend, which is a big deal.'

'Then that makes it a relationship, doesn't it?'

She continued to push, missing all the danger signals from him, which was rare for her. But she was upset about Thanksgiving and not being with him. It made her braver about challenging him and his 'rules.'

'A relationship is for people who eventually want to get married. I don't. I told you that. This is dating. It works for me.' She didn't say a word after that, and the next morning, she went back to her own place. He felt guilty all afternoon about what he'd said. It was a relationship. It had become one. He wasn't seeing anyone else, and as far as he knew, neither was she. He just didn't like admitting it, but he also didn't like hurting her feelings. And he hated not being with her on Thanksgiving. He hated all of it. And he felt like a shit. She was at work when he called her, and he left a loving message on her machine.

He never heard from her when she got off work. And she didn't turn up at the apartment. He called her that night, and she was out. After that, he called her every hour on the hour, until midnight. He thought she was playing games with him, until one of her roommates answered, and told him she was really out. The next time he called, they said she was asleep. She had never called him back. And by the following afternoon, he was beginning to steam. He finally decided to call her at work, which he rarely did.

'Where were you last night?' he asked her, trying to sound calmer than he felt.

'I thought this was only dating. Wasn't that the one where neither of us gets to ask questions? I'll have to look it up, but I think those were the rules, since this isn't a relationship.'

'Look, I'm sorry. That was stupid. I was just upset about Thanksgiving. I feel like a shit leaving you alone.'

'You *are* a shit for leaving me alone,' she corrected.

'Maggie, give me a break on this one. Please. I have to go to Long Island. Honest to God, I have no choice.'

'Yes, you do. I don't mind if you're with your kids. That, I understand. But stop going back to spend holidays with your parents, so they can punish you.'

'They're my parents. I have to. Look, come over tonight. I'll cook you dinner and we'll have a nice time.'

'I have something to do. I'll be there at nine.' She sounded cool.

'What are you doing?'

'Don't ask me questions. I'll get there as soon as I can.'

'What's that all about?'

'I have to go to the library,' she said as he fumed.

'That is the worst bullshit excuse I've ever heard. All right, I'll see you tonight. Get there whenever you want.' He hung up on her then, and wanted to tell her not to bother to come at all. But he wanted to see her, and he wanted to know what was going on. There were at least two nights a week when he called her and she wasn't home. If she was seeing someone else, he wanted to know. She was the first woman he had been faithful to in years. And he was beginning to wonder if she was cheating on him.

He was sitting on the couch waiting for her when she got in that night, having a stiff drink. It was nearly ten o'clock, and it was his second drink. He had been looking at his watch every five minutes. She looked at him apologetically when she walked in.

'I'm sorry. It took longer than I thought. I came as soon as I could.'

'What were you doing? Tell me the truth.'

'I thought we weren't supposed to ask questions,' she said, looking nervous.

'Don't give me that shit,' he shouted at her. 'You're seeing someone, aren't you? This is perfect. Absolutely perfect. For the past eleven years I've had a chorus line of women. You come along, and for the first time in years, I'm faithful to you. And what are you doing? Screwing someone else.'

'Adam,' she said quietly, sitting across from him

and looking him in the eye, 'I'm not screwing someone else. I swear.'

'Then where are you when I call you at night? You're out till nearly midnight. You're never god-damn home if you're not here.' His eyes were blazing, and his head was throbbing. He had a headache, and the woman he was crazy about was fucking someone else. He wasn't sure whether to cry or scream. It was poetic justice perhaps, for what he had done to other women, but it sure didn't feel good while it was happening to him. He was crazy about her. 'Where were you tonight?'

'I told you,' she said calmly. 'I was at the library.'

'Maggie, please . . . don't lie to me at least. Have the balls to tell me the truth.' Looking at the agony in his eyes, she realized she had no other choice. She had to tell him the truth. She hadn't wanted to. But if he thought she was seeing someone else, he deserved to know what she was doing when she wasn't with him.

'I'm taking pre-law classes at school,' she said quietly but firmly, as he sat in his chair and stared at her.

'You're *what?*' He was sure he had misheard.

'I want to graduate and go to law school, and it's going to take me about a hundred years to get my degree. I can only take two classes a semester. I can't afford to take more than that anyway. I got a partial scholarship.' She exhaled deeply as she said it. It was a relief to tell him the truth. 'I was at the library tonight, because I have a paper due. I have midterms next week.' He stared at her in disbelief and then his face broke into a grin.

'Are you kidding?'

'No, I'm not kidding. I've already been doing this for two years.'

'Why didn't you tell me?'

'Because I thought you'd laugh at me.'

'Why on earth are you doing that?'

'Because I don't want to be a waitress for the rest of my life. And I'm not looking for a man to save me. I don't want to be dependent on anyone. I want to be able to take care of myself.' What she said to him nearly brought tears to his eyes. Every woman he'd ever known, or dated, wanted to take some poor slob for a ride, including him. Maggie was out there working her ass off, waiting on tables, going to college and aspiring to law school two nights a week. She had never asked him for a penny. And more often than he wanted her to, she showed up with a bag of groceries or a small present for him. She was an amazing woman.

'Come over here,' he said, beckoning her to him. She came over to where he was sitting, and he put his arms around her. 'I want you to know that I think you're terrific. You're the most terrific woman

I've ever known. I apologize for being an asshole, and I apologize for leaving you on Thanksgiving. I promise we'll celebrate on Thursday, and I'll never bug you about what you're doing again. And another thing,' he said, looking at her matter-of-factly, but there was a tenderness in his eyes she had never seen before. 'I want you to know that I love you.'

'I love you too,' she whispered softly. He had never said that to her before. 'What does that do to the rules?'

'What rules?' He looked confused.

'You know, the rules. Does that mean we're still just dating, or is this a relationship now?'

'This is I love you, Maggie O'Malley. Fuck the rules. We'll figure it out as we go.'

'We will?' She looked thrilled.

'Yes, we will. And the next time I tell you what the rules are, remember to tell me I'm full of shit. By the way, what's your paper about?'

'Torts.'

'Oh, shit. Tomorrow let me see what you've got. I'm too drunk to deal with it tonight.' But they both knew he wasn't that drunk. He was more interested in taking her to bed and making love. He was definitely not too drunk for that.

'Will you really help me?'

'Absolutely. We're going to get you through college and law school in record time.'

'I can't do that,' she said seriously. 'I've got to work.' It wasn't a plea for help, it was a simple statement of fact.

'We'll discuss that some other time.' He scooped her up in his arms then and carried her into the bedroom.

'Did you mean what you said?' she asked him as he set her down on the bed. 'Or are you really drunk?'

'No, Maggie. I'm not drunk. And I meant it. I love you. I'm just a little slow at figuring things out sometimes,' although two months wasn't bad, especially for him. She smiled up at him, and he turned off the light.

17

Gray called Charlie in the office the week before Thanksgiving, and thought he sounded unusually glum.

'What are you doing for Thanksgiving?'

'Nothing, as a matter of fact,' Charlie said. He had been thinking about that himself. The holidays were always hard for him and he hated to make plans. For him, holidays were a time for people with families to gather around and share their warmth, and for people who didn't have any to feel the bitter chill of all they'd lost and would never have again.

'Sylvia and I were wondering if you'd like to join us for dinner. She's cooking the turkey, so dinner should be pretty good.'

Charlie laughed. 'Actually, I'd like that a lot.' It was an easy, painless way for him to spend the holiday with his friend.

'You're welcome to bring Carole, if you like.'

'That won't be necessary, but thanks anyway,' Charlie said, sounding tense.

'Does she have other plans?' Gray could hear that something was wrong.

'I assume so. As a matter of fact, I don't know.'

'That doesn't sound so good,' Gray said, worried about him.

'It's not. We had a major blowout two weeks ago. Carole and I are a thing of the past. It was fun, but not for long.'

'I'm sorry to hear that. I take it you discovered a fatal flaw.' He always did. You could count on him for that.

'You could say that. She lied to me. I can't be with a woman I don't trust.'

'I guess not.' Gray knew him well enough to know that once the fatal flaw had been discovered, Charlie was gone. His job was done. Gray told him to come to dinner at Sylvia's at six o'clock, and a few minutes later they hung up. Gray reported the bad news about Carole to Sylvia that night. She was sorry to hear it too.

'He always does that,' Gray said, looking unhappy. 'He always looks for that one thing, whatever it is, that means she isn't a saint and can't walk on water, and then bang, they're gone, and he hits the door. He just can't forgive women their frailties or accept that it still might be okay to love them, and give them a break for once. He never does. He's so fucking afraid that he might get hurt or they might die or leave him that he hits the ejector button if someone coughs. I've seen him do it every time.'

'I take it she coughed,' Sylvia said, thinking about it. Although she didn't know Charlie well, she felt as though she did from hearing Gray talk about him. He talked about him a lot. They were more brothers than friends. And in both cases, the only family each had. Gray had told her he still had a much younger adopted brother out there somewhere, but hadn't seen him in years, and was no longer sure where he was. Charlie was the brother of his heart. And from what she knew of his history, it was easy to figure out what happened every time. He was terrified whatever woman in question would abandon him, so he ditched her first.

'The guy just has no flex, there's no give in what he expects.' They both knew from their own lives that in a relationship one had to bend. 'He said she lied. Shit, who doesn't sometimes? It happens. People do stupid stuff.' Sylvia nodded, curious about what had happened.

'What did she lie about?'

'He didn't say. My guess, judging from past history, is that it wasn't something important, but he used it as an example, or an excuse, to illustrate that she could lie over something big. That's usually how it works. It's like Kabuki. He makes a lot of ugly noises and faces, and acts shocked. He "can't believe . . ." Believe me, I know the drill. It's just such a goddamn shame. He's going to wind up alone for good one of these days.' In fact, he already had.

'Maybe that's what he wants,' Sylvia said thoughtfully.

'I hate to see that happen to him.' Gray smiled sadly at her. He wanted to see his friend as happy as he was himself these days. Everything between him and Sylvia was great, and had been since they met. They laughed sometimes over the fact that they hadn't had a single disagreement, or even a first fight. They knew that something would come up one of these days, but it hadn't yet. They seemed to be perfectly matched in every way. The honeymoon was still in full bloom.

Charlie showed up at exactly six o'clock on Thanksgiving Day. He brought two fabulous bottles of red wine with him, a bottle of Cristal, and another of Château d'Yquem. They were all set for a terrific evening of great wines, good food, and good friends.

'My God, Charlie, we could open a liquor store with all this,' Sylvia exclaimed. 'And it's such fantastic stuff.'

'I figured if we were going to have hangovers tomorrow, we might as well do it on great stuff.' He smiled at her.

Sylvia was wearing black velvet pants and a white sweater, and had wound her long black hair into a knot. She was wearing small diamond earrings, and she smiled tenderly every time her eyes and Gray's met. Charlie had never seen his friend so happy, and it touched his heart. Gone were the nutcases and neurotics, the psychotic ex-boyfriends threatening their lives, the women who left him for someone else at the drop of a hat, or tried to set fire to his paintings on the way out. Sylvia was precisely what every man should have. And it was obvious to anyone who saw them that Gray meant just as much to her. Charlie was relieved to see that she treated him like a king. It warmed his heart to see it, but at the same time it made him feel left out. In the company of people who loved each other to that extent, one always felt the absence of all one didn't have. It was bittersweet for him. Sylvia had prepared a delicious meal with Gray's help. The table looked beautiful, the linens perfect, the flowers she had arranged herself just right. Gray was living well, and basking in the warmth of the love he shared with her.

The subject of Carole didn't come up until halfway through dinner. Charlie never mentioned her, but Gray finally couldn't stand the suspense anymore, and brought it up.

'So what happened with Carole?' He tried to sound casual as he asked him, but he sounded anything but, as Sylvia gave him a glance. She was sure it was a painful topic, and she didn't think Gray should ask. But it was too late to stop. He had jumped in with both feet. Charlie didn't react. 'What did she lie to you about?'

'Oh, just a minor matter, like who she is. She didn't even tell me her right name. Apparently, she's traveling through life incognito, and didn't think it was worth telling me the truth.'

'Wow, that's too bad. Is she hiding from an old boyfriend or something? Some women do that.' He was trying to make excuses for her. Knowing how terrific Charlie had thought she was, he hated to see yet another good one wind up in the trash. For his friend's sake, if nothing else, he wanted to give their failing romance CPR. But from the icy tone of Charlie's voice, it sounded like it was already dead and Gray's well-intentioned efforts came too late.

'No,' Charlie answered slowly, 'she's hiding from herself.'

'I've done that, so have you. Some people do it all their lives.'

'I guess that's what she had in mind. I found out by accident. I thought she was lying about her credentials at first. It turned out to be more complicated than that. She was concealing her identity from everyone. She pretends to be a simple girl who hates the fancy social world, and only respects people working in the gutters of life, as she is, which is admirable, but her humble origins are bullshit in her case. She had me feeling guilty for everything I am and have, how I live, and where I was born. I was even afraid to tell her about the boat.'

'So? She's not what she claims? She's a princess in disguise?' It didn't sound like a death penalty offense to Gray. But to Charlie, it was.

'It turns out she's a Van Horn, for chrissake. She's just as "fancy" as I am, if you want to call it that. I didn't even bother mentioning it to her, but as I recall, her grandfather had a bigger yacht than mine.'

'A *Van Horn* Van Horn?' Gray looked surprised.

'Yeah.' Charlie said it as though she had had sex with his best friend in plain sight in the lobby of the Plaza Hotel, while being filmed by the press.

'Wow! That's pretty impressive. The Van Horn thing, I mean. Shit, Charlie, that should make things easier for you. Why the hell are you pissed off? You're not playing Pygmalion here, which is hard to do. You know, "you can't make a silk purse out of a sow's ear" and all that stuff, although a lot of people try, but it's damn hard and usually doesn't work. She has a pedigree of her own, which may even be better than yours. Is that what's bothering you?' Gray said insightfully, as Sylvia winced. Gray was not hiding what he thought.

369

'No, of course not. I'm not jealous of her pedigree.' Charlie looked annoyed. 'I don't like the fact that she lied. She made a fool of me. There I was thinking that she was feeling shy about my kind of life, while I was tiptoeing around and apologizing, and it turns out she grew up just like I did. She may not like that world, but it's home base for her too. Simply put, she's full of shit. All that humble simplicity is just a lot of pretentious phony bullshit in her case.' He sounded furious as he said it, and Gray laughed.

'Don't hesitate to tell us what you really think,' he teased. 'Okay, so she's pretending to be a nobody. So fucking what? That can't be an easy name to wear with the kind of work she does. Neither is yours. Maybe she doesn't want to play Lady Bountiful coming down to the masses from on high. She wants to be one of them and not have to deal with all that shit. Can you blame her, Charlie?'

'Yes, I can. It's fine to lie to the people where she works, if that's what she wants. But it wasn't okay to lie to me. She told me she lived in a one-room studio. Hell, she lives in a ten-million-dollar brownstone on the Upper East Side.'

'Really, how disgusting of her,' Gray said scathingly. 'I'm shocked! And what do you think your apartment on Fifth Avenue with the breathtaking view of Central Park is worth these days?

Five million? Ten? And let's see, what did you pay for *Blue Moon*? I can't remember. Fifty million? . . . Sixty?'

'That's not the point.' Charlie glowered at him. 'The point is that if she lied to me about her name and who she is and how she grew up, she'd lie to me about something else, and probably already has.'

'Maybe not,' Gray said bluntly. It sounded like the proverbial tempest in a teapot to him. At Carole's expense. Charlie had poured the tea right over her head, and stormed out. It didn't sound like a fair fight to Gray. With Charlie, it never was. And in the end, although he didn't see it that way, Charlie lost. That much was very clear to Gray, especially now. His whole perspective on life had changed in the past few months. 'Maybe all she wanted was to be like everyone else. Don't you want that sometimes? Do you always want to be Charles Sumner Harrington? I'll bet you don't. Shit, Charlie, give her a chance. Okay, so you felt stupid when you found out who she was. But is that so terrible? You really can't forgive her something like that? How perfect are you, for chrissake?'

'I don't lie to people I love. I don't even lie to my friends. I've never lied to you.'

'Okay, that's why we love each other. But I'll tell you one thing right now, I'm not leaving Sylvia to marry you.'

371

'Damn,' Charlie said with a laugh, 'I was hoping you would.' He glanced at Sylvia. 'Sorry, Sylvia, I saw him first.'

'I'm happy to share him with you,' she said honestly, and then decided to put in her two cents, for whatever it was worth. 'I don't mean to butt in, and I see your point. It always worries me too when people do something I don't like. I figure there's more hidden somewhere that I don't know about yet, kind of the tip-of-the-iceberg theory. But I suspect in her case, her heart was in the right place, or it could have been. For people like you, and her, you never really know what people want, or who they see. I think Gray may be right in this case, she may have just wanted a clean slate. She should have told you at some point, and maybe sooner than she did. It's unfortunate you had to discover it for yourself. But she sounds like a terrific woman, from everything you said, and you have a lot in common. Maybe you should give her another chance. We all need a break sometimes. And you can always walk if you get another whiff of something you don't like. You're not committing for life. There are compromises in every relationship, as we all know. Unfortunately, none of us are perfect. You may need a bit of indulgence from her at some point. It's a trade-off in the end, a lot of things you love about someone, for a few things you don't. As long as the scale stays weighted on the positive side, it's worth putting up with a little shit. And it sounded to me, before this happened, that there's a lot about her you do like.' She fell silent as Charlie looked at her. She saw two deep pools of sadness in his eyes. There was a lot of pain in his soul that he never shared. There were tears in his eyes when he looked away.

'I just don't want to get hurt. Life is hard enough as it is.'

Sylvia reached out and touched his hand, as they sat next to each other at the beautiful table she had set. 'It's harder alone. I know,' she said, with a lump in her throat. He looked back at her and nodded, but he wasn't sure he agreed. It was hard alone, but it was harder still losing someone you loved. He knew she had been there too. Her last lover's suicide had nearly taken her down with it.

'I don't know,' he said sadly, 'maybe you're right. I was just so furious. I felt so ripped off. And I felt like such a fool when I found out. She has an absolute aversion to her own world and her own kind. She hates everything it represents. How healthy and normal is that?'

'Maybe her life wasn't so easy either as a kid,' Gray added. 'We all think everyone has it so great. We don't know who was dumped on, who was abused, who was kicked around, who was neglected, who was molested by their uncle. You just don't know. We all have tough stuff to live with. No one gets off scot-free. Maybe hers wasn't such a cakewalk either. I've read a lot about her father, he's a pretty important guy, but he doesn't sound like a sweetheart to me. I don't know, Charlie. Maybe you're right, maybe she's just a lying piece of shit, and she'll break your heart, and your balls. But what if she isn't? What if she's just a decent human being who got sick and tired of being who she is, and growing up as the kid of one of the richest guys who ever lived? It's hard to imagine for someone like me, but you of all people should know that the responsibilities that come with who you are aren't a lot of fun sometimes. To tell you the truth, I love the things you have, and I have a hell of a good time on the boat with you, but honestly, when I take a good look, I'm not sure I'd want to be you every day. Sometimes it looks like a lot of hard work and goddamn lonely to me.' It was as honest as Gray had ever been with him, and Charlie was touched. More than his friend knew.

'You're right, it *is* hard work, and lonely at times. But you don't get a choice in the matter. They pass you the baton at some point, sometimes sooner than later, as happened to me, and off you go. You don't get to sit on the sidelines and whine, and say you don't want to play. You do the best you can.'

'It sounds like she is. Maybe she just needed a break from being her.'

Charlie looked pensive as he pushed some crumbs around the tablecloth, thinking of what Gray and Sylvia had said. There was a possibility that it was true. 'The woman who told me who she is said that she'd nearly had a nervous breakdown when her marriage fell apart. She pretty much told me that herself early on. Her ex-husband sounds like an abusive bastard, and a sociopath. I've met him, and he's not a nice guy. He made plenty of money on his own, but I think he's a real shit. I have a feeling he may have married her because she's a Van Horn.' Gray had made a good point. Maybe she needed to take a break from all that. She had been living her life in hiding for nearly four years. She felt safer on the streets of Harlem than she did in her own world. It was a sad statement about her life, and all that had happened to her, some of which he knew she hadn't told him yet. It was just too hard for her. 'I'll think about it,' he said, and then they all breathed a sigh of relief as the subject of conversation moved on to other things. It had been heavy for all of them talking about his feelings about Carole. They all had issues of their own, scars and pain and fears. Life was about how you managed to get around the shoals and reefs of life without running aground and sinking the ship.

Charlie stayed with them until ten o'clock that night, talking and chatting about what they were all doing. They told funny stories about themselves and each other, about living together. He talked about the foundation, and the subject of Carole never came up again. He felt nostalgic and hugged them both when he left. It touched his heart to see them so happy together, but increased the sharp focus on his own loneliness too. He couldn't even imagine what it felt like to be like that, two people slowly weaving their lives together after so many years on their own. He would have liked to try it, he thought, but at the same time so much about it frightened him. What if they got tired of each other, or betrayed each other? What if one of them died, or got sick? What if they simply disappointed each other and the erosion of time and the ordinary agonies of life just wore them down? What if tragedy struck one or both of them? It all seemed so high-risk.

And then as he lay in bed and thought about them later that night, as though possessed by a force stronger than he was, he leaned over and picked up the phone. His fingers dialed her number before he could stop himself, and the next thing he knew he heard Carole's voice on the phone. It was almost as though someone else had called her, and he had no choice after that but to say hello.

'Carole?' He sounded almost as surprised to hear her as she did to hear him.

'Charlie?'

'I . . . I . . . I just wanted to wish you a happy Thanksgiving,' he said, nearly choking on his own tongue. She sounded stunned.

'I never thought I would hear from you again.' It had been nearly four weeks. 'Are you all right?'

'I'm fine,' he said, lying in bed with his eyes closed, savoring her voice. She sounded as though she was shaking, and in her own bed, hearing the sound of his voice again. She was. 'I had Thanksgiving dinner tonight with Sylvia and Gray.' Something they had said to him must have gotten into his soul somehow, or he knew he never would have called. For the first time ever, he had put on the brakes, stopped and looked around, and slowly doubled back. He was on the final turn, and land was in sight again. 'It was nice. How was yours?'

She sighed, and smiled at the sound of him. It was so wonderful to be speaking of mundane things. 'The way it always is. About all the wrong things. No one in my family is ever thankful. They're just embarrassingly overconfident about how wonderful they are. It never even occurs to them that other people don't have what they do, and maybe even wouldn't want to. It's not about family for us. It's about how wonderful we are for being Van Horns. It makes me sick. Next year, I'm just going to have Thanksgiving at the center with the kids. I'd rather eat turkey sandwiches, or peanut butter and jelly if that's all we've got after your money runs out, than drink champagne and eat pheasant with my family. It just sticks in my throat. Besides, I hate pheasant. I always have.' He smiled at what she said. Sylvia and Gray were right. Maybe he'd been wrong. It was hard work for her being a Van Horn. She wanted to be like everyone else. Sometimes he felt that way too.

'I have a better idea,' Charlie said quietly.

'What's that?' she asked, holding her breath. She had no idea what he was about to say, she just loved the sound of his voice. And everything else about him. She had right from the first.

'Maybe next year you and I can have Thanksgiving with Sylvia and Gray. The turkey was pretty good.' He smiled at the memory of the cozy evening he had shared with them. It would have been better yet if she'd been there.

'I'd love that,' Carole said with tears in her eyes, and then decided to tackle her perfidy again. She had thought about nothing but that for the past four weeks. Her motives had been good, but she knew what she'd done had been wrong. If she was going to be with him, and love him, she had to tell him the truth, even if he didn't like what he heard, or it scared her to say it. She had to trust him enough to let him see who she was, whatever the risk or cost. 'I'm sorry I lied to you,' she said sadly. 'It was a stupid thing to do.'

'I know. I do stupid things sometimes too. We all do. I was afraid to tell you about the boat.' It had been a sin of omission rather than commission, but he had done it for the same reasons. Sometimes it was just hard being out there, visible to all. It gave people a tremendous target to focus on and take aim at. Sometimes even he felt like he had a bull's-eye painted on his back, and apparently she did too. It wasn't an easy way to live.

'I'd love to see your boat some time,' she said cautiously. She didn't want to push, she was just grateful he had called. More grateful than he knew, as quiet tears of gratitude slid out of the corners of her eyes onto her pillow. She had even prayed about his coming back, and for once her prayers had been answered. The last time she had done that, they hadn't, when her marriage failed. In the end, God knew better.

'You will,' Charlie promised her. One day he wanted to spend time with her on the *Blue Moon*. He couldn't think of anything better. 'What are you doing tomorrow?'

'Nothing. I thought I'd drop by the center. The office is closed, but the kids are there. They get antsy on long weekends, and holidays are hard for them.'

'They're hard for me too,' he said, honest with her. 'I hate them. This is the time of year I hate most.' It brought back too many memories for him, of loved ones lost. Thanksgiving was hard. But Christmas was always worse. 'How about lunch tomorrow?'

'I'd love it.' She beamed as she lay in bed.

'We can go by the center if you want. I won't wear my gold watch,' he teased.

'Maybe you should wear your lion suit. You've earned it. This was very brave,' she said, with a voice filled with admiration that he had called her.

'Yes, it was.' It had been hard for him, but he was glad he'd done it. He knew they had Sylvia and Gray to thank for it. Thanks to them, he had gotten up the courage to call her. 'I'll pick you up at noon.'

'I'll be ready . . . and Charlie . . . thank you.'

'Goodnight,' he said softly.

18

The drive to Long Island was interminable, as Adam crawled along the Long Island Expressway in the Ferrari. He hadn't spent the night before with Maggie, because he didn't want to deal with her comments, however accurate, when he left to see his family in the morning. He had dropped her off at her place the night before, and knew she was spending the day alone. There was nothing he could do about it. He felt that some things in life couldn't be changed or avoided. It was his code of ethics, and sense of duty to his family, however painful they were for him. Thanksgiving with his family was a responsibility he felt he couldn't shirk, no matter how unpleasant. Maggie was right, of course, but even that didn't change anything. Going to spend the day with them felt like facing a firing squad. In spite of the aggravation, he was grateful for the traffic that slowed him down. It almost felt like a reprieve. A flat tire would have been nice too.

He was nearly half an hour late when he finally

arrived. His mother glared at him as he came through the door. Welcome home. 'Sorry, Mom. The traffic was unbelievable. I got here as fast as I could.'

'You should have left earlier. I'm sure if it was to meet a woman, you would.' Bam. First shot. More to come, he knew. There was no point trying to respond, so he didn't. Her score. And never his.

The rest of the family was already there. His father had a cold. His nephews and nieces were outside. His brother-in-law had a new job. His brother made cracks about Adam's work. His sister whined. No one ever talked about anything he cared about. His mother said she had read that Vana was on drugs, why did he want clients like that? What kind of firm did they run, catering to drug addicts and whores? Adam's stomach tied itself into the appropriate knot. No worse than usual, but uncomfortable all the same. His mother talked about getting old, one of these days she wouldn't be around, and they'd better appreciate her while they still could. His sister stared into space. His brother said he'd heard Ferraris were built like shit these days. His mother rhapsodized about Rachel. His father fell asleep in his chair before lunch. Cold pills, his mother said. His mother made a crack about his blowing it with Rachel, and that if he had been more attentive to her, maybe she wouldn't have left him for someone else, an Episcopalian yet. Didn't he worry about his kids being brought up by a Christian? What was wrong with him anyway? He hadn't even made it to synagogue on Yom Kippur. After everything they'd done to give him a decent upbringing, he never went to temple anymore, not even on holidays, and he went out with women who looked like prostitutes. Maybe he wanted to convert. As Adam listened, time stood still. He heard Maggie's voice. He thought of her alone in the apartment in the tenement in New York. He stood up, as Mae walked into the room to tell them lunch was served. His mother stared at him.

'What's wrong? You look sick.' His face was white.

'I think I am.'

'Maybe you have the flu,' his mother said, turning away to say something to his brother. Adam didn't move. He just stood rooted to the spot, looking at them. Maggie was right. He knew it.

'I have to leave,' he said to everyone in the room, but looking at his mother.

'Are you insane? We haven't eaten yet,' she said, looking right at him. But whatever she saw, he knew it wasn't him. She was seeing the little boy she had berated all his life, the one who had intruded on their lives and her bridge games. The one she had criticized since he was born. Not the man he had become, with accomplishments and achievements, disappointments and pain. Not one of them cared about his pain. Not even when Rachel left him. It was his fault. It always was. It always always always was, and always would be. And maybe he did go out with women who looked like whores. So what? They were nicer to him than anyone in his family had ever been. And they didn't give him any shit. All they wanted was boob jobs and new noses, and a couple of shots at his charge cards. And Maggie didn't even want that. She wanted nothing except him. His father woke up then and looked around. He saw Adam standing in the middle of the room.

'What's happening? What's going on?' No one in the room was moving. They were all looking at Adam. He turned to speak to his father.

'I'm leaving. I can't do this anymore.'

'Sit down,' his mother said, the way she would have if he'd been five years old and stood up at the wrong time. This wasn't the wrong time. It was the right one. And it was long overdue. Maggie was right. He shouldn't have come. He should have stopped coming years ago. If they couldn't respect him, if they didn't care who he was, and didn't even see him, if they thought he deserved all the shit Rachel had put him through and still was, then maybe they weren't his family after all, or didn't deserve to be. He had his kids, that was all he wanted, and they weren't there anyway. These people were strangers to him, and always had been. And they wanted it that way. He no longer did. He was forty-one years old, and he had finally grown up. It was time.

'I'm sorry, Dad,' he said calmly. 'I just can't do this again.'

'Do what?' His father looked confused. The cold pills had addled him a bit, but not as much as it looked. Adam sensed that he knew exactly what was going on, but wasn't going to deal with it. He never did. It was easier not to. Today was no different. 'Where are you going?'

'I'm going home,' Adam said, looking around the room at the people who had never failed to make him miserable for years. They had never let him in. So now he was choosing to stay out.

'You're sick,' his mother said as Mae stood in the door, not sure whether to announce lunch or not. 'You need a doctor. You need medication. You need a therapist, Adam. You're a very sick man.'

'Only when I come here, Mom. Every time I leave here, I have a knot in my stomach the size of my head. I don't need to come here and feel sick anymore. I'm not willing to do it. Happy Thanksgiving. Have a nice day,' he said then, turned, and walked out of the room. He didn't wait for further comment, or further abuse. He'd had enough. Mae caught his eye on his way out, and winked. No one tried to stop him, and no one said a word as he walked out the door. His nieces and nephews didn't know him. His family didn't care. And he didn't want to care anymore either, not for people who cared so little for him. He imagined that they sat staring at each other, as they heard the Ferrari drive away, and then they walked into the dining room. No one mentioned him again.

Adam gunned the car as he drove home. There was less traffic as he drove back into the city. He made good time, and was on the FDR Drive within half an hour, smiling to himself. For the first time in his life, he felt free. Truly free. He laughed out loud. Maybe his mother was right. Maybe he was nuts. But he had never felt less nuts in his life. And his stomach was feeling great. He was hungry. He was starving. And all he wanted now was Maggie.

He stopped at the supermarket on his way to her apartment. They had everything he needed. A prestuffed, precooked, prebasted, everything but pre-eaten turkey, with all the trimmings. He bought the whole shebang, cranberry jelly, sweet potatoes, biscuits that only needed to be warmed, mashed potatoes, peas, and pumpkin pie for dessert. For $49.99, he had everything he needed. Ten minutes later, he was ringing her doorbell. She answered in a cautious voice. She wasn't expecting anyone, and was stunned when she heard Adam. She buzzed him in immediately, and was wearing her nightgown when she opened the door to the apartment. She looked a mess, her hair wasn't combed, her face was streaked with mascara in patches. He could see that she'd been crying. She looked at him in confused amazement.

'What happened? Why aren't you on Long Island?' She looked confused.

'Put your clothes on. We're going home.'

'Where?' He looked like a madman. He was wearing a charcoal-gray suit, a white shirt, and a tie. His shoes were shined. He looked immaculate, but his eyes were wild. 'Are you drunk?'

'Nope. Cold stone sober. Get dressed. We're leaving.'

'Where are we going?' She didn't move, as Adam looked around the apartment. It was awful, worse than he had expected. It had never dawned on him that she lived in a place that looked like that.

There were two tiny unmade roll-away beds in the bedroom, and sleeping bags in the living room on two tattered couches. Both lampshades on the room's only lamps were broken. Nothing matched, everything was dirty, the window shades were broken and torn, there was a bare lightbulb hanging from a frayed wire in the middle of the room, and the carpet was filthy. The springs of the two couches they'd bought at Goodwill were sagging to the floor, and there was an orange crate as a coffee table. He couldn't imagine living like this, or her coming out of a place like that looking even halfway decent. There was dirty laundry all over the bathroom floor, and dirty dishes everywhere. The hallway when he'd come up had smelled of cats and urine. It made his heart ache just seeing her standing there in her nightgown. It was an old frayed flannel nightie that made her look like a little girl.

'How much do you pay for this place?' he asked her bluntly. He didn't want to say 'shithole,' but it was.

'My share is a hundred and seventy-five dollars,' she said, looking embarrassed. She had never let him come up before, and he hadn't asked, and now he felt guilty about that too. The woman slept in his bed nearly every night and he said he loved her, and when she left him, she came back to this. This was worse than Cinderella cleaning up her stepmother's house, scrubbing floors on her knees. It was a total nightmare, and the rest of the time she was getting her ass pinched at Pier 92. He had had no idea how she lived. 'It's all I can afford,' she said apologetically, as he fought back tears.

'Come on, Maggie,' he said softly, putting his arms around her and kissing her finally, 'let's go home.'

'What are we going to do? Don't you have to go to your parent's house?' She thought maybe he hadn't left yet, and had come to see her on his way out of town. In her dreams, he would ask her to come to his parents' with him. But she didn't realize the full extent of how miserable that would have been.

'I already went. I left. I walked out. I came home to be with you. I can't put up with that shit anymore.' She smiled at him as he said it. She was proud of him, and he knew it. At least someone was. And he was too. It was the ballsiest thing he had ever done. Thanks to her. She had opened his eyes, and when he looked and listened, he couldn't take it anymore. She had reminded him that he had a choice.

'Are we going out for lunch?' she asked, running a hand through her hair. She looked a total mess, and hadn't expected to see him till that night.

'No, I'm making you Thanksgiving dinner at my place. Let's go.' He sat down on one of the couches, and it sagged right to the floor. Everything looked so filthy, he hated to sit down. He couldn't even imagine living there. It never occurred to him that people lived like that. Let alone that she did. It made his heart ache for her. It took her twenty minutes to dress. She just put on jeans, a sweater, a Levi's jacket, and boots, washed her face, and combed her hair. She said she'd shower and put on makeup at his place, and she had decent clothes there. She hated to leave them in the apartment, because her roommates always took them and never gave them back, even her shoes. It was inconceivable to him now, having seen the place, that she ever looked as good as she did for him. You had to be a magician to come out of a hole like that and look, act, and feel like a human being, but she managed it somehow.

He followed her down the stairs, and two minutes later they roared off in the Ferrari and went back to his place. She helped him carry the groceries and cook dinner, after she showered and they made love. She set the table while he carved the turkey, and they had Thanksgiving dinner in his kitchen wearing bathrobes. After dinner they went back to bed, and he held her as he thought of everything that had happened that day. They had come a long, long way.

'I guess this must be a relationship, then,' he said, pulling her closer and smiling at her.

'What made you say that?' She smiled. He looked so beautiful to her, as she did to him.

'We just had a holiday together, didn't we? Maybe we even started a tradition. We'll have to get dressed next year though. My kids will be here. And I'm not taking them to my mom's.'

He still had a decision to make about Chanukah, but that was weeks away. He didn't want to keep his children from his parents, but he was no longer willing to sacrifice himself, or be burned at the stake to please them. Those days were over. There was a slim chance that his walking out might teach them to treat him better, but he doubted it. All he knew right now was that he was happy with Maggie, and his stomach didn't ache. That was a lot, and a vast improvement.

It was Sunday night before he asked her what had been on his mind all weekend. It was a big step, but having seen her apartment, he couldn't bring himself to let her go back there. It scared the shit out of him, but it wasn't marriage for chrissake, he told himself.

They were cleaning up the dinner dishes on Sunday night before she left. They had finished all the leftovers of their turkey at lunchtime. It had been delicious. His best Thanksgiving to date, and surely hers.

'What do you say you move in? You know . . . kind of try it out . . . see how it goes . . . you're here most of the time anyway . . . and I can help you with your homework . . .' His voice trailed off as she turned to look at him, uncertain. She was touched, but scared.

'I don't know,' she said, looking confused. 'I don't

want to be dependent on you, Adam. What you saw is all I can afford. If I get used to this, and you toss my ass out of here one day, it would be hard to go back.'

'Then don't. Stay here. I'm not going to toss your ass out, Maggie. I love you. And for now, this is working.'

'That's the point. "For now." What happens if it doesn't? I can't even afford to contribute to the rent.' He was touched by the thought, and looked pleased with himself when he answered.

'You don't have to. I own it.' She smiled, and kissed him.

'I love you. I don't want to take advantage of you. I don't want anything from you. Just you.'

'I know that. And I want you to move in. I miss you when you're not here.' He put on a basset hound face. 'I get headaches when you're not here.' Besides, he liked keeping track of her and knowing where she was.

'Stop giving me Jewish guilt.' She stood looking at him then and slowly nodded. 'Okay . . . I will. But I'm keeping my apartment for a while, just in case. If it doesn't work, or we get on each other's nerves, I'll go back.' It wasn't a threat, it was a sensible move on her part, and he respected her for it. He always did.

She stayed with him that night, and as he

cuddled up next to her, just as they were about to fall asleep, she tapped him on the shoulder, and he opened one eye. She had a way of wanting to discuss earth-shattering events with him, or life-altering decisions, just as he was drifting off to sleep. Other women had done that to him before, he figured it was something in the chromosomes, determined at birth. Women liked to talk when men wanted to sleep.

'Yeah? What?' He could barely stay awake.

'So what does this make it now?' She sounded wide awake to him.

'Huh?'

'Well, if we're living together and had a holiday, I guess this really really makes it a relationship, right? Or if you're living together, do you call it something else?'

'You call it sleep, and I want some . . . you get some too . . . I love you . . . we'll talk about it tomorrow . . . it's called living together . . . that's something good . . .' He was almost asleep.

'Yeah, I know,' she said, smiling to herself, too excited to go to sleep. She just lay there looking at him, as Adam rolled over, dead to the world, and snored.

19

Charlie picked Carole up promptly at noon on Friday and took her to lunch at La Goulue. It was a fashionable restaurant on Madison Avenue, with a good menu and a lively crowd. He felt less compelled to take her to simple down-to-earth restaurants, now that he knew who she was, and it was fun for both of them to go someplace nice. They had a delicious lunch, and then wandered up Madison Avenue, looking into the shops.

For the first time, she opened up with him about her early life. Gray had been right. Blue blood and fancy houses didn't necessarily make for a happy childhood. She talked about how cold and distant her parents had been, how chilly with each other, and emotionally and physically unavailable to her. She had been brought up by a nanny, never saw her parents, and she said her mother was a human block of ice. She had had no siblings to comfort her, she was an only child. She said she had gone weeks sometimes without seeing her parents, and they were deeply upset about the path she had chosen for her life. She had come to hate everything her world represented, the hypocrisy, the obsession with material possessions, the indifference to people's feelings, and lack of respect for anyone who hadn't been born into that life. It was obvious, listening to her, that she had been a lonely child. She had eventually gone from their icy indifference to her to the lavish abuses of the man she had married, who, as Gray had suspected, had married her because of who she was. When he left her finally, she had wanted to divorce herself not only from him, but from everything that had drawn him to her in the first place, and a set of values she had hated all her life.

'You can't do that, Carole,' Charlie said gently. There had been times when he wanted to do that himself, although not to the degree she had, but she had paid a higher price. 'You have to accept who you are. You're doing wonderful things for the children you work with. You don't have to strip yourself of everything you are to do that. You can actually enjoy both worlds.'

'I never enjoyed my childhood,' she said honestly. 'I hated everything about it from the time I was a little girl. People either wanted to play with me *because* of who I was, or *didn't* want to play with me because of who I was. I never knew which to expect, and it got to be too much work to figure it out.' He could see how that would happen, and it reminded him of something as they walked along. He hesitated to mention it to her so soon after they hadn't seen each other for so long. But it was as though they had never been apart. Her arm was tucked into his as they strolled up Madison Avenue, chatting as though he'd never left. He felt as though he belonged in her life, and she had exactly the same feeling.

'You're probably going to kill me for this,' he began cautiously as they crossed Seventy-second Street, heading north. The weather had turned cold, but it was crisp and clear. She was wearing a wool hat, and a cashmere scarf and gloves, and he had turned up the collar of his coat. 'I go to an event every year that you probably don't want to go to, given everything you've said. But I always feel I have to, and this year two of my friends' daughters are coming out. I go to the Infirmary Ball every year, where they present the debutantes. Aside from the obvious social complications, it's always a nice party. Would you come with me, Carole?' he asked hopefully, and she laughed. After the speeches she'd been making him about how much she hated 'their world,' she knew he was probably terrified to invite her to an event where blue-blooded young girls were presented to society and 'came out.' It was an archaic, snobbish tradition, but certainly one she was familiar with, as she turned to him and smiled.

'I hate to admit it' – she laughed ruefully – 'but I came out there myself. My parents go every year too. I haven't been since I came out. But it might be fun, with you. I wouldn't go otherwise.'

'Is that a yes?' he asked, smiling broadly at her. He was dying to go somewhere nice with her and show her off in a pretty dress. He loved seeing her at the center, but he still enjoyed formal events like that himself. It was fun dressing up once in a while, and the event was white tie.

'It's a yes,' she said, as they walked on. 'When is it?' She had to buy a dress. She hadn't worn a ball-gown in years, although she could have borrowed one from her mother, but didn't want to ask. They were the same size. She wanted to look beautiful for Charlie, and her mother's gowns would look too matronly on her.

'It's not for a few weeks. I'll look it up when I go to the office.' She nodded. Going to the deb ball with him was a big step for her, backward into her old life. But she also knew it was just a one-night oddity for her now, not a way of life. As a tourist, she could handle it, though she didn't want more of it than that. It was a compromise and gesture she was willing to make for him.

They fell silent as they continued to walk uptown

toward her house, and then turned east on Ninety-first. They were both ice-cold by then. It felt like it might snow. When they got to her front door, she turned to him and smiled. She could invite him in since he now knew it was her house, and no longer believed she was renting a small studio in the back.

'Would you like to come in?' she asked him shyly as she looked for her key and finally found it, at the bottom of her bag, where it always was.

'Is that all right with you?' he asked cautiously, and she nodded. She wanted him to. It was getting dark by then. They had been together since lunchtime, and had had a long lunch. They had a lot of time to make up for now, and had admitted over lunch how much they had missed each other. He had missed talking to her, knowing what she did, and sharing the excitement and complications and daily details of his own life with her. He had gotten used to her sage advice and wise counsel in the month they'd been seeing each other, and had felt her absence sorely once she was gone, as she had his.

They walked into a small distinguished-looking vestibule as they walked into the house. It had an elegant black-and-white marble floor. There were two small sitting rooms on the ground floor, one of which led into a handsome garden, and one flight up the stairs was a beautiful living room with large comfortable upholstered chairs and couches, a fireplace, and English antiques that she had taken from one of her parents' houses with their permission. They had more in storage. The house was elegant but at the same time warm and cozy, as she was, distinguished but playful. There were objects everywhere that were meaningful to her, even artwork by the children at the center. It was a wonderful mélange of old and new, expensive or priceless objects that had been made by children, or unusual objects found somewhere on her travels. There was a big comfortable kitchen, and a small, formal dining room with dark red walls and English hunting prints that had been her grandfather's. Upstairs, she had a large sunny bedroom and a guest room. She used the top floor as a small at-home office. She gave him a tour of the office, and he was greatly impressed as they walked back downstairs to the kitchen.

'I never invite anyone over, for obvious reasons,' she said sadly. 'I'd love to have people for dinner here some time, but I just can't.' She was pretending to be poor, and leading a secret life. Charlie knew it had to be lonely for her, just as his life was, for different reasons. She still had parents, but didn't like the ones she had, and had never been close to them. They had been emotionally absent all her life. He had no one. By different routes, they had arrived at the same place.

She offered him hot chocolate in the cozy kitchen, and they sat at her kitchen table while it got dark outside. He mentioned again how much he hated the holidays and was dreading them, as he always did. She didn't ask him what his plans were, she thought it was too soon to ask. He had only that day walked back into her life. He offered to light a fire in the fireplace then, and they settled down on the couch in the main living room once it was lit, and talked for hours. Their lives scattered around them like pieces of a jigsaw puzzle that they were slowly fitting together one by one, a piece of sky here, a tree there, a passing cloud, a house, a child-hood trauma, a heartbreak, a favorite pet, how much he loved his sister, how devastated he had been when she died, how lonely she had been as a child. It all fit together seamlessly, better than either of them could have planned.

It was after eight o'clock when she finally offered to cook him dinner. And he politely offered to take her out. It had just started snowing, and they both agreed it was much cozier inside. In the end, they made pasta and omelettes, standing together at the stove, with French bread, cheese, and salad. By the time dinner was over, they were both laughing at funny stories she told, and he told her about exotic places he'd been on the boat. And as they walked back into the living room, he took her in his arms and kissed her, and then suddenly he laughed.

'What are you laughing at?' she asked, sounding slightly nervous.

'I was thinking about Halloween and your green face. You looked so funny.' It was the first time he had kissed her, and they both remembered it well. All hell had broken loose between them shortly after that.

'Not nearly as funny as you with your lion's tail sticking up straight behind you. The kids still talk about it. They loved it. They thought you were really cool, and it gave Gabby something to hang on to, while she followed you around.' They hadn't gone to the center that day, and Carole said she was going the next day. Charlie said he wanted to go with her. He had missed the kids, especially Gabby. 'I told her you were away.' He nodded. He had missed all of it, but Carole most of all. And then, as he kissed her again, she looked into his eyes. There was something so gentle and peaceful there that she felt as though she'd come home. 'Do you want to go upstairs?' she asked him gently, and he nodded. He didn't say anything to her as he followed her up the stairs to her bedroom, and then he stood looking at her for an endless moment.

'Are you all right?' He didn't want to push her. He remembered how reluctant she had been to date, and that had only been two months before. A lot had happened in the meantime, and his four-week absence had told her that she loved him. She was willing to take the chance. For her, it had been a long, long time.

She nodded in answer to his question, and they settled comfortably into her big bed, where she slept in the middle when she was alone. She lay next to him feeling as though they had been there before. Their lovemaking was comforting and joyous, passionate and cozy at the same time. It was precisely what they both wanted so much, intimacy much needed and equally shared. And as the snow fell outside her windows that night, it looked like a Christmas card, and lying in each other's arms was like a dream.

20

The Thanksgiving weekend was easy for Gray and Sylvia. She went to the gallery on Saturday, and had errands to do. Gray went to his studio to paint, and on Sunday they sat in bed with *The New York Times* strewn around them, while he coached her on the crossword puzzle, and eventually they made love, and went back to sleep.

They hadn't heard a word from Charlie since Thanksgiving dinner, and they hoped he'd taken their advice, but they didn't know if he would. There were four inches of snow on the ground on Sunday morning, and that night Sylvia cooked dinner, while Gray read a book in the living room. They were chatting easily about nothing in particular over dinner when Gray asked her when her kids were coming home. He hadn't thought about it till then, and when he asked her, he looked worried. She knew he'd been anxious about meeting them, and afraid they might disapprove of their romance.

'A few days before Christmas, I think. Gilbert

said the twenty-third, but Emily is always a little vague. She'll catch a plane at the last minute, and blow in here like a hurricane. She always does.'

'That's what I'm afraid of,' Gray said, looking anxious. 'Sylvia, I just don't know if that's a good idea.'

'What, my children coming home for Christmas? Are you kidding?' She looked stunned. They were, and always had been, the light of her life. There was no way she was going to tell them not to come home, even for him. 'What are you saying?'

'I'm saying,' he said, taking a deep breath, 'that I don't know if I'm up to meeting them. I think I should stay at my studio while they're here.' She had a tiny studio apartment downstairs that they used when they were home. The rest of the time she used it for storage, so there was no reason why Gray couldn't continue to stay with her, and she had already explained that to him weeks before.

'Sweetheart, they're going to love you,' Sylvia said easily, trying to dispel his fears.

'I don't do well with kids.'

'They're not kids, they're adults.'

'That's what you think. Kids are kids, I don't care if they're eighty years old. If someone's hundred-year-old mother has a boyfriend, their eighty-year-old kid is going to be pissed. It's the law of nature.' He sounded convinced.

'Bullshit, they never gave Gordon any problems, and they were younger then.' Gordon was her lover who had died. 'Trust me, they're great kids, you're going to love them.'

'Maybe not,' he said sadly, and she looked up at him, worried.

'What are you saying?' She sensed that there was more to it than what appeared. She knew he was anxious about children, but not to this degree.

'I'm saying that that level of involvement makes me nervous. As long as we're just dealing with each other, I'm fine. But once you start dragging kids into it, I freak out.'

'Gray, for God's sake, that's insane. They'll only be here for a few weeks.' She was taking them skiing the day after Christmas, and she wanted Gray to come. They already knew there was a man in her life, and both seemed fine with it. They knew how lonely she had been since Gordon died.

'Maybe I should just stay out of the picture till they're gone,' he said firmly, growing more resolute by the minute, and Sylvia looked hurt, angry, and shocked.

'Let me get this straight here,' she said through clenched teeth. 'You don't want to meet my children, and you don't want to see me till they leave. Is that it? Did I get that right?'

'Yes, you did. You can come over to see me at the studio whenever you want.'

'Fuck that,' she said, as she strode nervously across the room and began to pace. 'I'm not going to be in a relationship with a man who won't even meet my kids. They're wonderful children, and I love them. And I also love you. They're part of me, Gray. You don't even know who I am until you know them too.'

'Yes, I do. And I love you too,' he said, looking more than a little panicked. He hadn't expected her reaction to be so extreme. 'But I'm not going to be forced into a situation I know I can't handle. I can't deal with that level of commitment. I just can't. I know myself. I've never wanted kids of my own, and I don't want anyone else's either.'

'Then you should be going out with a woman who has no kids.'

'Maybe so,' he said, staring at his feet.

'Just when did you decide all this?' She was horrified by everything he'd said. She had never expected him to be as unreasonable as this.

'As soon as you told me they were coming back here for Christmas. I just figured I'd bow out gracefully for a few weeks.'

'And what about next summer? You don't come to Europe with me either?' She liked having time

406

alone with them, but his reasons for it struck her as ridiculous, and even mean. He wasn't willing to make any effort whatsoever to meet her kids, or be part of her life, an important part of her life, in her eyes. 'I wanted you to come skiing with us,' she said, looking disappointed. She had rented a beautiful house for them in Vermont.

'I don't ski.' He remained unconvinced.

'Neither do I. But they do. And we always have a nice time together.'

'You will this year too. I just won't be there.'

'You're a shit!' she said, stormed into the bedroom, and slammed the door. And when she came out two hours later, he had gone back to his studio, to spend the night there for the first time in three months. It was a terrible situation, and when she called him, he said he was working and didn't want to talk.

'Fuck,' she said to herself, and paced some more. She had no idea how to win him over. She knew how bad his childhood had been, and how insane his family was. He had told her early on that family life was not for him. She just hadn't expected him to take it to these extremes. He didn't even want to see them. He only wanted her. She knew that if he remained firm on it, it would impact their relationship sooner rather than later. She wasn't sure whether to just let him be, and see if he'd relent on his own, or draw a line in the sand, and give him an ultimatum. Either way, she could lose him.

The Three Musketeers, as Sylvia now called them, met for dinner in a Chinese restaurant two weeks before Christmas. All of them were stressed and busy. Charlie said he had a million things to do for the foundation before he left on the boat. Adam's clients were all going nuts, and he was going to Vegas for the title fight of one of his clients that weekend. And Gray just looked depressed.

'So how are the lovebirds?' Charlie teased him as they started dinner. Gray just shook his head. 'What does that mean?'

'It means Sylvia and I are barely speaking to each other. It's been a tough couple of weeks since Thanksgiving.'

'What happened?' Charlie looked stunned. 'You two looked fine when I was there.' They looked better than fine. They were terrific.

'I don't do kids.'

'I know that.' Charlie smiled. 'That's Adam's department. Twenty-two-year-olds. Sylvia is adorable, but she's no kid.'

'No, but she *has* kids. And I don't want to meet them. They're coming in for Christmas, and I just can't go there. I can't. It makes me nuts. Every time

I get around families, it makes me nervous. I feel psychotic. I get depressed. I don't want to meet her kids. I love her, not her children.'

'Oh, shit. And what's she saying about that?' Charlie looked worried.

'Not much. She's pissed. I guess she's hurt. She isn't saying it, but I get the feeling that if I don't back down, it's going to be over with us, and I'm not backing down. I have to respect myself. I have limitations. I have issues. I grew up in the Addams Family on LSD. My sister is a Buddhist nun. My brother is a Navajo I haven't seen in a million years, and don't want to. And both my parents were head cases. I am allergic to families.'

'Even hers?' Charlie tested the waters.

'Even hers,' Gray confirmed. 'They're going to Vermont after Christmas,' he said as though they were going by rocket ship to another planet. 'To ski.' He made the electric chair sound more appealing.

'You might have fun.'

'No, I won't. They're probably not as nice as she thinks. Even if they are, I have my own problems. I don't want to be involved with her family, only with her.' But he also knew that if he stuck to that, he might blow the deal. Gray felt he had no choice, and Charlie felt sorry for them both. He knew how much it must mean to her. She was so proud of her kids. And also in love with Gray.

'I hope you guys work it out,' Charlie said gently. 'It would be a shame if you don't.' Gray had been so much happier since he'd been with her. And then he told him and Adam about Carole. 'I took your advice,' he said proudly, and then added, 'I hope you take mine, and compromise a little. I think you'll be sorry later if you don't.'

'I'm sure I will,' Gray said, looking resigned. He was fully prepared to pay the price for his decision, and lose her if he had to, rather than meet or get involved with her children.

'I have a little bit of news,' Adam said shyly, as the other two looked at him. 'Remember Maggie, from the Vana concert?' He reminded Charlie, and he nodded. 'She just moved in.' He looked half-proud and half-embarrassed as the other two stared at him.

'She *what*?' Charlie asked him. He remembered how she had looked that night, and feeling sorry for her. She had seemed like a nice girl and something of a lost soul. '*You*? Mr I'll-never-get-tied-down-again-I-have-to-have-my-freedom-and-a-million-women? How did *that* happen?' She hadn't looked like a conniver to him, but who knew? She had done something to turn him around, whatever it was.

'She's taking pre-law classes at night school, and I figured I could help her with her papers,' he said, trying to sound casual, and the other two guffawed, hooted, and jeered.

'Try that on someone else.'

'All right, all right . . . I really like her . . . love her . . . what do I know? One minute we were dating, and the next thing I knew, I didn't want her out of my sight. I haven't told her yet, but I'm taking her to Vegas this weekend. She's never been.' She hadn't been anywhere, and he was planning to change that soon.

'Have you told her about the boat?' Charlie asked him. Adam was flying to St. Barts to meet Charlie on the boat on December 26, as he did every year, after he spent Christmas with his kids.

Adam shook his head, trying to look un-concerned. 'I thought I'd tell her after this weekend.' He was hoping that she'd be so thrilled after the weekend that she wouldn't make a fuss about the boat. 'I can't change everything. We've been doing that trip for ten years. Have you told Carole?'

'No, but I will. I don't do holidays,' Charlie said firmly.

'I don't do kids,' Gray said just as firmly.

'Do you want to come to St. Barts with us?' Charlie suggested. 'If you're not going to be with Sylvia over the holidays, you might as well.'

'I don't do the Caribbean either,' he said

411

sheepishly, and then laughed at himself. 'Christ, among the three of us, we have enough baggage to start an airline.' But you didn't get to where they were in life, and come the long, hard road they had, without paying a price for it. They had all paid their dues.

'I don't do marriage,' Adam added with a grin.

'Tell me that this time next year,' Charlie said, laughing at him. 'Shit, you're the last person on the planet I would have expected to be living with a woman. What happened to all the others that you always juggle so expertly?' He was curious about it. Adam had never had less than four women going at once, often five, sometimes six in a good week. And once, seven.

'I gave them up for her.' He looked sheepish. 'I didn't want her doing the same thing to me. I thought she was. It turned out she was going to college. I thought there was another guy. To be honest, it nearly drove me insane. And then I realized I was in love with her. I like living with her.'

'I'm only staying with Sylvia,' Gray informed them. 'I'm still not living with her.' He sounded proud that he hadn't given in.

'That just means that your clothes are all over the city and you never have the right shoes in the right apartment,' Adam translated for him. 'And you're not going to be "staying" with her either, if you don't

412

meet her kids. Or at least that's my guess. I think that's a biggie for her. It would be for me too. I would have a fit if the woman in my life refused to meet my kids. It would be a deal-breaker for me.' It was insight for Gray, but he still shook his head.

'Have your kids met Maggie?' Charlie asked Adam with interest.

'Not yet. But they will. Probably before the holidays. I don't do mothers anymore either, by the way. Or at least I didn't on Thanksgiving. I went out to my parents', and I was sitting there listening to all the same bullshit getting dumped on me. I got up and walked out before lunch. I thought my mother would have a stroke if I ever did that, but she didn't. Actually, she's been very polite since then, whenever I call.'

'What did your father say?' Gray asked.

'He fell asleep.'

The rest of their dinner was uneventful. They talked politics, business, investments, art for Gray's sake. He was having a show in April, but they had already sold three of his paintings that they'd hung in the gallery in the meantime. Sylvia had done a wonderful thing when she opened that door for him, and he was grateful to her, but not grateful enough to meet her kids. Some things he just couldn't do. And Adam and Charlie talked about how excited they were about spending two weeks on the *Blue Moon*. They encouraged Gray again to join them, but he wouldn't. He said he had a lot of work to do to get ready for his show.

As usual, they were the last to leave the restaurant, and had had a fair amount to drink. None of them drank unduly on his own, but once together, all bets were off, and they let it rip.

Gray went back to his apartment that night. Maggie was asleep when Adam got in, and Charlie went home, smiling to himself thinking about the weeks he was about to spend on his boat. He was leaving four days before Christmas. It was the perfect way for him to pretend that Christmas did not exist.

21

Adam told Maggie about the weekend in Las Vegas the following morning, and she was thrilled. She had the weekend off from work anyway, and she had to do a paper, but she said she'd take her books with her and do it there whenever Adam was busy. She threw her arms around his neck and couldn't believe her good fortune. They were flying there on his plane.

And then she turned to him with a look of panic.

'What'll I wear?' Now that she was living with him, she no longer had access to her roommates' wardrobes, but they wouldn't have had anything appropriate anyway. Adam had already thought of it, smiled, and tossed a credit card at her.

'Go shopping,' he said generously, and she stood staring at it for a minute, and then handed it back to him.

'I can't do that,' she said sadly. 'I may be poor, but I'm not cheap.' She knew that other women had done that to him before her, and no matter what happened, she knew she never would. She'd make her own money one day. And in the meantime, she managed on what she had, which was the salary and tips she earned at Pier 92. 'Thanks, sweetheart. I'll figure out something.' He knew she would, but his heart always ached for her. Her life was so much harder than his, and always had been. He wanted to help her more than he did, and she never let him. But he respected her for it. She was an entirely different breed from any of the women he had known.

They were leaving for Vegas on Friday afternoon, and she was so excited she could hardly stand it. She threw her arms around his neck, and thanked him. He loved doing things like that for her. He was looking forward to showing her around, and making it special for her. He wanted to make up to her for all the hard times she'd had, and she was always grateful to him, and never took anything for granted. The following weekend, after the trip to Las Vegas, he told her he wanted her to celebrate Chanukah with him and his kids. He told his mother they wouldn't be there. Times had finally changed.

When Charlie picked Carole up to go to the debutante cotillion, she was dressed and waiting for him. She took his breath away when he saw her walking toward him. She was wearing a pink satin dress and silver high-heeled sandals, with her hair in an elegant French twist. She had borrowed a white mink jacket from her mother, and bought the dress at Bergdorf's. She hadn't been there in years. She was wearing diamond earrings and a diamond bracelet that had been her grandmother's, and she carried a small silver purse and long white kid gloves.

For a long, long moment, Charlie just stood there and stared. He was wearing white tie and tails. They made a spectacular-looking couple. Carole looked like a cross between Grace Kelly and Uma Thurman, with a dash of Michelle Pfeiffer thrown in. And Charlie was somewhere between Gary Cooper and Cary Grant.

Heads turned as they walked into the ballroom at the Waldorf-Astoria, and Carole looked absolutely regal. It was a far cry from the woman he'd met in blue jeans and Nikes at the center, or the green face and wig on Halloween. But the best part was that he loved all three sides of her. It was fun being out with her in public, and seeing her all dressed up.

They went through the receiving line and met all the debs, and Carole reminisced sotto voce about her own presentation there. She said she had been scared to death, but had fun in the end, in spite of herself.

'I'll bet you were gorgeous,' he said with an admiring look. 'But even more so now. You look absolutely beautiful tonight,' he said, and meant it, as he whirled her around the dance floor in a slow waltz. He was an exquisite dancer, and so was she. All their early life and training showed its colors at moments like that, dancing school, deb parties, all the things that Carole shunned and tried to forget now. But tonight she was back in her old world, though just for a brief visit. Charlie knew he wouldn't get her to do things like that often, and he didn't mind. He was somewhat tired of them himself. He just liked having the option to do them now and then.

They ran into her parents shortly before dinner. Carole pointed them out to him, and they made their way politely to her parents' table. They were sitting among the scions of New York, and her father stood up as soon as he saw them. He was a tall distinguished man and looked a lot like Carole. He held out a hand to Charlie when she introduced them, and his face looked as though it had been carved from ice. Charlie had met him years before, but he doubted that the older man recalled.

'I knew your father,' Arthur Van Horn said grimly. 'We were at Andover together. I was very sorry to hear about what happened. It was a tragic loss.' It was not a happy topic for Charlie, and Carole tried to get him off the subject. Her father had a way of casting a pall on everything, it was just the way he was. She also introduced him to her mother, who sat in glacial silence, shook his hand, nodded, and turned around. And that was it. Carole and Charlie went back to their table and then danced some more before they sat down.

'Well, that was a little daunting,' Charlie admitted, as Carole laughed. Their greeting had been typical of her parents, and had nothing to do with him.

'For them, that was warm.' They were caricatures of the upper class to which they belonged. 'I don't think my mother ever hugged or kissed me. She always walked into the nursery, as she referred to it, looking as though she was visiting animals in the zoo, and was afraid she'd be attacked if she stuck around, so she didn't. I never saw her for more than five minutes. If I ever have kids, I'm going to lie on the floor with them, get dirty, and hug and kiss them till they scream.'

'My mother was like that, the way you just described wanting to be with yours.' It made it that much harder for him when she died. She had always told him how much she loved him, as did Ellen. His father had been his mentor and best friend until he died. His hero. It had been a lot to lose. His whole world, in fact. He remembered his father as a happy, debonair man who looked like Clark Gable, and loved yachts. It was probably why Charlie had bought one in honor of him, when they died. He wanted to have boats that his father would have approved of, and commented to Carole how odd it was that those things followed one into adulthood, in fact all one's life.

'I guess we never get over wanting to please our parents,' he said as they sat down for dinner.

The evening was fun for both of them, the girls were pretty, the moments tender to watch. The girls danced first with their fathers, holding their bouquets, and wearing elaborate white gowns. It was almost like a wedding, and once upon a time it had been the precursor to that. Debutantes had been presented to society in order to find husbands. Now the girls just had fun, and at the end of the evening changed into miniskirts and went to discos with their friends.

'Technically, I disapprove of it,' Carole admitted to him, 'and everything it stands for. But the truth is, it doesn't mean much, it doesn't hurt anyone. It's not PC, but the kids seem to have a good time. So why not?' He was relieved that she saw it that way, and he looked at her again with pleasure, as they drove back to her house afterward in the limo he had rented for the occasion. The evening had been very grand, and they had both enjoyed it. 'Thank you for taking me.' She smiled at him, as he leaned over and kissed her. He thought she was the most beautiful woman he'd ever seen, and he was proud to be with her, although he'd been slightly horrified by her parents. He couldn't imagine growing up with two people like that. It amazed him that she was normal, and grateful that she was not like them. She was warm and kind and compassionate, gentle where they were stiff, and easy to be with. She was smiling at him happily as they approached her house. 'I can hardly wait to spend Christmas with you.' She smiled at him. 'I love the holidays. I thought I'd buy my tree tomorrow, and we can decorate it.' He looked at her then as though he had been slapped, and there was a strange awkward moment between them. He knew he had to say something now. If he didn't, he was a liar. He had to tell her the truth, just as he had told her, when they got back together, that he expected it of her.

His voice was very sad and soft as he spoke. 'I won't be here.'

'Tomorrow?' She looked startled, and he looked chagrined.

'No. For Christmas,' he said carefully. 'I hate the holidays, every moment of them, everything about them. I don't do Christmas anymore. It's too hard for me. I spend it on my boat every year. I'll be gone for three weeks.' There was a long silence between them as she stared at him, as though she found it hard to believe.

'When are you leaving?' she asked, looking as though he had hit her in the head with a brick. He almost expected to see blood trickling from her ear. It made him feel sick. He hated to disappoint her. But there were some things he just couldn't do for anyone, and this was one.

'Next week.' He sounded pained but determined.

'Before Christmas?' He nodded.

'I'm going to St. Barts with Adam. It's a tradition. We do it every year.' As though that excused it, but they both knew that in her eyes, it didn't.

'He leaves his kids for the holidays?' Her voice was filled with disapproval, it sounded incredibly selfish to her.

'He comes the day after Christmas. I always go down a week before.'

'Why don't you go down with him the day after? Then we could be together on Christmas.' It seemed like a reasonable compromise to her, but Charlie shook his head.

'I can't do it. I know myself. I just can't. I want to get out of here, before everyone gets maudlin, or I do. Christmas is for people with children and families. I don't have either.'

'You have me,' she said sadly. In some ways, she knew it was too soon to expect it of him, but they had a relationship, they said they loved each other, and Christmas was important to her. That was supposed to mean something. And apparently, to Charlie, it didn't. Or maybe it meant too much.

'We'll do something fun when I get back,' he said by way of consolation, but she was staring out the window, thinking.

'I can't get away then. I wasn't expecting to do anything spectacular.' She turned to look at him again. 'I just wanted to be with you. I have to work then anyway. I can't just walk out on the kids for no reason when you get back, just because you don't want to spend Christmas with me.'

'It's not about trying to avoid you,' he explained to her, looking unhappy. 'I hate the whole goddamn thing. It was designed to make people miserable and feel left out. Even kids, they never get what they want. People argue, children fight. Santa Claus is a lie we tell kids and then disappoint them later, when we think they're old enough to take it, and tell them it's not true. I hate the whole damn mess, and I won't do it.'

'Maybe love is always about disappointment,' she said, looking straight at him.

'I was hoping you'd be a good sport about it,' he

said, looking strained as they pulled up in front of her house.

'I was hoping you'd be here.' The prospect of spending Christmas alone with her parents depressed her even more, for obvious reasons. She was planning to spend most of it at the center, and the rest with him. So much for that.

He helped her out of the car and walked her to her front door. He had cast a pall over the evening with his announcement, and he was afraid to even kiss her. Although she hadn't said it in so many words, it sounded as though it was a deal-breaker to her. He feared it would be. But he knew this was one thing he couldn't do for her, and wouldn't.

'I'll call you tomorrow,' he said gently, as he walked her into her house. He didn't ask to stay, nor did she invite him. She was too upset about what she'd just heard. Apparently, it wasn't the relationship she thought it was. Not if he wouldn't spend Christmas with her. Or New Year's, if he was going to be gone for three weeks. She had another lonely New Year's Eve to look forward to as well.

'Goodnight,' she said quietly, as she kissed him on the cheek, and a moment later he left. She stood at the window watching, as the limousine drove away.

As they drove toward his house, Carole's words were ringing in his head. '*Maybe love is always about disappointment.*' It was a damning statement, and maybe he deserved it. But this time they were both disappointed. He expected her to understand how painful it was for him. She didn't. She expected him to be with her. And he couldn't do it. Even for her, no matter what the cost to them.

22

The weekend in Las Vegas was fabulous, and Maggie loved everything about it. The shows, the shops, the lights, the gambling, the people, and even the title fight. In the end, he had bought a dress for her and a little fur jacket, and she had worn them to the fight. She had won five hundred dollars on the slot machines on a fifty-dollar invest-ment of her own money, and she was thrilled. Flying back to New York, on his plane, she sat there feeling like a princess, as Adam smiled at her with pleasure.

'I'm glad you had fun.' He loved spoiling her, being with her, and showing her off. She had looked absolutely gorgeous in the new dress and fur jacket.

'I had a ball,' she confirmed again, and thanked him profusely.

They were about to land at JFK when for no reason in particular she brought up New Year's Eve, and said it would be fun to spend it in Las Vegas. She had loved it. She fit right into his world, instead of complaining about it like his mother.

'Yeah, maybe some time,' he said vaguely.

'What about this year?' she asked, looking excited. She knew he went often, and he had the plane, so they could go anywhere they wanted, which was a new concept for her. She felt like a bird with giant wings.

'I can't,' he said, looking out the window, and then, like Charlie, he knew he had to tell her. He had to sooner or later, and the time was now. 'I go away with Charlie every year, the day after Christmas.'

'You mean, like a guy thing, a hunting trip or something?' She looked disappointed.

'Yeah, sort of like that.' He was going to leave it at that for now, but she wouldn't.

'Where do you go?'

'St. Barts, on Charlie's boat.' Maggie stared at him in outrage.

'To the *Caribbean*? On a *yacht*? Are you kidding?'

'No, I'm not kidding. He hates Christmas. He goes down a week before I do. And I come after I have Christmas with the kids. We do it every year.'

'Yeah, and what? Screw every bimbo in the Caribbean?'

'Previously, yes. Now, no. I have you.' He said calmly. He didn't want a fight with her. Nor was he willing to change his plans. His trips with Charlie were a tradition that meant a lot to him.

'And you're not asking me to come with you?' she said, looking as though she was about to throw something at him. But fortunately for him, nothing suitable was at hand.

'Maggie, I can't. It's Charlie's trip, and he'll be alone. It's a guy thing.'

'Like hell it is. I know what guys do when they're alone. All the same shit you did till you met me.'

'Charlie's not like that. He's very proper. And he has a girlfriend now too.'

'Is she going?' Maggie asked suspiciously, as Adam shook his head in response.

'No, she's not. It's just the two of us.'

'For how long?'

'Two weeks.' He winced at her expression.

'*Two weeks?* You think I'm just going to sit here, while you go off picking up women for *two weeks?* If you think that, you're crazy.'

'Don't threaten me,' he said, looking angry. 'I know you're upset, but I can't help it. I can't let Charlie down. And I can't just ask Charlie if you can come. It would be weird for him, and he expects me to come alone.'

'Great, then have a terrific New Year's Eve, kissing him. Maybe that's what this is really all about. Is he gay?'

'Oh, for chrissake. We're friends. We travel together twice a year. I'm sorry it happens to be over New Year's Eve, but I didn't know you were coming. I'm sorry.'

'And next year will be different?'

'Maybe. I don't know. I'm not making promises now for a year from now. Let's see where this goes.' He tried to sound calmer than he was. Just listening to her, he was getting a headache. A bad one.

'I'll tell you where it's going. It's going right down the tubes, if you think you're going to dump me for holidays, and go off on trips with your buddies. If you don't want to spend holidays with me, fine, but then you can take your goddamn rule book about dating and shove it you know where. Because people in relationships spend holidays together, and especially New Year's Eve.'

'Thank you for the information.' He was holding his head by then and she ignored him. She was furious with him. 'Look, we just had a nice time in Las Vegas, let's not spoil it. I want you to meet my kids next week. I love you. I want this to work. I just have to go away for a couple of weeks. Can't you relax about it and be nice?'

'Nice people always get fucked over. And you don't *have* to go. You *want* to. What did Charlie's girlfriend say about it?'

'I have no idea,' he said grimly.

'I'll bet she's not happy about it either.'

The battle about not spending New Year's Eve together raged between them throughout the week. Maggie managed to put it aside long enough to meet Adam's children the following weekend, and after some initial cautious exploratory moves, they decided they loved her, and she was crazy about them. Adam was thrilled. The four of them went skating together, Maggie took Amanda shopping for a Christmas present for her father. They explained to her all about Chanukah. She even showed Amanda how to do her makeup, baked cookies with Jacob, and gave him tips about girls. They thought she was the best thing since sliced bread, she was young enough to have fun with them, and old enough to be someone they looked up to. Adam had expected some resistance to her, and got none. The three were fast friends when Amanda and Jacob left. And then the war began again. The cease-fire only lasted through the weekend.

Charlie had dinner with Carole twice after the debutante ball, and a decided chill had settled in between them. She didn't say anything about it initially, and then finally the second time she saw him, she asked him if he had changed his plans. He shook his head.

'Carole, I can't.' She nodded and said nothing. He had wanted to spend the night with her, but didn't have the courage to ask her, and went back to his place instead. He had the distinct impression that if he left for Christmas, their romance would be over when he got back. She particularly didn't understand what he was doing, since he was going alone for the first week, over Christmas. As far as she was concerned, there was no reason for him to go before the twenty-sixth, when he could have gone with Adam. He stopped trying to explain it to her, and decided to deal with it when he got back. If she was still speaking to him by then.

Adam called him in the office the day before Charlie was leaving town. Charlie was in a mad rush trying to finish everything on his desk. And Adam said his office was just as bad.

'All my clients fall apart at this time of year. If their marriage has been lousy, they decide to get divorced. If their mistresses have been cranky, they get knocked up. If their kids are crazy, they wind up in jail. If a singer hates her contract, she tears it up. And half my athletes get drunk over the holidays and go out and rape someone. It's a lot of fun. I really love it this time of year.' Adam sounded beyond stressed.

'Me too.' Charlie laughed. In spite of Carole's reaction to it, he was looking forward to their trip.

'I assume despite everything you just described, everything is still on track. You're still coming, right?' It was always good to check. And much to his surprise, there was a pause. It had been a rhetorical question, but suddenly he heard something in Adam's voice.

'I'm having a hell of a time with Maggie,' he admitted. 'She thinks we're going to be cruising the Caribbean picking up everything in sight, with our dicks hanging overboard. She's not too pleased.' Charlie laughed at his description, and then sobered quickly. 'She didn't voice it quite that way, but Carole is pretty upset too. She thought we'd be spending Christmas together, and I told her I don't do Christmas. I was hoping she'd understand, but she doesn't. This could be a deal-breaker for her.' But he wasn't willing to be forced into staying home. If she couldn't live with it, then that was that. He wanted her to accept him as he was, warts and all. And one of his warts was that he was phobic about the holidays ever since his parents' death, and worse yet since Ellen's.

'I'm sorry to hear it,' Adam said sadly. 'I'm worried that Maggie feels that way too. It's a shame that they can't just let it go, but holidays are a big deal to some people. There's something about holidays and women, if you don't do it right, they fire you.'

432

'Apparently,' Charlie said, sounding annoyed. But he was upset about Carole too. It had taken a big bite out of them ever since he told her. And he was planning to be gone for three weeks, which was a long time for her to stay upset with him. Particularly since they'd only just gotten back together. They didn't need another major bump in the road, and they'd already hit one. He was almost sure the relationship wouldn't survive another. He hated to lose her. He was afraid he would. But not enough to stay. His phobia was as powerful as her need for him to stay home with her.

'And to complicate matters further at my end, my kids just met Maggie this weekend, and they were crazy about her. To tell you the truth, Charlie, I hate to piss her off.' More than that, he hated to hurt her, and this would. A lot.

'What are you saying? That you can't come?' Charlie was shocked.

'I don't know. Maybe times have changed. For both of us. Me, in any case.' He wasn't sure how committed to Carole Charlie was at this point. It was hard to tell. And he suspected Charlie wasn't sure himself. He and Maggie were living together and further along.

'Let me think about it. I'll call you back.'

'Call me on my cell phone. I'll be out at meetings all afternoon. Believe it or not, all joking aside, I actually do have to bail one of my clients out of jail.'

'Lucky you! I'll get back to you,' Charlie said, and hung up.

It was nearly five o'clock when Charlie got back to Adam, and both men sounded strained. Adam had had a nightmarish afternoon, juggling both client and press. And Charlie was trying to chase elephants off his desk at year end. But beyond that, he was worried about Carole. He had paid close attention to what Adam said. Times had changed. And if he wanted more than he'd had in his life until then, he had to change too. He felt like he was leaping off a cliff. Hopefully, not into cement. That remained to be seen.

'Okay,' Charlie said, as though he were about to suggest they both jump out of a plane without parachutes. 'Let's do it.'

'Do what?' Adam sounded confused, and there was a lot of noise where he was. He was still at the jail, trying to keep the press at bay. It sounded like the birdhouse at the zoo. 'Why don't you bring Maggie to the boat? I like her. You love her. She loves you. We'll have fun. What the hell. Your relationship may not survive if you don't.' He didn't want to be responsible for that. He could tell that Adam had his back to the wall, and maybe even wanted her along. 'If you want to bring her, you can. It's up to you. I'm inviting Carole too.'

'Charlie, you're a hero.' Adam hadn't wanted to ask him, but he wanted to bring her. 'You're a prince. I'll tell her tonight. What about you?'

'I'm probably crazy, and I'm not sure we're there yet, either of us. But I'm going to invite Carole too. I would have liked it better if she could let me do this. But if she can't, or she doesn't, I think it will be a big loss for me. Maybe bigger than I think.' They had invested something in the relationship, honesty, truth, courage, love, hope, and he wasn't willing to cash it in. Not yet. And leaving her over the holidays might force him to, whether he liked it or not.

'Holy shit,' Adam said, laughing. 'What's happening to us?'

'I'm afraid to think,' Charlie said wanly.

'Yeah, me too. Scary stuff, bro. But you're a real mensch to do this. At least we won't have to worry about getting laid, or depend on the natives for help.'

'I'm not sure I would say that to Maggie if I were you.' Charlie laughed.

'No shit. When are you leaving?'

'Tomorrow morning.'

'Have a good trip. I'll see you on the twenty-sixth. *We'll* see you on the twenty-sixth. And by the way, I'll give Carole a ride down there on the plane, if she wants. Give her my number, and tell her to call me.'

'I will. Thanks,' Charlie said.

'No, thank *you*.'

They hung up then, and Charlie sat staring into space for a minute. Adam was right. Times had changed.

Charlie left his office at five-thirty, took a cab to the center, and got there at six, just as Carole was closing her office. She was surprised to see him, and wondered if something was wrong. Something else. There was a lot wrong lately. Christmas. New Year. Him away for three weeks. It had put a damper on her holidays. He hadn't even seen her tree.

'Hi, Charlie. What's up?' She looked tired. It had been a long day.

'I came to say good-bye,' he said as he walked in.

'When are you going?'

'Tomorrow.' She nodded. What else was there to say? She knew it would be over by the time he returned. For her anyway, if not for him. She felt as strongly about this as he had about her lying about her name. If you were in a relationship, as far as she was concerned, you spent the holidays together. He didn't see it that way. They didn't even exist for him. And maybe neither did she. She needed someone emotionally available, not someone who couldn't allow himself to feel anything, because it hurt too much. Life hurt too much, but was to be lived. Together, hopefully.

'Have a good trip,' she said, as she stuck a fat file into a drawer.

'You too,' he said quietly.

'Me too what?' She didn't get his drift. She was too tired to play games with him.

'You have a good trip too.'

'I'm not going anywhere.' She stood up straight and looked at him.

'Yes, you are, or at least I hope you are . . . or I hope you will. . . . ' He stumbled over his own words as she stared at him. 'If you're willing, I'd love you to come down with Adam and Maggie on the twenty-sixth. He's flying down then. And he's bringing her. We worked it out today.'

'And you want me to come too?' She looked stunned as she smiled at him. 'Are you serious?'

'Yes, I am.' Perhaps even more so than he wanted to be. 'I'd love you to come down, Carole. Will you?' he asked, looking at her. 'I hope you can get away.'

'I'll try. And I hope you know I wasn't trying to shove my way into your trip. I just wanted you to be here over Christmas, and leave on the twenty-sixth with him.'

'I know. I can't do that. Not yet anyway. Maybe one day. But if you can do it, we can have two weeks together there.' It sounded fantastic to her, and even to him now. It was a great idea. He was glad Adam had called him.

'I don't think I can stay for more than a week. I'll see.'

'Whatever you can do,' he said, and then kissed her. She looked at him longingly and kissed him. And then they took a cab back to her place, and spent the night together before he left the next day. He even saw her tree.

When Adam got home that night, he handed Maggie a credit card. She was sitting over her law books and didn't look up when he came in. He dropped the credit card on the desk.

'What's that for?' she asked, without looking up. She was still angry at him over the trip. Their weekend with his kids had only been a brief respite from open warfare. Now they were back to the cold war.

'You need to go shopping,' he said, as he took off his tie and threw it on a chair.

'What for? I don't use your credit cards. You know that.' She threw it back at him, and he caught it, and stood holding it.

'You need to use it this time.' He set it down next to her again.

'Why?'

'Because you need a lot of stuff. You know,

bathing suits, wraparounds, sandals, girl stuff, what do I know? You figure it out.'

'Figure what out?' She still didn't get it.

'What you need for the trip.'

'What trip? Where are we going?' She wondered if he was taking her to Vegas again, as a consolation prize.

'We're going to St. Barts on Charlie's boat.' He said it as though reminding her, and she stared at him.

'No, *you're* going to St. Barts on Charlie's boat. *I'm* not. Remember?'

'He called today and invited you too,' he said gently, and she stared at him and put her pen down.

'Are you serious?'

'Yes, I am. So is he. I told him I didn't want to upset you, and I don't think he wants to upset Carole either. He's going to invite her too.'

'Oh my God! Oh my God! OH MY GOD!!' She kissed him and ran screaming around the room and then jumped into his arms, as he laughed at her.

'Does that do the trick?' He could see that it did. And then some.

'Are you kidding? Oh my God! I'm going on a yacht with you to the Caribbean! Yes yes yes YES!' And then she turned to him with a grateful look. 'Adam, I love you. I'd have loved you anyway, but I was so hurt.'

'I know,' he said, kissing her again.

'I really love you,' she said, clinging to him. 'I hope you know that.'

'Yeah, baby . . . me too. . . .' And then he kissed her.

Come December 26, they'd be off to the Caribbean.

23

The argument between Sylvia and Gray, over his seeing her children, continued until nearly Christmas. He was staying at his studio now nearly every night, and she wasn't pressing him to stay at her apartment. She was too angry at him. She understood that he had 'issues,' but as far as she was concerned, he was taking it too far. He wasn't even trying to deal with them. Gilbert was arriving in two days. And Emily the day after. And Gray had dug his heels in. He was not going to meet them.

'If you're that upset about it, then go to counseling,' Sylvia had shouted at him in the course of their last fight. They were having them nearly daily. It was a hot topic, for both of them. 'What's the point of reading all those goddamn self-help books, if you're not willing to help yourself?'

'I *am* helping myself. I'm respecting my boundaries, and so should you,' he said grimly. 'I know my limitations. Families freak me out.'

'You don't even know mine.'

'And I don't want to!' he had shouted, and stormed out.

Sylvia was profoundly depressed over what had happened, and the position Gray had taken. It had been going on for nearly a month, and had taken a toll on the relationship. The joy that they had shared in discovering each other had all but disappeared. And when Gilbert arrived two days before Christmas, she hadn't seen Gray in two days. She tried to explain it to her son, when he asked about him, but it sounded nuts even to her. As she had pointed out to Gray, people their age were supposed to be saner than that, but apparently he wasn't, and was making no attempt whatsoever to get his neuroses in check. He was reveling in them. Like a pig in slop.

The only good thing about it, for him, was that he was so upset, it was driving him to paint more. He hadn't stopped painting in weeks, and had finished two paintings since Thanksgiving, which was fast for him. His dealer was thrilled. The new work was great. He had always said that he did his best work when he was unhappy. And he was proving it. He was miserable without her. He couldn't sleep. So he painted. Constantly. Day and night.

He was hard at work late one night, after their most recent argument, when his bell rang. He thought it was Sylvia, come to drive her point home one more time, and without asking who it was, he hit the buzzer and let her up. He left the door to his apartment open, and braced himself for another round as he stared at the canvas, frowning. It was almost becoming a game between them. She begged him to see her kids. He said no. Then she blew her top. And so did he. It had become a vicious cycle. She refused to let go, and he refused to give in.

He heard the door open, and looked up, expecting to see her, and saw a wraithlike young man looking at him instead. 'I'm sorry . . . the door was open . . . I didn't mean to interrupt. You're Gray Hawk, aren't you?'

'Yes, I am.' Gray looked startled. Whoever the young man was, he looked sick. His hair was thin and short, his face looked like a cadaver's, and his eyes were sunk deep into his head. His skin was concrete colored. He looked like he had cancer, or something just as bad. Gray had no idea what he was doing there, or who he was. 'Who are you?' He wanted to ask him what he was doing in his apartment, but he had left the door open so it was his own fault that there was a stranger standing there.

The man hesitated for a moment and stood where he was. 'I'm Boy,' he said softly, as though he didn't have the strength to say more.

'Boy?' Gray said, looking blank. It took a

443

moment to register, and then he looked like he'd been shot. He went almost as pale himself, as he stood rooted to the spot. 'Boy? Oh my God.' He had thought about him, but not seen him in so long. He was the Navajo baby his parents had adopted twenty-five years before and named Boy. Gray walked slowly toward him and then stood in front of him, as tears rolled slowly down his cheeks. They had never been close. There were twenty-five years between them, but he was a ghost from a piece of history that had haunted Gray all his life, and still did. It was at the root of his battle with Sylvia now. He wondered for a moment if it was a hallucination. Boy looked like the Ghost of Christmas Past. Gray put his arms around him then and just held him as they cried. They were crying for what might have been, what had been, and all the insanity that they had experienced separately but in the same place and for the same reasons. 'What are you doing here?' he finally managed to choke out. Gray had never even tried to see him, and probably wouldn't if he hadn't been standing there.

'I wanted to see you,' he said simply. 'I'm sick.' Gray could see that. His whole being was almost translucent, as though he were disappearing and filled with light.

'What kind of sick?' Gray asked sadly. Just seeing him brought it all back.

'I have AIDS. I'm dying.' Gray didn't ask him how he had gotten it. It was none of his business.

'I'm sorry,' he said, and meant it. His heart went out to him as they looked at each other. 'Do you live here? In New York? How did you find me?'

'I looked you up. You're in the phone book. I live in L.A.' He didn't waste time telling Gray about his life. 'I just wanted to see you . . . once . . . you're the reason why I came here. I'm going back tomorrow.'

'On Christmas?' It seemed like a sad time to travel.

'I'm in treatment. I have to get back. I know this sounds stupid, but I just wanted to say good-bye.' The real tragedy was that they had never said hello. The last time he had seen Boy, he was a child. And then once at their parents' funeral. Gray had never seen him again, nor wanted to. Gray had spent a lifetime closing the door on the past, and now this man had put a foot in it, and was keeping the door open, and shoving it wider, with his deep sunken eyes.

'Are you all right? Do you need anything?' Maybe he needed money. Gray didn't have much. But the young man shook his head.

'No. I'm fine.'

'Are you hungry?' Gray felt as though he should do something for him, and then asked him if he wanted to go out.

'That would be nice. I'm staying at a hotel nearby. Maybe we could go out for a sandwich or something?'

Gray went to get his coat, and a few minutes later they were outside, walking toward a nearby deli. He bought him a pastrami sandwich and a Coke. It was all he wanted. Gray had a cup of coffee and a bagel, and slowly they began talking about the past, as they each knew it. It had been different for Boy, their parents had been older then, they didn't move around as much, but were just as crazy. He had gone back to live on the reservation after they died, then to Albuquerque, and finally L.A. He volunteered that he had been a prostitute at sixteen. His life had been a nightmare. And nothing their parents had done before that had helped. It amazed Gray that Boy was still alive. Looking at him, it was hard to make sense of any of it, and the memories came flooding back. They scarcely knew each other, but they cried for each other and held hands. Boy kissed his fingertips, and looked into his eyes.

'I don't know why, but I just had to see you. I think I wanted to know that one person on this earth will remember me when I'm gone.'

'I always did, even though you were only a kid the last time I saw you.' He had only been a name to him, and now he was a face, a soul, a heart, one more person to lose and to cry for. He didn't want it, but it had come to him, like a gift. This man had come three thousand miles to see him to say goodbye. 'I'll remember you,' Gray said softly, engraving him on his memory as he looked at him, and as he did, he knew that one day he would paint him, and he said as much to Boy.

'I'd like that,' he said to Gray. 'Then people will see me forever. I'm not afraid to die,' he added. 'I don't want to, but I think it will be fine. Do you believe in Heaven?'

'I don't know what I believe in,' Gray said honestly. 'Maybe nothing. Or God. But for me, it's kind of free-form.'

'I believe in Heaven, and in people meeting each other again.'

'I hope not.' Gray laughed. 'There are a lot of people I've known that I don't want to meet again, like our parents.' If you could call them that.

'Are you happy?' Boy asked him. Everything about him was surreal and ethereal and transparent. Just being there with him was like being in a dream. He didn't know how to respond to Boy's question. He had been happy, until lately. He had been miserable for the past month, over all the bullshit with Sylvia. He told Boy about it.

'Why are you afraid to meet them?'

'What if they don't like me? What if I don't like them? Then she'll hate me. What if we like each other and I get attached to them, and then we break up? Then I never see them again, or I see them but I don't see her. What if they're a couple of spoiled little shits and they make trouble for us? It's all so fucking complicated, I don't need the headache.'

'What have you got without the headache? What would your life be like without her? You'll lose her if you don't see them. She loves them. And it sounds like she loves you.'

'I love her too. But I don't love her children, and I don't want to.'

'Do you love me?' he asked then, and Gray was suddenly reminded of the Little Prince in the Saint-Exupéry book, who dies at the end of the book. And not knowing why he said it, he answered him. He was honest, as though they had been friends and brothers for years.

'Yes, I do. I didn't love you until tonight. I didn't know you. I didn't want to know you,' he said honestly. 'I was afraid to. But now I do. Love you, I mean.' He hadn't wanted to know him for all those years, or even see him. He had been afraid of the pain of caring about him, or having a family. All Gray knew was that families hurt, and disappointed you. But Boy wasn't disappointing, he had come to see Gray, as a gesture of pure love for him. It was the gift of love no one in his family had ever given him. It was both painful and beautiful, as only love could be.

'Why do you love me? Because I'm dying?' Boy's eyes were haunting as they bored into Gray's.

'No, because you're my family,' Gray said in a choked voice as tears rolled down his cheeks and wouldn't stop. The floodgates of his heart had opened totally. 'You're all I have left.' It felt good to say it. The two men held hands across the table.

'I'll be gone soon,' Boy said matter-of-factly. 'And then she'll be all you have left. And her children. They're all you've got. And me.' It wasn't much, and Gray knew it. He didn't have much to show for fifty years on the planet. As crazy as they were, his parents had more. Three kids they'd adopted and made a mess of, but they tried at least, to the best of their limited abilities. They had each other. And all the people they touched as they roamed the world. Even Gray's paintings, and the agony that had inspired them, were somehow an outcropping of the two people who had adopted him and Boy. They had done a lot. More than Gray had ever thought or admitted. He saw that now. His parents had been crazy and limited, but at least they tried, even as messed up as they were. And Boy had tried too. Enough to come and see him. In comparison, Gray felt he had done far less with his emotional life, until Sylvia, and now he was limiting that too, and hurting her because he was scared. Terrified in fact.

'I love you, Boy,' Gray whispered as they sat holding hands across the table. He didn't care who saw them or what they thought. Suddenly he was no longer afraid of everything that had frightened him for so long. Boy was the final living symbol of the family Gray had run from for years.

'I love you too,' Boy said. He looked exhausted when they finally got up, and cold. He was shivering, and Gray gave him his coat. It was his best one. He had grabbed it on the way out, but it seemed a fitting gesture for the dying brother he had never known. He wished he had gone to see him before that, but he hadn't. It had never occurred to him, or in fact it had, and he had run from the idea. He realized now that he had run from so much, and all of it to avoid life, and getting hurt again. His family had become the symbol of all he feared. Boy was slowly lifting the fear from him.

'Why don't you stay with me tonight?' Gray offered. 'I'll sleep on the couch.'

'I can stay at the hotel,' Boy said, but Gray didn't want him to. They went to pick up his things and went back to Gray's place. He said he had to leave by nine in the morning to catch his plane.

'I'll wake you up,' Gray promised as he tucked him gently into bed and kissed him on the forehead. He felt almost as though Boy were his son.

Boy thanked him and was asleep before Gray closed the door.

Gray painted all night. He did sketches of him, dozens of them, so he wouldn't forget every detail of his face, and laid down the foundation for a painting. He felt as though it were a race against death. He never went to bed all night, and he woke Boy at eight and made him scrambled eggs. Boy ate about half, and drank some juice, and then said he had to leave. He was taking a cab to the airport, but Gray said he'd go with him. Boy just smiled, and then they left. He had to be there at ten for an eleven o'clock flight.

They stood close together after Boy checked in, and then they called the flight. Boy looked panicked for a moment, and then Gray reached out and pulled him into his powerful arms, and held him there while they both cried. They were tears not only for the present but for their lost past, and all the opportunities they'd missed, that they had tried to recapture in a single night. They had done well, both of them.

'It's going to be all right,' Gray said, but they both knew it wouldn't, unless Boy's theories about Heaven were right. 'I love you, Boy. Call me.'

'I will.' But he might not, Gray knew. This could be the last moment, the last time, the last touch. And now that Gray had opened his heart to him, it would all hurt so much. So much too much. But it was a clean hurt this time. The clean sharp sword of loss. It was like severing a limb surgically, instead of having it torn off.

'I love you!' Gray called after him as he boarded the plane. He said it again and again so Boy would hear it, and when he reached the door to the plane, Boy turned and smiled. He waved, and then he was gone. The Little Prince had vanished, as Gray stood watching the place where he had been, and cried.

Gray walked around the airport for a long time. He needed to think, and to catch his breath. All he could think of now was Boy and the things he had said. What if he had never existed, if Gray had never seen him again? If he hadn't come all this way to see him. He seemed like a messenger from God.

It was noon when Gray finally called Sylvia on his cell phone. He hadn't talked to her in two days. And he hadn't slept all night.

'I'm at the airport,' he said, sounding gruff.

'So am I.' She sounded surprised. 'Where are you?' He told her what terminal, and she said she was at the international terminal picking Emily up. It was Christmas Eve. 'Is something wrong?' Yes. No. It had been. Now it was fine. It wasn't fine. It never had been, but at least he was now. He felt whole for the first time in his life. 'What are you doing at the airport?' She was suddenly worried that he was leaving to go somewhere. Everything between them had totally fallen apart.

'I was seeing my brother off.'

'Your brother? You don't have a brother.' And then she remembered, but it sounded crazy to her, and it was.

'Boy. We'll talk about it. Where are you?' She told him again, and he hung up.

She saw him walking across the terminal toward her, and he looked a mess. He was wearing an old sweater and jeans, and a jacket that should have been thrown out years before. Boy had left in his good coat. Gray wanted him to have it. He looked like a madman, or an artist, and he looked as though he hadn't combed his hair in days. And then suddenly he had his arms around her and they were crying and he was telling her he loved her. He was still holding her when Emily walked out of customs with a big grin as soon as she saw her mother.

Sylvia introduced them, and Gray looked nervous, but shook her hand with a cautious smile. He asked her how the flight was, and picked up her bag. They walked through the airport with Gray's arm around Sylvia's shoulder, and Emily holding her mother's hand. They went back to the apartment, where Gray met Gilbert, and Sylvia fixed them all lunch. Gray helped her cook dinner that night, and he told her about Boy in bed that night.

They talked for hours, and the next morning, they all exchanged gifts. He had nothing for her, but Sylvia didn't care. The children thought him eccentric but nice. And much to his own surprise, he liked them. Boy was right.

They called Gray on Christmas night. Boy was gone. The friend who called said he was sending Gray his journal and a few things. The next morning, Sylvia and her children left for Vermont. Gray went with them, and he walked out into the snow one afternoon at dusk, and stood looking at the mountains. He could feel Boy near him, and hear his voice. Then quietly, he walked back to the house where Sylvia was waiting. She was standing on the porch, watching him and smiling. That night, as he stood outside with her, he looked at the sky, saw the stars, thought of Boy, and the Little Prince.

'He's up there somewhere,' he said sadly. She nodded. They put their arms around each other, and walked back into the house.

24

Carole, Maggie, and Adam flew down to St. Barts on Adam's plane. It was the first time either of them had met Carole, and it was a little awkward at first, but by the time they landed in St. Barts, Carole and Maggie were fast friends. They were as different as two women could get. But while Adam slept, Carole talked about the center and the children she met there, and Maggie talked about her early life, the time she'd spent in foster care, her pre-law classes, her job, and how lucky she was to be with Adam. Carole loved her long before they got off the plane. She was genuine and honest, kind, and incredibly bright. It was impossible not to like her, and Maggie felt the same way about Carole. They had even giggled conspiratorially about how furious they had each been that Charlie and Adam had wanted to go off on their own over the holidays, and how grateful they were that they hadn't.

'I was *really* pissed!' Maggie confessed in a whisper, as Carole laughed.

'So was I . . . actually, I was more hurt. Charlie says he doesn't do Christmas. That's really sad.' They talked about his lost family then, and how close the three men were. Maggie was glad they had finally met. She knew they had broken up for a while, but she didn't tell Carole. And then she talked about spending Christmas Day with Adam's kids. It had been great. They were taking them skiing in January over a long weekend. They had covered all the bases by the time Adam woke up, just before they landed.

'What have you two been cooking up?' he asked with a yawn.

'Nothing,' Maggie volunteered with a guilty grin, and then she said she hoped she didn't get seasick. She had never been on a boat before. Carole had. She had been on lots of them, though mostly sailboats. Maggie was amazed at how down-to-earth she was, since Adam had told her who she was. He was struck by Carole's beauty, her gentleness and kindness. How normal she was. Charlie had done it right this time. Adam just hoped he didn't blow it, or chicken out. It was going to be fun being a foursome for a change. It was a major difference in their lives.

Gray had called him just before they left. He was on his way to Vermont, and said he had met Sylvia's kids. Everything was fine. Adam had no idea how it had happened, but Gray had said he would tell him about it over lunch when he got back.

Charlie was waiting for them at the airport with two crew members and the captain, and he already had a tan. He looked happy and relaxed, and thrilled to see Carole. When they got there, Maggie couldn't believe the boat. She walked from one end to the other, looking at everything, talking to crew members, asking questions, and she said she felt like Cinderella all over again when she saw their cabin. She said it was going to be like a honeymoon, and Adam gave her a dark look.

'Oh, relax,' she teased him. 'I don't want to get married. I just want to stay on this boat forever. Maybe I should marry Charlie,' she said, jokingly.

'He's too old,' Adam said as he pulled her onto the bed with him. They didn't go back on deck for several hours, and when they did, Charlie and Carole were relaxing. Carole looked totally at home. She had brought the perfect wardrobe of white jeans and shorts, little cotton skirts and blouses, she even had deck shoes, which Maggie checked out, and was impressed. She had brought a lot of really dressy stuff, along with bikinis, and shorts, but Carole assured her she looked great. She was so young and pretty and had such a great figure, she could have worn garbage bags and looked terrific. Her style was completely different from Carole's, but in her own way, she was exotic and sexy, and her look had toned down a lot in her months with Adam. What she had bought wasn't expensive, but she'd paid for it herself.

They went to their cabins before dinner to change, after a quick swim, and then came back up to have drinks on the aft deck as they always did. Adam had tequila, Charlie a martini, and the girls both had wine. They were leaving for St. Kitts the next day, but not until the girls had a chance to do a little shopping in the port, as Charlie had promised. That night they went dancing. Everyone came back exhausted and happy, and slept late the next day.

They had breakfast together, and then Charlie and Adam went windsurfing while Carole and Maggie went shopping. Maggie didn't buy much, and Carole bought *pareos* at Hermès to wear on the trip. She offered to lend some to Maggie. By the time they left port late that afternoon, all four felt as though they had been traveling together forever. The only dark cloud on the horizon was that Maggie got seasick on the way to St. Kitts, and Charlie had her lie down on deck. She was still a little green when they anchored just outside the port. But she was fine at dinner, and they all watched the sunset together. Everything was perfect day after day, and their only complaint was that the trip went too fast. It always did. Before they knew it, it was the last day, the last night, the last swim, the last dance. They spent their last night on the boat, and Charlie teased Maggie about getting seasick, but she'd been a lot better for the last two days. Adam had even taught her how to sail. Charlie had taught Carole to windsurf, she was strong enough to do it, Maggie wasn't. They all hated to see the trip end.

Carole had only been able to stay a week, and Adam and Maggie had to go back too. His clients were complaining, and Maggie had to get back to work. They all did, except Charlie, who was staying on. He had been quiet for the last two days. Carole had noticed it, but didn't say anything until the last night, after Maggie and Adam had gone to bed.

'Are you okay?' she asked him quietly, as they sat in deck chairs in the moonlight and he smoked a cigar. They were at anchor that night, instead of in port. Charlie always preferred it, and it was more peaceful on the water than having people walk by all night on the quay. Carole preferred it too. She'd had a wonderful time with him and the others.

'I'm fine,' he said, looking out at the water, the lord of his domain. She could see why he loved being on the boat. Everything about the *Blue Moon* was perfect, from their cabins to the food, and the impeccably trained crew. It was a life one could easily adjust to, it seemed a million miles away from real life and all its problems. It was a life of being constantly and totally pampered.

'I've had a wonderful time,' she said with a lazy smile. It was the most relaxing week she'd spent in years, and she loved being with him. Even more than she had expected to. He was the perfect companion, perfect lover, perfect friend. He glanced over at her through his cigar smoke, looked at her strangely, and worried her again. He looked as though he had something on his mind.

'I'm glad you like the boat,' he said with a pensive expression.

'Who wouldn't?'

'Some don't. Poor Maggie, she got so seasick.'

'She got used to it in the end.' Carole stuck up for her new friend. She was looking forward to seeing her again, and she was sure she would. Maggie wanted to come up to the center to see what they did. She said she wanted to be an advocate for children when she graduated from law school, which was years away.

'You're a good sailor,' Charlie commented. 'And a good windsurfer.' She had learned quickly, and she'd gone scuba diving with him several times, and snorkeling with Adam. They had all taken full advantage of the comforts and delights of his boat.

'I used to love sailing as a kid,' she said, looking

wistful, she hated to leave him the next day. It had been so nice sharing a cabin with him, waking up with him in the morning, and cuddling up to him at night. She was going to miss that when she went home. For her, it had been one of the great advantages of conjugal life. She hated sleeping alone, and in good times had enjoyed the constant companionship of marriage. Charlie had seemed to enjoy sleeping with her too, and didn't appear to mind the intrusion in his cabin. 'When are you coming back?' Carole asked, smiling at him. She thought he was staying for another week.

'I don't know,' he said, looking vague. He seemed troubled, and then glanced back at Carole. He'd been thinking about them all week. She was so perfect in so many ways, she had the right breeding, right background, she was intelligent and fun to be with, gracious, thoughtful, nice to his friends, and made him laugh. He loved making love to her, in fact there was nothing about her he didn't like, which scared him to death. The most terrifying thing about her was that there was no fatal flaw. There had always been one that he could use as an escape hatch. But not this time. He was worried that in the end, he wouldn't want to settle down. And then everyone would get hurt, they always did. He had finally met a woman he didn't want to hurt, nor did he want to be hurt by her. There seemed to

461

be no avoiding it if you got close. He didn't know what to do about it.

'Something's bothering you,' Carole said gently, wanting to know what it was.

He hesitated for a long time and then nodded. He was always honest with her.

'I've been thinking a lot about us.' The way he said it sounded like a death knell, and she was frightened the moment she saw his face. He looked tortured.

'What about?'

He smiled through the cigar smoke again. He didn't want to worry her unduly, but he was concerned. 'I keep wondering what two commitment phobics like us are doing together. Someone could get hurt.'

'Not if we're careful of each other's wounds and scars,' and she was. She knew the things that upset him now. Sometimes he just needed space. He had been alone all his life. At times she sensed that he wanted to be alone, and had left the cabin, or left him to his own devices on deck. She tried to be sensitive to his needs.

'What if I never want to get married?' he asked her honestly. He wasn't sure he did. Maybe it was too late. He was almost forty-seven, he wasn't sure he could make the adjustment anymore. After a lifetime of searching for the perfect woman, now that he seemed to have found her, he wondered if he was the right man. Maybe not. He was coming to that conclusion.

'I've been married,' she said calmly. 'It wasn't so great.' She smiled sadly.

'You should have children one day.'

'Maybe. Maybe not. I have children where I work. Sometimes I think that's enough. When I got divorced, I told myself I'd never get married again. I'm not pushing for marriage, Charlie. I'm happy the way things are.'

'You shouldn't be. You need more,' he said, feeling guilty. He didn't know if he was the man to give it to her, and if he wasn't, he felt he owed it to her to let her go. He had been thinking about it a lot. The great escape. One way or another, in the end, it always came to that.

'Why don't you let me decide what I need? If I have a problem, I'll tell you. For now, I don't.'

'And then what? We break each other's heart later? It's dangerous to just let things drift along.'

'What are you saying, Charlie?' Listening to him, she was scared to death. She was getting more attached to him by the hour, especially after the last week of living with him. He could easily become a habit. And what he was saying was panicking her. He sounded like he was about to bail.

'I don't know,' he said as he put his cigar out in

the ashtray. 'I don't know what I'm saying. Let's go to bed.' When they did, he made love to her, and they both fell asleep without discussing the matter further.

The next morning came too soon. They had to be up at six, and Charlie was asleep when she got out of bed. She took a shower, and was dressed when he woke up. He lay in bed, looking at her for a long time. For a terrible moment she had the feeling that she was seeing him for the last time. She hadn't done anything wrong on the trip, or been too clingy or too attached. She had just allowed life to take its course. But the look of fear in his eyes was unmistakable, and guilt and regret. Ominous signs.

Charlie got up to see them off. He put on shorts and a T-shirt, and stood on deck watching as they lowered the tender to take them into port. He was going to Anguilla that day, after they left. He kissed Carole before she got into the tender, and looked into her eyes. She had the feeling he was saying more to her than just good-bye. She hadn't pressed him about when he was coming home. She thought it was better not to, and she was right. She had the feeling that he was poised at the edge of a terrifying abyss.

He patted Adam on the shoulder and gave him a hug, and then he kissed Maggie on both cheeks. She apologized for getting seasick. They thanked him, and he waved as they got off.

Carole turned to watch him from the tender as it sped away. She had the terrible feeling, as he waved at them from the deck, that she'd never see him again. She put on her dark glasses as they pulled into the port so no one would see her cry.

25

Life moved into high gear for Adam and Maggie when they got back. He had three new clients, his kids said they wanted to see him more often, especially now that they knew Maggie, and his father had a heart attack. Life. He was out of the hospital in a week, and his mother was on the phone to him ten times a day. Why wasn't he coming to see them more often? Didn't he care about his father? What was wrong with him? His brother was there every day. Adam pointed out in a tone of exasperation that his brother lived four blocks away.

Maggie was just as crazed. She was studying for finals, had two papers to write for her classes, and was working her ass off at Pier 92. Adam told her she needed to get a better job. But the tips were great. And for the first two weeks they were back, she had the flu.

She still had it and couldn't shake it, when she went back to work anyway. She couldn't lose any more days, or they'd fire her. She was still at work one afternoon, when Adam came home from the office, and found a note that the cleaning woman had quit. The apartment was a mess. He knew how tired Maggie was, so he decided to take out the garbage and do the dishes before she got back. He emptied the wastebasket in her bathroom into a big plastic bag, and just as he was about to tie a knot in it, something caught his eye. It was a bright blue stick. He had seen them before, but not in a while. A long while. He stopped what he was doing, gingerly fished it out, and stared at it in disbelief. He sat down on the toilet and stared at it, before throwing it back in and then tied the knot, but when he did, his face was grim. He looked like a tornado when Maggie got home. She went straight to bed, saying she felt like shit.

'I'll bet you do,' he said under his breath. He had cleaned the entire apartment, and was vacuuming when she got home.

'What are you doing?' she asked as he whizzed through the room.

'The maid quit.'

'You don't have to do that. I'll do it.'

'Really? When?' He was furious with her.

'Later. I just got home from work. For chrissake, Adam, why are you running around like a rocket ship with a burr up its ass?'

'I'm cleaning the house!' he said through clenched teeth.

'Why?' And then suddenly he turned to her with fury on his face.

'Because if I don't, I may kill someone, and I don't want it to be you.'

'What are you so pissed off at?' She had had a terrible day at work and she felt sick.

'I'm pissed at you. That's what I'm pissed at.'

'What the hell did I do? I didn't tell the maid to quit.'

'When were you going to tell me you were pregnant? Why were you saving that little piece of news? For chrissake, Maggie, I found your pregnancy test in the garbage, and it was *positive*, for God's sake!' He was out of his mind with rage. 'When did that happen?'

'On Yom Kippur, I think,' she said softly. They had been careful ever since. It was the only time they hadn't been. Since then, without knowing it, they had been locking the barn door after the horse escaped, or got in, or something like that.

'Oh, great,' he said, tossing the vacuum down at his feet. 'On Yom Kippur. My mother was right. I should have gone to synagogue, and I never should have called you.' He threw himself into a chair as she started to cry.

'That's mean.'

'It's meaner for you to be pregnant and not tell me. When were you going to tell me, for God's sake?'

'I just found out this morning. I didn't want you to get mad. I was going to tell you tonight.'

And then suddenly he looked at her and realized what she had said. 'Yom Kippur? Are you *kidding*? Yom Kippur was in September. This is January, for chrissake. Do you mean Chanukah?' She wasn't Jewish, she obviously had her holidays mixed up.

'No, Yom Kippur. It had to be that first weekend when I came over. It was the only time we weren't careful.'

'Wonderful. Did you notice that you didn't get your period for the last three months?'

'I thought I was nervous. I've always missed it a lot. Once I didn't get it for six months.'

'Were you pregnant?'

'No. I've never been pregnant till now.' She looked devastated.

'Terrific. A first. We just don't need this headache, Maggie. And when you get an abortion, you'll be crying and whacked-out for the next six months.' He had been through it all before, too many times. He didn't want to go through it with her, or with anyone ever again. And then he looked at her darkly, with suspicion on his face. 'Are you trying to trap me into marrying you? Because that's not going to work.'

She jumped off their bed then, and stood glaring at him. 'I'm not trying to trap you! I never asked you to marry me, and I won't now. I got pregnant. This is your fault too, not just mine.'

'How the hell could you not know you were pregnant for three *months*?' It was unbelievable. 'You can't even get an abortion at this point. Not easily anyway, it's a big deal after three months.'

'Well, then I'll deal with it. And I wasn't trying to marry you!'

'Good! Because I won't!' he shouted at her, and with that she stormed into the bathroom, and slammed the door in his face.

She was in there for two hours, and when she came out, he was in bed, watching TV, and didn't say a word to her. Neither of them had had dinner. She had thrown up when she was in the bathroom, crying on her own.

'Is that why you got sick on the boat?' he asked without looking at her.

'Maybe. I kind of wondered, and when I got sick when we got back, I thought maybe it was. That's why I did the test.'

'At least you didn't wait another six months. I want you to see a doctor,' he said, finally looking at her. She looked a mess. He could see that she'd been crying, her eyes were red, and her face was pale. 'Do you have a doctor?'

'I got a name from a girl at work,' she sniffed.

'I don't want you seeing some quack. I'll get a name tomorrow.'

'And then what?' she asked, sounding scared.

'We'll see what he says.'

'What if it's too late for an abortion?'

'Then we'll talk about it. I may have to kill you in that case.' He was only kidding, he had calmed down a little, but she burst into tears again. 'Come on, Maggie . . . please . . . I'm not going to kill you. But I'm upset.'

'So am I,' she said, sobbing. 'It's my baby too.' He groaned then, and flopped down on the bed.

'This is not a baby, Maggie. Please. It's a pregnancy, that's all it is right now.' He didn't even want to say the word 'fetus,' let alone 'baby.'

'What do you think that leads to?' she said, blowing her nose in a tissue.

'I know what it leads to. That's what I'm upset about. Just get some sleep. We'll talk about it in the morning,' he said, as he clicked off the TV and turned off the light on his side of the bed. It was early, but he wanted to sleep. He needed the escape. This was the last thing he needed. This happened to his clients, not to him.

'Adam?' She spoke softly just as he closed his eyes.

'What?'

'Do you hate me?'

'Of course not. I love you. I'm just upset. This was not a good idea.'

'What wasn't?'

'Getting pregnant.'

'I know. I'm sorry. Do you want me to leave?' He looked at her then, and felt sorry for her. This was going to be hard on her too, especially after three months. He knew there were doctors who did it, but it was a much bigger deal than if you caught it right away.

'No, I don't want you to leave. I just want to deal with this, as soon as we can.' She nodded her head.

'Do you really think I'll be a mess for six months?' She sounded worried. This was scary for her too. More than for him. He hated the inconvenience, she had to deal with it, either way. It was traumatic for her.

'I hope not,' he answered her question. 'Just go to sleep.'

She tossed and turned all night, and when he woke up in the morning, she was in the bathroom and he could hear her getting sick. He stood outside the bathroom door, wincing. It sounded rough.

'Shit,' he said out loud and went to shower and

shave. She came out ten minutes later. He had kept his bathroom door open so he could see her when she did. She looked green. 'Are you okay?'

'Yeah. I'm great.'

He made her tea and toast when he was dressed, told her he'd call her from the office, and kissed her before he left. And then he thought of something terrifying on the way to work. She was Catholic. What if she refused to have an abortion? Now that really would be a mess. What would he tell his kids? Or his parents? It didn't bear thinking. He made the necessary calls as soon as he got to the office, and called her at work at noon. He gave her the names of two doctors, in case one was too busy to see her, and told her to try and see one of them as soon as she could. She called both that day, used his name as he had told her to do, and got an appointment for the following afternoon. Adam offered to go with her, but she said she could handle it alone. At least she was being decent about it. But they hardly talked to each other that night. They were both too stressed.

The following night, after her appointment, she was in the apartment when he got home. It was her day off, and she was doing homework when he walked in.

'How did it go?'

'It went fine.' She didn't look up at him.

'How fine? What did he say?'

'He said it's a little late, but they can say that my mental health is at stake if I threaten suicide or something like that.'

'When are you doing it, then?' He sounded relieved, and there was a long pause as she looked up at him with huge eyes in a pale face. She didn't look well.

'I'm not.' It took a long moment for it register, and he stared at her.

'Say that again.'

'I'm not having an abortion,' she said carefully, and he could see from the look on her face that she meant it.

'What are you going to do about it? Give it away?' That was a lot more complicated and took a lot more explaining, but he was willing to do that too, if she preferred. She was Catholic after all.

'I'm having the baby. And I'm keeping it. I love you. I love your baby. I saw it on a sonogram. It's moving. It was sucking its thumb. I'm three and a half months pregnant. Sixteen weeks, the way they figure it, and I'm not giving it away.'

'Oh my God,' he said, letting himself fall into the nearest chair. 'This is insane. You're keeping it? I'm not going to marry you. You know that, don't you? If that's what you think is going to happen, you're crazy. I'm never getting married again, to you or anyone else, with or without a baby.'

'I wouldn't marry you anyway,' she said, sitting up very straight in her chair. 'I don't need you to marry me. I can take care of myself.' She always had before. Although she was terrified now, but she wouldn't admit it to him. She had spent the whole afternoon figuring out how she was going to pay for it. She was determined not to take anything from Adam. She had to do this herself. Even if she had to quit her job, give up school, and go on welfare. She wanted nothing from him.

'What are my kids going to think?' he said, with a look of panic. 'How are we going to explain that to them?'

'I don't know. We should have thought of that on Yom Kippur.'

'Oh for God's sake, all I was thinking about on Yom Kippur was how much I hate my mother. I wasn't thinking about a baby.'

'Maybe it was meant to be,' she said, trying to be philosophical about it, but Adam didn't want to hear it.

'This was not meant to be. This was both of us being sloppy.'

'Maybe. But I love you, and even if you leave me right now, I'm having this baby.' She had dug her heels in and she wasn't moving an inch. The sonogram had done it. She was not killing their kid.

'I don't want a baby, Maggie.' He tried to reason with her.

'I'm not sure I do either, but that's what we've got. Or what I've got.' She sounded calm and unhappy. It was a lot to deal with, for both of them.

'I'm going to Vegas this weekend,' he said miserably. 'We'll talk about it when I get back. Let's take a break from it till then. Let's both think some more, and maybe you'll change your mind.'

'I won't.' She was a mother lion defending her young.

'Don't be so stubborn.'

'Don't be so mean.' She looked at him sadly.

'I'm not being mean. I'm trying to be a good sport about this, but you're not making it easy. It's mean to have a baby that no one wants. I'm just not prepared to have a baby, Maggie. I don't want to get married again. I don't want a baby. I'm too old.'

'You're just too mean. You'd rather kill it,' she said, bursting into tears, and he wanted to cry himself.

'I'm not mean!' he shouted after her as she ran into the bathroom again, as much to hide from him as to be sick.

The rest of the week was no better. They stayed off the subject, but it hung between them like a nuclear bomb ready to go off. He was relieved to leave for Vegas on Thursday. He needed to get out.

He stayed over on Sunday night. He was waiting for her when she got back from work on Monday. He was sitting in a chair with a look of resignation.

'How was your weekend?' she asked, but didn't come over to kiss him. She had been upset all weekend, and wondered if he was cheating on her because he was upset. She hadn't left the apartment, and she had cried herself to sleep every night, thinking that he hated her and would probably leave her and she'd be alone with their baby, and never see him again.

'It was fine. I did a lot of thinking.' Her heart nearly stopped as she waited for him to tell her that she had to move out. She had become an embarrassment to him.

'I think we should get married. You can come out to Vegas with me next week. I have to go back anyway. We'll get married quietly, and that'll be that.'

She stared at him in disbelief. 'What do you mean, "that'll be that"? Then I leave, but the baby is legal?' She had thought of a thousand terrible scenarios, and not one good one. He had.

'No, then we're married, we have the baby, and we live our life. Together. With the baby. Okay? Now are you happy?' He didn't look happy either, but he was trying to do the right thing. 'Besides, I love you.'

' "Besides," I love you too, but I'm not going to

marry you.' She looked quiet and determined.

'You're not? Why not?' He looked stunned. 'I thought that was what you wanted.'

'I never said that. I said I was having the baby. I didn't say I wanted to get married,' she said resolutely as he stared at her.

'You don't want to get married?'

'No, I don't.'

'But what about the baby? Why don't you want to get married?'

'I'm not going to force you to marry me, Adam. And I don't want to get married "quietly." When I get married, I want to make a lot of noise. And I want to marry someone who wants to marry me, not someone who *has* to. Thank you very much, but my answer is no.'

'Please tell me you're joking,' he said, dropping his head into his hands.

'I'm not joking. I'm not asking you for money, and I'm not going to marry you. I'm going to take care of myself.'

'Are you leaving me?' He looked genuinely horrified at the thought.

'Of course not. I love you. Why would I leave you?'

'Because you said I was mean last week.'

'You're mean if you want to kill our baby. But you're not mean if you ask me to marry you. Thank you for that. I just don't want to, and neither do you.'

'Yes, I want to!' he shouted. 'I love you. I want to marry you! Now will you do it?' He looked desperate, and she looked calmer by the minute. She had made up her mind, and he could see it too. 'You are the stubbornest woman I've ever met.' She smiled at him, and he laughed. 'That wasn't a compliment. Oh, for God's sake, Maggie.' He came and put his arms around her and kissed her for the first time in a week. 'I love you, please marry me. Let's just get married, have the baby, and try to do it right.'

'If we'd done it right, we would have gotten married, and then had the baby. But you'd never have married me then, so why do it now?'

'Because you're having a baby,' he nearly screamed.

'Well, get over it. I'm not getting married.'

'Shit,' he said, and went and poured himself a shot of tequila, which he downed at one gulp.

'You can't drink. We're pregnant,' she said primly, and he gave her an evil look.

'Very funny. I may become an alcoholic before this is over.'

'Don't,' she said gently. 'It'll be okay, Adam. We'll work it out. And you don't have to marry me. Ever.'

'What if I want to marry you someday?' He looked worried.

'Then we'll get married. But you don't want to right now. I know it. You know it. And one day the baby would know it.'

'I won't tell him.'

'You might.' People did things like that sometimes. *I had to marry your mother.* . . . She didn't want that for her child. And she didn't want to take advantage of him, even if he was willing to do the right thing.

'Why are you so fucking honorable? Every other woman I've ever known wants me to pay their bills, marry them, get them jobs, and do a million other things for them. You don't want shit from me.'

'That's right. Just your baby. Our baby,' she said proudly.

'Could they see what it is?' he asked with sudden interest. He didn't want this baby, but as long as they were having it, it might be nice to know what it was.

'I'm going back in two weeks for another sonogram. They can tell me then.'

'Can I come?'

'Do you want to?'

'Maybe. We'll see.' He had spent all weekend thinking he was marrying her, and now he was almost disappointed he wasn't. Everything about their life right now was weird.

'What are you going to tell your mother?' Maggie

asked him that night at dinner, and he shook his head.

'God knows. At least now she'll have something to really bitch about. I think I'll tell her that I knocked you up on our first date, and you're Catholic, so she won't want me to marry you anyway.'

'How charming.' He leaned across the table, kissed her, and smiled at her.

'Maggie O'Malley, you're crazy to have my baby and not marry me. But I love you. So what the hell. Wait till I tell Charlie and Gray!' He smiled at her, and she laughed as they finished their dinner, and talked about how crazy life was sometimes. Theirs surely was, but they both looked happy that night as they finished the dishes and went to bed. This wasn't what they'd wanted or planned, but they were going to make the best of it, whatever it took.

26

Charlie didn't call Carole after she left him on the boat in St. Barts. She sent him a fax thanking him, but she felt awkward calling him, after the things he'd said the night before she left. She had no idea what conclusions he was coming to, the only thing she was absolutely certain of was that he needed space. She gave him a wide berth. It was all she could do. She grew more frightened every day. It was a full two weeks before he finally called her. She was sitting in her office when the phone rang. He said he was back. But he sounded strange. He asked her if they could meet for lunch the next day.

'That would be wonderful,' she said, trying to sound light-hearted, but she wasn't even fooling herself. He sounded terribly and profoundly upset. He seemed cool and businesslike, and after she'd agreed to meet him for lunch, she wondered if she should cancel. She knew what was coming. He hadn't asked her out to dinner, or said he wanted to see her that night. He wanted to meet her for lunch the next day. Distance. Space. It only meant one thing. He was meeting her to be polite and tell her it was over. The handwriting was on the wall so loud and clear it looked like graffiti. All she could do now was wait.

She didn't even bother to put on makeup the next morning. There was no point. He didn't care anyway. If he loved her, and wanted her, he would have called her from the boat in the past two weeks, or seen her the night before. He hadn't. He might love her, but he didn't want her. All she had to do now was get through the agony of hearing him tell her. She was a wreck by the time he showed up at the center.

'Hi,' he said, standing awkwardly in her office doorway. 'How've you been? You look great.' But he was the one who looked great, in a gray business suit with a deep tan. After worrying all night, and lying awake, thinking about him, she looked and felt like shit.

'Where do you want to go for lunch?' She wanted to get it over with, and was sorry now she hadn't called him to cancel. He obviously thought he had to do it in person. He didn't. He could have called her on the phone to dump her. 'Do you really want to eat?' she asked, looking discouraged. 'Do you want to just talk here?' But he knew as well as she did that there were constant interruptions. Kids walked in, counselors, volunteers. The whole world walked into her office. It was the hub of the wheel.

'Let's go out.' He was being painfully polite and looked strained. She grabbed her coat and followed him out of the building. 'Mo's or Sally's?' he asked her. She didn't care. She couldn't eat anyway.

'Whatever you like.' He picked Mo's, it was closer, and they walked down the block in silence. Mo waved at her when they walked in, and Carole tried to smile. Her face felt wooden, her feet felt like cement, and there was a brick in her stomach. She could hardly wait to get it over with, and go back to her office so she could cry in peace.

They sat down at a corner table and they both ordered salads. He didn't look hungry either. 'How was the rest of your trip?' she asked politely, and then they spent the next half hour picking around at their salads, and eating little. She felt like she was going to the guillotine.

'I'm sorry if I upset you before you left the boat. I thought about us a lot after you left,' he said. She nodded, waiting for it to happen. She wanted to tell him to hurry up, but just sat staring into space, pretending to listen. She didn't want to hear what he was going to say. She just had to sit there and take it. 'There are a lot of reasons why this could work. And a lot of reasons why it couldn't.' She nodded, and wanted to scream. 'We come from the same background. We have many of the same interests. We both have a strong philanthropic bent. You also hate my way of life. You want a much simpler lifestyle' – he smiled at her – 'although your house is no simpler than mine. I think you like my boat, and you're a good sailor. We're not after each other's money. We both went to Princeton.' He droned on until she thought she was going to die, and finally she looked at him, wanting to put them both out of their agony. It had gone on for long enough.

'Just say it, Charlie. I can take it. I'm a big girl. I've been divorced. Just get it over with, for chrissake.' He looked shocked.

'What do you think I'm saying?'

'That it's over. I get it. You don't have to dress it all up and gift-wrap it for me. You didn't even have to take me to lunch. In fact, I wish you hadn't. You could have called me or sent me an e-mail. "Get lost." "Fuck you." Something. I can pick up the clues if you give me a hint. You've been hinting for three weeks. So if you're going to dump me, just do it.' It was a relief to spit it out. He was staring at her strangely, as though he didn't know what to say now. She had said it all for him.

'Is it over for you?' He looked deeply unhappy as he waited, and she hesitated, but decided to tell him the truth. She had nothing to lose now.

'No, it's not over for me,' she answered him. 'I love you. I like you. I enjoy you. I think you're terrific. I have fun with you. I like talking to you. I love sharing my work with you. I loved being on the boat with you. I like your friends. I even like the smell of your cigars. I love sleeping with you. But that's how *I* feel. Apparently, that's not how you feel. If that's the way it is, so be it. I'm not going to sit here and try to convince you of something you don't want.'

He sat there and looked at her for a long time. He was looking into her eyes intently, and then he smiled. 'Is that what you thought? That I came here today to tell you it's over?'

'Yes. What else was I supposed to think? Before I left the boat, you told me a lot of mumbo jumbo about being worried about us. Then I left and I didn't hear from you for two weeks. You called me yesterday, sounding like the executioner, and invited me to lunch, not dinner. So I guess we've got it pretty well covered. Go for it, Charlie. If you're going to do it, do it.' She wasn't even scared anymore. She could deal with it. She'd survived worse. She'd been reminding herself of that all day.

'That was the conclusion I came to on the boat. If you're going to do it, do it. Stop fooling around. Stop waiting for the other shoe to drop. To hell with the fatal flaw, and getting hurt, and worrying that the person you love is going to die or walk out or turn out to be a lemon. If you're going to do it, do it. And if it's a mess, we'll pick up the pieces later. Together. Carole, will you marry me?' He was looking her right in the eye, and her mouth fell open as she stared at him.

'What?' She looked stunned.

'Will you marry me?' He was smiling at her as tears filled her eyes.

'You're asking me that at Mo's? Now? Here? Why?'

'Because I love you. Maybe that's all that matters in the end. The rest is window dressing.'

'I mean why did you ask me here, at Mo's? Why didn't you take me out to dinner, or see me last night or something? How can you ask me something like that here?' She was laughing through her tears as he took her hands in his across the table.

'I had to see my lawyers last night, for the foundation, and close out our fiscal year. I couldn't do it last night. And I didn't want to wait till tonight. Never mind all that. Will you?'

She sat looking at him for a long time with a broad smile on her face. He was a little crazy. Nice crazy. But crazy. He had absolutely terrified her and convinced her it was over. And instead he wanted to marry her. It was totally nuts. She leaned across the table and kissed him. 'You damn near gave me an ulcer. And yes, I'll marry you. I'd love to. When?' She got right down to business, and she was smiling from ear to ear.

'How does June sound? We could honeymoon on the boat. Or any other time you want. I was so damn scared. I was afraid you'd say no.'

'Of course not. June sounds great.' She still couldn't believe he had asked her. It felt like a dream, to both of them.

'It doesn't give you much time to plan a wedding,' he said apologetically, but now that he'd decided, he didn't want to wait too long. It was time.

'I'll work it out,' she said as he paid the check, and they walked slowly back down the street to the center. It wasn't the way she'd expected things to work out at all.

'I love you,' he said as he kissed her, standing right outside the center. People walked by and smiled at them. Tygue walked past them on his way back from lunch, and teased them.

'Having a nice day?' he asked as he opened the door to the center.

'Very,' Carole said, and smiled at him, and then kissed her future husband again before he left to go back downtown. Mission accomplished.

27

Things settled down to a dull roar with Adam and Maggie. They decided not to tell his children until the baby showed, which was a couple of months off yet. And they weren't going to tell his mother till after the children knew. Adam wanted to do them the honor of telling them first. It was still going to be hard to explain. And he was sure Rachel would have plenty to say.

He was busy with his clients, but he managed to go to the sonogram with her two weeks later. The baby was healthy, looked fine, and it was a boy. When they watched him moving around, Adam and Maggie cried. She was four months along.

He had to go to Las Vegas the week after that, and he asked her if she wanted to go with him. Coincidentally she had two days off, which worked fine for her. He had been in surprisingly good spirits, given the amount of tension in his life, and he had been a good sport about the baby. Maggie was sleeping a lot, and sick almost every day, but she tried not to complain. It was for a good cause.

The night they flew to Las Vegas, she was feeling slightly better. One of his major musical acts was playing there for two days. But he said he only had time to stay there for two nights, and Maggie had to be back at work anyway.

They flew to Vegas on his plane, and stayed at the Bellagio, which she loved. And much to her delight, Adam said the hotel had given them the Presidential Suite, which had a dining room, conference room, and the biggest bed she'd ever seen. It had a grand piano in the living room, and they got there early enough to spend some time in bed before dinner. The act they had come to see wasn't going on till midnight, and just before they went downstairs for dinner, Adam said he had to do some business in the room. He told her he'd use the conference room, and closed the doors. Two men in suits arrived, and as Adam had asked her to, she showed them into the room. When she opened the conference room doors to let them in, there was an enormous bouquet of red roses on the table, and a bottle of Cristal chilling in a bucket, as Adam smiled at her.

'Come on in, Maggie.' He beckoned her in with the two men, who were smiling too.

'What are you doing?' Something strange was

happening, and she didn't know what it was. Everyone seemed to know what was going on except her. 'What's going on in here?' She looked around suspiciously. She was dressed for dinner, in a pink dress and high heels. Adam had told her to wear something nice. Everything was getting tight on her, but the baby didn't show yet. Her figure was as good as it had been before, just fuller, and she was spilling out of the top of her dress.

'We're getting married, that's what's happening,' Adam said to her. 'I'm not asking you. I'm telling you. And if you give me any trouble, Mary Margaret O'Malley, I'm not letting you out of this room until you do.'

'Are you kidding me?' she asked him, grinning. She was stunned.

'I've never been more serious in my life,' he said as he came to stand next to her proudly. 'You're not having that baby without me. This is Judge Rosenstein, and his assistant, Walter. They're here to perform the ceremony. Walter is going to be our witness.'

'We're getting married?' She looked at him with tears in her eyes.

'Yes, we are.'

'Does your mother know?'

'She will tomorrow. I want to tell the kids first.' He had thought of everything and overridden all her objections. She had always wanted to marry him, but not because he thought he should. He had taken it out of her hands now, and it was obvious to her that he wanted to do it too.

The judge performed the ceremony, and Maggie cried as she gave her responses. Adam put a narrow gold band on her finger that he had bought at Tiffany the day before. He had bought one for himself too. And Walter signed the marriage certificate as their witness. By eight o'clock that night, the deed was done. He kissed her as they stood alone in the room. She had only sipped the champagne since she wasn't supposed to drink.

'I love you, Mrs Weiss,' he said, smiling at her. 'I'd have married you sooner or later anyway, even if you weren't pregnant. This just speeded things up.'

'You would?'

'I would,' he said firmly. She was still in shock.

They had dinner at Picasso's, and went to the midnight show, and she looked at her ring about a million times. She loved seeing his too.

He was just drifting off to sleep that night, after he made love to her, when she poked him in the shoulder. He stirred, but was too far gone to fully wake up.

'. . . Uh? . . . I love you . . .' Adam mumbled.

'I love you too. . . . I just thought of something.'

'. . . Not now . . . too tired . . . tomorrow . . .'

'I think I should become Jewish. I want to convert.' She was wide awake. He was within milliseconds of sleep, but managed to nod his head.

'... Talk about it tomorrow ... love you ... 'night ...' And then he fell asleep. She lay there next to him, thinking about everything that had happened. It had been the most wonderful night of her life.

28

The next day when Adam called his mother, you could have heard her from Long Island Sound to the Brooklyn Bridge.

'*O'Malley?* She's *Catholic?* Are you trying to kill me? You're a sociopath! You'll give your father another heart attack!' She pulled out all the stops and accused him of everything she could.

'She's planning to convert.' She barely stopped screaming long enough to hear what he said. She told him that he was an utter and complete disgrace.

'Is that where you were going when you walked out on Thanksgiving?' she accused him, and this time he laughed. He wasn't going to let her give him headaches anymore. He had Maggie now, his lover, ally, and best friend.

'As a matter of fact, it was. Best decision I ever made.'

'You're insane. With all the nice Jewish women in the world, you marry a Catholic. I guess I should be grateful you didn't marry one of those *schwarze* singers you represent. It could have been worse.' For the remark she had just made, and for disrespecting Maggie, he decided to let her know it *was* worse. She had it coming. And had for forty-two years.

'And, Mom, before I forget. We're having a baby in June.'

'Oh my *God*!' You could have heard the screams all the way to Nebraska that time. 'I just thought you'd want to know the good news. I'll call you soon.'

'I don't even have the heart to tell your father, Adam, it will kill him.'

'I doubt it,' Adam said calmly. 'But if you tell him, be sure to wake him up first. Talk to you soon, Mom.' And with that, he hung up.

'What did she say?' Maggie asked, looking worried, as she walked back into the room. They had just gotten back to New York. He had called his kids before his mother, and they were fine. They had said they liked Maggie a lot, and were happy for him.

'She was thrilled,' Adam said with a broad grin of victory. 'I told her you were going to convert.'

'Good.'

* * *

The three couples met for dinner at Le Cirque a week later. Charlie had invited them, and had given them a clue. He said he had important news.

They all arrived on time, and were ushered to a well-placed table. The three women looked lovely, and everyone was in a good mood. They ordered drinks and chatted for a few minutes, and then Charlie told them that he and Carole were engaged and getting married in June. Everyone was thrilled. And then Adam looked at Maggie with a conspiratorial grin.

'What do you two have up your sleeve?' Charlie had seen them exchange the look.

'We got married last week,' Adam said, beaming at his wife. 'And we're having a baby in June.' There was a small roar from the group.

'We've been upstaged!' Charlie said, and laughed. He was pleased for them. Carole and Maggie consulted immediately about the date the baby was due. The wedding was set for two weeks before her due date, so Maggie said she'd be fine. Fat but fine.

'What about our August trip on the *Blue Moon*?' Gray asked, looking worried, and everybody laughed.

'Works for us,' Charlie said, looking around the group, as all the others nodded their heads.

'Can we bring the baby?' Maggie asked cautiously.

'Bring the baby and a nanny,' Charlie confirmed. 'Looks like everybody's on. And Sylvia, I hope you'll come too.' They all agreed it would be a cozy group of six with all their ladies along, different than before, but a lively group nonetheless.

'Oh, and by the way,' Gray said, smiling happily, 'I just moved in last week. Now I'm *living* with Sylvia, not just *staying* with her. I have a closet, I have a key, my name is on the bell, and I answer the phone.'

'I remember those rules.' Maggie laughed. 'Do you have holidays yet? It's not a *relationship* till you do.' She glanced at Adam, and he winced.

'I just did.' Gray answered her question about holidays. He said he'd gone to Vermont with Sylvia and her children, and celebrated Christmas with them. It had made him nervous once or twice, but he had done fine. Emily and Gilbert had gone back to Europe the week before, and he had promised to go to Italy with them for a week before he and Sylvia went on the *Blue Moon*. He had assumed Charlie would invite her now, since he'd had Maggie and Carole on the boat over New Year's.

He was hard at work on the portrait of Boy, and moving full steam ahead for his April show. He wanted the portrait of Boy to be the most important piece in the show, but it wasn't for sale. He was planning to hang it in Sylvia's loft, and referred to it as a family portrait. In death, more than he had ever been in life, Boy was his brother. They had found each other at the eleventh hour, thanks to Boy.

'What about you two?' Adam teased him, since everyone else was getting married. 'When are you going to tie the knot?'

'Never!' they both said in unison, and everybody laughed again.

'You should do it in Portofino next summer, where you met,' Charlie suggested.

'We're too old to get married,' Sylvia said convincingly. She had just turned fifty, three days after Gray turned fifty-one. 'And we don't want babies.'

'That's what I thought too,' Adam said sheepishly, with a grin and a loving glance at Maggie. She'd been feeling better for the past few days.

'No wonder you got seasick on the boat,' Charlie said as he figured it out.

'Yeah, I guess,' Maggie said shyly. 'I didn't know then.'

They were a congenial group and toasted each other liberally all evening. As usual, the men drank too much. And given the occasion, the women made no attempt to keep them in control. It was all in good fun. They drank an impressive amount of very fine French wine.

By the time they left each other at the end of the evening, plans were made, dates were set. Everyone had made note of the date of Charlie and Carole's wedding, Maggie had shared her due date, and they were all set for the *Blue Moon* on August first, as always. Life was sweet. And good times were ahead.

29

After much debate, in spite of the fact that it was Carole's second wedding, and Charlie's first, she acceded to her parents' wishes, and they got married at St James. It was a small, elegant, and formal event. Charlie got married in white tie and tails. Carole asked Sylvia to be her matron of honor, and Maggie to be her bridesmaid. Carole wore a simple but elegant gown in the palest mauve, and lily of the valley in her hair. She carried a bouquet of white orchids and roses. She looked absolutely regal as she came down the aisle on her father's arm. Gray and Adam were Charlie's best men. After the ceremony, all two hundred guests attended the reception at the New York Yacht Club. The wedding was as traditional as possible, except for the flock of children from the center who came, with Tygue and a handful of volunteers to keep them in control. Gabby and Zorro were there, of course, and Carole had hired a group of fabulous gospel singers from Harlem. The dance band played until three A.M.

Carole had done the seating of all the tables herself, and even her parents looked as though they had a good time. Charlie danced with Mrs Van Horn after he danced with the bride, and Carole danced with her father. Unlike most weddings, there wasn't an army of unwanted relatives there. In fact, other than her parents, there were none. They were surrounded by their friends.

Sylvia looked beautiful in a lilac gown that she and Carole had chosen together at Barney's. She carried lilacs and tiny white roses. It had been more challenging to find something for Maggie to wear. They had finally settled on an evening gown that was somewhere in color between Sylvia's lilac and Carole's pale mauve. It was lavender, and she carried lavender roses. By the day of the wedding, the dress was so tight she could hardly breathe. The baby was huge, but she looked beautiful anyway. She had youth and motherhood on her side, even though she looked like she could hardly move.

Carole said she had a fabulous time at her wedding, and she looked as though she did. She danced with Charlie, Adam, Gray, Tygue, some of her old friends, but most of the night with Charlie. Everyone agreed they had never seen a happier couple in their lives. They ate and danced and laughed all night.

The music was so good that even the Van Horns

couldn't stay off the dance floor. Sylvia and Gray did a tango that put everyone else to shame. And Adam couldn't keep Maggie down. Every time he turned around, she was dancing with someone else, at arm's length of course. In order to keep track of her, he finally kept her on the dance floor with him. She never sat down. She was having a lot of fun. She danced and danced and danced. And when she finally sat down at the end of the evening, she told Adam she couldn't tell what hurt more, her back or her feet.

'I told you not to overdo it,' he scolded her.

'I'm fine.' She grinned at him. 'The baby's not due for two weeks.'

'Don't count on it, if you keep dancing like that. I don't know how a woman who's eight and a half months pregnant can look sexy, but you do.' They were among the last to leave.

Carole had thrown her bouquet by then, straight at Sylvia, who caught it with a groan. Charlie and Carole were staying at her place that night, and leaving to meet the boat in Monte Carlo the next morning. They were taking the boat to Venice for a three-week honeymoon. She was nervous about leaving the center, but Tygue had agreed to run it while she was gone.

The last of the guests threw rose petals at the bridal couple as they got into the car and drove away, and Adam helped Maggie into their rented limousine. She couldn't get in and out of the Ferrari anymore.

She was yawning as they rode up in their elevator, and for once she was asleep before Adam. She had totally worn herself out, and looked like a small mountain as she lay beside him. He kissed her cheek and her stomach, and turned off the light. Cuddling these days was more of a challenge. He went right to sleep, thinking of his friend's wedding, and was in a deep sleep two hours later, at five o'clock in the morning, when Maggie poked him.

'. . . Mmm . . . what?'

'I'm having the baby,' she whispered to him, in a voice that was slightly panicked. He was too tired to wake up. Like everyone else at the wedding, he had enjoyed the unlimited torrent of great wine. 'Adam . . . sweetheart . . . wake up. . . .' She tried to sit up in bed but was having too many contractions. She poked him again with one hand. She was holding her enormous belly with the other.

'Ssshhhh . . . I'm sleeping . . . go back to sleep . . .' he said, and turned over. She tried to take his advice, but she could hardly breathe. It was getting scary and it was happening so fast.

It was nearly six when she not only poked him but shook him, and by then she was having to pant through the pains. Nothing was working. It hurt too much.

'Adam . . . you have to wake up . . .' She couldn't get out of bed, and she tried to move him, but he blew her a kiss and slept on.

It was six-thirty when she finally pounded on him and shouted his name. That time he woke up, with a start.

'What? What?' He picked up his head and set it back down on the pillow just as fast. 'Oh shit . . . my head . . .' And then he looked at her. Her face was contorted in pain. And headache or not, he woke up. Fast. 'Are you okay?'

'No . . . I'm not . . .' She was crying by then, and she could hardly talk. 'I'm having the baby, Adam, and I'm scared.' By the time she finished her sentence, she was having a contraction again. The pains were running right into each other and never stopped.

'Okay. Give me a minute. I'll get up. Don't be scared. Everything's fine.' He knew he had to get out of bed and put on his pants, but his head felt like cement.

'It's not fine . . . I'm having the baby . . . now!'

'Now?' He sat bolt upright and looked at her.

'*Now!*' She was crying.

'You can't be having the baby now. It's not due for two weeks . . . dammit, Maggie . . . I told you not to dance so much.' But she was beyond hearing him. She looked at him with wild eyes, and he jumped out of bed.

'Call 911!' she panted at him through the contractions.

'Oh shit . . . okay. . . .' He called them, while he watched her. She was starting to push. He told the operator at 911, and they said they'd send the paramedics right away, unlock the front door, stay with her, and tell her to blow, not push.

He did what they said, and told Maggie to blow, not push, and she was screaming at him through the contractions. There was no time in between anymore.

'Maggie . . . come on, baby . . . please . . . blow! Blow! Don't push! . . .'

'I'm not pushing, the baby is,' she said, making a terrible face, and then she screamed a blood-curdling scream. 'Adam! He's coming out . . .' He was holding her legs and watching their son come into the world as the paramedics arrived. The baby had delivered itself, and Maggie lay breathless against the pillows as Adam held him. As they looked at him, they both cried.

'Nice job!' the head paramedic said, as he took over from Adam and another one cleaned the baby up, and put it on Maggie's stomach. Adam was looking at them both in wonder, and couldn't stop crying. Maggie was smiling and peaceful as they covered her, as though nothing had happened. They cut the cord then, and the baby looked at him as though they had seen each other somewhere before.

'Does the young man have a name?' the second paramedic asked.

'Charles Gray Weiss,' Adam said, looking adoringly at his wife.

'You were fantastic!' he whispered to Maggie, as he knelt on the floor close to her head.

'I was so scared,' she said softly.

'And I was so drunk.' Adam laughed. 'Why didn't you wake me sooner?'

'I tried!' She was smiling and holding their baby.

'I promise, next time you talk to me when I'm falling asleep, I'll listen.'

The ambulance was waiting for them downstairs, but before they left, they called Carole and Charlie. They woke them up and told them that the baby had been born, and they were thrilled to hear it. They had to get up early anyway to leave for Monaco that morning.

Adam called Jacob and Amanda from the hospital, and the doctor let Maggie and the baby come home that night. They were both fine, and she wanted to be home with Adam. Maggie said it had been the most beautiful day of her life. The baby was perfect.

As Adam drifted off to sleep that night, with the baby in his bassinet next to them, Maggie poked him, and he gave a start and sat straight up and looked at his wife.

'What? Are you okay?' He had kept his promise. He was wide awake.

'I'm fine. I just wanted to tell you I love you.'

'I love you too,' he said, as he sank back into bed and pulled her closer. 'I love you a lot, Maggie Weiss.' He smiled as he fell asleep, and so did she.

30

Everyone boarded the *Blue Moon* on August first, as planned. Maggie and Adam brought their baby and a nanny, as Charles had invited them to do. They started in Monte Carlo, as they always did, gambled for a night, moved on to St Tropez, and when they'd had enough of it, left for Portofino. The girls shopped, the men drank, they all swam, they walked in the piazza at night, and ate gelato. They danced in the discothèques, and between outings and meals, Maggie nursed her baby. He was two months old on the day they left, had big bright eyes, and a sturdy little body. He was blond like Maggie.

On the morning after they arrived in Portofino, Sylvia and Gray walked up to the Church of San Giorgio, and that night they all had dinner in the restaurant where they'd met. They had just come back from a trip with her kids, and this time Gray was more relaxed. He and Emily had talked about painting techniques, and he and Gilbert had truly become friends. Sylvia had been right, he admitted to Charlie, she had great kids. 'She was right about a lot of things,' he confessed to his friend. The others toasted them that night. It was the one-year anniversary of the day they'd met.

'I still think the two of you should get married,' Adam said as they opened another bottle of wine. They'd been living together officially for seven months. Sylvia said that wasn't long enough to count. They'd only known each other for a year. The others hooted and jeered, Charlie and Carole had dated for eight months before they got married, and Adam and Maggie for four. And everything seemed fine. Better than fine. They were the happiest they'd ever been, all four of them.

'We don't need to get married,' Sylvia insisted, and Gray laughed at her and told her she sounded like him when he was afraid to meet her kids.

'I don't want to screw up a good thing,' she said softly.

'You won't,' Charlie said. 'And Gray's a good man.'

'I wouldn't even think about it for another year,' she said blithely.

'Fine,' Adam said. 'We'll be back here next year, same time. Let's see what you do then.' The others toasted them again.

31

The day was incredibly hot and the sky perfectly blue. If you stopped talking, you could hear insects and birds. There wasn't a cloud in the sky as the ragtag group made their way up the hill. It was almost too hot to move, and it was only eleven o'clock in the morning.

A woman in a white eyelet peasant skirt and a full-sleeved white blouse was carrying a bouquet of red roses, and wearing red sandals. She was wearing an enormous straw hat, and an armful of turquoise bracelets. Beside her, there was a man in white trousers and a blue shirt, with a mane of white hair. And behind them, two couples, both women heavy with child.

All six of them walked into the Church of San Giorgio in Portofino. The priest was waiting for them there. It was her second marriage, but she hadn't been married in the church before, and he had never been married at all.

The bride and groom stood at the altar, looking

solemn as the priest had them exchange their vows, and their four friends looked on. When the priest told the groom he could kiss the bride, the groom cried.

Sylvia and Gray turned to their friends then. Maggie and Carole were both pregnant. Charlie and Adam looked proud, not just of the women they had married, but of their two friends who had done it at last. They stood talking in the church for a long time, lit some candles, then walked slowly down the hill again, and stopped in the piazza. Sylvia and Gray were holding hands.

They had their wedding lunch in the restaurant where they'd met two years before, to the day. It had been a long time and a long journey for all six of them. They had come far and done well, and had been blessed to find each other.

'To Sylvia and Gray and a lifetime of happiness!' Charlie toasted them, and then looked at his wife. Their baby was due in December, their first. Maggie and Adam's second was due in October, two years after their life together began.

The past two years had been happy and busy and full, for all of them, with babies and weddings, their other children had done well. Their careers were flourishing. Maggie was in college, and still headed for law school. Carole's center had grown. And so had their hearts. They had carried heavy baggage

511

and set it down, and traveled on better and lighter for loving each other.

They went back to the boat that afternoon, and swam, all of them. And they had dinner that night on the boat. Sylvia and Gray loved sharing their honeymoon with them. It seemed appropriate for all of them to be together. And when they left Portofino, and headed for other ports, the bachelors that had once been were finally no more.

THE END